DURANGO LIGHT

by Ed Williamson

Cliff -
Climb to the top
then come back
all in one piece.
— Ed Williamson

Library of Congress Catalog Card Number 97-70881
ISBN 1-878936-03-4

Printed in the United States of America

Mader Consulting Co., 1049 Kamehame Drive;
                    Honolulu, HI 96825-2860

1 2 3 4 5 6 7 8 9

Chapter One

The August sun was straight overhead and we were high above timberline in the mountains of southwestern Colorado. My partner Buck and I had started our climb with clear skies as we went up a mountain called Jupiter Peak that morning. We had been to the mountaintop and we were on our way back down, but now the clouds were gathering on the western horizon like soldiers uniting for a battle.

I stopped for a moment and tugged the faded straps of my weathered red daypack forward, out and away from my shoulders, giving my aching muscles a rest. I breathed in deep mouthfuls of the thin, crisp air. It tasted cool and dry, normal for late summer at this altitude.

As I surveyed the scenery, I studied the approaching clouds. They looked like flat, white-gray puffs of cotton, floating along out there a few miles away. Some were rolling, expanding, turning a darker shade of gray as they gathered and merged into larger clouds. They could mean trouble for us. If Buck and I didn't get down from the mountain soon, those nasty-looking clouds would build into a thunderstorm. Inevitably, it would send sheets of cold rain and bolts of lightning down on the mountains. Neither of us wanted to be caught up here in such a storm.

Buck Corwin, my companion and fellow climber, was a hard-bodied man in his mid-fifties with a big round head and a burr haircut. He glanced back at me. Buck was never one for subtlety in his words.

"Can't you move it any faster, Mike?" he said, his eyes taking in the advancing clouds.

"Sure," I said. "You in a hurry or something?"

He flashed me a toothy grin. Behind his mirrored sunglasses, I knew Buck's hard black eyes were measuring me. His face was streaked with sweat, tanned from many days in the outdoors. He was breathing hard now. "In case you hadn't noticed, we're about to get rained on."

"Come on, take it easy," I replied. "We've got a little time before those storm clouds get serious."

A moment later we heard a clap of thunder booming off the mountain walls. It was much louder than I had expected.

"Does that tell you anything?" Buck asked with a cold grin. "Time, we don't have. Let's move it."

"Okay, maybe you're right," I laughed. "It could get wet up here. Lead on."

We began walking faster down the ridge line now, pushing it, but watching our footing on the narrow, rocky trail. You had to be very careful on a ridge like the one we were descending. There were plenty of loose rocks here and we didn't want to slip and fall down over the steep cliff face a few feet away on our right.

I thought about our excursion as we ambled along. It had been a good climb all through that morning. We had moved strong and well on the ascent, right up to the rocky summit of Jupiter Peak. Scrambling up the last big boulders toward the top had been the toughest part of our work, and the effort had taken a lot out of us. Now, as we hiked down the approach trail, I turned and glanced back up at the brilliant noonday sky above me. The heavens were a deep blue bowl overhead, beautiful but somehow unreal in their azure purity. Soon that peaceful sky would be filled with the approaching swirling clouds, and the summer weather would change to that of winter, even in August.

I walked faster, following Buck, but I turned my eyes to the cold granite summits on the skyline around us. Patches of snow gleamed from the rocky walls. It was a beautiful sight. But it was not the place to be when the storm screamed in like a hurricane with its wind, rain, and lightning ripping through the crags.

The mountains in this corner of Colorado were some of the steepest peaks in the San Juans, a sub-range of the Rockies. These particular mountains were named "The Needles" because of their jagged, sawtooth profiles as seen from a distance. They were the kind of mountains you imagined in your dreams of mountains.

Buck caught me inspecting the scenery. "Come on now, let's keep a move on. This ain't no time to rubberneck." "I know. I just needed one last look from up here on top."

He sighed. "We haven't got the time, buddy."

"Okay, I hear you." I began to match his pace, moving even faster over the rocks.

He was right, of course. Still, it was hard not to take a moment and look up at the mountains. This was a stark but beautiful world here on the ridge, some thirteen thousand feet high. The sharp peaks had a special character, with their red-gold granite spires and their cloud-grazing stillness. Few plants grew above timberline among these barren crests of stone and snow. Only marmots, pikas, eagles, and a few other hardy creatures lived here.

"It's funny," Buck said, leaning his big, stocky body forward against his ice-axe as he hurried along, "I sometimes go climbing with a friend named Bob. He's a laid-back kind of guy, mentally real tough, but real quiet. Bob always says that up here is where he feels the most alive. What do you make of that?"

"I know what he means."

Yes, I knew the sentiment well. You could lose yourself in the extraordinary beauty and the spell of these high peaks, where so few humans ventured. It was a landscape out of a fantasy. Yet, though the mountains might be beautiful, you got the feeling that they expected to exact a toll of some kind from you for entering their rare domain. It was as if they wanted to test you, try you, to see what you were really made of. They might even want to take everything you had. You could not help regarding them with awe, and perhaps, a healthy sense of fear as well.

"It's too tough to leave this place, Buck," I said. He snorted. "Maybe so, but remember, these hills can be mean, Mike. They can kill you."

"You make them sound like they're enemies."

"No, they're not enemies. Sometimes I think they're the best friends I've ever had. But you'd better respect them. Remember, any mountain can kill you, even the little ones. Never relax completely with them."

"I know," I replied, following him on down. In a way, it was always a contest between you and the mountain you were climbing. And if you died, the mountain won.

I had once seen, up close, what was left of a climber when the mountain won. I had helped bring his body down. The dead man had been climbing with a partner, and they were nearing the summit, but apparently something unnerved him. He froze. His climbing partner told him to stay put and wait for him while he went on up to the top, but the fearful climber decided to go back down alone. Trying to descend from the ridge too rapidly, he had moved carelessly, not testing the footing, and had slipped off and fallen. His partner, up on the summit, had neither seen nor heard a thing, and when he came back down he thought his friend had returned to their camp and had somehow gotten himself lost.

A search party looked for the man for two days, but they could not find him. He had simply vanished.

Several months later, however, a backpacker bushwhacking off-trail near the base of the mountain saw a patch of clothing against some rocks. Coming nearer, he saw a bony hand sticking out of a rocky talus bed. Then he found the body wedged down in a crack in the rocks there at the base of the peak.

I was camping with some friends a half-mile from the mountain at that time. The backpacker came running into our camp, white-faced, and told us about his grisly discovery. We followed him through the woods to the death scene.

The sight of that body engraved itself in my memory. Animals had obviously found the now-skeletal corpse, and I remembered seeing a length of taut, dried, gnawed, yellow flesh stretched over broken bones. I remembered how the skull still had scraggly patches of blonde hair on it. Hollow eye-sockets stared upward from that skull at us from between the crack in the rocks. The jaw was missing, the bones lying on the ground a few yards away where some animal had probably dragged it.

After that incident, I knew full well that the mountains could kill. Today though, coming down from Jupiter Peak, it looked like a time for winning. Buck and I felt blessed to be enjoying such a gloriously beautiful day, even if a storm was coming.

As we moved along the ridge, we could see where the deep snows from last winter had been melted away, except in the deep couloirs and on the northern slopes of the mountains. Shielded by the shadows, north-face snow is the last to melt, if it ever does.

Marmots stared at us as we quickly hopped over the rocks, making our way on down. On the higher plateaus we saw thousands of tiny wildflowers, profuse in a dense array of color. The view of distant mountains, valleys, and far-off plains was as clear as could be.

I am taller than most people, and I have always been blessed with strength and good health. Buck said I was a natural climber. Ever since I was young I had loved mountains, and had dreamed of climbing them. Though much of my life was spent in the flatlands, I still kept the dream of someday testing their heights. And now I was here among them.

"How high did you say Jupiter Peak was?" I asked Buck.

"Something over thirteen-nine. It's one of the 'Centuries', the one hundred highest peaks in Colorado, but it's not quite a Fourteener."

Colorado had 54 mountains called "Fourteeners," peaks more than 14,000 feet high. Buck had climbed them all. I had done most of my own climbing on lower peaks up until a few months ago, and had yet to summit my first Fourteener. Buck and I had climbed several lower summits together, as I learned from my new friend the ways of these higher peaks. Jupiter had been a warmup climb for me on the way to the Fourteeners.

"Buck, I think I'm ready for a Fourteener, now," I said as we walked on. "If they're anything like Jupiter, I want to see what the big ones are like."

He laughed lightly. "You'll get your chance. Let's get on down out of harm's way right now."

The clouds kept advancing on us. It was nearly one o'clock now as we made our way on down to a long, flatter area on the ridge. We had reached the top of Jupiter by nine o'clock that morning, and had spent a restful half-hour on top before beginning the downclimb.

It was Buck's custom to gain the summit of the mountains we tried by ten o'clock in the morning. On a clear day the cool, still morning air normally kept the rain-filled cumulus thunderheads from forming until late morning or early afternoon.

Neither of us wished to try our luck with those dark clouds that so often delighted in throwing lightning down on unsuspecting climbers. Both of us knew people who had been struck by lightning in the mountains, and we knew it could happen to us as easily as to the next climber.

Once, I had pressed my luck with such storm clouds. I normally don't climb alone, but on that day I was by myself and it seemed like the thing to do. I had started my solo climb on a mountain called Lost Arrow Peak, a 12,000-footer. It was late in the morning, and I was almost up to the summit. Then a drifting, errant thundercloud strayed toward the peak. I was only a hundred feet or so from the top when I saw the black shadow of the cloud overhead.

I heard the ominous "buzzing of the bees," the ionized air on the peak readying to receive a bolt from the cloud. My hair stood up on my neck.

That was enough for me. I scrambled back down as carefully as possible. I found safe refuge below a tall cliff and huddled there in a fetal position, as I had learned to do. It was good that I did, too, because minutes later hail and lightning began to pummel the mountain. The lightning cracks and the booming thunder were like artillery shells exploding all around me in a war zone. I was terrified, but the storm passed, and I survived, and went back down, shaken. I could have gone on up to the summit, I suppose, but I had lost my taste for it.

So I lost the summit that day, but I got to keep my life. Now I observed Buck's "ten-o'clock rule" as religiously as he did. There was only one thing you did if you were caught in the death-zone of a thunderstorm: you retreated. Otherwise, you could be barbecued, the mountain way.

Buck and I had started climbing together the previous April. We were a pretty good team, and our personalities were well-suited to each other. Our first meeting came one afternoon when he walked into The Aspen Leaf, the outdoor sports store where I was the manager. Buck had come in to buy a climbing rope.

I was new to the Durango area at the time. I had been looking for a regular climbing partner, but I hadn't found the right person. I might have gone out climbing with one of my store employees, for some of them were very good climbers. But friendship with individual employees can be a problem and can cause jealousy among the troops, so I wanted to find someone else to go backpacking and climbing with.

That day when I met Buck, we started talking about mountains. I liked him; he was my kind of friendly. I sized him up as a possible mountaineering partner. We talked for a while about ropes, and then climbing, and he offered to take me on an outing he was planning the next weekend.

We found that we got along well together on that first trip, and so we started going out to the wilderness together whenever we got the chance. It was a good mix. I got his climber's experience; he got my younger man's strength. And both of us got a new friend out of the deal.

When it came to mountains, Buck really was much more experienced than I was, and I found him to be a good teacher. A little brittle and autocratic, maybe, but when it came to mountaineering he didn't play games, and he knew what he was doing and why he was doing it.

He taught me the basics of simple climber's ropework, such as how to tie in, how to belay, and how to rappel. He taught me other tricks as well, like how to keep from stepping on the braided nylon rope so you didn't weaken it by pressing rock granules between the strands with your boot. I took a lot of security in my new training.

After years of climbing, Buck knew what worked and what didn't, and he had his own peculiarities. He had discarded some of the traditional practices other backpackers and climbers used. For example, when going on a two-person outing, many people took only one tent, the parts of the tent divided between the two campers, to save weight in the backpacks. That meant you slept with your buddy. But Buck liked his privacy when he was out and away from it all. He carried his own complete tent and suggested I carry one for myself as well. It meant an extra three or four pounds, but having your own private tent proved to be worth it.

When you went to bed at night, alone in your own tent, you were in blessed solitude. No phone, no TV, and no obligatory conversation with the guy in the sleeping bag beside you. Hermit-like, yes, but out there it was a virtue. In your tent it was just you, alone, with your thoughts and your own ways. We liked it like that.

The thoughts you had in those dark hours of solitude could be good or bad, but they were yours alone. You thought of where your life was going, what it all seemed to mean. It was a good kind of thinking that let you uncoil the kinks in your life and usually it made for restful sleep.

Normally, on the evening before, we hiked in to an area below our mountain and made our base camp in the evening at high altitude, say 9,000 to 11,000 feet or so. That way we knew we would only have somewhere between 3,000 to 5,000 feet of ascent on the summit attempt planned for the next day.

Then, hours later, we would awaken and stick our heads out of our respective tents in the cold air of the pre-dawn early morning darkness, and check the sky. If it looked like favorable weather, and we both agreed on going, we would get our climbing clothes on. We dressed in layers, wearing thin shell parkas over warm, insulating clothes underneath. After dressing, we ate a quick breakfast, slipped on our daypacks, grabbed our ice-axes, and then left camp for the ascent.

In the darkness we would begin our chilly trek up some dirt
trail, aided by small flashlights that helped you stay on the pathway. Sometimes the moonlight helped.

The small daypacks we both wore were in fact portable life-
support systems. The daypacks contained extra clothing, food,
water, first-aid stuff and other small gear items designed to help
us survive if the unexpected should happen. Smart climbers prepared for the worst, even if conditions looked good at the start.
The rule was: if you can't take the weight of the stuff in the
daypacks, don't make the climb.

As the early-morning sun rose and the air warmed, we would
usually stop and take a break. The coldweather clothes, the
sweaters and parkas, would find their way into our daypacks. If
it grew cold again the warm clothing came back out. Clothing
was taken off or put on as the temperature and weather dictated.
Stopping to add or subtract clothing was something you did in
climbing as commonly as taking a frequent bite of food to give
your body a small but continuous supply of energy.

Beginning the morning climb normally meant slowly trudging
up some trail shown on our topographic map. The trail shown on a
typical topo map often disappeared into an ambiguous landscape
of broken rocks as you rambled higher, out of the aspens and
pines, above the timberline.

There, beyond the more obvious trail, one often discovered
piles of rocks called cairns, stone markers piled by past climbers to
mark the way to the summit. You then followed the cairns across
the broken rocks on up to the top of the mountain. Sometimes you
had to look hard for the cairns, for occasionally they were small
and they weren't always placed where you thought they should
be. But they were always somewhere nearby and you could find
them if you kept your eyes open.

On the mountain summit, if the weather was holding, we
would first shake hands. Then we would rest a while and sign
in on the summit register if one was to be found. The summit
register was simply a notebook or sometimes a sheaf of papers
tucked into a box or a plastic tube. You would write down the
climb date and then add something like "Mike Rader, Durango.
Reached Summit 10:00 A.M.. Weather: Clear."

Perhaps then you would sit down, eat a snack, take a few

pictures of the world below, and think of starting back down. Buck and I had done this many times.

We observed a tradition all our own before leaving the top. Somewhere, Buck had discovered a non-carbonated canned lemonade, and we always carried a couple of cans of the drink with us on every climb. After summitting, we toasted our accomplishment with the clink of the two cans. After that, it was time to leave.

We would carefully make our way back down, and would try to arrive back in camp by mid-afternoon. I was always glad to get back to my tent. I would be drained of physical and emotional energy and ready to let my mind and body go.

Climbing dehydrates the body, so I drank a lot of water when I got back to camp. After that I would stretch out on the grass beside my tent, my head propped on my daypack. A hat shielding off the sun's hot rays from my face, I would take a long nap. After a couple of hours like that I always felt restored.

Toward evening, we got out the little one-burner white gas stoves we brought with us. Then we cooked hot meals as we discussed the climb, watching while the sun slipped down behind the steep walls of the mountains.

After supper, we made a small campfire and sat beside it, like a couple of hunters after the hunt, watching the twilight come. This was a special time for us. Maybe we sensed some primeval mood in the approaching darkness, the coming of the unknown, perhaps, or death, or simply a vague loneliness. It was in these moments that Buck and I, two essentially solitary men, often had our deepest talks, the ones that brought us close.

You could say anything to your buddy at such a time, it didn't matter what it was. It might be something sacred or irreverent, it just did not matter. You were two beings who had been to the mountain and had won, together. In victory, you were totally liberated in mind and speech, and it was good. Everything else about your existence was stripped away. The primitive, deep-down thoughts inside you came out. You felt like your climbing buddy understood you, knew your moods, your fears, your dreams, your joys. You could laugh or sing or shout at the moon, and your brother climber would just smile and laugh at you, and with you. Yes, he understood. For a brief window in time, you thought you were the two sanest men in the world. And, perhaps, you really were.

Today, on the long trek down from Jupiter Peak, my mind was starting to get tired. I was craving the water and the nap and the hot food and the chance to unwind and let go. Nothing else mattered except to get the dull ache of the downclimb over.

Jupiter Peak had not really been difficult, but it had required a certain concentrated, sustained effort. Now, on the descent, we were weary and a storm was coming. I just wanted to avoid the storm, get back to camp, and get some rest and sleep.

We made our way on down to a broad, gently down-sloping ridge that led to a steeper hillside and a grassy meadow far below us. On my right, a few paces away, I saw the stark edge of a cliff. It fell several hundred feet to a broad shelf of rock that curved over to other mountains. As long as we stayed on the ridge, we could get down to the valley floor with little trouble. Lower down the ridge, one could go down the grassy inclined slope to the meadow at any point, although negotiating the steepness would stress the muscles of your knees. I wasn't looking forward to the knee-jarring descent, but it was all part of climbing.

I scanned the landscape beyond the ridge to the west. Down below was a glaciated valley named Chicago Basin, encircled by the tall mountains, with melting snowfields in the shadowed hollows. Groves of pine trees grew along the sides of that horseshoe-shaped valley. From the ivory sparkling waterfalls near its head the crystalline waters of Needle Creek formed a small rushing stream that ran through the middle of Chicago Basin. Miners who came there a hundred years ago to look for gold had named the area after their home town, Chicago.

Rising skyward, across the basin, was a tall peak named Mount Eolus. It was a tall but wide oblong mountain, and mists veiled its summit. Mount Eolus had been named by early surveyors for Aeolus, the god of the winds and weather. To those pioneer surveyors, Mount Eolus appeared to be a peak where storms were continually being "manufactured."

I had read and heard about Mount Eolus. It was a Fourteener. Veteran mountaineers who climbed it had graded it as "moderately difficult" to ascend, but as I had not yet climbed it, I didn't know what that description entailed. What I did know was that Eolus could be treacherous.

A lot of people tried to climb Eolus, and most people made it. But once in a while someone got hurt or died falling off the mountain. It was steep, with lots of loose, rotten rocks on its upper slopes. As I stood watching the mountain now, it almost seemed to be looking back at me, taunting me to climb it.

"Buck," I said, "what about Eolus?"

From behind his sunglasses, Buck glanced across the basin toward the mountain. "What about it?" he asked, matter-of-factly.

"Can we climb it tomorrow?"

Buck laughed. "Eolus? No. One of these days, maybe. But not yet. You'd better warm up on something tamer first. Maybe Sunlight Peak or Mount Windom. Let's let Eolus wait."

"You're sure?"

"Look," he answered, with a trace of sarcasm in his voice, "you can go ahead and try it tomorrow if you really want to. Just don't drag me along with you. You're not ready yet, friend. Trust me on that. I don't want to be responsible for what might happen to you. Eolus requires experience you just haven't had the chance to absorb yet."

I persisted. "Not tomorrow, then?"

"I don't think so. Look, maybe you could do it okay. The thing of it is, you've got to get mentally ready for a mountain like Eolus. It's a progressive thing, a confidence thing. Let yourself grow a little, head-wise, confidence-wise, before we do it. If you'll take my word for it, you'll do some easier stuff before you tackle Eolus. I know what I'm talking about. Understand what I'm trying to say?"

"I understand. Just a thought."

We walked on down as the wind from the gray clouds now darkening the whole sky whipped at us. Out of the corner of my eye, something caught my attention. I forgot about Eolus and stared down the ridge trail past Buck, on farther down. I saw something pink there, moving among the rocks. Then I recognized it for what it was. It was a young man clad in pink flamingo-colored tights with gray shorts over them. I smiled. Such clothing was the kind of trail outfit favored by a lot of young rock climbers.

Rock climbers were a different breed from Buck and me. Most rock climbers were good people, often young, adventurous, and brave, and I had several friends among them. They loved to do their climbing in a style decidedly different from the way Buck and I did ours.

Buck and I almost always took the path of least resistance in
our climbing, going up along the flat trails and slopes and ridges.
Rock climbers, on the other hand, usually looked for the steepest
and most challenging way to go up a mountain. They loved to
find ways to go straight up the cliffs, taking the hard way, loving
the adrenaline high of the steeps.

Our kind of mountaineering meant mostly a lot of high-
altitude uphill hiking. Oh, in places we sometimes had to do
some scrambling, some rope-work, and occasionally, as on mountains like Wyoming's Tetons, a good bit of rock climbing, too. But
we didn't crave the steep stuff like the dedicated rock climbers did.
It was just a difference in taste. And, to some of them, it was a
matter of courage.

I watched the man in the pink tights approaching, and saw
that a young woman was following him. Like her friend, she wore a
similar tights-and-shorts outfit. Her upper body and leg clothing
were colored powder blue, and her shorts were fluorescent green.

The woman was a blonde with a slender body; she might
have been a dancer. As they neared us, I saw that she was quite
attractive. She had deep blue eyes, friendly young eyes that were
full of life. I could see that her graceful curves all moved together
in effortless harmony.

As the two of them approached they looked like they were
heading up the ridge to Jupiter's summit. I wondered why they
were starting their attempt so late in the day with a storm moving
in.

They were near us now. The young man was short and stocky,
wiry black-haired, with a beard and glasses. His face looked florid
above his beard, sunburned and pitted with old acne scars. There
was something about the way he looked that put me off a little.
Maybe it was the trace of arrogance I saw in his eyes, which
darted about uncertainly. Whatever it was, I had a bad feeling.
The man's small blue daypack looked nearly empty. The girl with
him had no daypack at all.

You could sometimes tell a lot about a climber by simply
looking at his clothing and gear. This was not without its excep-
tions though. A man many had judged as the best climber in the
world often made his ascents with surprisingly little equipment.
Still, the average climber often revealed his wisdom through what
he carried.

I knew that all climbers have their own ways of doing things, but the apparent lack of gear these two carried made me uneasy. The weather could turn on you very quickly up here. Still, it was a part of the protocol among climbers not to give strangers advice about their equipment unless it was asked for. Yet I wondered if these two understood what they were getting into with those thunderheads moving in on our mountain.

"Hello," the young man called out with a funny smile playing on his lips. "Did you guys do the summit?"

Buck stopped and leaned on his ice axe, nodding to the two. He breathed hard as he looked at them from behind his silvered glasses. "We got there about ten this morning. Spent a little time on top. We're on our way down."

The man glanced up beyond us to the mountain. "Looks easy," he said. "We did a wall this morning, and that took it out of us. We thought we'd relax and hike up Jupiter the easy way this afternoon. The guidebook said something about some scrambling near the summit though."

Buck studied the man. "It's not bad," he told the man, "Just some big rocks. You might...uh...want a rope, though."

The man grinned, his eyes blinking. "You two may have needed one, but I don't expect we will. We're used to steep places. I've been doing free climbing for a couple of years now, and Jill's a natural at it. We can make it."

Buck looked away. "Suit yourself," he said softly.

I knew what Buck was thinking. He had them pegged as a couple of crazies, or at the least, naive, to be heading up the mountain with a storm coming. But I knew he wasn't going to say anything about it.

The pretty blonde-haired girl smiled. "It looks like a good day for climbing for us all," she said cheerily, but a bit nervously. She looked strong and lean, fit, but I couldn't help wondering if she was beginning to question her partner's wisdom.

I glanced up at the sky, and toward the peak. "It was a good day, for a while," I said, "but it's starting to look a little dicey up there now. The clouds, you know."

The man dressed in pink smiled, and it was a toothy, over-confident smile. My bad vibes returned.

"Yeah, I guess we'd better get going, Jill," the guy said. "We don't want to get wet. Maybe we'll see you, uh, older guys, down at the bottom."

"Sure," Buck mumbled as the two of them passed. I was sure the "older guys" remark was intentional, for the girl's sake; the macho man showing his girl he was made of sterner stuff than the old geezers. We silently watched them go as they made their way on up the ridgeline trail.

"What do you make of that?" I asked.

"Trouble," Buck said simply.

"Yeah, that's what I think. But what can we do about it?"

Buck spat on the ground. "Nothing. They've got it all figured out. That guy thinks he knows it all, because they're younger, smarter, and faster than us decrepit old fossils. Anyway, it's their necks, not ours. Let's get off this hill before the rain sets in."

"I'm with you," I replied, though still concerned about the other two, who were moving fairly fast now toward the summit. Maybe, I mused, they'd make it after all. Luck was often with the young.

Buck and I headed on down the trail, and then we ambled down the last tough part, the grassy slope. The incline was indeed hard on our knees. I was glad we had the ice axes with us as we used them like canes for balance. We took our time.

Normally climbers use such axes only on snow and ice, but Buck had employed his for years on all kinds of terrain. I had followed his example. Even if you did not encounter snow, an ice axe still made a good walking stick. It was like a third leg on steep sections where you needed to watch your balance. We took our time.

An hour later, we came down off the steep part and wandered out onto a soggy meadow. We crossed it, ambling through a waist-high forest of leafy skunk cabbages. We were soon in the trees only a half-mile or so from our camp. The afternoon breeze had by now grown to a strong wind. Hard drops of rain began striking us like bullets, splashing cold water on our tired faces. We stopped and hurriedly pulled our parkas over us as the foul weather set in.

We were near our camp when we heard a shout from behind us. Turning, we saw, through sheets of rain, the young man who wore the pink tights crazily running after us across the muddy field of skunk cabbages.

"Please! Wait! I need your help!" he shouted as he came upon us.

"What's wrong?" I asked, wiping rain from my eyes.

"It's Jill. We had an accident!"

"What happened?" I asked. "She fell up there—down a cliff!"

The young man was wide-eyed, his body shaking with exhaustion and fright. The cold rain made him look like a drowned rat, his hair streaming wet down over his face.

"A fall? How did that happen?" Buck asked, surprised and a bit angry.

"I...we...it all happened so fast! We were near the top, scrambling, in the rain...the rocks were wet, real slick... and she...she just slipped over the edge!"

My memory flashed back to the image of that dead climber of long ago. The old fear stiffened me as the rain fell on us and thunder shook the mountains. Not again, I thought. I don't want to see any more death.

I looked at him. "How is she? Is she...?"

The guy was almost in tears now, really losing it. "Dead? Oh, man, I don't know. She landed on a ledge. I couldn't get to her...she was down too far. She wasn't moving and she didn't answer when I called to her."

He got his words out and then doubled over and vomited, emptying his stomach onto the wet mud at his feet.

"Blazes!" Buck shouted, disgusted. He turned away, muttering to himself. I grabbed the young man by his shoulders and helped him up. The cold rain was falling harder now, hail mixed in with it. The hail pummeled us like tiny marbles.

I turned to Buck. "What now?"

Buck tried to stare up through the blasting rain and hail at Jupiter Peak, but the dark mountain above us was invisible in the storm's fury. I knew it would take hours to notify a mountain rescue team far away in Durango. Buck looked at the guy, then to me. He seemed to read my thoughts.

"He looks wasted, Mike. He's done in and he's already half frozen. You know that the girl's probably dead by now."

"Maybe. Maybe not, though, Buck. She might still be alive up there."

Buck shook his head and sighed. "Look at the storm, Mike. Think, man. If you and I go back up there, there might be three bodies on that mountain instead of just one."

I nodded. "Or none, if we get to her in time. Look, Buck, we can't just leave her up there. If it was you or me we'd want somebody to come looking for us. We've got to go back after her."

Buck spat. He thought it over for a moment. Then turned to me. "Oh,..okay, hero, if that's the way you want to play it. I'll go with you. Like you say, if it was you or me up there..."

"Yeah, that's right. We'd want some help. And quick."

He leaned close. "Maybe so," he murmured. His sunglasses were put away now and his eyes were as serious as a heart attack. "But you listen to me, Mike. And listen close, good buddy. I've been in stuff like this before. It ain't fun. If I say we turn back, you'd better come with me or I'll leave you up there."

I nodded solemnly. "We'll do it your way, Buck. You're right. You know the mountains better than I do. You pull the plug and we'll come back down, pronto. Let's get moving."

"Okay. But what about this guy?"

I looked at the climber. "He can stay in my tent."

"Better yours than mine."

I grasped the young man by his trembling shoulders and turned him so I could look into his glassy eyes, and so he could see that I was dead serious. "Listen to me. Are you still thinking halfway clearly? Got a few neurons still moving around in that head of yours?"

The guy coughed and blubbered some crazy words I couldn't understand, but then nodded that he understood.

"Okay," I said to him, "here's what you do. Our camp's just down the way there, a quarter of a mile or so. Follow the trail. When you see a green tent, crawl inside. Get those wet clothes off, and get warmed up in my sleeping bag. Eat something if you can; there's some food there. But don't make yourself any sicker than you already are. Try to call out to someone if you see anybody, another camper maybe. Try to get a word down to someone at the trailhead about what happened. Durango has a mountain rescue team; maybe you can get word to them. If you can do all that, tell them we need a chopper."

"A what?"

"A chopper , you know, a helicopter. They've flown up from Durango before for rescues when they could. This storm may make that impossible, but if Jill's still alive, a chopper's her best ticket out of here to a hospital."

"Okay," the man replied. "I understand."

"Good. Now get this straight and don't forget it. We're going to try to go back up after her. We may not make it, but we'll give it our best. If you get some rescue people in here, you tell them all about us and where we're going. You tell them every detail. Where we went, when we left, and how long we've been gone. You got all that straight in your head?"

The young man looked almost comatose now. I slapped him hard. "I said, did you understand me?"

His eyes grew wide and he nodded. "Yes, I got it...but...what about Jill?"

"Look, we'll do what we can. I'm not promising anything. Now you get down to my tent before you freeze to death."

He started stumbling toward the trees in the direction of our camp. Buck pulled his parka tighter about himself.

"This is nuts," he said disgustedly to me.

Just then I didn't want to think about what we were going to try to do. All I wanted to do was get going. "I know it's nuts. Come on, let's go."

"You really think we can save her?"

"I don't know, Buck. I just don't want to go away from this thinking of her still up there, knowing she might still be alive, and knowing we might have done something."

He grinned darkly. "You know, I thought I knew you after all these weeks together. You're either a lot crazier or else a lot tougher than I would have given you credit for. Okay, Let's find out what you're made of."

"Fair enough. Lead on."

It was the hardest, most strenuous piece of climbing work I had ever done. Jupiter Peak normally was not a difficult climb. But working our way back up the mountainside in the cold, torrential rain and wind, it was a nightmare simply to make one boot follow the other up the meadow to the steep slope above. Along with the fear in my gut, I felt an inner ache coursing through my body like a hammer blow with each step. But I kept at it.

Booming thunder echoing off the mountains told me we were inviting a strike on ourselves, even if we weren't up high yet into the death zone. As we pulled ourselves on up over the wet rocks of the slope, our pace slowed. The footing was almost as slick as ice, and several times we slipped and fell back several feet and got muddy and lost ground and shouted in frustration. Still, we strained ourselves upward, on upward, into the cold, icy teeth of the lashing storm. I prayed to God that our climb was not just a foolish exercise in gross stupidity and false heroics.

We finally gained the rocky ridge after what seemed like horrendous hours, and still the relentless rain beat against us. I was thankful that we wore waterproof protective clothing. If we had not, hypothermia would have had us on the ropes by now. Every new step upward was a triumph of perseverance over fear.

Then, almost as suddenly as it had begun, the rain stopped like a shower faucet turning off. The clouds moved on and took the storm and its thunder to other nearby mountains. The wild winds were still with us though. The ridge was white with icy verglas and hail. We were still in danger of the errant lightning bolt, but less so now as the clouds moved away. The roaring winds wailed, blowing hard in occasional gusts capable of carrying a man off the ledge. At times it was easier to crawl along the ridge than to fight the wind walking upright. Remembering the girl, Jill, we pressed on.

Then the feeling of danger somehow caught up with me again. I felt craziness and despair mix in my mind. I found myself wavering. I wanted, desperately now, to tell Buck that our rescue attempt was a mistake, that we should turn back. But I remembered that feelings are just feelings, and something kept my mouth clamped shut. We kept going, dogged step after step. I wasn't going to let fear take over.

Brighter light suddenly shone upon us. The low sun sent its red rays under the flat blanket of gray clouds to the mountainside as we finally reached a point near the summit blocks. The wind howled ominously through the crags, taunting us.

There were huge steep rocks piled crazily near the top of the mountain. My eyes caught a little bundle of blue by the base of the nearest boulder, and as I came closer I saw that it was the young man's meager daypack. I looked at the edge of the cliff, and turned to Buck.

"She ought to be near here," I yelled to him over the wailing noise of the wind, gesturing toward the cliff. My fingers were numb, even in my gloves.

"We hope she is," Buck said doubtfully. He had his nylon climber's rope out of his daypack now and he handed it to me. I tied it in a bowline around my waist with one hand and crawled to the edge of the cliff. Buck secured himself, straddling a rock in a sitting belay position as he fed me the rope. I tried to look down, but the harsh wind blurred my eyes with tears. I wiped the tears away, and stared downward into the dark abyss below.

Thankfully, it was still light enough to see what was down there. The girl's still body was some forty feet below, lying precariously on a narrow ledge. Her legs hung down over the rock where she lay, and beyond her was a dizzying four hundred foot drop.

From what I could see of her, she didn't look good. Her skin was bluish-white. Her eyes were closed, the jaw slack, the mouth open. She was like a drenched, lifeless, rag doll, unmoving, as her body lay sprawled on the rock ledge. I shuddered. I felt certain that she was stone dead.

"I see her," I yelled dejectedly back to Buck. Or what's left of her, I thought.

Buck nodded, the hood of his dark blue parka bobbing. In the dim light he looked like a crazy monk in a cowl, sitting there as if in meditation.

"I'm going down to her!" I yelled.

"Is she alive?"

"I don't think so, but I've got to find out!"

He shook his head. "Better to wait till tomorrow, Mike! That wind may blow you off. Let the rescue people check her out!"

The wind shrieked in my ears. "No! We're the only rescue people she's got, if there's anything left to her. I'm going to rappel down to her and check her out and see if she's alive! I can do it, Buck!"

Buck reluctantly nodded his head. "Okay, but be careful, you dumb peckerwood!"

I had to smile. "Right!"

I never really liked rapelling, even under good conditions. I know some people love it, but I'm not among them. It looks like fun if you've never tried it. But once you lean back, the cliff down there behind you, you know you're dead if a weak spot in the rope tied to a loop around your middle breaks. Your whole life, all your past, present, and future days, becomes the sole responsibility of that nylon cord tied to the loop there at your belly. You're betting your entire natural life on a tiny strand of plastic fibers, and that's all you've got. It always gives me the willies, but there are times when you have no alternative. Like now.

I stood on the edge of the cliff with my back to the depths below. I felt Buck pull the rope taut. The old fear seized me like a manic phobia, but I tried to ignore it. It wasn't easy.

I'm going to die doing this, I thought to myself. I gritted my teeth. Then I remembered the girl below me. I readied myself to lean back into thin air, the tightness of the rope holding me.

"Okay, on belay!" I shouted nervously as I swayed in the gusty wind.

"Belay on!"

"Downclimbing!"

"Climb!"

I leaned farther back against the rope, almost horizontally, feeling it tighten more, one hand holding the rope, and stepped down the rock face. Black fear went through me like a tidal wave as my gloved hand held the wet rope. My boot found solid rock, and then I balanced myself and took another step down, keeping my legs wide for stability. The rock was slippery, but the lug soles of my boots found the purchase they needed. The gusting wind threatened to blow me off my stance and I swayed and struggled for balance.

Easy now, take it slow, I thought.

Buck's eyes were staring at me over the cliff-edge. Strangely, I felt Buck's presence inside me now. Buck had taught me how to do this the right way, and Buck would follow my every move each time the rope pulled out. He was somehow with me, and I knew it. Slowly, I rappelled on down the black, wet, rock like some crazy, erratic crab. It was like a tedious descent into hell.

The cliff's edge above me was some distance away now, and a moment later I felt that I must be near the ledge where the girl lay. I reached my free hand back to try to touch it, and I felt something soft. Her body.

Shocked, I pulled my hand back and an involuntary groan escaped my lips. I felt sick. Then, trembling, I grasped the ledge and huddled securely against the cliff wall, forcing myself to turn and stare at the girl's body. The old memory-image—the remembered dead climber's skull with empty eye-sockets—seemed to be looking straight at me. Then my vision cleared. This was Jill, not that guy back in the past.

"Belay off!" I cried, not sure Buck could even hear me over the moaning wind. A moment later I heard the faint, wistful return call, "Off Belay!"

I leaned forward toward her body. I took off my glove and felt her neck for a pulse. Her skin felt like a cold fish. Under the cold flesh, though, I could somehow feel a faint rhythmic pulsing. Her heart was still beating!

I looked up and down her unmoving body and saw no signs of massive bleeding. She had scratches and bruises, but at least she was still alive. Or, more accurately, she was probably closer to death than life. But still alive!

I carefully felt her head and neck for injuries, but found nothing irregular there, no bones out of place that I could tell. Still, I knew, she could be badly injured. It was always a terrible judgment call to know what to do in a moment like this. Moving her could kill her if she were broken up inside, I well knew. But leaving her here on the mountain overnight until the other rescuers came would certainly mean she would die from hypothermia.

I touched her face again to see how cold the flesh was. Suddenly, like an electric shock, her face tightened into a horrible grimace. She moaned, and her eyelids parted.

"Jillll! Wake up, girl!" I shouted.

"C-c-cold," she murmured weakly, frowning up at me. I was cold too. Very cold. I pulled off my parka and covered her as well as I could, glad I had on my heavy wool guide sweater underneath.

"Take it easy, Jill," I said. "We're going to get you out of this." Her eyes looked pleadingly at me as she felt her pain again. "What?...Where? Oh, but it hurts..."

"Listen Jill. My name's Mike Rader. You met me earlier today. You've been in an accident...a fall. How's your brain? Can you think clearly now?"

"S-sort of," she mumbled. "So cold."

I wondered if I could keep her alive. Her whitened face and her crumpled body lay still. It didn't look good.

I looked down the cliff, then back at her. "Don't you dare try to move yet. Just listen to me."

"Okay."

"Look. We have to decide something here. We're on a ledge and it's getting dark. I don't know how badly you're hurt, and if I try to move you, and you have internal injuries, it could be really bad. But I can't let you freeze to death up here either. Understand?"

She nodded, comprehension now welling in her eyes.

"Good. Okay, I want you to try to see if you can move your neck, and then your arms and legs. Take it real slow."

"Okay," she answered, and she was slowly able to move her neck and her extremities without any trouble. I felt more hopeful.

"Now try moving your back. Again, take it real slow."

She gave a slight move and moaned, but she could do that too. What I had to do next would be a gamble, but I didn't see any way around it.

"Okay, you don't seem to be too bad. Now let's try to get you up and out of here."

I grasped her upper body, slowly helping her to sit up on the ledge. When she looked down over the edge at the four hundred foot drop, she almost passed out.

"Oh! I...I could have died..."

"But you didn't, Jill!" I said quickly, sternly. "You were real lucky. Now let's see if your luck holds. We've got to climb to that ridge above us."

She stared up at the forty feet of steep wet rock above us. It must have looked like forty thousand feet to her.

"But I...I can't," she protested. "So weak...there's no way, the way I feel..."

It was time for my pep talk. "Look, Jill. You're supposed to be a good climber. Think positive. Let your strength all come back to you now. Look, this is life or death. You've simply got to do it. It's the only way. One short climb and it's all downhill from there to safety. I'll help you make it. You've got to trust me. We can make it together."

"No..."

"Try!" I said impatiently, almost angrily.

Finally, she nodded. "All right. I'll...I'll try."

I looked up toward the cliff above us. I saw Buck's face staring down at us like a faint gray moon.

"We're coming up, Buck! Get ready!"

"Okay!" he shouted. He disappeared beyond the edge and I knew he would be getting back in his sitting belay position, straddling the rock.

I tied Jill into the rope with a bowline around her waist. I had purposely left a long piece of rope on the end and I tied myself in with this. I pulled the line tight as Buck helped me, and I helped her slowly rise to her feet. She was shaking badly and it was difficult to steady her.

"Okay, Jill, here we go. Just take it easy as you go."

"I will."

"On belay!" I shouted up the cliff to Buck. "Belay on!" Buck shouted back.

"Climbing!"

"Climb!"

It was getting much darker now, dreadfully dark. I made Jill go ahead of me so I could watch her and help her. She was extremely weak, but the holds were there and she remembered how to climb on rock. She made better progress than I thought she would.

Then, after twenty slow feet of ascent, she stopped climbing, as if her strength had played out. She was breathing unevenly, a gurgling sound coming from her lips. Her head was nodding weakly. She looked to me like she was about to give out completely.

"Come on, climb, Jill! This is no time to stop."

"I'm sorry...so weak...," she murmured.

"You've almost got it made. Just a little way to go yet. We're almost there now. Just a few more feet and we're home free. Keep climbing."

She struggled on up the rocks, and once or twice she fell back against me, but I caught her. Finally, finally, we were at the edge of the cliff. I pushed her limp body up over the edge, rolling her over, and she lay gasping and moaning. I climbed up beside her and unfastened the rope.

I suddenly felt drained and frozen, but seeing her there alive at my side made the effort worthwhile. Buck helped her put on a sweater, and then I helped her put my parka on over it. Buck also took off his wind pants and helped her slide them on over her wet tights.

"You are one very, very lucky young lady," I said. "But if you can still climb like that after the fall you took, I know you can make it on down the mountain."

"I'm not sure," she mumbled, shaking terribly. Her face was pale as chalk.

"Oh, yes you will," Buck replied. "We've got you this far and we don't intend to leave you here now. And I, for one, don't intend to bivouac on this mountain tonight."

He tried to give her a bite of chocolate for energy, but her stomach just couldn't handle it. She spat it out.

I shook my head at him. "Forget it, Buck. Come on, let's go."

"She'd be better off if she could eat something."

"But she can't. Maybe later."

He nodded and we all stood up. The three of us moved as quickly as we could go down the ridge in the darkening twilight. As I stumbled along, I felt my consciousness fading several times and I pinched myself to remain alert. I trembled wildly from the cold. Hypothermia was stalking me now.

"You want to take a turn with my parka?" Buck asked me.

"No, let's just keep moving. Let's not waste the time," I said. "I'll stay warm enough if we're on the go."

The wind was colder than before, and I felt my fingers growing numb. It was darker, too, but we had the flashlights out and they were invaluable. The blessed ice axe came to my rescue time after time, too, steadying my steps as we brought the girl down the final grassy slope toward the swampy meadow.

We got down to the more level ground. As we crossed the bog of swamp cabbage, we suddenly heard the drone of a helicopter approaching. The dark shape of it was coming in low, up the basin. I was never so glad to see such a chopper. My spirits rose and now the cold was a little easier to take.

"Somebody send for a chopper?" Buck asked. "We could have used one back up there on the top of that mountain."

I steadied Jill. She was like a jellyfish now, barely able to walk. "I don't think it would have made much difference, Buck," I said. "It was way too windy for the chopper to hover near that summit ridge. And remember, watch out for that son-of-a-gun when it lands. I hear that more people get killed walking into chopper rotors in rescue attempts than in falls."

Buck looked at Jill, whose eyes were half-lidded now. He grinned at me.

"Thank you, Mister Safety First. We will be careful, won't we, Jill?"

She tried to speak, but she was unable to get any words out. Buck gripped her arm. "Don't worry, Jill, we'll put you on that chopper with tender loving care, believe me. After what we just went through on that hill, we aren't about to screw up now. In a few minutes they'll have you aboard that chopper and they'll thaw you out. Then they'll have you on your way to a Durango hospital and they'll really fix you up, good as new."

I pointed my flashlight up to the night sky. The chopper pilot saw it as I signaled him with the beam. He found a flat place on the meadow a hundred feet from us and set the helicopter down with a soft thud, the dark rotors blurring overhead.

It was not a hospital helicopter, as I had hoped. I saw from its paint job that it was a private bird from a luxury dude ranch down the valley. That didn't matter, of course. It was the ticket out of this hellish night for Jill, the way to keep her alive.

The pilot got out of his helicopter and ran over to us, stumbling through the muddy grasses, his arms swinging back and forth in his haste. He was short and slightly pudgy. He wore tan overalls with the dude ranch's logo patch on the upper right pocket. Beneath his baseball cap, his gray eyes were full of intense excitement as he stared at us. From the expression on his face, he looked like it was the first time he had ever tried this sort of thing.

"You people are just darned lucky," he said, as he helped us guide Jill toward the craft, her feet stumbling. The pilot looked up at Buck, staring him in the eyes. "Don't you overgrown boy scouts know anything? These mountains can kill you! You shouldn't go out climbing in weather like this!"

I fully expected to see Buck explode like an atomic bomb after all that had happened that day. Buck simply stopped, looked at the ground, then he shrugged and smiled down at the pilot as serenely as he could manage.

"Why, yes," he exclaimed softly as the wind howled around us, "I guess we've got a lot to learn, mister."

The pilot quietly seemed to sense that Buck was not the kind of man to suffer fools gladly. Buck was smiling, but his cold, squinting eyes reminded me of a rattlesnake tensed and ready to strike.

The pilot swallowed hard. "Well, uh, anyway, like I said, you're just darned lucky."

We moved Jill closer to the chopper, helped her through the doorway, and strapped her into a passenger seat. I shut the door. The pilot turned and looked at me. He was a bit more relaxed, now that he didn't have Buck staring him in his eyes.

"Uh, either of you two want to go to the hospital and get checked out yourselves. I've got room for one more in the bird, you know."

He looked at me hopefully. I knew he was wishing if it were a choice between Buck or me, it would be me.

I shrugged. "No thanks. Just get the lady there quick. I've been in helicopters. They make me airsick."

Buck smiled at me and shook his head. He laughed loudly. "You'd better go with them, Mike. You've had a full day, friend. That rappel was a killer and you look like you're frozen to the gills."

I glanced back at Jupiter Peak. "No," I told him. "I'll be okay." Maybe it was a macho thing to say, but I wanted to tough it out. I wanted to walk away from this mountain on my own, not be flown away by some magic bird. I was angry at what the mountain had tried to do, but I wanted to leave it the same way I had approached it, one bootstep after the other.

"Hero to the end, huh?" Buck taunted.

"No, all I need is a cup of coffee down at camp. I'll be fine."

He shrugged. "Okay, suit yourself."

Then, to our surprise, Jill's friend, the rock climber, came stumbling up through the wet grass behind us. He had some of Buck's clothes on, and they didn't fit well. He looked somewhat comical in the oversized pants and shirt. He seemed dazed, but he was more in control of himself now than when we had left him before.

"Jilly!" he yelled, "Where's Jilly?"

I restrained a laugh as I looked at him wearing the ill-fitting clothes. "She's in the chopper, man, alive but hurting pretty bad. Looks like you've recovered okay though."

"I'm...I'm okay," the guy said, looking through the chopper's window at Jill. "I found some people going down the trail and I told them what happened. I'm sure glad I got that helicopter up here. I guess I...I really helped rescue her, didn't I?"

I looked at the ground, too tired now even to laugh at his words. "Yeah, you sure did."

"I..I guess I'll fly back with her...if that's okay. I'm still awfully cold. I got our camping stuff together and it's all down by your tents. By the way, could you...could you carry it out for us tomorrow?"

I turned and looked at Buck. In spite of our numbness from the cold and heavy fatigue, this was just too much. It was a comically absurd request. Buck and I closed our eyes and laughed hilariously, shaking our heads.

"Did I say something wrong?" the guy asked.

Buck sighed and looked at him. "No. Listen, pilgrim. Right now, you're lucky to still be breathing. What say my friend and I cache your gear in the bushes. You can come back for it later. Right now, why don't you just haul your carcass inside that whirlybird and get out of here before your girlfriend buys the farm while they're waiting for you?"

"You're...you're right, I just thought..."

Buck lost all pretense of civility then. "Inside! Now!" he snapped, so loudly I thought I could hear an echo off the mountain walls.

"Okay, okay! I'm going!" the guy said, putting motion to his words.

The pilot and the young man got in, and Buck and I stood back out of the way as the chopper's engine roared to life. It thundered as its engines gained lift speed. Then it shuddered, rose, and wavered ten feet off the ground, its strobe light beams flashed wildly through the darkness. I looked up and saw Jill staring down at me through the plexiglass window.

"Thanks," her lips formed the word. I waved my gloved hand to her. The chopper swung its bulbous metal nose around in the night sky. It leaned forward through the air with a lift of its tail rotor and roared off down over Chicago Basin like some giant, lighted insect, the cold stillness of the mountains returned, save for the low moaning of the wind. We were alone again.

"Well," Buck murmured, "looks like it's going to be one cold night."

"Yeah, and there went my parka and half your clothes." Buck shrugged. "My backpack'll be that much lighter on the hike out of here tomorrow."

I sighed and laughed. "Well at least we've got a way to get our clothes back from him. We can always hold their camping gear for ransom."

Buck snorted. "I'm not carrying their stuff out. Come on, hero, I'm starting to turn into a popsickle in this wind. And you already are one. Let's go make that coffee you were talking about."

"I'm ready," I answered. I was colder than I had ever been, but I felt good inside anyway. Our part of the mission was done. We had gotten her out.

As we walked through the trees down the path to our camp, I said, "Buck. I want to ask you about something. When we went back up the hill for the girl, you said you'd have left me up there if you called it quits and I didn't want to come. Did you really mean that?"

Buck spat on the ground and sighed. "What do you think?"

"I think you're one mean and ornery...well, you know."

"You're darned right I am. That's why I'm still alive and kicking to tell about it too, Mike. Pure meanness keeps me going."

I laughed. "Mean? No, I don't think so. You're really just a pussy cat at heart, Buck."

He smiled, but did not reply.

We made our way down to our camp, to the tents, and I entered mine and struggled to strip and put on warm, dry clothing. No amount of clothing could take the chill away though. There is a certain kind of chill that just takes you over, and I had it now. I shook to my core.

Reality hit me. I wished now I'd gone on with the chopper. But I'd made my choice.

Buck made some coffee and brought me some. I didn't begin to feel halfway warm until I had my third cup of the coffee, and then the heavy fatigue hit me again. I knew I needed to lie down. I headed for my sleeping bag.

"You sure you'll wake up in the morning?" Buck asked. "I hate to admit it, but I'm a little worried about you going to sleep and freezing to death. I'll stay with you if you want me to."

"No, I'm okay now, Buck," I replied, knowing it was only half- true. The cold was hard to shake.

I knew I must have looked like death warmed over. I ran a hand through my wet, bedraggled brown hair. My face felt cold, gray, dry, salt-stained, and bewhiskered to the touch, and my body craved comfort and sleep. My mouth was dry, the taste of blood there, and my head ached all over. I knew I had to get warm or I really might die. So when I crawled into my sleeping bag and stripped off my clothes, I cheated. I had a little plastic bag filled with liquid in my backpack that I kept there for such possible emergencies. Exhausted, I gathered my waning strength and pulled the bag out, squeezed it, and it got hot like a little hot water bottle.

It was a chemical-reaction heating pad made for hikers, and I'd never used one before. As I passed it over my torso and limbs, I was thankful I had it now. It was indeed warm, like a warm summer rain, a God-send. Gradually the chills left me.

Later, as I lay there in the darkness, I knew one last part of our trip would have to wait till another day. We had originally planned to attempt a climb of one of the two nearby Fourteeners, Windom or Sunlight, tomorrow. The way things stood now, there was no sense in trying to go climbing at dawn. We were absolutely beat after the rescue climb. And I knew I might yet be sick by tomorrow morning from all the exertion. Besides, we would want to check on the girl we had rescued, once we were back in Durango. Windom and Sunlight, and Eolus, for that matter, could wait for another day.

I pulled on my two-layer underwear and covered my head with my wool balaclava. Weariness took me down like a lead weight. I surrendered to the black curtain of sleep, hoping I wouldn't freeze to death in my slumber.

I awoke several times in the night. It was very cold, and from time to time even my sleeping bag and the chemical-warmer weren't enough to keep me warm. I knew I should have eaten something before I went to sleep, I thought. The body needed the calories to make heat. But I was nauseated, and even the thought of the chocolate in my food bag was not very appetizing.

My fear returned as I lay there. The realization of how near we had come to Jill's death, and possibly our own, kept me awake and uneasy through the remaining long hours of darkness. That old picture in my memory of the dead climber's corpse kept coming back to me. Jill's face, crazily, kept superimposing itself onto the corpse's skull, making me shake with fright. I knew sleep was only going to be a wistful hope for the rest of the long, cold night.

So I made the best, or maybe the worst, of it.

Morning finally came, dawning clear. I felt a little better with the coming of the sun. After daybreak we slowly packed up, not caring that the tents were still wet as we stashed them into the pack bags and prepared to leave the campsite. We would dry them out and sort out the gear later. Normally, we dried the tents out and packed them neatly before breaking camp, but at the moment we simply wanted to get down from the basin and go home.

Sunlight caught the frost on the grass around us. We hid Jill's and Ray's camping gear behind some bushes and left it there. Then we ate a cold breakfast and pulled our heavy packs on for the six- mile hike down out of Chicago Basin.

Before leaving the campsite, we turned and looked up at Jupiter Peak one last time. The sky was cloudless now. From where we stood, we could see an outline in its cliffs that was like the laughing face of Jupiter, the old monarch of the gods himself. The face seemed to be mocking us.

"The mountain almost won, Buck," I said softly. "It almost got that girl named Jill."

Buck stared up at Jupiter and gave a short laugh. "Not this time, buddy. It didn't get Jill and it didn't get us, either. You ready to make tracks?"

"Yeah. Let's go. Another time for Windom or Sunlight. And Eolus."

We headed out, one tired bootstep at a time, across Needle Creek and up to the green meadows beyond. Then we plodded down the morning trail, the crisp air and the brilliant sunlight leading the way.

We caught the narrow-gauge train at the trailhead, a whistle-stop called Needleton. Durango has a narrow-gauge tourist train that goes several miles up to the old mining town of Silverton. The train is mainly for those who want to catch the scenic views of the mountains from the windows of the nostalgic old passenger cars pulled by a steam engine. Backpackers and climbers like us often use the train to gain access to places like Chicago Basin.

We lifted our packs to an attendant in the baggage car and walked to the passenger cars. Excited sightseers filled the seats next to us as we got on. We sat down in a couple of empty seats and sighed, the walking over at last.

The ride on the train was a once-in-a-lifetime excursion for many of these people. After having ridden the narrow-gauge train several times, all it meant to me was an easy way to get in and out of the wilderness. I nodded my head against the window and fell asleep as the train clacked slowly along down the tracks.

Late that afternoon we arrived back in Durango. We unloaded our backpacks and gear and I found my Blazer at the parking lot where I had left it. We put the stuff in the Blazer and I drove Buck to his house. I didn't get out as he got his gear out of the back.

"I'll call you in the morning," Buck said to me as he stood there on the sidewalk beside my window.

"Make it tomorrow afternoon," I replied. My legs were stiff and tired now.

Buck smiled and leaned on his ice axe. "Sounds like you're going to sleep in."

"You got it. After all we've done I think I deserve it."

"You going to check on the girl?"

"Jill?"

"Yeah, Jill."

"I don't know, Buck. Probably, maybe tomorrow. Right now I just want to go crawl into something warm and crash for a while."

"Okay, I'll see you."

"Fine."

I slapped myself awake and drove through the streets of Durango. It was summer, the tourist season, and many license plates told of Texans and New Mexicans visiting the old western town. I pulled onto a back street and drove toward my house.

Then, on impulse, I changed my mind and turned down another street. Maybe, I thought, just maybe, Tracy might be home. It was worth a try.

Chapter Two

The warm, frothy water in Tracy's hot tub soothed my sore muscles as I closed my tired eyes. I leaned back against the redwood siding, trying to stay awake. My whole body was exhausted now, stretched beyond anything I had required of it in a long time. But it was my mind that was truly numbed, jumbled and disturbed from the events that had happened when we were back in that storm on Jupiter Peak. Now I was letting go, finally un-coiling the tightly controlled strands of tension I had been holding in check.

Now that the rescue attempt and all that went into it was over, I felt a deep, gnawing sense of dread settling in on my mind. I had repressed that feeling back there in Chicago Basin and on the train ride out. Now it had overrun the ramparts of my denial and was having its due revenge. It was like some strange, mythic beast was sinking its blood-drenched saber teeth into the back of my brain. The beast was chewing away there, making a meal, reminding me in unmistakable terms how close I had come to ending it all.

There had been far too many unknowns back there on Jupiter Peak, too many ways to die. Now that I had the time to add them up, I knew that it was a miracle that we had lived through the experience. Indeed, the mountain had almost won.

Okay, I told myself, we did the right things, and the rescue worked. We made the climb, the storm passed over us, and I had enough daylight to rappel down to the girl. She could climb, we made it down off the mountain okay, and the chopper got to us in time. Lastly, I had survived a case of hypothermia. But it all was so lucky. If any of those variables had tipped the scales the wrong way, our little rescue attempt probably would have ended in a tragedy.

The ominous feeling stayed with me. It had all been just too close. The sightless eyes of that dead climber, back there in my memory, were staring at me again, taunting me. I tried to blot out those eyes and return to reality, but it was like clawing at broken glass with bloody fingertips. Somehow the role of hero did not suit me. I wanted to crawl back into time, back into the safety of the womb. I strained to get away from the feeling as I remembered where I was now.

The smell of eucalyptus in the room filled my nostrils. I opened my eyes. Through the dim light, the humidity, and the shadows of the green plants around me, I saw a woman's face smiling down at me. It was Tracy, standing there like an angel.

"I wondered where you went," I said to her quietly. Her smile warmed me. Her short brown hair framed her face and her brown eyes were friendly, full of warmth. A moment before, I had felt alone and shaken. Now I began to feel the anchoring warmth of someone who understood me. It was a blessing, indeed, a release.

"I was in the kitchen," Tracy said. "You must have drifted off in here. Are you feeling better now?"

"I don't know," I said, honestly. "After our fun back there in the mountains, I'm still sort of numb. We made it down, but it was...it was close, Tracy. Now that it's all over I guess I'm getting a little weary."

Her eyes looked at me with a deepening awareness. "Hey," she said, "I understand. You went through a rough time. It's only human for you to feel wrung out now. You're just letting down. That's only natural. You'll be okay in a while."

I gave her a small smile. "Maybe you're right."

"You know I'm right."

I sighed heavily. "Maybe I shouldn't have come over tonight. My head's still buzzing from the trip. I'm probably not very good company right now."

She grinned at me, wrinkling her nose. "Don't be silly. You need a friend tonight. We both know that. Especially if you're all frazzled from what you went through out there."

I tapped my fingers on the redwood siding and stared at her. "My therapist. Yeah, maybe you're right."

"Of course I am," she replied. "Here's your tea. You said no sugar, right?"

I took the cup of hot herbal lemon tea from her slim, graceful hand. My own hand, I noticed, was trembling.

"That's right," I said. "No sugar. Like I've told you before, sugar kills the taste. I like my tea straight up."

She gave me an amused look and brushed my brow with her fingertips. "My, what a purist you are, Mike," she teased, tossing her short hair back.

"Purist?" I said, my eyes on her, "that's what I like about you. You're the one who's the essence of purity."

She laughed lightly. "Purity? Me? You're making some very rash assumptions about my character, Mr. Rader."

"I am?"

She laughed again and dropped the blue terrycloth robe she was wearing. My tired eyes widened in appreciation as she climbed down into the hot tub. In her ivory swimsuit, her elegant feminine shape brought me back from my hazy state to full alertness again. The dreamy curves and swells of her made my mouth tremble, and I knew I was alive once more. Tracy was more than a friend. She was extremely feminine, a woman whose nearness had the power to bring me to life with all my senses acutely operative.

I watched her as she settled into the hot water. Her sensual manner was strikingly, hauntingly lovely to me, and she moved on down into the water with a languid grace. I liked the casual way she smiled and brushed the droplets of water from her smooth cheek as she settled in across from me.

She was exactly what I needed right now. Maybe, I mused, for different reasons, tonight she needed me as well.

She sighed quietly, and looked down at the bubbling waters of the hot tub. I eased myself a little higher and hesitated before taking a drink of the cup of tea she had brought me. She stirred, and I could sense that something was on her mind.

"What is it?"

"Oh, nothing. It's kind of funny. I'm glad you came by this afternoon. You really had that lost dog look about you when I let you in, all wrung out from your adventure. I guess I'm a sucker for tending to men in need. That's what got me in trouble with my ex- husband, you know."

"What do you mean?"

"He was always coming in from his exploits with a hang-dog look on his face, expecting me to kiss his wounds and make everything right again."

I frowned and set my tea cup on the deck. "I remind you of your ex?"

She grinned at me, gently kicking me under the water with her foot, and laughed. "No, silly man. Not really. My ex was like that most of the time. You know, all clingy and dependent and whiny, trying to get stuff out of me. You, sir, are definitely unlike

him. You are so strong, Mike, so strong inside. I like what's on
the outside, of course, you know that. But I really like what's
inside of you. This is just a tough time for you. I know that.
You're exhausted. You...yes, you're different from him. Oh, man,
are you different."

"Well, that's a relief. I mean, I guess it is, anyway."

She smiled confidently, showing her fine white teeth. "Believe
me, you're nothing like him. Do you feel like talking about the
trip– the climb, I mean, and about rescuing the girl?"

My smile faded and I felt a chill within. I shook my head.
"Let me...let me just rest a while, if that's okay. I'll tell you about
that later. Right now, I just need a little space to let my brain
settle out a bit."

"Fine," she said, nodding. "Take your time. Just don't fall
asleep on me here in the hot tub. I don't think I could lift you
out by myself."

I liked the way she had about her. She was easy and she gave
me freedom. I sipped my tea in silence for a while as she settled
in across from me. Our legs touched comfortably now under the
warm water, and neither of us really minded that. It was good
to be with her, to know that the warmth of another human being
was there. Yes, I needed it. More to the point, I needed her.

Tracy closed her eyes and gave in to the spell of the warmth
and the water, relaxing from the strain of her own day at work. I
enjoyed the quiet of the evening, enjoyed her nearness. I had been
all pulled in on myself, tightly wrapped in a ball within. Now,
with her, my friend, I was letting go, opening myself by degrees,
a little piece at a time.

"You need anything?" she asked after a while, opening her
eyes.

"No, I'm fine."

She closed her eyes again. I remembered how she had met
me at her door that afternoon. She had given me a hug, told me
I smelled like a bear, but she had let me come in anyway. I had
asked her if I really smelled bad. She looked up at me, blushed,
and said no.

While Tracy cooked supper, I had called the Durango hos-
pitals. I found out that Jill was at Mercy Hospital. A nurse I
knew there checked on her and called me back. My nurse friend
technically wasn't supposed to give out that sort of information,

but we were good friends. She knew I was one of the men that got Jill down. She trusted me to keep my source confidential.

She said Jill had some broken ribs and was suffering from hypothermia, but it looked like she was going to be all right. I thanked her and told her I wouldn't tell on her. I thought about going over to Mercy and visiting Jill the next day as I put down the phone.

Later, Tracy and I had dinner together in her kitchen. She had fixed chicken soup, the universal cure-all, and she had embellished it with some special spices. It tasted wonderful. I devoured three bowls of it, and she teased me about my impressive appetite.

After dinner, she suggested we take a soak in her hot tub. I needed little encouragement. I had left a swimsuit at her place from other soaks, so now I put it on and went to the tub.

Now, all was quiet. It was indeed good to be with her tonight, here in the warm waters that were gradually calming my nerves, washing away my feelings of dread.

Tracy was a very private woman. Some might have called her cool, or even aloof. Yet she was very friendly once you gained her trust and got to know her.

I knew why she acted quiet and withdrawn. She had her reasons. We had met six months before, not long after she had moved to Durango and had rented her small Victorian house.

The house was in an old residential section of town, a couple of blocks from downtown Durango. It had an ambiance, a certain charm, as did many of the early Victorian houses you saw in the old Colorado mountain towns.

She told me that it had been placed on the rental market by a couple only a short time before the day she found it on a realtor's listing. An architect and his wife had come from California to Durango, awed by the beauty of the small town and its alpine scenery. They had bought the house the previous summer. It was pretty run-down then and needed a lot of repairs, but it was the kind of house they wanted.

The couple had restored it from top to bottom, first taking care of new plumbing, wiring, shingles and siding. Retrofitting, the process was called in the brochures. Then the couple had added niceties like stained glass windows here and there, a new fireplace, and the redwood hot tub in a special room near the back. They had good taste. It was to be their cozy little home in the mountains, far from the hectic life of their former home in Los Angeles.

But there was a small problem. The Californians had never actually stayed in the Colorado mountains all year round until after they had fixed up the house. Maybe they had spent too much time in sunny California, but they became discouraged by Durango's prolonged spell of gray winter weather.

Long, cold, winter days can be depressing to people who have been drenched in California sunshine for years. The Durango climate, so pleasant in the summer, can turn bone-chilling cold under winter's gray sky, and sometimes the storms left snow piled several feet deep along the streets. Shoveling snow day after day and driving the messy streets can wear away at you. The couple had moved back to California, leaving a realtor to rent out the dream house for them. Lucky for Tracy.

Tracy had been looking for a place to live, and when she discovered the Victorian, she called the realtor, checked over the house, and quickly put down a deposit. After she moved in, she added a little interior decoration all her own, with plants and southwestern paintings and Indian rugs. Under her care, the house was always neat and clean, and she preferred to keep it that way. I admired the way she had beautified the house, and I felt right at home there whenever I came over.

I had lived in Durango for almost two years now. Arriving in town more or less by accident, in a way, I was fortunate to find a job in an outdoor sports store called The Aspen Leaf. I had started as a floor salesman, but after a few months I had been promoted to store manager.

In the warmer months, The Aspen Leaf catered primarily to backpackers, climbers, and car-campers who visited the many campgrounds of Southwestern Colorado. In the winter the ski crowd flocked in to shop and buy their equipment and ski-clothes. I liked working there; you met all kinds of people.

The work itself was extremely interesting to me. The Aspen Leaf stocked a large selection of high-quality outdoor gear, and they were practical items, not the cheap kind. I found that I liked learning about all the stuff, and I spent time studying it in detail. Maybe the owners had sensed my natural interest in useful camping items. I guessed that's why they had brought me up from my initial job as a floor salesman to the position of manager in a relatively short time.

Oh, I'm sure they had other reasons. They knew from my job application that I had supervised people before, when I was in the service. I got along well with the other employees, too. There was an opening, and they put me in it. It had worked out well.

I often left my office in the back of the store and went out on the sales floor with my clerks to give the customers personal help. I enjoyed teaching and learning from the clerks about the merchandise, too. If there was one thing I hated, it was to go into a store, any kind of store, where the salespeople didn't know the details about the merchandise on the shelves and racks. So I encouraged the clerks to be sensitive to the customer's needs and to know all they could about the store's products. I felt that if you were going to work at a place, you at least had to have enough interest in the business to know what you were selling and how it worked. And to show some enthusiasm about it, too.

I had met Tracy the day she came into the store looking for a special kind of fleecy coat we call a pile jacket. I had, months before, purchased such a jacket of my own, made of a synthetic material called Patagonia Synchilla. In cool weather I wore my pile jacket everywhere; it was my favorite garment.

I found Tracy in one of the aisles looking at the display of this type of coat on a rack. I told her how I wore mine at work and at play, and she asked me all manner of questions about it. She tried one on, and it fit her perfectly. As we discussed the jackets, her eyes caught my own with a look that touched something deep within me. Call it chemistry; whatever it was, I felt moved.

Tracy had deep brown eyes that were wide and full of mirth and life, with a hint of promise. I felt a strange perception about her, as if I had known her somewhere before, somewhere back there in my past, long ago.

Many attractive women came into The Aspen Leaf, but something about Tracy drew me to her. She had no rings on her fingers, so I knew she was probably single. She was obviously intelligent; but there was also a sense of freedom, humor, and yet, too, a suggestion of wistful sadness to her.

Before I had moved to Durango, I was living in Texas and I had been engaged to a woman. Yet for no apparent reason, my fiance had broken off our engagement. She never gave me a clear reason. She just said goodbye one day. No amount of persuasion on my part could make her change her mind. The whole experience blew me away.

For a long time the pain of that break-up kept me away from all women. I just didn't trust them. To be honest, my pride was hurt and my confidence was shaken. For a long time, I simply wasn't ready for any new relationship. Then, on the day Tracy came into The Aspen Leaf, I felt something click on inside me like a furnace coming to life on the first cold night of a Durango fall. It was sudden and surprising, and I was skeptical of it. But I let it happen, wondering where it might go.

As I talked with her that day about the pile jacket, Tracy seemed to sense my attraction to her, but she didn't seem bothered by it. In fact, to my surprise, she acted quite receptive to it. I wasn't prepared for her openness, and it both pleased and perplexed me.

As we talked, she told me she was new in Durango. I'm usually not very impulsive, but I sensed an opportunity with her. Before I really knew what I was doing, I offered to take her out into the town right then and there and show her around, to acquaint her with Durango.

"Right now?" she asked, a little surprised.

"Sure," I said, feeling a bit apprehensive at the risk I was taking. This was unlike me, unlike the way I had been. "I'm...I'm the store manager. I can take off when I feel like it. And right now...I feel like it. If you've got the time, let's go."

She tilted her head to the side and gave me a little smile. "Well, you're rather direct, Mr...."

"Rader," I said. "But call me Mike. As for being direct, well maybe I am. I apologize for that. But look, I won't bite. And I feel like taking a break. Besides, I belong to the chamber of commerce. Think of it as my civic duty."

I fully expected her to say no. That would have been the expected response to say to me, someone she hardly knew. Yet a tiny bridge of trust must have been growing between us as we talked in those few moments we had together there in the store. Maybe it was in the eyes, the body language, but something good was there.

She smiled and tilted her head again. "Okay...Mike, is it? I'll go. I don't really know Durango that well, and it might be fun to have a 'local' show me the sights. But let me buy this jacket first before I forget it. It feels comfortable and I want to keep it."

"You won't be disappointed," I said. I was hoping she wouldn't be disappointed in me either. I rang up the sale for the jacket on the cash register, told a clerk I was leaving for the day, and we went out the door.

For the rest of the afternoon I drove Tracy around in my Blazer and showed her Durango. I pointed out the tourist places and all the colorful stores, souvenir shops, and restaurants. We drove up the hill to Fort Lewis College, looked it over, and then we went into a newer part of town.

We were relaxed with each other as we drove along, like old friends, which I found both surprising and yet uplifting, wonderful. It had been so long since I felt that way with a woman. She made me feel things I had kept locked away inside, things like silly little bursts of humor, and banter, and I felt better than I had for weeks. We laughed and talked in good spirits the whole time. I really liked the lady.

Later in the day, we were both getting hungry. I took her to Roma's, a quiet Italian restaurant where the specialty was tasty pizza. I parked and we went in and found a table.

"This place has a warm, friendly feel to it," she said, looking around after we were seated.

"I know. I've got a lot of good memories connected to Roma's," I said. "I come here a lot in the winter with friends after skiing."

Her eyes grew wide with interest. "You like to ski?"

"Sure. I'm not what you'd call an expert skier, Tracy, but I do enjoy it. Do you ski?"

"Sort of. But I'm not very good at it," she confessed.

I liked her way of tilting her head as she smiled at me. The hair framing her face and the dancing light in her eyes were definitely alluring to me. Maybe, I thought, we might become friends. Or more.

"If you stay here in Durango long enough," I said, "you can get pretty good at skiing."

"I hope so. I'm really just a snowplower. I first learned up at Stowe, in Vermont. To tell you the truth, I'm still just a beginner."

"Everybody has to start some place. That'll probably change if you stay here. Skiing in Colorado snow really gets addictive.

The snow's dry and fluffy here, nice dry powder. It's friendly and forgiving, even on the steep runs. And you get better at skiing as you do more of it. You get your turns and the feel of the snow and the balance down and all that. Just go for it, as they say."

"My, but you're persuasive," she said, teasing. "You were pretty good at selling me that fleecy jacket. Are you going to try to sell me some of your ski equipment next?"

"No," I laughed. "But I meant it about the skiing. Like anything else, skiing's basically a matter of getting in enough practice. A good instructor helps a lot. At first you feel really awkward; everybody does. But if you stay with it, that all passes away. You work out the kinks and the awkwardness and get into the natural flow of it with time. Then it all starts to become second-nature. Maybe we could go up to Purgatory together some time next winter."

Then I hesitated, and looked away. For some reason I felt I had put my foot in my mouth.

"What is it?" she asked.

I shrugged. "Oh, I don't know. I was just thinking. You hardly know me, Tracy. We just met today. Here I am talking to you about taking you skiing. I guess I sound pretty presumptuous."

She laughed. "What's wrong with that?"

"Oh, nothing...nothing, I guess. Maybe I'm just going a little fast for you. I don't want you to get the wrong idea about me, that's all. I don't mean to rush things."

I looked down at my hands. It had been such a long time since I had said such words to a woman. But when I looked up at her, her wide, friendly eyes were inviting.

She smiled. "What if I told you that I'd like that very much...I mean, to go skiing with you?"

I stared at her, wondering where all this was heading. "Then I'd say that would be fine. I just don't want you to think I'm being too forward, too impulsive."

"Mike," she said softly, "impulsive...is fine. Don't worry."

I was genuinely surprised, both with myself and with her. It was so effortless. Maybe I had been simply out of the loop too long. Or, on the other hand, maybe I had let my broken heart drive my feelings for too long. Perhaps there really was more to life than rejection.

You sometimes forget that there really are a lot of fish in the sea, as they say. And one of those fish might have your name written on it. But still, I was doubtful, cautious, and it was hard to break free from my old pattern of feelings. The memory of my failed almost-marriage, the pain of it, had been like such a wall inside me for so long. That night the wall was slowly beginning to melt away within me as I looked across the checkerboard tablecloth at her.

Tracy told me she was a freelance photographer. From the description of the pictures she told me she had published, it was apparent that she was very good at her work. She had worked for a few years in New York City. She said she had passed through Durango on an assignment for a magazine a year or two earlier. She fell in love with the locale, and had decided she wanted to come back and do a book of photographs on the area. Then, when the chance came, she had moved here to work on her book.

"Why Durango?" I asked. "Surely you might have gone to a lot of other places. What makes Durango special?"

She stared at me for a while, as if she was wondering if I could appreciate the fullness of what she was about to say. Hesitantly, she said, "It's the light."

"The what?" I asked, wondering what she meant.

She hesitated again, considering her words. "I like...well, the quality of the sunlight here, the light. Photographers and artists are always looking for special kinds of light, Mike. I know that may sound funny..."

"No," I said, "it doesn't sound funny at all. I think I know what you mean. But tell me more of what you mean about the light."

"Well, you see, there's this...a sort of special...I don't know exactly how to describe it...maybe it's the high altitude or something, but there's this special rich quality of sunlight here, in these mountains. I don't know what it is, but on certain days it gives, well, a unique kind of mood or character to the landscape. It helps create a good picture for me when I'm lucky enough to catch the play of the light just right. I call it 'Durango Light'. It's hard to put this all into words, but maybe I can show you what I mean if I show you some of my pictures."

"I'd like that," I said. I had never really paid that much specific attention to the light she talked about, but now, as I thought about it, I saw that she was right. I wasn't an artist or a professional photographer, but there were days when the sunlight, especially in the mountains where I climbed, evoked a peculiar kind of mood. You never forgot how a certain scene looked because of that strange and beautiful light. The images etched themselves in your memory.

After dinner at Roma's, we drove over to her house. We went in, and she pulled out her portfolio and spread her photographic prints on the coffee table in front of me as we sat on a sofa together.

I took in her work, letting the images reach deep within me. The pictures were of beautiful landscapes of mountain scenes, shot from several interesting angles. Some showed sunbeams filtering through the green leaves of aspen trees. Others were of views up snowy valleys. Several of the pictures were of old mining cabins.

The photographs had a unique point of view to them, too; I could see that. The light she had described was there all right, and I could see now how she used the light like paint on a canvas. It glowed golden in the scenes, playing an important role in the composition, in the angles, and in the shadows. It spoke of something the photographer-artist could see with a special vision. You wanted to study those pictures a long time.

Now I knew why she was considered good, and why her pictures sold well. Anyone can snap a picture of a mountain, but Tracy had a gift of, well, of actually drawing you inside her photographs. You wanted to know what she was thinking when she released the shutter. Why had she wanted those old boards to be in the foreground of a picture? Why had she wanted that bird on the stretch of barbed-wire fence in another? When I would ask her about this print or that one, she would only smile enigmatically and say, somewhat evasively, "It means whatever the viewer wants it to mean. When it works, the viewer herself...himself...sort of, well, interacts and participates in the image. My picture then becomes your story. That's part of the creative, or if you will, the re-creative adventure."

I nodded, trying to follow her reasoning. I felt like her photographs were almost a religious thing for her. I wanted to ask her more, to see how much she would reveal about her work. I pressed her.

"But what do you, the photographer, see in your pictures?"

She smiled at the question. "I'll never tell. I have to let you guess that part. Part of the fun of good photography is the mystery, of letting the viewer invite his own story into the scene."

She laid the pictures aside after a while and as we talked she told me more about her life. She told me about living in New York, of her travels.

"You've had an interesting life," I said.

"Yes," she said. "But I had to get away from New York. I came to Durango for another reason besides wanting to do a photography project, Mike."

"Am I allowed to ask what it was?"

She hesitated, and sat back on the couch, crossing her arms. She seemed to turn rather cool and distant.

"Did I say the wrong thing, Tracy?"

"No, not really. I went through a divorce. It was a nasty one, too."

She turned her eyes away, and I saw her wipe away a tear from her eye. "It ground me down into pieces. It really made me hate myself for a long time."

She faced me again. I could see that her eyes were wet and I watched as her hands shook. I knew that the hurt was far from over for her.

"It was tough, Mike, but it's better now. Coming to live in Durango opened another chapter in my rather strange life. I'm ready for something new now. I'm just drawn to that beautiful light. It heals me and renews me when I get out into the mountains to work with it."

"But...do you still feel badly about yourself because of the divorce?"

She shook her head. "No, not as much anymore..." Then she paused and looked at me in embarrassment. "I..I don't know why I'm telling you these things. They probably bore you."

"No, no, they don't," I said quietly. "I've got a few scars of my own inside, Tracy. Fairly recent scars at that. I was supposed to get married a few months ago, but my fiance broke off the engagement. She never gave me a good reason for it either. It was like going from heaven to hell all in one afternoon. I've felt like, well, like something of a failure ever since. So I know a little about pain."

She smiled. "So that makes us kindred spirits, huh?"

I nodded. "Something like that, I guess."

It was two a.m. when I glanced at my watch that first night with her and I decided it was time to leave. The hours had raced by. I was as surprised by the swiftness of how the time moved when I was with her as much as by how we had fallen into this little window of togetherness. We seemed to be a couple of wounded people seeing a little, well, light, for the first time in a long time.

We often spent time together after that, taking it slow, both of us simply content to relax and learn little bits and pieces about each other. Thus, a comfortable companionship slowly built between us. We knew that we liked each other as friends, then as more than friends, though we weren't sure exactly where our relationship was headed.

Caution ruled us, though. Whenever we felt the feelings of romance stirring, both of us seemed to want more, yet we pulled back from the edge. I suppose it was simply that we had each survived a taste of our own private hell when it came to the opposite sex. Neither of us wanted to explore that place in the heart again just yet. When you're healing, you don't want to risk losing what you've gained.

The mood was different tonight, though. As we sat soaking in her hot tub together, I felt the degrees of separation between us starting to slip away. When I looked into her eyes, there was a new look there, telling me anything might be possible. It was like some last barrier between us had finally fallen.

It's funny how that happens, but when it comes you both know it. I put my tea cup aside.

I sighed. "Can I ask you something?"

"What?" she asked, returning my sigh.

"I'm really tired tonight, Tracy, you know that. But right now... when I look at you...do you know what...what I want to do?"

Her smile came slowly, cautiously. "I think so. You were out there in the wilds for a day or two, all alone. Is that loneliness...or maybe lust that I see in your eyes, mountain-man?"

I laughed. Sometimes she could read my mind. "Oh, probably," I said. "But we're adults, Tracy. We're both too old for games. But..." I paused.

"But what?"

"But...oh, it would probably ruin everything we've got going for us to tell you what I'm thinking. Don't get me wrong. You're as attractive a woman as I've ever seen. I guess...I guess I'm afraid if I followed up on what I'm thinking...feeling right now, it might kill that something special between us. I wouldn't want that."

She nodded. "I know what you mean. I've been down that road before. I've felt what I think you're feeling. I don't want to lose you as a friend, either, remember. I'd have to really be...in love with you...and to be honest, I'd really have to trust you before I wanted anything serious to happen for us. I don't think I'm ready."

"I know," I said.

She smiled lightly. "Can I tell you something about yourself, though, now that we're on this rather...delicate subject?"

"Go ahead."

"Mike, I like the way you...you don't threaten me. I mean, well, about sex. You haven't ever made demands on me. It's been like that from the beginning for us. I really like that. It's good to...just be friends with a man, and not have to worry about whether or not he's going to come on to me. You make me feel...well, safe."

I laughed gently. "Hmm, 'safe.' Now that's an interesting word. Some women might wonder why I was so 'safe'. They might even wonder what kind of man I really am, that is, if I'm a normal man."

"You mean because you don't try to come on to me?"

"Yeah."

She rubbed my foot under the water with her toes. "I know what you're like. I knew that the first time we met. I could see the way you looked at me. Don't forget, Mike, I have feelings of my own. The chemistry is good between us. But I know something else about you, too. You aren't in this for yourself, just trying to seduce me so you can say, 'Well, I nailed her.'"

"No," I said, "I'm not."

"Ironically, that makes me feel very tender toward you, and strange as it may sound, very vulnerable to you. I might be easier to seduce than you think."

I waited a moment, conflicting emotions suddenly making my mind hazy. "I don't want to seduce you, Tracy. Call it respect. And yet, to be honest, completely honest, in spite of my...restraint...or whatever it is, right now...right now when I look at you, I'd like to..."

"Like to what?"

I hesitated. It was hard to get the words out, but I forced them forth. "I want to kiss you, Tracy."

Her eyes widened in surprise She shook her head. Her flirtatious smile disappeared. Suddenly, she was serious.

"No, Mike. Please, don't."

"Why?"

She stared at me nervously now, trembling. "Because a kiss is...well, it's a sexual thing to me."

I stared back at her with questioning eyes. "Hey, I...I didn't mean it...sexually, Tracy."

She gave a small laugh. "Don't try to hide it. Of course you did."

I was flustered now. I was sure I had said the wrong thing. I started to get up, but she touched my arm.

"Wait a minute," she said. "Relax. You're allowed to feel what you feel. I'm just not...ready. Understand?"

I wasn't sure what to say. "I'm sorry, Tracy. Tonight I just...have this feeling of, well, caring...tenderness...for you. Does that make any kind of sense at all?"

To my absolute surprise, she came over to me and took my face in her hands. Then she kissed me full on the lips.

Her lips were warm. And incredibly dangerous. Her kiss and her nearness and her warmth were somehow suddenly perfect, and were drawing me in like I was...home. Home, yes, after a long, long time.

I felt as if I were on fire. I felt my own body responding, reaching out to her. My mind went blank. For a brief moment in time I was lost, out of control, lost in a dream.

"There," she said, pulling her lips from mine, but moving against me. "Now. Is that what you wanted."

I caught my breath. "But...why? I didn't think you...you wanted a kiss."

"A lady...can change her mind, can't she?"

"Yes, but...so fast?"

Her beautiful eyes flashed me a passionate look. "Sometimes it doesn't take long."

I circled my arms around her and started to kiss her in return, but then she pushed back away from me, a worried look on her face. I wanted to kiss her so badly, but I restrained myself. I looked down at her.

"You were right before," I said. "We're not ready yet. We need more time. I'm sorry. I shouldn't have said anything about it. Forgive me."

She moved toward me again and pressed her cheek against my chest. "Now you're going to make me cry."

I was baffled. "Why?"

"I don't know. I just...don't know."

I pulled her hard against me as warm tears streamed down her face, onto my chest. She felt quiet and warm. I shook my head. "Well, I guess I messed up our evening, didn't I?"

She hugged me desperately. "No. Please don't say that. Give it...give me time, Mike. Please. I just need to think...to feel. I'm still working out my crazy, mixed-up feelings inside my head. I'm...I'm learning all over again what it means to...to trust a man. Do you understand that?"

I sighed. "I understand. Believe me, I really do," I said. "Anyway, it's late. I'd better be going."

"Not yet," she said.

Again she surprised me. "Why?"

She brushed the tears from her eyes. "You said you were going to tell me about the climb and the rescue. Let's get out. I...I want to hear all about it."

I shrugged. "Okay. We'd better get dressed though. With you so near like this, my mind's all caught up in you. I can't think straight. After we're dressed I'll tell you all about it."

"Okay," she said with a sigh. There was a pained reluctance in her as she backed away from me. I felt the same yearning, yet the same reluctance. The flesh was willing, but we both knew the emotional complexities within each of us, and we knew we were simply not ready. Better to go with the flow than to rush things.

After we had dressed, we sat in the living room. I was sober and alert again. I told her the story of the climb and how we had rescued Jill. Going over the events with her was helpful to me now for some reason. Talking it out with her, I found I could sort through the facts better. She listened intently, asking questions here and there as I covered the details. I finished and she sat back.

"Mike, do you realize that you could have been killed up there?"

"Tell me about it. That's what finally caught up with me tonight. But we had to do what we did, Tracy. We couldn't stay down there at the foot of that mountain and leave that girl up there to die."

"But what a risk you took."

"I know. But I had Buck with me. He's more experienced and even more conservative than I am when it comes to stuff like we did. We would have called it off if we really thought we were getting in over our heads. If the rain and lightning hadn't let up on us we might have turned back, but I guess it all worked out somehow."

"And Jill...the girl's all right?"

"I guess so. Sounds like she cracked a few ribs and she had suffered some bad hypothermia, but she'll recover."

Tracy nodded and sat back against the sofa. Then she looked at me differently. "What's she like? Is she pretty?"

I smiled. What was Tracy thinking now? "Yeah, I suppose she is. I guess so, anyway. I really didn't get much of a look at her. Things were pretty crazy up on that ridge."

"And she's at Mercy Hospital? Are...are you going to see her?"

"If I can. I just want to make sure she's going to be all right."

She looked away. Something was bothering her.

"What is it?"

"Nothing."

"No, what is it?"

"Mike, just...well, just don't fall in love with her."

I smiled down at her. I almost laughed. "Fall in love...with Jill? What do you mean by that? You're the one I'm hung up on. What do you mean? Are you actually jealous of her, Tracy?"

She darted her eyes at me quickly and turned away. "I don't know. I might be. I've heard that sometimes heroes fall in love with the women they rescue, like in the movies."

I felt like laughing. "Oh, Tracy, Jill's just a kid. And I sure don't feel like much of a hero now that it's all over. More like a fool who got lucky."

"You're not a fool. You've got to admit, when you really look at it, what you did was pretty heroic. She's sure to be grateful to her gallant hero."

"Look," I said, sighing. I took her hand. "Get this down. I'm not a hero, dear lady. We just did what anyone else might have done if they'd been there. That's all."

She pulled me close and hugged me. "Well you're a hero to me. And maybe I am a little jealous. I just don't want to lose you to some damsel in distress. I'm the only damsel I want you concerned about."

I returned her hug. "Thanks," I said. "I'll be your hero if you want me to be. Just don't ask anyone else to call me that."

The fatigue was catching up with me. "Tracy, it's late. I've got to get some sleep. I think I'll be going home."

"Want me to drive you back to your place? You really look wrung out. I don't want you to crash into a street lamp on the way home."

"I can make it."

"You sure you don't want me to drive you? I'm concerned about you, big fellow."

I thought about the night before, when Buck had admitted that he, too, had been worried about me. I grinned. "No, I'm okay, Tracy. I'll call you tomorrow."

I left her and went back to my house, driving on instinct through the darkened streets. I was thankful when I came to my driveway that I had not, as Tracy had feared, clobbered a lamp post or something else with the Blazer. I felt like a zombie. Going into my darkened house, stumbling down the hallway, and falling into bed was a dizzying experience.

I felt like it was another person I was seeing as I closed my eyes. I watched that other person falling asleep, and then I knew that the person I had been watching was me.

I had been asleep about an hour when the phone beside my bed rang. Slowly awakening, I thought it was a phone ringing in a dream. It wasn't until the seventh ring that I realized that the ringing was coming from a phone in reality, and I woke up.

I glanced at the clock. Midnight. I thought the phone call was probably the police or a reporter or someone else asking for details about the rescue. Maybe Tracy. I picked up the phone and was surprised to hear a feminine voice, not Tracy's, that I knew quite well.

"Mike?"

"Ruby?"

"Yes, it's me, Ruby Carpenter. I'm sorry if I woke you up. I know it's late."

Ruby Carpenter was my guitar instructor. She was a retired school music teacher who taught guitar and piano in her home.

I had run across Ruby through the advice of a customer at the store. I had always wanted to learn to play the guitar, and Ruby became my teacher. I had taken lessons from her for several weeks. In the process, we had become pretty good friends. It was strange for Ruby to call me in the middle of the night.

"What is it, Ruby?"

"I called to thank you, Mike."

I sat up in bed. "Thank me? For what?"

"You know that girl you rescued up there in the mountains, Mike? That was my daughter Jill."

"She's...your daughter?"

"Yes. You remember I told you once I had a daughter named Jill?"

I searched my memory. "Well, yes, I remember you saying something about her once."

"I've never told you very much about her. She lives here at home with me, but I don't like to talk about her. She's had a lot of trouble in her life, Mike. Anyway, she's the girl you rescued in the mountains. I wanted to thank you for saving her life."

I was fully awake now. This was a strange coincidence. But then, Durango was a small town.

"Ruby, I didn't know she was your daughter. If I had known who she was I would have called you when I got in."

"I know that. I tried to phone you several times tonight, but I guess you were out."

"I was with a friend."

"I understand. I just had to call you and thank you though, Mike. I'm sorry it's so late, but I couldn't sleep. You don't know how thankful I am to you. Was Jill really in danger?"

I stared at the phone. "Yes, she was, Ruby." I told her what had happened, trying not to make the story sound too alarming. Just your everyday heroic rescue, I thought to myself. When I finished there was a sigh of relief on the other end of the line.

"Oh, Mike, I'm so glad you were there for her."

"I wasn't the only one involved. My friend Buck Corwin had a big part in it."

"I understand that. I've heard you speak of him, but don't know Mr. Corwin. I'll call and thank him tomorrow. I just felt I had to call you tonight. Do you understand?"

"Sure, I understand. Thanks. I called Mercy Hospital. They say she's doing all right."

"Yes, they told me that when I went up there this evening. I stayed at her room for several hours. I just hope that this whole thing shook some sense into her. After this maybe she can...can get out of the trouble she's been in."

I hesitated before asking the question. "What do you mean?"

"I...I hate to even talk about it. Jill was a good girl before my husband George died. Ever since he passed away two years ago she's been like a completely different person. It's those people she's been with, Mike. Her so-called 'friends'. They're bad for her. She...through those 'friends' of hers...she's been involved with drugs and all kinds of terrible things."

I frowned. "Drugs? Wait a minute, Ruby. Jill's a climber, an athlete. Surely she knows what drugs can do to her body."

"Yes, I know, you'd think so. But it's a long, crazy story, Mike. She's young. I guess she thinks she's invulnerable. You know how young people can be. I guess she thinks she can beat the odds, even when it comes to drugs, and still be an athlete too. You and I know that's stupid, but she's young and she just can't see it.

"That's not too smart, Ruby."

"I know. This is nothing new, I've been over it with her a thousand times. I've done everything I know to help her, to get her straight, but she's an adult now and even though she lives with me, I just can't seem to reach her, to get through to her. She lost her job last week at a convenience store. The manager caught her when she was high on something. He fired her on the spot. She came home and she was very depressed about it. That's why she went out climbing. I think she thought going climbing would help her get over her depression and forget being fired."

"I can understand that. Who was that guy she was climbing with, anyway?"

"His name's Ray Hamby. But he's one of them...one of those bad people. I don't know for sure, but I suspect she gets her drugs from him."

Now I remembered more about the other climber, Ray, the guy who had been with Jill. He was the one who went down to my tent when Buck and I went back up the mountain. I remembered the bad vibes I felt about him, too. Now I knew why. Call it intuition.

"You think Hamby's her drug connection?"

"Yes, I think so. He's probably one of her 'connections', anyway. Mike, I'm so worried about her. Hamby is the one she spends most of her time with, because she likes climbing and so does he. But there's another man in her life, too, a friend of Ray's. I think he's the big drug dealer from whom Ray and a lot of other people get their stuff. His name is Dil Cullen."

I frowned. "Dil Cullen?" I asked, surprised. I knew the name. Dillard Cullen, Jr., was an aggressive, very chamber-of-commerce- type businessman in Durango. He was well-connected with the town civic officials and, it was rumored, also the state-house people in Denver. He developed residential real estate and was currently involved in putting in a new subdivision west of town. His picture was often in the Durango newspaper. There was some talk around town in the coffee shop circles that Cullen might run for mayor or state representative one of these days.

Buck had mentioned Dil's name, not in overly-friendly tones, several times, when he was talking about his own real estate dealings. He didn't like the younger man's piranha-like, take-no- prisoners competitive style. I had met Cullen casually, bumping into him occasionally at chamber of commerce parties and other civic events. Every town seems to have a few men of his type. But I was surprised to hear that he might be mixed up in drugs.

"I know Dil Cullen, Ruby."

"I thought you might. He's got that land development business, but I think he brings in drugs, too, as a kind of secondary business, on the sly. You don't often hear about that side of him, of course. He wants to look good in the eyes of everyone. I think he brings in his drugs from the outside and people like Ray Hamby sell them for him."

I thought about what she was telling me. This was serious, dangerous talk. It could get Ruby hurt if it were true. "How do you know about all this, Ruby?"

"Jill told me. She let it slip out. A few weeks ago she said she was finally going to get straight and get her life sorted out. I only wish she really meant it. We had this really teary mother-daughter talk, and she told me all about it. She told something else too. She said she liked to go climbing with Ray, but that Dil Cullen was the man who really wanted her...uh, you know. Hamby knows that, and he won't touch her, because he's afraid of Cullen."

I frowned. "So you think Cullen's attracted to Jill? Ruby, from what I've heard, Dil's supposed to be an upstanding family man. He's got a wife and kids."

"I know that. But apparently that doesn't stand in his way where girls like Jill are concerned. That solid-citizen image is just for show, Mike. Then there's those terrible drugs, too. That's the worst part of it all."

I felt very tired. "I'm sorry, Ruby. I wish I could help you in some way. But right now I'm not sure what I could do."

"I know. There doesn't seem to be anything anyone can do. It's all up to Jill. Maybe I shouldn't even be telling you these things. I don't want to involve you in my troubles."

"I can understand, Ruby," I said.

"Well," she said, "at least she wasn't killed in that fall. Maybe there's hope in this thing somewhere. Maybe the fall really will frighten her into thinking about how short life is, and maybe it will somehow scare her straight. Anyway, thanks, Mike. Thanks...for saving my baby."

She began to cry, and for a while I said nothing, trying to think.

"'You're right. Maybe there is some hope here. What about you? Are you all right? You want me to come over or anything?"

"No," she said through her tears. "I'll be all right."

"You sure?"

"I'm sure. Mike, there's just one other thing. Saving Jill, that means so much to me. I want you to know something. Your guitar lessons are free from here on out."

I smiled. "Hey, that's okay. No, Ruby, forget it."

"No," she said, "it's something I want to do. It's the least I can do to thank you for saving my little girl's life."

This was not the time to argue with her. Sometimes it's better to let people do things for you like that. It gives them a way to feel like they're paying some kind of debt, even if you have a different way of looking at it. I decided I'd sort it out with her after the incident had settled down. "Okay, Ruby, we'll talk about it later," I said.

"Fine. Again, Mike, I'm...I'm sorry I called you so late, but I felt I had to talk to you. I didn't think you'd mind."

"It's okay, I understand. Look, I'll talk to you tomorrow."

"Mike, there's...there's one last thing. I want to ask a special favor of you. Jill, well, she'll probably be grateful to you for saving her life. She may listen to you. If you go see her, could you...could you say something to help her in some way?"

I sighed. Why me, I said to myself. "What do you want me to say?"

"I'm not sure. I don't want you to talk to her about the drugs or anything, but could you just...just be friendly to her? Maybe you could tell her that, well, that life is worth living or something?"

I groaned inwardly. I didn't want this, but there it was. "I'm not much of a preacher, Ruby. But I'll...I'll give it a try."

"That's all I ask. Just be friendly to her."

"Okay, I'll do what I can, Ruby."

Rader, I thought to myself, what have you gotten yourself into this time?

She seemed relieved, grateful. "Thanks. I'll let you get back to sleep now."

"You sure you're going to be okay?"

"Oh, I'll be all right. You know me pretty well by now. I may get all teary-eyed, but I'm pretty tough underneath it all."

"Well, okay then, Ruby. Goodnight."

"Goodnight, Mike."

I hung up the phone and looked at it. Drugs, I thought. Maybe Jill's fall on the mountain had somehow been connected to them. Was she on something when they were climbing? No, that would have been incredibly stupid. No one in their right mind would be doing drugs while climbing the tricky part of a mountain, especially in a storm. That was worse than driving a car on ice when you were drunk. In climbing, you needed every sense alert, not dulled by drugs. But then again, some drugs were supposed to make your senses sharper, or so some people said. Knowing what I knew about drugs in general, I was skeptical. I lay back down and thought about it some more.

It had been a long time since I had personally known anyone involved with drugs. But I did know, very intimately, the problems narcotics could cause a person.

Not that I myself had ever taken such drugs. No, I guess I had my chances to experiment like a lot of folks, but I believed all the stuff they told you about how such drugs could screw up your head. I didn't even like to take aspirin. No, I had never been a user, but I knew someone very close to me who once had been. I would never forget him.

It had happened when I was a soldier, many years ago, back in my Viet Nam days. I was young then, in the infantry, in a Ranger unit, right in the thick of that long-ago war. That time now seemed like a dozen lifetimes ago.

Like many who had come out of that ugly war alive, I had tried to bury the memories of it. Now they came back to me. I remembered the fear, the faces, the smell of the jungle, the dead and dying people on both sides. I recalled the lonely nights where you were afraid of just about everyone and everything.

You couldn't even trust your own people half the time. Somebody was always trying to hustle you. All you thought about was how long it would be until you shipped out and got back to what we called "The World," life in the states, again.

But there was one man I trusted through it all. He was my buddy, Joe Eggars. Joe was a black man from Helena, Montana, big in body like me. We were thrown into the same platoon together. Joe and I liked to talk about cars when we weren't playing soldier. Maybe that's where our friendship began.

Joe and I came to depend on each other in the fire-fights as well as the rest of it. We enjoyed each other in the card games, the bars, the joke R-and-R shuttles, and laughing our way through the daily routines. When our tired eyes met, we knew we were like brothers, brothers who could check things out with each other and help each other keep our heads on straight in the midst of the insanity of war.

There was a lot of racism in 'Nam, of course, but not for Joe and me. We knew in our gut that we were both members of a common race. Call it warriors. We shared the warrior spirit, and that was enough for both of us. He was one of the bravest men I'd ever known.

I owed Joe my life as well as my sanity. Once, we were out in the jungle, clearing tunnels the Viet Cong had used. Joe had seen the trip wire to a booby trap, hidden in the leaves, just before I snagged it, and he warned me. The shaped-charge munition the Cong set up would have cut me in half. Bobby, one of our buddies, had bought it that way the day before. Joe waved me off and disarmed the little trinket, smiling his big toothy grin at me. So I owed him.

Some of the mean days in that war went on and on like eternity. They tore away at your mind like sandpaper wearing away at a board, until you were nothing but dusty, gritty, painful emptiness down inside yourself. In spite of our best efforts to keep from going nuts, it was plain hard at times.

And then it happened. Drugs were available. They were an escape from the pain. They were everywhere if you knew where to look. Even the bravest of men can crack. Joe did.

He somehow got into heroin. Though he tried to stay strong, I guess something just snapped inside him one day and he took the plunge into the hazy euphoria of smack. He started out easy, but before long it had him.

It was easy to get heroin on almost any Saigon street corner if you knew who to ask. I was tired of the endless, futile war, too, but I couldn't believe it when I discovered that Joe was hooked on smack. It made me madder than ever at how the war was destroying us, but I felt powerless to do anything. I told Joe what a fool he was; tried to get him to quit. I even helped him hide his habit from our squad leader and prayed that he could keep going and wouldn't get himself, or us, killed.

It got worse, of course. One night something went really bad for Joe. We got assigned a particularly tough patrol along a river. We got shot up and lost two men. Though Joe and I survived, after it was over he seemed to go berserk, all twitchy and mean and full of craziness. He even turned on me and tried to slash me with a knife. I knew I could no longer cover for him. I told the squad leader Joe was cracking from combat fatigue, and the lieutenant told me to get him out of there, to take him to a hospital.

With Joe kicking and screaming, I dragged him to the doctors. I stayed close to him, visiting him often through long days and nights at the hospital where they kept him. Finally, through it all, somehow he got straight again.

Later Joe thanked me for standing by him. Thanks to a sympathetic doctor, we got his records fixed up and he came through the rest of the war okay. When we got back to the states Joe hugged me and said he owed me. I reminded him about the booby trap and told him we were even.

So I knew first-hand what it was to watch someone you love lose it to drugs. Joe survived, but too many other good people didn't. So I had a reason to hate drugs.

Now, years later, I didn't want to get mixed up with helping Ruby's daughter with the same kind of problem. One drug rehab experience was enough for me. My life was relatively peaceful now, and one thing I didn't need was playing Mother Teresa to another druggie. And I for sure didn't want to have to mess with pushers and dealers or anything else connected to the drug scene. I wasn't a cop, and those kinds of folks can definitely be hazardous to your health.

Yet there it was. Ruby had asked for my help with her kid. Was there a way I could help Jill and still stay out of the intrigue of it all? Probably not, I knew. But maybe there was a shred or two of hope in the whole mess somewhere. I hated to think of what Ruby had gone through with the girl. Ruby was a friend; and I don't like my friends to hurt, though sometimes, whether you like it or not, that's the way things play out.

I was tired from thinking about it. I decided to distract myself, to change the focus of my thoughts, and think about Jill and her problems later. My thoughts, strangely, returned to Mount Eolus, up there in Chicago Basin.

Eolus, the misty mountain, the mountain of death and dreams. It was a mountain you could remember, a mountain to mesmerize you. I was already thinking of going back up there, of climbing that tough baby. With the mountain on my mind again, luring me into dreams, I drifted off into ragged sleep.

Chapter Three

I awoke at six the next morning, feeling like I had regained most of my strength, although some of my muscles were still sore. It would take a few days to get my body and mind back into balance. Turning over in my bed, I saw the morning light flowing in through the glass of the wooden-framed window. It was a welcome sight, dappling the green leaves on the tree outside my window. I knew it was time to get up.

I go running to keep myself in shape. Normally, I do a five-mile run on most mornings, but that day I decided to give it a rest. You have to listen to your body and treat it well. The body has its own voices, and today those voices told me to let it rest from exertion a while longer.

So I lay there in bed, recalling my late-night telephone conversation with Ruby Carpenter; and I thought about her daughter Jill, up there in that room at Mercy Hospital. I hoped Jill had slept well and was healing okay. Then I remembered Ruby's request that I go up and talk to the girl.

I really didn't want to. I was reluctant to get involved in Jill's drug situation in any way, shape, or form. My life was going well now, and I didn't need some new intrigue bringing trouble into my placid existence. But I had promised Ruby I'd talk to Jill, and I have a deeply ingrained habit of honoring my promises to my close friends. I wondered how to go about it, however. Maybe I could just give the girl a little encouragement, leave her, and that would be the end of it. The promise would be kept; end of story. It would be the simple way out.

I got out of bed and combed my hair. Then I faced the big, dumb question I usually faced in my bleary-eyed mornings: whether or not to wear a shirt with a tie to work. I know it sounds crazy, but it's one of those little stumbling blocks I always get hung up on when I consider society's customs. I often wore the old shirt-and-tie uniform to work like all the other guys in my class of managers, but I hated it, even though I knew it probably was the socially correct custom. Social correctness and I don't always get along.

The shirt-and-tie thing vexed me in one of life's minor ways. Neckties appeared to me to be a concession to an outmoded tradition, a dress code whose time had run its course. There probably was a time back in history when there was a practical need for a necktie, that little belt of cloth around your neck to keep your collar closed, or for the sake of fashion or something. Yet to me, it seemed that the day for neckties had long passed. Even if ties were decorative, I wasn't much on decoration. I preferred the practical freedom of an open-necked shirt. But usually I gave in to conformity and wore the shirt-and-tie to work anyway. It was only a minor compromise.

I dressed in a clean, light-blue shirt, plaid necktie, tan slacks, argyle socks, and brown loafers. I smiled mockingly at myself in the mirror. Mr. Friendly Manager, I thought, ready to impress the customers.

I had a bowl of cereal in the kitchen, and as I ate I glanced over at my kitchen wall, which needed a new coat of paint. My house is old and a little run-down, but it's homey and comfortable. It has character. It is located in an enduring and congenial neighborhood full of big shade trees and other old houses and narrow streets. My neighbors all knew each other and we watched out for each other.

Durango is a fairly cosmopolitan town. All kinds of people live here. Doctors who moved here for the skiing rub shoulders with old ex-hippies who run mountain bike and rollerblade shops. The old guard, the Durangoites who have lived here for generations, reside next to expatriates from places like Chicago and New York City. The newcomers were people like Tracy and me, folks who came out West to escape their old Gothams and find peace in the more predictable small town atmosphere. The one trait we all had in common was a love for the town and the mountains around it.

When you live in a small town like this you learn to be tolerant and accepting of other kinds of people. You exercise your sense of humor about all the different cultural ideas people have sometimes. I liked this feel of the town, though. Even if it was old, there was always a sense of excitement in the air.

I ate my cereal and scanned the morning paper. There was a story on page two about the rescue of Jill Carpenter. I had to laugh aloud at the part that read: "Ray Hamby, a local climber, coordinated rescue efforts from a camp near Jupiter Peak. Two other local men, Buck Corwin and Mike Rader, helped Hamby in the rescue." They must have interviewed Hamby first. What a guy, I thought. I finished breakfast and left the house. I got to the store at eight- thirty.

When I had first come to Durango, I wasn't planning to stay long. At that transitional time in my life I was just drifting, dazed actually, more or less on the rebound from my broken engagement. After leaving my home back in Texas, I had vague but half-hearted notions of going to California, looking up some old army buddies, seeing what I might find there. I had no well-defined plans about doing anything at the time. I was just looking for some kind of newness in my life, some way to put my lost love and busted dreams behind me.

I drove northwest from Texas to Colorado on a whim, and I stopped for the night in Durango. Something about the place hooked me, and so I decided to stay on a few days longer to see what it might be.

I don't know how this sort of thing happens, but something about Durango just felt right, felt like...me. I guess some call it karma, intuition, or whatever you want to call it. Like Tracy, I simply felt like it might be the kind of place I was looking for to get my head back together. Durango was comfortable, the way an old pair of faded jeans are comfortable. So I stayed on there, trying to find some kind of a job and see if the feeling would last.

While ambling through the downtown streets, I found myself wandering into The Aspen Leaf. There was a "Help Wanted" sign next to the cash register. I had always been an outdoor sort of person; and so I felt that the store, like the town itself, called out to me in a funny way. On an impulse, I asked to meet the store manager, and after talking a while he hired me as a floor salesman. It turned out to be a lucky move.

I enjoyed learning the ways of the store, and in the days that followed I worked hard, though it wasn't like work to me. I got along well with the other clerks, and they didn't bother me with nosy questions about my past. They just accepted me and let it go at that. Maybe it was because they, too, were mostly people going through changes in their lives. Nobody pressured you about where you had been or what you had done. If people talked about such things, it was because they wanted to tell you.

After a few months as a store hand, I had compiled a good record of sales and a reputation for help with the customers. It all came easy for me, like I was made for it. I liked the customers who came in to buy the outdoor equipment. I spent a lot of time talking with them and helping them. Without really trying, I became popular with most of the shoppers I dealt with, and they came back again and again to talk and to buy. I suppose the store manager took note of this, because he soon moved me up to assistant manager. Then the manager himself had to move, so the owner promoted me to store manager.

There were nine people on the staff. The crew included the assistant manager, a secretary, a bookkeeper, five salespersons, and me. The whole arrangement had a comfortable feeling of teamwork, of balance. It was one of those situations where the workers got along well and we all felt we were in a quality place and time.

Surprisingly, there had been little jealousy from my co-workers when I was so quickly promoted to manager. The others were glad to have someone else taking over the supervisory and paperwork responsibilities, and they liked the way I handled the business. The workers were all outdoor-oriented people; skiers, backpackers, and climbers. They mostly worked at the store to support themselves so that they could pursue their real loves, their sports. Management, with its white-collar headaches and desk time, did not excite them.

I enjoyed running the store and supervising the workers. Management fitted me well, and I liked it even more than being a store hand. I had been given command positions years before, in the army, and I knew how to supervise people. It was enjoyable work, and I found I had enough time of my own for my own outside interests.

That morning I was sitting in my office, reviewing the sales reports of the last few days, when Barry, our assistant manager, came in. He was in one of his typically jovial moods.

Barry was a lean, muscular fellow in his late twenties. He had large green eyes that were almost always full of good humor. His short, sandy hair and glasses made him look a little like a young and eager high school football coach. He worked out a lot at the health club with weights and it showed. Barry was an expert skier, and he lived for the perfect run down a mogul field. He also liked the ski bunnies. His store work was done efficiently though, because he was a fanatic when it came to helping people have fun.

He was a likable fellow, single, and he knew his way around the night-life world of the bars and diversions of Durango. We had grown to trust each other well.

"Morning, boss," Barry said, ambling into the office.

"Hi, Barry," I replied, looking up from my stack of papers.

"Heard you got in some mountain rescue work on your hike up to Chicago Basin."

"Did you read that story in the paper?"

"Yeah, and I heard what really happened last night when I went to a meeting of the Mountain Rescue Club over at Zonker's. They think you and your friend Buck were nuts for going back up that hill in the storm."

I smiled. "They're probably right, Barry."

"Was it cold up there?"

"Colder than a witch's nose in a brass mask. Glad we got down in one piece. Did everything go okay here at the store while I was away."

"Yeah, no problems to speak of. Oh, one thing did happen I should tell you about. You remember Denise Rippy, that new girl I hired a couple of months ago? She quit. She met some Texan and she took off with the guy. Said it was true love. She sure looked like it, all warmed up and rosy-faced like a June bride. Anyway, she's history for the store, I guess. Want me to go ahead and try to hire someone to replace her?"

I thought about Denise's departure as I leaned back in my chair. "No, Barry, let it ride for a few days. I want to check something out first."

Barry knew me fairly well. He grinned and said, "You've got somebody in mind for the job?"

"Maybe. We'll see."

He smiled more broadly and nodded. "Okay, boss. Whatever you think. I'm going out to open those boxes of fall clothing that came in the other day."

"Fine," I said. "I'll take a look at them with you later."

What was I doing? I wondered what made me tell him to hold off on the hiring. Was I starting to get soft in the head? Was I thinking about hiring Jill Carpenter, the lately unemployed convenience store clerk? Forget it, I said to myself. I scratched my head. No, don't forget it. Selling outdoor equipment wasn't that hard, and maybe Jill might have a knack for it. If she really was trying to get free from the drug life, a job here might give her the motivation she needed.

The drug thing could be a problem though. Hiring her could be risky, of course, but I was used to risks. And if we hired her, and by some chance it did work out, I'd have done a truly good deed for Ruby Carpenter, too. If Jill were hired and she didn't work out, it could be sticky though. It's tough to fire anyone, but especially a friend's kid. Yet maybe it was worth a try, I thought. Or was I just playing games with myself?

I turned my attention to the sales summary sheets again. The Aspen Leaf was having a good year so far. The previous winter had cooperated with lots of snowy weather, so the skiers got plenty of the white stuff to play in, and that helped our balance sheet. We had experienced a record sale of skis, bindings, boots, and ski clothing in the last ski season. Now that summer was here, the car-campers, backpackers, and climbers were giving the store lots of business, too; and that kept the staff on the go.

There were a number of other outdoor stores like ours in Durango, but there seemed to be enough business to go around. We had one of the best locations of such stores, here in a downtown shopping mall, but location is not as important as giving good service. I encouraged the staff to outdo the competition in service to our customers. By my reckoning, we had been successful at it.

Oddly, I had mixed emotions about all the tourists that came to Durango, though, customers or not. You might say that my capitalistic ambitions were in conflict with my environmental concerns. Then again, maybe I was just selfish about the tourists' impact on the mountains and on our beautiful little town. Sure, the tourists kept our businesses humming along, but every year there were more and more of them. That put pressure on the town as well as the wilderness around it. Too many people and you have no more wilderness, or wilderness as I chose to think of it.

I had been up to Aspen a few weeks back, and the tourists up there were wall-to-wall in the streets, impacting everything like a horde of banshees. Aspen was a strange, gilded little Colorado mountain village unto itself. It marched to the beat of its own drummer, catering largely, it appeared to me, to celebrities and wannabes and the shorts-and-camera crowd. I hoped Durango could avoid becoming Aspen-ized, but it looked like things were headed in that direction at full tilt. C'est la vie.

The telephone rang. I put down the sales summary and picked up the receiver. It was Jeannie, my secretary.

"Yes, Jeannie?"

"Mike, it's Buck Corwin on line one."

"Thanks, I've got it."

I punched in the line and heard the familiar husky voice of Buck on the other end.

"You got back to work, I see."

"Yeah. A little worse for wear, Buck, but I'm generally okay."

"And you didn't get sick after being halfway frozen?"

"No. I went over to Tracy's house when I got in. Tracy's hot tub fixed me right up. Nothing like a long, hot soak in a hot tub to get your juices flowing."

Buck laughed. "Got your juices flowing, huh? Did Tracy fit into that somewhere?"

I laughed. "Watch your mouth, you dirty old man. You know Tracy and I are just friends."

"Pretty close friends, I'd say. If you ask me I'd reckon that your single status is in mortal danger."

"Not really. We're just good friends, Buck. Really. What's up?"

"Oh, the newspaper called me. They want an interview with me about the rescue. You know I'm not much for newspapers and interviews. Bunch of baloney. Do you want to talk to them?"

"No way. You go ahead, Buck. You can use the free publicity. You might get a few new real estate contacts out of the story."

I heard him snort. "Baloney," he repeated. "I might wind up telling them the truth about what happened. That wouldn't sound real nice, would it, considering what they've already printed. Did you read what that guy Ray Hamby told the paper about the rescue? About how he made himself out to be a big hero?"

"I saw it."

"I couldn't believe it. He made himself look like some kind of super mountain expert. Hey, you were the one that went down the cliff in that storm to get the girl out. You did all the hard work, Mike."

"Not really. Remember, Buck, you were the fearless mountain guide on our expedition. You led the way and called the shots. You were the guy holding the rope. You got us up the cliff face and got the three of us back down again alive. I'd say you were the point man, and the one the news media should be talking with."

There was some off-color muttering on the other end of the line. "Oh, give me a break," he said. "I'm serious, Mike, I don't want to do some stupid newspaper interview. All the dramatic crud aside, I always worry that they'll get the facts in the story all mixed up."

"Then tell them no. Tell them the truth, that you're a hard-nosed, foul-mouthed old man and what you would tell them might be unprintable."

He laughed. "You're not much help, you know."

"I know. And on this one I don't want to be much help either."

"Oh, come on, give me a hand on this thing. I thought it might look good to have a newspaper story showing the manager of our town's most wonderful outdoor store looking like an expert mountain jock. Think of the backpacker and climber angle for the Leaf. Good public relations. Might bring you some new business, buddy."

"Nope," I said. "I don't like the limelight any more than you do, Buck. When I was back in 'Nam, I was mixed up in an operation, once, that the media hacks thought looked pretty dramatic. I remember it only too well. They got the story all wrong and turned it around. Made us look like stupid dopes. Ever since that little debacle I've sworn off getting my name in the news."

There was a silence on the phone line. I knew Buck was remembering the war, when I mentioned it. He had a son who went over there and came back more a vegetable than a man. He was now living out his days in a nursing home.

" 'Nam was years ago, Mike," Buck said slowly. "This is today."

"I know, times have changed. But I haven't, Buck. I'm still gun-shy of the newshounds. Let's just let the whole matter drop, shall we?"

"You really think we should?"

"I think."

"Okay," he snorted, "if you say so. I guess I understand. Boy, that's a relief."

"Yeah. Have you heard anything more about the girl, Jill?"

"No. Why? Have you?"

"Well, I found out who she is. She's the daughter of my guitar teacher, Ruby Carpenter. Ruby called me last night and thanked us for saving her kid's life."

"My, my. Your guitar teacher. Small world, huh?"

"Small town."

"I guess."

"Yeah. By the way, when do you want to go back up to Chicago Basin? I've still got the itch to do those Fourteeners we missed up there."

Buck chuckled. "My, my. I do believe you've got the bug. You got a belly full of mountain climbing the other night, but you're ready to go back. Still thinking about old Eolus, are you?"

"Yes. And the other two hills, Windom and Sunlight. I'd like to do them first, like you recommended."

"Okay," he said. "I guess I'll be ready when you are. It's just a matter of finding some clear dates when we can get away."

"Fine, I'll look at my calendar and we'll talk about it."

"Okay," he said. "Talk to you later."

"Yeah. See you." I hung up the phone.

When noon came, I decided to skip lunch and drive over to Mercy Hospital to check on Jill Carpenter. I thought I might as well get it over with. I still had that job opening on my mind, but I was unsure whether I'd really go ahead and talk to her about it. I wanted to feel out the situation first.

As I drove north along Main Avenue, I thought back to what Jill had looked like lying there on that ledge on that cold, windy evening high on Jupiter Peak. Again I reminded myself how luckily the experience had worked out for all of us.

I turned onto Park Avenue and drove toward the hospital parking lot. I was about to pull into the lot. Suddenly, I saw a black Pontiac GTO, an old '68 model, approaching down the street. I had to smile. It was a looker, obviously well taken care of, no doubt repainted and restored.

I was a sucker for the old muscle cars from the '60's, like this lumbering old GTO I now saw. I wondered, idly, if it had the big original 389 Pontiac engine in it. A real classic might even have the three/two carburetor setup. The open hood scoop made me wonder even more. The GTO had been the car to beat back in the street rod days when I was a kid growing up back in Texas.

The windows on the GTO were tinted very dark, so you couldn't see the driver. It moved past me like a shark gliding through a lagoon, its low exhaust rumble burbling as I watched it slowly pass. A tingling feeling coursed through my spine as I watched it. I felt a little like a dog facing off another dog with a growl in its teeth. It was that old feeling of the challenge, of street race competition that caught me. I laughed at myself.

In my teen-age days back in Texas, back before I went into the army, I had run many late-night street races in my '62 Olds 88 with the slicks and the Isky racing cam. If I saw a GTO like this one back then, it was enough to get my heart pumping fast, thinking of taking him on. The old tingling feeling was still there, but that part of my life was ancient history now.

I shook my head and said to myself, Mike Rader, you're not some young kid cruising the late-night drive-ins anymore. Those were the days of night-games, of laughter, of burned-rubber squeals, of gushy girls, of speeding away like fools from the cops down two- lane blacktops. That was a world away, another life-time, an innocent but delinquent time, and, on reflection, probably a stupid one. We were lucky we didn't get killed. Years had passed. I was another person now, Joe Solid Citizen. Or was I?

That old part of my mind couldn't help wondering, could I take that GTO in a street drag? The Olds was long gone, of course, sold when I went into the army. And it was laughable today to think of racing the GTO with my big old Blazer, of course. Yet, I mused, I might give that big black piece of hot Detroit-iron a run for the roses with my other car, the one I kept in the garage.

My other car was as close as it came to a hobby for me. It wasn't pretty and shiny like this ghostly black GTO. To the casual observer, my other car probably looked like some old worn-out sportster that was a candidate for the junk yard. But if you knew cars, and you looked closer, if you recognized my other car for what it really was, your eyes might widen and your pulse rate might quicken a bit. It was a vintage Cobra sports car, a 1966 289.

Back in the Sixties, some people said that a 289 Cobra could hit 60 miles per hour in 4.3 seconds from a standing start. That may have been all dealers' hype, but yes, it could move. Well-tuned Corvettes back in the old days did the zero-to-sixty dance in about six seconds. So a Cobra got your attention. It got my attention when I found it.

The Cobras did well, very well, on the racing circuits back in the Sixties. My own semi-restored Cobra was a far cry from the ones that had roared into the record books back in those halcyon days, turning the sports car racing world on its ears.

The one I owned was old and ugly, dented in a few places, and it had mottled patches of gray primer-paint on its aluminum skin. It was all Cobra, though, and it still had a lot of the old fire left within its heart. When I drove it, if I ever desired it to do so, it could still make most of the other cars on the road seem to be standing still. Yet on those very rare occasions when I actually took it out of the garage for a spin, I gave it a light touch on the throttle when I cruised the Durango streets and surrounding highways. I didn't like the thought of visiting the local traffic court.

I found the Cobra by accident a few years back. I discovered it, of all places, when I was poking around one afternoon under a pile of wrecked Detroit sedans at a junk yard on the outskirts of Fort Worth, Texas.

The old man who was running the junk yard that day was minding the yard for his son-in-law. The son-in-law was tied up in divorce court. This was probably lucky for me, because the son-in- law might have understood what the wrecked car really was.

The old guy stood beside me in the junk yard, scratching his chin whiskers and looking at the wrecked Cobra. He said it looked to him like some dinky little European sportster some rich kid had bashed up in a late-night joy ride. I didn't enlighten the man otherwise as to its true pedigree, and I bought it from him "for parts" for $850. Vintage Cobras in good running condition sell for considerably more than that. Blind luck, I guess.

We used the junk yard's wrecker to pull it out from under the other old beat-up cars. I rented a car carrier at a U-Haul place and towed it behind the Blazer to Dallas, where I was living at the time.

I asked a friend who was a better mechanic than me to help

me fix it up. My friend whistled when he saw it. He recognized what a find it was, and readily agreed to help with the project. Working on a Cobra was going to be like being a part of history.

The big question we faced was whether or not we could actually do anything with it. It was pretty well smashed up, with a bent frame and with bodywork so damaged that it looked like it a couple of Mac trucks had run over it a few times.

Our good luck held though. Although the wrecked Cobra was badly mangled, over the course of a year we got the frame straightened out and we had the old original 289 Ford engine revving almost like it did when it was new. I had the transmission overhauled at a tranny shop. We smoothed out the bodywork, reworked the suspension, added new tires, put in many new internal parts, and soon it began to look and sound roadworthy. Rebuilding the beast was a long and tedious process, and it took a lot of my extra cash. But in the end, it was worth every scraped knuckle and unexpected expenditure.

Early one bright Dallas morning, after working all night adjusting the quirky twin-quad carburetor, I sat at the wheel and turned the ignition key. The 289 engine let out a hearty rumble from its new exhaust headers that made the walls of the garage vibrate. My hands shook as I gripped the steering wheel. I slowly pulled out of the driveway and wheeled the car around the block. I could tell by the pure animal growl from the engine that the old Cobra fury inside was still there, waiting to be set free. It was pure Cobra, ugly or not, and it was mine.

A few days later I acquired the license tags and somehow we got it through safety inspection. Then, one day, when I felt sufficiently brave, I took it out onto the back roads several miles from town, checked for smokies, and let the hammer down.

Driving the Cobra at speed, shifting and downshifting, was a pure, ripping, adrenaline-pounding ego trip. You were in a wholly different state of existence when you turned it loose. It ran like it had wings of fire. But it wasn't finished, and I wanted to complete the job. Like a prospector hiding his cache of gold, I kept it hidden away and rarely took it out on the road after that.

When I moved to Durango, I drove up in the Blazer, and then I rode the bus back to Dallas. Then I drove the Cobra up to my new Colorado home. I kept the unfinished Cobra in the garage at my house and rarely took it out on the road.

It was my one foolish pleasure in life. I had worked on it for a long time, and now only the paint job was left undone. Yet for some odd reason, I kept putting off completing that final touch. I had been hooked on the whole adventure of rebuilding it. Maybe I thought if I did that final act of painting it, the fun and magic of restoring it might leave me. So I left it as a work in progress.

When I did occasionally feel stressed out from work, I would go out to the garage and tinker with the Cobra. It was a joy to go out there, to lift the hood and check everything. I would run my fingers over all the metal surfaces, making sure they were clean and that the car could run at its fastest if I ever felt the need. Touching it was pure tactile pleasure, almost sensual. Cobra magic had saved me on many a lonely evening.

Now, today, in the hospital parking lot, looking at that beautiful black GTO moving on down the street, it was easy for me to wonder how the Cobra would do, going up against that shark from Detroit. My reveries of street racing were kid stuff, I knew. Grown men left such childish games behind. It was the time in life to be respectable.

I stepped out of the Blazer and looked down the street at the disappearing taillights of the GTO. It was just another car on the street, I thought. Today, I had best turn my attention toward that girl up in the hospital.

I entered the hospital. There was a volunteer lady in the pink uniform at the patient information desk. I asked her for Jill's room number. She told me, and I took the elevator up to her floor. Jill's name was there on a label on the hospital room door. I knocked on the door softly.

"Come in," I heard a feminine voice say.

It was a private room. Jill was sitting up in the bed, pillows behind her, eating lunch from a tray. She turned her eyes to me. I could see that she didn't recognize me.

"Who are you?"

"I'm Mike Rader, Jill."

She raised her chin and gave me a warm smile. "Oh, I remember you now. You look different from the way I remember you in your climbing clothes. You were one of the men that got me down off that mountain. You saved my life."

I sat down in the chair beside her bed. "We just did what had to be done, Jill," I said.

She looked like she was recovering well. She had good color in her face. I saw now, much better than on the mountain, that she really was a lovely young woman. She was all clean now and her hair was combed. Her facial bones were delicately carved, her mouth full. She resembled her mother. Wisps of her ashe-blonde hair framed her face.

"How do you feel?" I asked.

She sighed and smiled. "I'm a lot better than I was two nights ago, I can tell you that for sure. When you and Mr. Corwin brought me down off that mountain, I thought I was going to die right then and there, I hurt so bad. I must have seemed like a zombie or something to you. I was completely out of it. I still can't believe I made it down with you guys."

I smiled at her. "Well, you did make it down. You remember what it was like when I found you on that ledge? I know I gave you a pretty rough pep talk, but for a while there I honestly didn't think you could climb back up to the ridge. But you did. You found the strength somehow, and you made it the rest of the way down okay too. I guess the human body can do a lot of things that seem impossible when it has to."

She nodded woodenly. "I guess so. Man, but I feel like such a stupid schmuck, though, falling like that. I guess I just slipped or something."

"It happens."

"But that's never happened to me before in climbing. I mean, I thought I was pretty good. I've been rock-climbing on things that make that mountain seem like a cakewalk by comparison. Ray and I had done a hundred-foot wall earlier that morning. After that, we decided to do Jupiter because it was supposed to be easy and close, a walk-up. I don't know. I guess the storm had a lot to do with my fall. The rocks were all wet. We thought we could make it to the top before the weather got really messy. We should have taken the hint when you and your friend acted doubtful about us going ahead with that storm coming."

"Yeah," I said. "You and Ray were lucky the lightning didn't get you, too."

"That's probably why I fell. The lightning was getting close and we were scared and in a hurry. We were rushing things. That's when I slipped on the wet rock. It was crazy."

I nodded. It was so different here, now, in her quiet hospital room, far from the mountains and the horror of that night on Jupiter. That had been like a war zone. Here in this quiet place of rest, that stormy night was like a bad dream.

"Another thing, Jill," I said, "if you don't mind my saying so, neither of you were carrying extra clothes or other things in case you got caught in a storm. You've got to be prepared for bad weather, kid. Next time take some survival stuff along."

She nodded. "I know. At least I know now. But Ray and I, well, we've always been able to get down off the hill in a hurry before the really bad weather comes. Ray says if you only carry the clothes on your back you can move quicker."

I crossed my arms and shook my head. "Ray's wrong, Jill. Sooner or later some storm is going to catch you in a place where you can't retreat, or some other nasty situation will happen. A lot of people don't come back because they don't prepare for the worst. You've just got to be prepared for the bad stuff, Jill. It's only a question of time before the odds turn against you."

She smiled faintly. "Well, I guess I found that out, didn't I?"

"I guess so." I hesitated. "I don't mean to pry, but is Ray your boyfriend or something?"

She stared at me for a long moment, then wrinkled her nose and shook her head. "Not really. Oh, he'd probably like to be my boyfriend. But we're just friends, that's all. He came by earlier, and he said that he and a friend of his are going to bring our camping stuff back down from where you left it. No, he's not my boyfriend, Mike. Ray and I, we just like to climb together. At least we have until now."

I raised my eyelids in curiosity. "There's been a change?"

"Yes," she said. "When we got near the summit of that mountain, I didn't want to go on. I saw that the storm was getting too near. We argued about it, and I guess I gave in to him. And look where it got me. I think I've had it with him. Do you...do you do a lot of climbing, Mike?"

"Not as much as I'd like to. I haven't been at it long. I'm working on trying to climb some of the Fourteeners up in Chicago Basin."

Her eyes grew wide with interest. "Really? I know this may sound funny, but...do you think maybe I could go up there with you some time? I think I need some new climbing partners."

"Well, maybe...," I said, feeling like she'd trapped me. Taking

Jill climbing had definitely not been in my plans.

"Good," she said. "I really would like that."

"Wait a minute, Jill," I said, "look, you hardly know me."

Her smile was warm, intriguing. "I know that. But I find you interesting. So is that other guy who was with you, Buck. I think I'd like to get to know the two of you better."

She was indeed attractive, even lying in a hospital bed. And now she was working on me.

She smiled again. "Who are you, anyway? The paper said you work at The Aspen Leaf. I go there occasionally to get some of my climbing gear, but I've never seen you there."

"That's probably because I'm not always out on the sales floor, Jill. I'm the store manager, and I spend a lot of my time back in the office. By the way, I'm not sure if you are aware of it, but you and I have a mutual acquaintance."

She nodded. "I know. My mother."

"Uh-huh. She told you?"

"Yes. Mom told me you were one of her guitar students."

"She called me last night when I got in. I like your mom, Jill."

Her smile faded. "Yeah. And she...she said she told you about me, about my problem with...well, I might as well spell it out for you." Her voice grew very quiet. "With drugs."

"She told me."

She pushed her half-eaten food tray away and pulled the sheet tighter around her. "I'll bet you really think I'm something, don't you? A stupid young climber and a druggie to boot."

I leaned forward in my chair. "Look, Jill, let's get something clear between us. I can see you're not stupid. Your mother told me you had put the drugs behind you. If that's true, then what you were in the past doesn't bother me now. That is, if you're really trying to change your life. I know people who've closed the book on the drug chapter on their lives. It can be done. Your mother said you were working on staying straight, and I believe her. It's who you are now that makes you real, not who you used to be."

Her eyes narrowed. "You really think so?"

"I know so. Your mom has a lot of faith in you."

"Sometimes I wonder."

I sat back. "She also told me you were recently fired from a job."

She rolled her eyes upward. "Oh, great. I guess she told you everything about me, didn't she?"

"Enough."

She looked away. "It's a wonder she doesn't hate me, after all I've put her through."

"She doesn't hate you," I said. "Oh, sure, you've disappointed her. But she loves you, kid. She loves you the way any mother as good as she is would love her daughter."

Then, without warning, the hospital room door opened. A tall man with a slim, athletic-looking build came through the door, a bouquet of flowers in his hand.

The man's ruggedly handsome face had a brilliant, toothy smile. His head was massive, balding a little, and above his Roman nose his eyes were deep-set and serious, very businesslike. I recognized him. He was Dil Cullen. He ignored me and smiled warmly at Jill.

"These are for you, pretty lady," he said in a quiet, deeply resonant voice. Some women I knew would have called it a bedroom voice.

"Dil...," Jill said, sitting up higher in the bed. She pulled the sheet against herself again. "Thank you Dil, but you...you didn't need to bring me flowers. I'm getting out of here today."

Cullen calmly put the flowers on a shelf with slow deliberation and spread out the blossoms to show off their beauty. "I'm glad they're releasing you, hon. You can take the flowers home with you. Just remember that I gave them to you because I care about you, Jill."

Jill looked embarrassed. For some reason, I felt it was an awkward moment. Maybe it was because Cullen was so oppressively direct, so controlled, when he came in. He had not knocked; he had just entered the room as if he owned the place. And he wanted to make certain Jill got the point about his concern. I had the feeling he didn't want me to miss it either.

Jill looked over at me. "Dil, I want you to meet someone. This is Mike Rader, one of the men who saved my life."

Cullen slowly turned, studying me, and smiled down at me. In spite of his warm look, there was a raw-boned coldness to him. His eyes were measuring me, friendly but not without a reserve of suspicion. I knew that he was a highly competitive businessman. I thought: this guy is more than a competitor; he's a predator. But at the moment he was all charm. He extended his big hand to me, and I felt his strong, crushing grip.

"I'm Dil Cullen. Glad to...meet you, Mike. You look familiar. Have we met before?" The smile lounging on his lips was like that of a half-sleeping lizard.

I shook his hand and withdrew mine before my fingers went numb. "Yes, we've met before, Dil. I work at The Aspen Leaf."

"Mike's the manager, Dil," Jill said.

Cullen's brow wrinkled as he searched his memory. "Oh yes. I know the store well. But, for the life of me, I can't recall ever meeting you there, Mike. Where exactly was it that we met?"

"Chamber of commerce Christmas party last year. I think you were the master of ceremonies."

"Oh yes, now I remember that party," he said, laughing lightly, carefully. "I probably had a few too many drinks that night, and there were a lot of people there. Sorry if I didn't connect on your face and name. Lots of people there, you know. Anyway, it's good to meet you again. And yes, you were one of the men who rescued Jill, weren't you? You don't know how very grateful I am to you for getting Jill down off that mountain."

"Think nothing of it," I said.

Cullen was very, very skilled with his charm. I could see him mentally changing gears as he made his judgment of who I was now, and what I represented. He seemed to relax, and he gave me a look that tried to make me feel like I was the most important person he had ever met. Yet it was just a bit too stilted, too calculated. He had a quick way of glancing back at you to see how well the glow of his charm had registered.

"Think nothing of it?" he said softly. "On the contrary, Mike, I feel that I owe you a great deal. Jill is...well, she's a very good friend of mine, very precious to me. You've done me a great service."

A service for him, I thought. How selfless. Cullen slowly turned his eyes back to Jill, and I could see something new in them now. Slick or not, I could tell that he wanted her, and I suspected that if he wanted something, he usually got it.

"Mike," he said, turning his theatrically warm eyes to me once again, "look, if there's ever anything...anything...I can ever do for you, all you have to do is ask."

Far back in the brain, there is a warning light that blinks on when you sense some ominous, monstrous presence. It's the fight-or-flight thing. I felt that warning light flash on now, that little red light that starts the adrenaline pump, sending the caution juice into the bloodstream. I said nothing, but the adrenaline was roaring through me now, and my thoughts were racing. You really want to help her, you creep? You can stop supplying her with drugs.

I held back my emotions and forced a smile. "Thanks, Dil, that's good of you. I'll remember that. But seeing that Jill is recovering well is really all the thanks I need."

"No," he said, shaking his large head, "I'm serious. Listen, I have a lot of friends here in Durango. Maybe I can do a favor for you, maybe help your store or something some time. If you ever need a favor like that, just call me, any time. I've been known to help people."

He handed me his business card. For the moment, I decided to play along. "I may take you up on that some time, Dil," I said calmly. "Thanks."

Cullen smiled, and in his practiced, patronizing way, he nodded to me. I knew that in his mind some kind of corner had been turned with me. I had submissively accepted the gesture of his patronage. The line of authority was established in his mind: big man will help the little man. It was important to him to demonstrate to Jill, even now, who had the power.

Jill smiled nervously at him. "Dil, Mike's offered to take me climbing with him."

He cast a quick, nervous glance at me. For a fraction of a second, I saw a glimmer of surprise and jealousy in his dark eyes, as if I had threatened some plan he had brewing. But then, quickly, the gleaming smile and the gracious look returned.

"That's very thoughtful of you, Mike. After the accident, Jill may, well, she may need someone new to help her pursue her love of climbing. I'd do it myself, but I run on such a tight schedule these days. Ray Hamby is, well, a bit reckless at times. I intend to speak to him about that. You're probably the right sort of fellow for her to be with on a mountain."

Jill had caught me by surprise. "Well," I said, "I'm not sure we actually had it all worked out."

"Oh?" he said. "Well it sounds like a very practical idea. Jill's a fine girl. I guess I'm a little overprotective of her, though. Sometimes I feel like a...a big brother to her."

I sensed a small opening in his defenses. "Or a father?" I asked.

I saw a sheen of tightness flicker over Cullen's face.

"Something like that," he said, covering his reaction with his 24-karat smile. "No, I rather like the idea of her going climbing with you. That was a good bit of rescue work you and your partner did. Have you had much experience climbing?"

"Some," I said. "I'm just getting the hang of it. Why? Do you climb?"

He nodded. "Yes, Actually, I've been doing it for several years now. I do some fairly technical climbing with ropes and chocks. I even get in a little ice-climbing on occasion. It gets your blood pumping when you're a couple of hundred feet up a frozen waterfall with only your crampons and your ice hammers holding you into the ice. Maybe you and I could go climbing together one of these days. I know you may think of yourself as a beginner, but we could do something easy, something down on your level."

Bingo, I thought. He was good. Here was another one of his subtle put-downs, another way to assert his superiority over me after that remark I had made about him being like a "father" to Jill. He enjoyed these little power games, but I was getting tired of them. Maybe because he was so obvious with them. I must have pushed a button on him somewhere, and now he was getting just a little too transparent.

Sometimes it's best to humor the jerks. I smiled innocently and said, "From the sound of it, Dil, you really are a lot more advanced than I am when it comes to climbing. But maybe someday I'll take you up on that. That is, if you don't mind me holding you back."

"Good," Dil said, smiling like he'd just won the state lottery. "I doubt if there'll be any holding back, though. I'll take you up something...interesting."

"Sure," I said. Yes, he knew the game well.

Cullen turned to Jill again. "Jill, did...did Jimmy Rowe come by to see you earlier? I looked for his GTO on the parking lot and I thought I might catch him, but I guess I missed him."

Suddenly there was a trace of fear in Jill's blue eyes. Nervously, she ran her fingers through her hair. What's she afraid of, I wondered.

"He...he was here a while ago. Dil, I really don't like that man. I don't know why you have him working for you. He's not at all nice, like you are. I wish he would just stay away from me. There's something about him. He gives me the chills."

Cullen smiled. "Oh, Jimmy's all right, Jill." He stepped closer to her bedside, and he reached out and carefully smoothed her hair on her brow possessively. When I saw him touch her, I felt a twinge of disgust. My fists clenched. My pulse pounded in my head, but I tried not to show what I was feeling.

"No, don't worry about Jimmy," Dil said to her, as if she were a child. "He's a little rough around the edges, but he's really a hard worker. He can be a little, well, blunt at times, that's just his way. I'm sorry if he disturbed you though. I'll speak to him about it."

She still had that look of fear in her eyes. "Dil, I wish he'd just stay away."

"We'll see." Cullen stepped back from her. "Oh, there's just one other thing. You'll be needing a job now, won't you. Come down to my office when you get out. I want to fix you up with something nice. I'm sure we can work out a position. We'll find something suitable."

Jill stiffened. "I...I'd have to think about that."

"What's there to think about? Be a good girl and come on by when they release you. You know me. I'll take care of everything."

"No," she said, "I want to think it over, Dil."

"Jill...," he said, an intimidating tone creeping into his voice.

I looked straight at him. "Dil," I said quietly, "why don't you let the lady rest. She's been through a lot."

He turned quickly and flashed me a look that was meant to intimidate me, I suppose, but I could see right through him. He was just a school-yard bully dressed in an expensive suit. I was relaxed about it, but now I had him pegged. And now that I had his number, I wanted to take him apart.

He knew it, too. He stared at me for a long moment, measuring me, perhaps sensing my lack of fear, and then he backed off. The quiet, almost imperceptible tension eased. He turned his attention to Jill again.

"Yes, I suppose you're just tired now, Jill. But do give it

some thought. If you need anything...anything, just let me know. I'm here for you. You know that."

He looked at his watch. I noticed that it was a Rolex, of course. "Lunch meeting with the zoning board chairman coming up, my dear. I'd better be going," he said.

Cullen, smiling, turned to me again. The charm was switched back on. "And thank you again, Mike. You remember what I said about my owing you one. Come see me. I'd like to repay you for what you've done. Take care."

"Sure, Dil," I said. "See you around."

Cullen said good-bye to Jill and then he left, walking quietly out the door.

A moment or two after the door closed, Jill let out a long sigh. "Thanks," she said, relieved that Dil had gone.

"For what?" I asked.

"For helping get me off the hook about that job he offered."

"No problem," I said. "I don't like to see people being pressured. You look like you need some space."

"I do," she said. She regarded me with wide, serious eyes.

"I've got my reasons," she said.

"That's pretty obvious. Are you really in the market for a new job?"

"No. I mean, well, yes, maybe I am, at that."

I sighed. "How would you like to work for me?"

She laughed lightly. "Work for you? Doing what?"

Okay, I said to myself, here goes. "I've got an opening at my store for a clerk's position. You'd be selling climbing gear and other things. Would you be interested?"

She sat up straight in her bed and looked me squarely in the eyes. "I definitely would be interested. But why?"

I shifted in my chair. "Well, it's a question of needs. You're a climber. You know what climbers need. You need a job. I need a new employee. So we take care of three needs at once. Simple."

She stared at me with suspicion in her eyes. "Did my mother ask you to offer me the job? Did she put you up to this?"

I shook my head. "My, but you're suspicious. No, your mom had nothing to do with it. I really am short-handed at the store, Jill. I need someone knowledgeable to take the job quickly and it sounds like you need the work. Like I said, you're a climber, so you probably know the kind of stuff we sell. I think it could work out to our mutual advantage."

She shook her head. "I don't know. I seem to bring people trouble everywhere I go."

"I don't believe that, Jill."

"It's true. I'd be bad luck for you. Maybe I ought to go ahead and take Dil up on his job offer."

I shook my head. "Look, let's be honest. You know you don't want to go to work for Cullen. We both know that. Cullen has another business on the side. He's a land developer, sure, but we both know he deals in more than simply parcels of land. His other merchandise comes in little plastic baggies. And I'd be willing to bet that you've been one of his customers. Am I right?"

She gave me a look of resignation. "Mother again. She told you all about Dil, didn't she?"

"Not everything, but enough. Cullen's a nice guy on the surface, Jill. But if he's the kind of man I think he is, he may not be so nice underneath that successful businessman image he tries so hard to sell. He might even be downright dangerous. But what really complicates things is that he's obviously very interested in you. He may even be in love with you, or whatever passes for love with a man like him."

She looked at me seriously for a moment, then laughed heartily. "You're very perceptive. You know, that's the funny part. I've never had to buy the stuff from him. He gives it to me free."

I laughed. "Figures. But it's not really so free, is it?"

She frowned and shook her head. "No, it isn't like that. He's never made any demands on me. He...he says he loves me."

I nodded. "I think that's probably the one thing he would say that would be the truth. But eventually he'll want more, Jill. His little gifts are just to grease the skids for other plans he has for you."

She sighed. "I know that."

"But that's not what you want, is it? Look, maybe this is none of my business. We both know how he feels about you. But what about how you feel about him? Are your feelings mutual?"

She colored. "That's none of your business!" Then she bit her lip and shrugged. "Oh, so what. I guess if you know this much and you're still willing to hire me, maybe you're all right."

Her eyes caught me head-on. "No, Mike, I don't love him. Sure, I was flattered at his attentions at first. He's an important man in town. He made me feel like I was worth something, like a princess or something. I guess I let myself get a little carried away with him at first, but I'm through with that now. Dil is married, and he could have a lot of women. Why he picked me, I don't know."

"Love's a funny thing, Jill. Don't take this the wrong way, but any fool could see why he'd be attracted to you. You're young and good-looking. He really does want you."

"That," she said, shaking her head, "I'm very well aware of. But thanks for the compliment. And no, I didn't take it the wrong way. Anyway, I guess I'm really in a bad spot where Dil is concerned. He won't stay away and I don't know how I can keep him away. If I take the job you're offering, it would probably just make matters worse."

"Why? Remember what they say, 'just say no'."

She smirked. "Oh, that's cute . It really is. But it's not that simple, Mike. Dil Cullen is a very powerful man in town. He can hurt people. People like you. He's done it before."

I sighed. "Look, Jill, I hardly know you. And I don't want to sound as overprotective as Cullen does, but if it's any comfort, don't worry about me. I've had my share of dealing with jerks like him. Maybe I can help you."

She frowned. "You? What can you do?"

"I don't know. But I just don't like to see you intimidated by a man like Cullen. By the way, speaking of intimidation, who's this other guy, the one that works for him? 'Jimmy Rowe,' I believe his name was. You really don't like him at all, do you?"

She made a face. "Jimmy? No, I don't like him one bit. He's the main man in Dil's 'other business,' as you called it. Dil never directly gave me those 'gifts' I was telling you about. Jimmy–or sometimes Ray–gave them to me."

"Figures," I said. "Dil's covering himself there. So what was Jimmy Rowe doing here visiting you at the hospital? I can't imagine it was just a get-well visit."

"No, it wasn't," she said. "Jimmy was asking me some questions. I got my name in the paper because of the accident and Jimmy wanted to make sure I hadn't told the doctors or anyone about my little habit, about those 'gifts' and where they came from. Maybe he was worried that I might have let something slip in a weak moment when I was so out of it, on the anesthesia or something."

"So friend Jimmy was just making sure there were no leaks in the old pipeline. I'm sure he was just the sort of person you wanted to talk to here while you were in the hospital."

She frowned. "He's awful, Mike. Ugly and smelly. He actually threatened me. Really was smooth about it, of course, but I could tell by the way he said it, he wanted me to keep my mouth clamped shut."

I nodded. "Well look, don't worry about me saying anything about this. I'm on your side, Jill. I will say one thing for your friend Jimmy, though. He's got a nice set of wheels."

"Please don't call him my 'friend.' You mean that old GTO of his?"

"Yeah. I thought I was the only person in town with an old muscle car from the '60's. Too bad a slimeball like Rowe is driving it. The car deserves better."

"'I think he lives in it," she laughed. "He sure smells like he does. Dil says that GTO can outrun anything on the road."

I smiled softly. "Maybe. I can see why Jimmy likes it though. If he's a veteran player in the midnight pharmaceutical business, a fast car might come in handy at times. Of course, it does tend to stand out if you know your cars. Any good cop would peg it on sight."

"Jimmy doesn't seem to worry about cops. He likes for people to know when he's around. Jimmy...he's the one who's really dangerous, Mike."

"Nope. Both of them are trouble. Cullen just hides his dark side better. Jimmy may be his street muscle and Dil's friendly neighborhood distributor, but Dil still holds his leash. Whoever holds the leash in that kind of game has the juice over the street-man. Dil's got the big money and the influence. That means he's got legal talent to protect guys like Jimmy. But any trouble from Jimmy and little Jimmy might get cut from the team, the hard way, so Jimmy plays along. Assuming Jimmy's loyal, he's the buffer, the fall guy if there's a bust. And Jimmy knows it and accepts it. Dil could get another Jimmy Rowe any time he wants to. Again, Jimmy knows that, so he follows orders. He may threaten you, but as long as Dil's got his lusty eyes on you, you're going to be safe. It's like protective custody."

She nodded. "You're probably right. You seem to know a lot about it."

"Not really," I said. "Let's just say I've been through scenes like this a time or two."

"Where?"

"A lot of places. Drug people are pretty much the same all over. They all suck blood out of people the same way. They don't see it that way, of course. They make it all good in their minds, like they're helping people. But garbage is always garbage when you hold it up to the light."

"That's for sure," she said. "But...where do you come in on all this, Mike? I can't help wondering about what you want out of helping me."

I got up, went closer, and took her hand. "Look, Jill, you're a nice young lady. But I'm not offering to help you with the job because I want anything from you. You know that, don't you?"

She stared up at me. "Yeah, I guess I do. You seem okay. And I guess by now I know a man on the make when I see one. You don't seem the type. But what's your real angle in this, Mike? What's in it for you?"

I grinned sheepishly. "I've been wondering the same thing. I came here today thinking I'd do a favor to your mother by giving you a pep talk of some kind. At first, that's all I was going to do. I know offering you the job seems like one way to help you, although I told you the truth when I said your mom hadn't asked me about offering it. She didn't even know I needed someone at the store. But I do need a new salesperson. That's the truth."

"I believe you."

"There's more, though," I said. "Now that I've seen Cullen in action, how he talks and how he does things I just don't like the thought of you under his thumb. And, if you'll pardon me, I don't like the idea of you on the way to his bed either. Lady, I've seen what happens when that kind of thing goes down. You deserve better than that. As for your former drug habit, I suppose you've got to make your own decision about that. I know there are no guarantees about all this. But I'll help you in whatever way I can. Fair enough?"

"Sounds okay to me," she said, nodding. "But Mike— aren't you afraid of Dil?"

I smiled. "Sure. But he's got more to lose than I do. Guys like Cullen don't like to attract attention, at least the negative kind. And right now he's vulnerable in one area of his life: you. He wants to keep you happy, so he'll make little compromises in his control game to keep it that way. He doesn't see me as a threat. I'm just a minor annoyance to him. He's probably figured that he can handle me some way. So I doubt if he'll lose any sleep over me."

"You're sure?"

"No," I said stiffly. "You're never really sure with a man like Dil. But we'll see. Let's just try to forget it. Come by and see me at my store when you get out of here."

"Okay, I will," she said. "I like how you think. I think I might like working for you."

"I hope so. Let's see where it goes. Get well first though."

"I'm feeling better already."

I left the hospital and went back to the store, wondering about what I had done. I wondered if Jill would really come in for the job. To be honest, I guess I had mixed emotions about what I had done and said. She probably would mean trouble for me of one kind or another. Still, I hoped she'd take the job.

As for Cullen and his bully-boy, Jimmy, time would have to sort that one out. Usually, I knew, those types kept their distance as long as you didn't interfere directly with their business and come straight at them like someone stupid. Same as dealing with a rattlesnake. Unfortunately, I have a bad habit of being direct with people like that. I hoped giving Jill the job at the Leaf wouldn't be seen as a straight challenge, but you never knew.

The rest of the afternoon I sorted through paperwork at the store. At about four o'clock I called Barry into my office.

"Barry, have you got any leads on that new clerk yet?"

"No. Why?"

"Just wondered. Hold off on hiring anyone. Like I told you this morning, I have an idea."

"You have somebody in mind?"

"Yeah, maybe," I said. I wasn't quite ready to tell him I'd offered Jill the job.

"Whatever you say, boss."

He left my office and I phoned Tracy. I was ready to get away from what had happened and relax. It had been a nervy day.

"Hi," I said. "I think I owe a you a dinner."

"No you don't," she said. "The other night was on me."

"You're forgetting our little agreement."

When we first started seeing each other, Tracy had made it clear from the beginning that as long as our relationship was platonic, she didn't want me picking up all the tabs for our meals together. She told me that if I started buying her dinners she would feel obligated to me, and she wanted an equal setup with no strings on our friendship. She was adamant about it, too.

"That meal I cooked for you was on the house, Mike. Call it a dinner at Mother Diamond's Charity Kitchen for Lost and Foolish Mountain Climbers."

I laughed. "Lost? Foolish? No, Tracy, I don't take charity. That's the deal, right? Nope, no free lunch—or dinner either. Especially from you. Let me even the score. I'll fix you dinner tonight."

She relented a little. "What did you have in mind?"

"How about a couple of big steaks from Rader's Backyard Barbecue Grill. Garlic toast, buttered and seasoned, of course. Baked potato and a big tossed salad on the side."

"Go on," she said, "It's calorie and cholesterol city, but I'm weakening."

"Good. Weakening you is my intent, sweet lady. How about key lime pie for dessert? The last, of course, from The Purple Pieman down on Water Street."

"Okay, I'm sold, you hustler. Deal."

Three hours later, we were sitting in the lawn chairs in my back yard, and had eaten our fill. Dinner was behind us now and we were relaxing, finishing the helpings of key lime pie with coffee. Two black cats were sitting on the top of my high wooden 4X4 fence, watching us like sentinels as the sky turned darker in the glow of twilight.

"Where did the cats come from?" Tracy asked.

"They own a single lady next door. She's the business manager for a nursing home. The cats just like to come over and check out who is having dinner with me. I think you pass inspection."

"Hmmm," she said. "Black cats make me nervous."

"Superstitious, Tracy?"

"Not really."

"They're good cats. I think they must like you. If they didn't like you, they'd come down here and rub my legs and purr and try to make you jealous."

She lifted her eyebrows. "Well, I'm glad they approve, even if it's two cats who are doing it. I don't need any more rejection in my life. I had kind of a rough day."

"What happened?"

"My editor got mad at me down at the paper."

To have a steady paycheck while she worked on her landscape photography book, Tracy had taken a job as a photographer with the local newspaper. She had never had any trouble there before.

"What happened?" I repeated.

"He told me we needed some human-interest shots, so I took a few pictures of some kids down at the trout hatchery. You know me. I couldn't just take your normal children-having-fun pictures. I tried to make them interesting – low angle shots – 'artsy', my editor called them. He said they were too – what was the word he used – too aesthetic for the local paper. Naturally, I argued with him about them, and in the end he went along with me and they ran the shots."

I scratched my chin. "Well, at least you struck a blow for True Art. Have you recovered by now?"

"Yeah, I think so. It was all so stupid. The pictures were pretty good, Mike."

"I know they were. You were the photographer."

"But I hate stupid arguments."

"How well I know," I said, winking at her.

She gave me a wicked smile, sticking out her tongue at me. I laughed, and then there was a long silence between us.

"Tell me something," she said at length, "that girl you rescued, Jill Carpenter. Did you see her today?"

"Yes, I saw her. I did something else, too. I hired her for a job with the store."

Tracy set her plate down on the wooden picnic table near her. "You did what? Why did you do that?"

"Her mother asked me to help her. She needed a job, so I guess I saw that as a way to help her. She's had some trouble with drugs, but I think she really wants to go straight. And oh, yes, there's one other thing, too. She got mixed up with this guy, a businessman named Dil Cullen. Now she's trying to untangle herself from him. The job ought to be a fresh start for her all the way around."

Tracy searched my face a long moment, sitting there with crossed arms. There was a serious edge in her voice when she spoke. "Mike, look, don't take this wrong. I'm not trying to tell you how to run your life or your business. But I don't know if you should help her that way. I know you mean well, but if she's mixed up with Dil Cullen, that could mean a lot of trouble for you."

I sat back in my chair. "What do you know about Cullen?"

She glanced around, perhaps wondering if anyone was within earshot. "Cullen's a land developer. That's his legitimate job. Most people in town think he's a respected businessman. But...well, you know Reverend Foster, the minister at the church where I go?"

I remembered the name. Tracy attended a church on the northeast side of town, and she had been after me for some time to go to services with her some Sunday. The minister there was named Harry Foster.

"Sure, I remember him. What's your Reverend Foster have to do with Dil Cullen?"

"Reverend Foster – Harry – is a member of the Drug Abuse Task Force here in town. He told me once about Cullen. Harry said that Cullen is suspected to be the major cocaine distributor for this area."

"I've heard the rumor."

"It's more than a rumor, Mike. Cullen's very slick, and nobody can pin anything on him. He gives plenty of money to charitable causes; it's good public relations. He even donates to the Drug Abuse Task Force, believe it or not, so he can look like a knight in shining armor to the town leaders. The cops all know he's behind a lot of the drug trade, though. He must handle it all indirectly so they can't get to him. He has others to sell the stuff, and he's insulated from the street deals. At least, that's the confidential word from Harry."

I shrugged. "Has Cullen bought off the police?"

"As far as I know, the answer to that is no. The Durango cops aren't like that. But they just can't get a handle on him. He's big-time. Harry says he's supposed to get his stuff from the bad guys in Colombia and Peru. If that's true, he's bound to have ways to keep his business in line. And if...if you get in the way, if you get mixed up in some way with Jill Carpenter, it could be rough for you."

In the growing darkness of the evening, Tracy didn't see my face muscles tighten. She didn't see the coldness that suddenly came over my eyes. I blinked and said in a soft voice, "Cullen could get in my way, too, Tracy,"

She turned and stared at me. "What do you mean?"

I shrugged. "Nothing. I saw Cullen today. He came up to Jill's room. I don't like him."

"But what made you say...he could get in your way?"

I hesitated. "I just don't like the thought of him controlling Jill's life. Or anybody else's, for that matter."

"But what could you do, Mike? You're just one man. He's probably a professional, a criminal with an organization. And that means he no doubt has some very tough people working with him. Mike, I know I called you a hero, but don't be a dead hero. I want you alive and in one piece."

I sighed. "Tracy, you go to church. Isn't there a story in the Bible about a fellow named David taking on a guy named Goliath? It's all about one simple little guy standing up to a giant and his army of bad guys. Sometimes all it takes is one person willing to stand his ground against a bully-boy. Maybe Cullen just needs to meet a David."

I could see the rising anger in Tracy's eyes. "Don't be an idiot," she said. "Come down to earth. Be realistic. Cullen's probably a much bigger Goliath than you think. And he may have some other Goliaths with him. It could be very dangerous."

"Maybe so," I said. "All I know is, if Jill wants a job and she wants to get straight, he'd better stay away from her. She deserves a chance at a life; her own life."

Tracy shook her head in frustration. "Do you know what you sound like? You're talking all macho and stupid tonight. And you could get yourself hurt, or worse. Look, for my sake, at least, please don't do anything dumb."

I laughed. "You've already called me foolish once tonight. Maybe I am, Tracy. But let's forget Cullen. Come on, it's getting cold out here. Let's go inside."

The chill of the mountain night air made her shiver as we got up and carried the dishes inside. Somehow, I felt that the shiver she was feeling was more than from the cold.

I thought about her warning, and I felt a little shiver all my own. Time would have to decide if my words had been foolish.

Chapter Four

It was early morning, and I was a few miles north of town in shorts and tee-shirt, now on the return leg of my daily run. I ran easily along a quiet two-lane blacktop road, feeling the cool air on my bare arms and legs. The soft breeze was chilly and humid, lifting from the river running alongside the road, but my body was warm now from the exertion of the run. I didn't mind the chill of the air. I liked the bright clear light of the morning, the way the sunlight flashed though the leaves of the trees as I passed along. The morning light made me think of Tracy.

Funny, that lady, I thought. She wanted me close to her, but not too close just yet. And she didn't want me getting too close to Jill Carpenter, either. Not to worry, pretty lady, I told myself. Jill's too young and she's really not my type. But I would help Jill start her life over if that's what she wanted. Tracy would somehow just have to understand.

I had run four miles so far that morning, and my knee wasn't bothering me. In fact, the easy running seemed to help it. I had twisted the knee two weeks before, jumping over a log fallen in the middle of a trail, but now the soreness was easing. I had not noticed it so much when I was mountain climbing, but in running, where your feet and legs pounded the hard pavement, it had been bothering me until today. I had another mile more to go before I finished the run, and I was feeling better than I had for days.

The run was refreshing my inner spirit as well. The night of the rescue had left me with a lingering fatigue that lasted for a while, but now I was feeling whole again. I felt renewed this morning, regenerated.

I glanced over at the river nearby. The water level was low now, much lower than back in June when the snowmelt had nearly filled it to its banks. This was the Animas River, "El Rio de Las Animas Perdidas," or "The River of Lost Souls," it was called. Yet on this morning, its crystalline gurgling and splashing filled my own soul with a new sense of energy. The rapids flashed in the sunlight, and beyond them, I could see the ever-beautiful San Juan Mountains.

As I gently jogged along, I noticed a car approaching along the blacktop road. I could see that it was a large car, coming toward me rapidly. I always was cautious about cars when I was out running. I always ran on the left side of the road, facing the traffic, and the cars usually pulled over a little and gave me a wide berth. But I was continually prepared to get out of the way if an approaching car looked like it was not going to give way.

As the car neared, for some reason I felt a tingle of fear running down my spine. The person driving the car seemed to be steering it straight at me. Oh no, I thought, one of those.

Sometimes you encountered crazies who liked to scare the bejabbers out of runners just for fun. I stopped and hesitated by the roadside. I waited to see what would happen next. The car kept racing toward me.

I moved quickly well off the road, onto the taller grass. When the car was at its nearest to me, the driver swerved off onto the grassy verge, barely missing me. It roared past, spraying gravel, and rocketed on up the road.

"Crazy idiot!" I said, as I stood there, breathing hard. I recognized the car and I knew who the driver was. It was that black GTO I had seen at the hospital, and I knew the driver was probably Dil Cullen's "associate," Jimmy Rowe.

As I watched the GTO disappear, I wondered what was going on. Had Rowe done it just for kicks, not knowing who I was? Or had he known exactly who I was, and had done it to scare me? If so, why?

I wondered if it might have had something to do with Jill Carpenter. Was Cullen so possessive of her that he would send Rowe out to scare me, or do worse? No, it didn't seem likely. Maybe Cullen knew by now that she was coming to work for me. But simply giving her a job wouldn't cause such a reaction. Or would it? Maybe Rowe was just out for a morning drive and he got his jollies scaring runners that way. He wouldn't be the first low-life to do it.

I could go looking for him later in town, of course, but he would probably just deny it or laugh and tell me he was only playing with me. Whatever the reason, I didn't like the game. And I didn't like him. I decided to let it go, though. Maybe I was being baited. Better to wait and see. I continued my run uneventfully, and when I got into the city I made my way back to my house. I took a shower, got dressed, and went to the store.

Before I got lost in my work, I called Barry into my office.

He was as cheerful as ever.

"Hi, Boss," he said.

"Hey, good morning, Barry. I think I've filled our sales clerk position." His brow was wrinkled in curiosity. "Who'd you hire?"

"I haven't officially signed her on yet. She's that girl who took the fall on the mountain, Jill Carpenter."

Barry sat down in a chair beside me and scratched his jaw. "You sure about doing that, Mike?"

"Is it a problem?"

Barry looked at me as if he wondered if he should tell me what was bothering him. I guess he decided to tell me anyway. "Boss, look, she's...well, this sounds funny to say, I know, but the word on the street is that she's a druggie. Ask anyone in town that knows her. She can't keep a job, either. She could be trouble."

I nodded. "I know the story, Barry. Look, she's trying to get straight. I think we should give her a chance. Believe me, I've thought it through. I'll take the responsibility if anything goes wrong. She's Ruby Carpenter's daughter. I'm just trying to help out a friend. I think it can work out."

He whistled softly. "Look, Mike...," he said, pausing, "I know you're the boss. You call the shots around here. But this really smells bad to me."

"If it means trouble, I'll be the one to deal with it. If she messes up, I'll let her go and we'll get somebody else. But let's give her a chance. Fair enough?"

He bit his lip. "Whatever you say, Mike," he said doubtfully. "I just didn't know we were in the drug rehab business."

I laughed. "Barry, look, I know it's a gamble. But I'll cover it one way or the other. Okay?"

"Sure. You're the boss, Mike."

Barry got up, shaking his head, and left me. I knew he wasn't happy about my hiring Jill, and I had some lingering reservations about it myself, but I still thought it was a gamble worth taking.

I looked out the window. The blue sky of the summer beckoned to me. There were fluffy white clouds grazing the tops of the nearby mountains. I wished I was back up in Chicago Basin right now, climbing one of those big ones we'd left behind. I picked up the phone to call Buck.

"Hey, Buck," I said, "how about lunch together today?"

"Today?"

"Why not?"

"Well, I'm showing a house on the north side of town. I think I'm near to closing the deal on it. Can we get together about 1:30?"

"That'll be fine. Where?"

"Is the Lost Pelican okay?"

"Sure. I'm in the mood for seafood."

"I'll see you then."

"Great."

I put the phone down and got up and went out onto the sales floor. I was in a conversation with some car-campers from Oklahoma when I saw Tracy come into the store, carrying a camera. She looked worried.

"Got a minute, Mike?" she asked, walking up to me.

"Sure, Tracy. Let me take care of these folks first."

"Fine. I'll wait," she said.

I helped the car campers get their stuff and then I motioned to Tracy to come with me to my office. I dropped into my chair and she sat down next to my desk.

"You look worried, Tracy. What's on your mind this morning?"

She ran a hand nervously through her hair. "I hear you're evading my newspaper on that story about the rescue."

My smile faded. "Is that why you're here? To get me to do a story for your paper?"

She laughed. "No. I'm a photographer, Mike, not a reporter, remember? I leave the stories to the other people. I just heard a couple of reporters at the office talking about you and Buck giving the paper the cold shoulder on the rescue story. I was curious as to why."

"You think I should talk to them?" I asked, smiling.

She returned my smile. "I'm just curious. But no, you don't have to talk to them if you don't feel like it."

"Thanks. I thought you were going to twist my arm."

She leaned back and looked at me intently. "You know me better than that by now. But what's the harm in giving them your take on the story?"

"Call it my need for privacy. I just don't feel like talking to the reporters about it. Neither does Buck. Besides, it's old news by now."

She looked away, then back to me. "Okay, fine. Forget it," she said. "I understand. Look, it's getting toward noon. Do you want to have lunch or something?"

"I'd like to," I said, "but I've already got a date."

Her brow furrowed and she pursed her lips. "With Jill Carpenter?"

I paused, enjoying her suspicion. "No, it's Buck. I'd invite you along but we're probably just going to talk about some climbing."

"Guy stuff, huh?"

"Yeah. Us guys, anyway. How about dinner tonight?"

She nodded, relieved that I wasn't taking Jill to lunch. "That'd be nice. I've found out some more about Dil Cullen you might find interesting."

I gave her a long look. "That...I would be interested in hearing."

"How about my place at six-thirty."

"I've got some work to do at the house. Car work. I might get a little dirty. It'd be better if we ate there, if that's okay. Would you consider doing the cooking?"

"Yes, that'd work. I'll come over after I get off."

"Fine."

She left the office, and the rest of the morning went well. I arrived at The Lost Pelican shortly after one-thirty. The place was packed and noisy, as usual, even after the lunch hour. Buck was waiting for me at a table.

"Did you sell the house?" I asked as I sat down.

"Yeah," he said. "Got the paperwork done. They got a good deal. Nice couple from down in New Mexico. They're retiring here."

"There you go, pushing the population figures up in our pretty little town. You real estate people keep that up and we'll be just like Aspen one of these days, full of jet-setters and other hangers-on. Do these folks know about the winters here?"

"They talk like they do. They used to live down in Aztec, about forty miles south of here. They've skied some at the local areas. I think they'll be all right."

"Okay," I said. "I suppose we can let a few New Mexicans in."

He laughed. "I'm glad you approve. Remember, we let you in, even if you were from Texas."

"Something wrong with Texans?"

"Not really. They do keep Colorado green. With their green-backs, that is. Texans do get a little loud and tacky sometimes though."

"Aw, we're not all that way."

"Like I said, we let you in."

"And I do appreciate it."

He flexed his fingers and sat back. "What's on your mind, anyway?" he asked.

I saw the waiter coming over to take our orders. "I'll tell you after we order."

We made our selections with the waiter without bothering to check the menus. We'd both been to the Pelican many times before and we knew what we wanted. After the waiter left, I turned back to him.

"I'm ready to go back up to Chicago Basin, Buck."

"I was afraid you'd say that. When do you want to go?"

"Soon as we can. I've been thinking a lot about Windom and Sunlight Peaks."

Buck smiled. "And Eolus?"

"Yes, and Eolus."

"You're still not ready for Eolus, amigo. Take my word for it. But Windom and Sunlight, probably. You say when, and I'll try to work it out with Amaryllis."

Amaryllis was Buck's wife. She was a strong, single-minded woman. She liked me and I liked her. She was always happy to have Buck go climbing with me because she knew I was cautious, and both of us would come back. She told me once that the outdoors was what kept him sane. Climbing got his kinks out, she said.

"Amaryllis won't mind," I said. "She'd probably be glad to get rid of you for a day or two."

"Yeah, I know. I'll talk to her about the trip."

We talked on for a while about how long we wanted to be gone, where we should set up our base camp, and other details. Our plates arrived and we ate as we talked. After a while, Buck turned the conversation to the subject of Jill Carpenter.

"Did you go up to the hospital and see her?"

"Yeah. She's doing fine."

"You sure?"

"Uh huh. There's something else too, Buck. I'm giving her a job at the store."

He frowned as he took a bite of his shrimp. "You're what?"

"We lost a salesperson, a floor clerk. I need somebody for the position. Jill needs a job and she knows climbing. I thought I'd take a chance with her."

He shook his head. "Mike, I don't know. I've heard more about this girl. She's got a reputation for being a drug user. From what I've heard, she's also mixed up somehow with that guy Dil Cullen. He's trouble."

"I know," I said, nodding. "People keep telling me that."

He lowered his voice so the other restaurant patrons could not hear him. "Then do you also know that Cullen is supposed to be pretty big in the drug trade in these parts?"

"Where'd you hear that, Buck?" I asked softly.

"Word gets around."

"Is that so? Look, I ran into Cullen. He came up to Jill's room in the hospital while I was there. He was pretty happy with us for saving her."

Buck was unmoved. "He's trouble, Mike. Trouble with a capital 'T'. I wouldn't hire her if I were you."

I looked at my food, then glanced up at him. "Maybe you're right, but it's too late. I've already hired her. She's coming into the store this afternoon. What's done is done, Buck. And I...I really don't think I'll have any trouble with Cullen."

His eyes fixed me with a cold stare. "If you hire that girl, you may be messing with someone he has in his plans."

"Well, I guess I'll find out about it if he does."

"I just hope you don't find out the hard way. I was starting to enjoy knowing you."

I laughed. "Buck, I really don't think he'll be a problem." He gave me the same skeptical look he always gave me when I said I wanted to do something he thought too risky. Often, his skepticism was well grounded in experience. But he knew it was my call, and he didn't press the matter further.

After lunch, I went back to the store. The mail had arrived, and I leafed through the envelopes as I sat at my desk, dropping the junk mail into the trash can. I put the other envelopes on my desk. I opened the ones that looked worthwhile, and they were the usual flyers; wholesale notices, new product come-ons, and the like. Then I picked up an envelope with the return address: "Businessmen In Action." I opened it and read the letter inside.

It was an invitation to a luncheon a few days away. "Businessmen in Action" was a group of Durango townspeople involved in the local anti-drug campaign. A year ago, the mayor had set up the Drug Abuse Task Force, the one Reverend Foster was on, and out of that effort several actions had come about. We now had good drug education programs in the schools. An old building had been converted into a youth center, to give the kids a place to meet their friends and have good times and, hopefully, stay away from drugs. Some of the town merchants had been organized into the group called "Businessmen In Action." In spite of the word "Businessmen" in the title, several businesswomen were involved in the project, too. Gender awareness had not yet gotten through to some of the town fathers when it came to organizational titles, I suppose.

I was normally a little skeptical of such groups. Citizen do-gooders sometimes have good intentions but they were a little short on the knowledge it takes to make anything really worthwhile happen. Still, I thought, maybe the organizers had their hearts in the right place. If it kept people away from drugs, it was probably all right.

I filled out the return postcard that said I would attend their luncheon, put a stamp on it, and tossed it into the outgoing mail tray.

The phone buzzed again. My secretary said It was Ruby Carpenter. I punched in the line.

"Hello, Ruby," I said.

"Hi, Mike. How are you feeling? Have you recovered?"

"Yeah. I'm okay. How about you?"

"Oh, I'm all right. I'm just glad Jill got out of the hospital. That's what I wanted to talk to you about. Mike, I asked you to talk to her, but I didn't expect you to give her a job. Are you sure you want to do that?"

I didn't tell her that Tracy, Barry, and Buck had also expressed reservations about what I had done. "I think it'll be all right," I said.

"I hope so, Mike. Anyway, I'm grateful."

"Don't thank me too soon, Ruby. I know she's your daughter, but I'm only giving her a chance. If she doesn't work out, I may have to let her go. If I do, I want to be clear with you here at the start that it's strictly a business decision. I wouldn't want it to interfere with our friendship if it comes to that."

"I understand, Mike. I'd say the same thing to you if I were in your place. I want you to know that. You've got to do what's right for your business, and I know Jill. But I think she'll work out for you. For once, she's acting seriously about a new job. She loves outdoor sports. And I think she respects you. I must confess, though, that I'll believe it when I see it."

"Yes, the proof will be in what she does here at the store, Ruby. But I wouldn't have hired her if I thought she wouldn't work out. I think she will. But we'll just have to wait and see."

"That's fair enough. Are you coming in for your lesson this week?"

"I plan to."

"Good, I'll see you then."

We hung up and I turned my attention back to the paperwork again. I wished somebody besides me and Ruby had a little faith in Jill. So far most of the people I trusted were skeptical. I really hoped I hadn't gotten myself boxed into trouble. But, as I had reminded myself before, sometimes you have to follow your hunches and go on faith.

Jill came in later that afternoon. She was neat and clean, well dressed in a blouse and jeans. She acted as if she was eager to go to work.

"So, do you still want the job?" I asked.

She beamed. She really was a pretty girl. "I really do. I've thought it over and I think it's the right thing to do."

"Good. I'm glad. And I'm glad to see you looking like you're feeling halfway human again after your stay in the hospital."

"Lots of sleep helps. I do feel good."

"Glad to hear it."

She hesitated and frowned. "Mike, I hope you'll be patient with me. I may be a little slow at first. I'm still recovering from the fall. And I'm...I'm a little nervous about all this."

"I'll be patient," I said. "We'll take it slow, one step at a time."

"I really do want to make a good employee for you. But I want something else too, and I've been thinking about it. I want to get out and do some climbing one of these days. Which reminds me, by the way. You did promise me you'd take me on one of your climbing trips, didn't you?"

I sighed and coughed. "I'm not exactly sure it was a promise, Jill. But I guess it's a good possibility. I normally go climbing with Buck Corwin, you know. Since taking you with us would make it a threesome, I'd want him to feel okay about it. I'll just have to talk to him about it."

"I understand. But if you guys think it's okay, I'm ready to go whenever you are. Any time you say. Just let me know. That is, if you'll give me the time off from the store, of course."

I nodded. "That brings up another consideration, too, Jill. I normally don't climb with my store employees. Friendship and work don't always mix very well. Even the most understanding workers can get a little jealous. But I'll make an exception to my rule if Buck feels all right about you coming along. I'd appreciate it if you didn't advertise the fact too strongly to my other employees, though. Do you understand what I'm saying?"

"Yes," she said, nodding.

"Okay, now one more little item. Shut the door for a minute. I want to ask you about something else."

She went over, closed the office door, and sat back down. Her eyes were wide. "Did I say something wrong?" she asked me.

"No. I want you to have this job, and I want you to do well in it. But you need to be aware of something important. The people you'll be working with, well, they know you used to do drugs."

She nodded and sighed. "I was afraid of that."

I smiled reassuringly. "I don't think it will be a big problem after they've gotten to know you and can see that you are, well, reformed. Just show them you can do it. Just walk the line and do your job well."

She laughed lightly to herself. "That's funny."

"What?"

"You said 'walk the line'. It just hit me a little funny. I've done quite a few 'lines' of cocaine. But I'll walk the line you mean."

I gave her a long look. "Is it hard for you?"

"You mean staying off the coke?"

"Uh-huh."

She nodded. "Of course it is. I'd be lying if I told you it wasn't hard. Occasionally, I get the old hunger. I look down the street and I get a feeling, a pull, to get back into the coke scene again."

"What's down the street?"

"I don't know if I should tell you."

"Then don't, if you don't feel like it."

She shook her head. "No, maybe it will help if you know. Mike, I...well, sometimes I see him down the street, standing there on the street corner, you know. I see the man who usually supplied me with my coke..." She didn't finish.

I leaned forward. "Anybody I know?"

She took a deep breath. "Yes. Jimmy Rowe. He makes me feel so dirty. I mean, when I was heavy into the blow he knew they had me on a string. He never did anything to me, though. He knew Dil was, well, interested in me, so he left me alone. But he always had that mean, hungry look anyway."

"So Rowe was your pusher?"

She smiled. "Mike, that word went out years ago."

"Okay, so my age is showing. He's a supplier, a dealer, a candyman, a player, whatever they call themselves these days. But he's the guy who gave you your nose candy. How exactly did this start with you and Cullen and Rowe?"

She sighed. "Okay, I got into marijuana in high school. Nothing very heavy. Then I discovered coke. It's expensive, but I got it anyway every now and then, from some friends, and I liked it. Two years ago I was at this party. I met Dil there, and I was only vaguely familiar at that time with who he was. As we talked, he started coming on to me. Then we were interrupted by a man I did know. It was Jimmy Rowe. He came over to Dil and me."

"That was the first time you saw them together?"

"Yes. Jimmy told Dil that business had been good that night. It was like a progress report to a supervisor. That's when I figured out that Jimmy worked for Dil. Dil tightened up when Jimmy said that, like he hadn't wanted Jimmy to say anything about his 'business' in front of other people. Jimmy saw Dil's look, and he clammed up like he knew he'd made a mistake."

"A little flaw in the arrangement, huh?"

"I guess so. That's when I knew that Dil must be a guy who controlled the drug action."

I leaned back in my chair. "Jill, I still don't understand something here. Dil Cullen's a rich man. He's apparently pretty successful as a businessman here in town. He's got it made. Why should a guy like him risk it all in the drug trade?"

She shook her head. "I don't know how or why Dil got into it, Mike. It seems odd to me, too. Most of the time Dil seems as different from Jimmy as daylight is from dark. I mean, he's always been a polite and kind man, at least to me."

"Yeah," I said. "I remember how polite he talked to you in the hospital. He was like the proverbial steel claw in the velvet glove. Did you go out with him after that incident at the party?"

"No. Oh, he wanted me to, but I saw the wedding ring on his finger. Like I told you, I was attracted to him. After all, he is good-looking, athletic, and rich. And he really is a charmer, at least with women. But I draw the line with married guys. He kept asking me out though."

"Persistent, huh?"

"Very."

"He knew you were a user?"

"Of course he did. I suppose it's easy for a man like him to find that out. After that day...well, I didn't have to pay for it anymore. Cullen had Jimmy bring me as much as I wanted. Since it was free, I used it more and more. Jimmy always said it was a 'gift.' Some gifts, huh?"

I thought about Dil and his "business." Like most towns, drugs probably came into Durango through various sources. Most likely, a lot of it made it here in the backpacks of transient hitch-hikers or in the trunks of the cars of small-time drug peddlers. But if a man as powerful as Dil Cullen was involved in the trade, that meant he handled big volume. Cullen had a reputation for doing everything in a big way. I suspected he had his game set up so that he was well-insulated from vulnerability to being arrested, too. The big dealers were like that. They let their street sellers take the hits, but they almost always stayed clear and clean.

"Jill," I said, "thanks for leveling with me about this. Look, I can't tell you how to live your life. But I'd try to stay away from those two from now on, if I were you."

"Hey, Mike, I'm straight now, remember?" she said. "I really am. And I'm staying that way, believe me. All I want to do is be the best worker in your store. When are you going to put me to work?"

"Right now," I said. I called Barry in and told him to take care of her application paperwork and to show her the ropes. Barry was friendly to her, but I could tell from the look he shot me, he was still worried about her.

After she left with him, I looked at the letter from the "Businessmen in Action" again. The luncheon was three days away. Yes, I wanted to be there. It might be interesting, and I might learn something new.

I drove home after work and parked the Blazer out front, along the street. I went on into my house and tossed the keys on the desk in the living room.

My house is small but comfortable. I had been slowly redecorating it as time and my budget allowed. I am partial to stained-glass tiffany lamps, and a couple of these hang from the ceiling in the living room. I also like southwestern stuff, and I have Indian rugs on the hardwood floors that sure feel good under my bare feet on a cold winter night. The furniture is also southwestern, oak-and-textured-fabric chairs and sofa. I collect prints of western scenes, like those of Remington and Russell, and these are framed on the pine-panelled walls. Sometimes I mused that my love for western decor came from all those John Wayne movies I saw as a kid. Then again, maybe it was just my way of affirming all the Durango ambiance, and my new life here.

I had three of Tracy's photographs on the walls, too. They made me smile, and I thought of her whenever I looked at them. They made me think of her, out in the mountains, working away with her cameras.

I walked into my bedroom. I sleep on a big, king-sized waterbed I built, covered by a large wool Navajo blanket. At night, in the darkness, I would lie awake and hear the boards creaking, and wonder what tales the old house could tell about its lifetime here in Durango.

I undressed and put on my coveralls. It was time to relax with something I knew and loved.

I went out to the garage, lifted the garage door, and stared at the Cobra. Just looking at the car was an escape for me; it made me think of speeding over winding mountain roads with the wind in my hair.

The Cobra, as always, looked fast just sitting there in the dark garage. It looked like it was as hungry for a challenge as I was. Though I loved to drive it, I sometimes thought I loved to work on it even more, to feel its engine's metal surfaces under my fingertips. It was a purely sensual thing, knowing all that power was there.

Grabbing a clipboard that hangs on a nail on the wall of the garage, I set to work on my mechanic's checklist. For a long time I inspected everything; the oil, the filters, even down to the timing and the valve clearances. The tires had plenty of tread on them and the suspension was adjusted right where I wanted it, good and tight. It made for an pretty stiff ride, but the Cobra cornered better that way. Most cars you see on the road have cushy suspensions that make the ride soft as a cloud. But in a racing car, you want it hard and stiff, so everything moves together in close harmony when you're cruising through the turns.

I checked over everything for an hour or so, and I got dirty with grease, oil, and dust in the process. I turned on the engine and sprayed a little carb cleaner down the chrome breathers of the 8- barrel Weber setup. Everything was synchonized there. I pondered taking the car out for a run, to see how it felt and sounded on the street. But I didn't want to miss Tracy when she arrived. I shut off the ignition.

Looking down at my work clothes. I saw that I was all sweaty and dirty now, and there was grease on my coveralls. I felt hot and thirsty, ready for a glass of something cold. I was putting my shiny chrome tools back into their box when the sound of gravel crunching came from behind me. I turned.

Tracy stood in the doorway of the garage, looking clean and fresh in her white blouse and blue jeans. She looked very relaxed and happy. I wondered why.

"How's the master mechanic doing?" she asked, a grin playing on her lips. She had her hair pulled back in a short ponytail and she looked like a teenager.

"Well, if it isn't Tracy Diamond, my favorite photographer and mystery woman," I teased.

"Mystery woman? Where'd that come from? I thought you knew nearly all my secrets by now."

I laughed. "I wish I did. You said you had some mysterious

stuff to tell me about Cullen, though, didn't you?"

"Oh, that. Yes, I'll tell you about it later. Right now I'm intrigued by you, though. I've never seen you dressed up like a shade-tree mechanic."

She walked up close to me, and I saw that she was going to kiss me. This surprised me. I backed away.

"Something wrong?" she asked.

"Tracy, I'm all dirty and grungy from working on that relic," I said, gesturing toward the Cobra's engine. "I've got grease all over me and I sure don't want to add some color to your pretty white blouse."

"Your lips look clean enough to me. Lean forward a little, handsome."

Her kiss was warm and sweet. She must be in some mood, I thought, quite a different mood from the other night.

"This isn't fair," I said. "Let me clean up if you're going to send off skyrockets inside me."

She smiled in pure mischief and tossed her dark hair back from her eyes. "I don't know," she said. "I find you rather appealing this way, smelling of masculine sweat and motor oil. If you got cleaned up, I might change my mood."

She had me cornered, helpless, and we both knew it. As much as I wanted to, I wasn't about to embrace her while I was covered with filth. She knew it too, and she was enjoying having me at her advantage.

"Lady, you're asking for it," I said.

"What do you have in mind, big-boy?"

"If you want me this way, you just might get me this way. What do you think of that?"

"Don't tempt me," she laughed.

"I knew it," I said. "Underneath that cool professional veneer of yours, there lurks a woman who gets turned on by the smell of motor oil."

"Pretty romantic, huh?"

"Pretty kinky if you ask me," I said. "What's gotten into you this afternoon? I've never seen you like this."

She looked over at the Cobra. "Maybe I'm just a little breezy today. Maybe I should have been a blonde. Aren't blondes supposed to be breezy?"

"You mean air-headed?"

"Oh, now that's a low blow."

She rushed at me with mock anger in her eyes and with her fingers like claws. She grabbed at my coveralls, and immediately drew her hands back, looking at the grime on them.

"Wow. You really are filthy. Look what you've done to my nails."

"I tried to warn you," I said, laughing.

"Do you keep any hand cleaner around here? You know, for all the women who can't keep their hands off you."

"Right over there on the shelf," I gestured. "It's a special formula for the passionate women who attack me when I'm at my dirtiest. Come on, tell me what's got you in such a la-la mood this afternoon. I know it isn't me."

"Don't be so hard on yourself," she said, rubbing her hands with the hand cleaner and a rag. "It might be you. But I must admit, I feel like celebrating right now. My agent called me just before I left the office down at the paper. He said a New York gallery wants to do an exhibition of my photographs."

I took some hand cleaner and quietly rubbed a spot on her wrist she had missed.

"What's the matter, Mike?" she asked. "You don't look too thrilled."

"No, I'm happy for you," I said. "Does this mean you'll be going back to New York?"

She made a face. "No, I don't think so. A trip back east, yeah maybe, but I'm not moving away from Durango. I'm hooked on the clean air out here."

"And– the light?"

"And the light. The pictures wouldn't be what they are without it. I'm going to call the exhibit 'Durango Light'. Like it?"

"Uh-huh. But I like the idea of you staying here more, Tracy."

She turned and looked up at me. "Well that's good to hear. I was afraid maybe Jill Carpenter had gotten to you by now."

I shook my head. "You know what? You don't seem good as the jealous woman. Look, like I told you before, Jill's just not my type. Take my word on that. She came to work at the store today and I think it's going to work out okay. I'm just trying to help her."

"That's all?"

"That's all."

"Want to tell me more about her?"

I put the can of hand cleaner away. "Maybe after I get cleaned up. That is, if you can stand me when I'm cleaned up. I rather like being attractive to you. I wouldn't want to see you change your mood just because I got clean."

"I'll suffer through it. You get cleaned up, and I'll go fry us some chicken, okay?"

"It's a deal."

She got her groceries out of her car, and we went into the house. She disappeared into the kitchen while I showered and put on clean clothes.

She was working at the stove when I walked into the kitchen. I sat down at the dining table and waited until she turned around.

"Well, you look different, now," she said.

"You like me this way? Without all the oil and grease?"

She sniffed at me. "I don't know. You seem to have lost some of your appeal."

"You really are in a sassy mood."

"Yes, I know I am. That call from my agent put the old fire back in me."

"Gee, and I thought it was just seeing me."

"Egotist."

I smiled and drummed my fingers on the tabletop. "Maybe so, maybe so. How's dinner coming?"

"Coming right up. Would you fix the salad and iced tea?

"Sure." I got up and busied myself, and a few minutes later we were eating. Tracy was a good cook. She had made some kind of special batter for the chicken, and it was tasty. I had been avoiding fried foods to keep my weight down, but you had to break training sometimes.

"Mike," she said as we were finishing, "why do people get married and then divorced."

I wondered what had brought that on. "The divorce coming back to you again tonight?"

"Every once in a while I think about it. Here we are, having dinner like a couple of old married people. Maybe that made me think about it. The old memories from when I was married sneak up on me some times when I least expect it."

"Sorry. I don't know why people get divorced. Divorce just seems to happen for some people."

She took a drink of tea and looked at her glass, then set it down.

"I've turned it over in my mind a thousand times. I was really in love with the guy, you know. We were having some problems, but basically we were doing okay, doing things together, enjoying life. Then he just seemed to change right before my eyes. He began withdrawing from me. It got to where he'd come in from work, sit down in front of the TV, and just stare at it. He wouldn't speak to me unless he had to. I tried everything. I even asked him to go to counseling with me, but he just acted like I wasn't there anymore, like I was a wall or something. Then he walked out and a few months later we got divorced. I still just don't understand it."

I sighed. "Let's go into the living room."

We sat on the sofa together, and I put my arm around her. She shivered when I touched her, cool again after being so warm before. It bothered me, because I was hoping she had somehow hung onto that playful and warm mood she had been feeling before. I took my arm away.

"Tracy," I said, "I don't understand what happened to you either. I think some people get married for the wrong reasons. They want someone who'll give them what they need. They find someone who satisfies them. They're friendly, the loving's good, the whole picture looks like it's perfect. But I guess they leave something out of the picture."

She asked, "What?"

"They forget to give themselves to the other person. I look at Buck and Amaryllis and what they've got. They get a little grouchy with each other at times, but you know it's only to act a little tough. Most of the time they treat each other good. He'd never hurt her or ignore her. They really do care about each other, and they give themselves away to each other. Buck won't do a thing without first thinking of her, and she's the same way for him. They're there for each other. Maybe that's what it's about."

She rubbed her neck and looked down. "I thought it was that way for me and my husband, too, before he turned into an iceberg. I thought he was there for me, but I guess I was wrong. Maybe the change I saw in him was just his true colors coming out."

"Maybe so," I said.

She turned and looked at me. "Mike," she said, "I want you to try to understand something. Part of me wants to really let go with you...to really fall in love with you. You seem so much like the best thing I've ever had. But I have this other part of me, this little voice inside that keeps crying out, 'It could happen again, don't get close, Mike might change'. I know that's stupid, but I'm caught in the middle. Do you know what I mean?"

I put my hand on her shoulder and rubbed it. "I think so. I knew a guy in the war who was all gung-ho to go out and fight and win for his home and country. A real patriot. He had done real well in basic training and in the Ranger school, and he had all the skills of a steely-eyed killer, a real soldier. Well, the first time he went into a fire fight he took a bullet in his leg. The wound wasn't really bad, but the guy just froze up. He was almost catatonic."

"He flipped out?"

"Yeah. I saw a lot of other guys get wounded, but this guy just went ape. The medics could hardly do anything with him because he was scared stiff. He kept saying, 'I don't want to die, I don't want to die,' over and over. They took him back to a MASH hospital and his leg wound healed quickly, but he just wouldn't return to combat. I talked to the shrink about him. He said the man had this notion in his head that war was like some movie where everybody else might get shot, but he, the hero, would come through it okay. He knew he should go back to combat, but he was afraid he'd get shot, maybe killed, the next time. Maybe he was like you are, caught on a fence."

She was staring at me. "So what happened to him?"

"The shrink got him to look around at the other guys in the hospital beds. He saw that those other guys were healing up and going back after they got better. I guess he decided that if they could do it, he could, too. He finally accepted that he could get hurt again, but he learned to live with it. He went back to the fight."

"Did he get killed?"

"No. He became a good soldier. He forgot about himself and he started thinking about his platoon, about working together on the team. He finished his tour of duty and made it back to the states okay."

Tracy took my hand. "Was that soldier you?"

I shook my head. "No. Not me. The guy saved my life. I was a little carried away one night, chasing some NVA regulars into a tunnel. He pulled me back. I had seen some friends die, and I was real angry, and I wasn't thinking. The guy just slapped me hard, made me cool off. Then he told me his story. He said I wasn't much good to the team if I went off on my own and got myself killed. He said I had to control my anger, for the sake of the other guys."

"Whew," she said. "It sounds scary."

"It was. I really don't like to tell old war stories. But for some reason when you told me about how you were hesitant about letting go, I thought about him."

She relaxed a little. "I'm glad you told me the story. It helps."

"Well, anyway, you'll get off the fence one of these days. You see, that guy had a ghost haunting him, and he had to get rid of his ghost before he could get on with his life. Your ex is like a ghost haunting you. But you'll lose him in time."

Her eyes looked straight into mine. "Can you bear to wait it out?"

"Sure I can," I said, kissing her brow. "I've got all the time in the world."

She smiled and snuggled against me. She felt warm. "I just need time, Mike. Do you feel like telling me about Jill Carpenter now?"

I held her close and told her about how Jill had seemed to be eager to go to work at The Aspen Leaf. Then I told her about how Jill had gotten involved with Cullen.

"You said you wanted to tell me something about Cullen," I said.

"Oh, yeah," she said. "I had a long talk with Harry Foster—Reverend Foster—about him. Cullen really is one dangerous dude, Mike."

"He probably wants people to think that. What did you learn about him?"

"He's big-time. This is all confidential, but Harry tells me Cullen's the major dealer for this part of Colorado and probably northwestern New Mexico and parts of Utah, too. How much do you know about drugs around here?"

"Only what I read in the papers. I'm no expert, Tracy, but

I'd expect you'd find a number of users in this part of the world. Most of the folks in Durango are straight and law-abiding, but not all of them. There are a few counter-culture people and non-conformists living around here, too, who do drugs. Ex-hippies and swinging yuppies, corporate types who get up on coke for fun and the buzz at work. Occasionally you hear about some guys bringing in a carload of the stuff to sell and getting busted."

She nodded. "They're small-time operators, freelancers, mostly, next to Cullen. He's a pro at this. According to Harry, the cops think his shipments come in by plane, from places like Cartegena to Miami and then up here. Harry says they've tried to track it and bust a load, but Cullen must have some kind of system worked out. With his money and smarts, he'd know how to set it up. Once it gets here, he stays away from it. He handles everything through his people."

"I figured as much. Slick. He doesn't even inspect the shipments?"

"I don't know about that. Harry says he probably gets a report on the size and type of shipment when it's ready to be air-expressed from the drug lords in Colombia. When it gets here, somebody else checks it out and lets him know. He probably directs everything on a secure phone and in code. And nobody talks, either; he sees to that."

"What do you mean?"

She stared at me. "I mean, well, Harry tells me that some people have disappeared, Mike. Contract murders, just like in the gangster movies. Right here in river city."

I thought about Jimmy Rowe. From everything I knew and could surmise about him, Rowe seemed fully capable of that sort of thing. When he tried to run me down, there was no hesitation. He had acted like he enjoyed it. Muscles R Us, made to order for Cullen.

"If Harry Foster and the people on his drug task force know all this, why doesn't somebody just blow the whistle?"

She shuddered. "Same old story. It's a combination of fear, sophisticated evasion, civic influence, and legal talent. I told you that people have disappeared. Nobody knows if Cullen's connected to any other organized crime operations in the country, but it's a safe bet. The big dealers are in bed together. So, that adds to the fear factor. He's protected and yes, he's slick. If the cops try to get him, he's probably got a hundred ways to get off. Add to that the fact that he's probably a sort of hero-outlaw figure to a lot of local people who like their recreational drugs. Then you've got one untouchable drug dealer."

I scratched my head. "I still don't understand it. The guy's probably a brilliant businessman. He's got a family. He makes lots of money in his businesses and in land development. He may appear to be to be bombproof, Tracy, but it's still got to be risky for him. It's crazy. Why does he even mess with drugs? Know anything about that?"

"Harry thinks he may just need a lot of capital for promoting and setting up his projects, and drugs are a very lucrative cash source. And then, you know he likes risks. He's into technical mountain climbing, so he's probably an adrenaline junkie. Maybe he just gets high on the action, whether it's smuggling or climbing."

I shook my head. "I still don't understand it. You'd think he was smarter than that."

"Well, understand this. Don't mess with him. He could make it rough on you, Mike Rader. You could get hurt. Maybe even killed. Surely, you realize that by now."

I sighed. "Okay, I see that. I'll stay out of his way as best I can."

"Do you promise?"

"No. It gets me in my gut to think he could get away with what he's doing, right here in Durango. Tracy, do you remember why I told you I liked Durango?"

"Why?"

"Because it's clean here. It's a clean and free and beautiful place. Drugs are scum, Tracy. I hate the idea that drugs are something fouling up the atmosphere of this beautiful place."

She shook her head. "Then you'd better get real, Sir Galahad. Durango might be nice, but drugs are here to stay. And until some bigger dealer moves in on him, Dil Cullen is here to stay, too."

"Maybe," I said. "But even Dil has to back off occasionally. I just want him to back off from Jill."

"And if he doesn't?"

"Then I'll try to persuade him that he should."

"And then you might disappear. From me. From everyone. Is that what you want?"

"No. You know that."

She looked at me long and hard. "Mike, I think a lot of you. But in all these weeks I've known you, one of the things I've liked about you the most is that you know how to survive and get along in the world. You know when to cut your losses and move in another direction. Now I'm really beginning to wonder about you."

"What does that mean?"

"I don't know. I'm wondering...about us, Mike. I'm wondering if I should really let my heart get serious with a man who is willing to take his life so trivially."

I frowned. "Oh, Tracy, don't worry about it. I'll be all right. Jill's just, a well, a romance he wants, for heaven's sake. He may try to scare me away, but it's not like I'm about to hand him over to the cops or move in on his little coke business. Those are the kinds of threats guys like him send their hit men after. I'm a nothing target to him."

Her eyes were still full of worry. She got very quiet. "Maybe," she said. "But let me ask you something. If it came down to it, just you and Cullen, and he tried...he tried to kill you, what would you do?"

"I'd probably try to stop him before he did it."

She shook her head. "I was afraid you'd say that."

"Why?"

"Because that's always the macho way to handle things, isn't it? Kill or be killed."

"I guess so. What other choice would I have?"

"If he came after you, you might try to talk it out with him. You could try to reason with him, maybe even change him, Mike."

I stiffened. "Change him?" I asked, unbelieving. "You think I could change a hardened drug dealer who's probably responsible for murder? Tracy, in 'Nam, I found out that if someone wants to kill you, you don't worry about changing him. You defend yourself."

"Anyone can change," she said, "even men like Cullen. He's smart. Maybe it could happen."

I laughed. "Now you're the one who needs to come into the real world, Tracy. Look. If someone acts like a mad dog and comes after you, teeth ready to tear you apart, you deal with them. Changing a man like Cullen would take more than I've got up my sleeve."

She gripped my arm. "But Cullen isn't a mad dog. He's a man, a man who went bad. He can change and go good, too."

I was genuinely surprised at her. I had been drawn to her in part because of her compassion for people, but this was unreal. "Why are you defending him, Tracy?"

"I'm not defending him," she said. "I just know that bad people can get straightened out. I've seen it happen."

I snorted. "Not very bloody likely, in his case, Tracy. If what you say about him is true, he's been out in the cold too long. He's a hard case, frozen over."

She said nothing for a long moment. "Mike, I think I'd better be going," she said finally.

"Okay," I said. "At least we've found something we disagree on."

"You're right. Very much so. I'll see you later."

She got up and left, with me watching her go down the sidewalk. It was a rotten way to end what had been a pretty good evening, but there it was. I watched her get in her car, wishing the words had come out differently.

After she left, I went to bed. I lay there and thought about what she had said about Dil Cullen. He was so obviously a leech, a scumbag under his tailored suits and outstanding-businessman-of- the-year facade. Oh, sure, he had a wife and family. But deep down, I knew he was as dirty as they come. If I knew a legal and quiet way to erase him from existence, it would seem like an act of charity for the world. But Tracy, strangely, thought he ought to live, to be changed. Probably some idea she got from her religion.

Sorry, Tracy, I thought. Guys like Cullen never change. They just get worse. And they hurt a lot of people in the process. If he comes at me, I'll deal with him on his own terms. That is, if I can.

Then I thought some more. You sound like a drill sergeant in the Rangers, Rader, I said to myself. The tough-nut soldier ready to get it on. Had I let that old me back out again? I thought I'd left all that behind. Annihilation of the enemy had been my game back then in that war. I became pretty good at it, too, maybe too good. At the time it seemed like the thing to do. It was like some manic fever within, killing and destroying like some ancient merciless barbarian, using every weapon, every instinct, every dark skill they had taught me. I lost all trace of compassion, of feeling, for the people on the other side. They ceased to be people to me; they were just things, gooks, and the more of them dead, the better.

Yeah, the old me, the warrior me, really knew how to lay out a body count. But, in time, all the death I was dealing out caught up with me. Being that kind of warrior, where you don't care what's right and wrong anymore, just kill the things coming at you, became for me a form of unrestrained insanity. I became drunk on the madness. I lived for the next kill.

The madness got me through the mess in Southeast Asia, but had exacted a price: it had stolen my soul. I lost what it was to be human. Yes, I was a "good combat soldier," I did my killing best, but that "good combat soldier" stuff nearly took my soul away permanently. It had for lots of guys.

Those guys became strangers to themselves, and some of them had never gotten over it. They gloried in the old brutality even when they came home, and it transformed them into disoriented animals, never free. It destroyed who they were as persons, and they wandered as strangers, nervous and blind to the reality around them.

At first I was like that, too. I tried long and hard to get my head back together again on my own after the war, to forget how many NVA and VC soldiers I had taken out. Guilt ate away at me as I remembered the bodies, the graves, the looks on the faces as I cut them down. I lived in a twilight somewhere between life and death.

Finally, I got smart enough to know I couldn't deal with it alone. I needed someone to help bring me down out of the nightmare.

So, using my VA benefits, I plugged myself into a good shrink. I spilled out all the horror and guilt of it and tried to make the pieces that were me fit again. I've never done anything that took more courage, that drained me so much, that turned me inside out, but it more or less worked.

With the shrink's help, I slowly opened my mind, and I discovered that all the "things" I had killed were not things at all, but human beings, people fighting for their country. Sure, they were smaller and their skin was a different color and they thought and spoke a different language. But strip all that away, and they were just like me, men and women doing a job.

Hate slowly turned to understanding, forgiveness, and finally respect. And through it all, I even lost my guilt for killing them, too. I saw that I had simply been caught in the sickness, in the madness, and I forgave myself for that. I somehow jumped the war years and I finally found that boy within that was back on the hot Texas nights in the '60's. I found that man I had once been, again, now fully grown, head intact. Through the shrink's help, the memories of the rest were reduced to a bad dream, flushed away. I was free.

And now this bully-boy Cullen and his trained dog Rowe were pulling that old killer persona out of the long-buried depths of my mind and memory again. They were resurrecting the death-dealing creature I had once been. I didn't need that. I liked being human again. But the locked door to the dark closet of my past had been opened, and I knew the demons wanted to come spilling out. I was disgusted with myself.

It made for a fitful sleep that night. I had dark, bloody dreams, where the demons were at play. And my very soul was on the line again.

Chapter Five

Ruby Carpenter strummed her guitar along with me as I worked my way through an old gypsy folk song on my Gibson. My fingertips were getting calloused from long hours of practice now, and I was making some progress. One of these evenings I was going to give Tracy a private guitar recital in my back yard, at sunset. I even had a line saved up for her. I would finish my songs, she would clap, and I would say, "You see, you're not the only creative artist around." And she would smile. Ruby and I finished the song and she set her guitar aside.

Ruby was one of those women in her early sixties who could easily pass for forty-five. Her short gray hair was always neatly combed and she was partial to silver earrings and tasteful clothes. She smiled in a gentle, caring way, and she could joke with you and make you laugh at yourself. She had a calming effect on me. She was a gifted teacher.

We often had long talks together, during and after these class sessions. Ruby had always been an adventurous woman, and it showed in her speech and enthusiasm. We talked about all kinds of things, but mostly about music, though.

"You're doing pretty well," she said. "I don't know when you've found the time to practice, as busy as you are."

"Maybe I've just got a good teacher."

"Maybe so. But you really do have a good ear for music. You seem to excel at getting into the feel of it."

"I don't know about that," I said. "If you like the music, it just plays itself in your head. I just play what I hear inside. I guess it helps if you really enjoy what you're playing."

"That's the secret," she said, nodding. "What I like about you is that you seem to like everything I give you to learn."

"Maybe. That's where you come in though, Ruby. If you like the person teaching you anything, you learn to like their choices, what they give you. At least that's the way it is with me. It probably wouldn't be the same if I didn't like you. But I do like you, so I like your music. Transferred enthusiasm, I guess."

"You're right. It's that way with anything. Are you ready for a break yet?"

"I was waiting for you to ask."

I set my guitar down in its case and she brought me a cup of coffee.

"I was wondering," she said, "how's Jill working out for you down at the store?"

"She's working out pretty well. It's kind of like what I was telling you about the guitar playing. She's a climber, so she's naturally interested in the climbing gear and the other merchandise she's selling. I can see the enthusiasm in her. I think she's going to make us a good hand."

"I sure hope so," Ruby said. "Maybe that's the sort of work she should have been doing all along."

I sipped my coffee and set the cup down. "It's probably a big part of it. But maybe it's good she took those other jobs, though, like working at the convenience store. Sometimes it's good to work at places you discover you don't really care for. That way, when you find a job you like, you learn to appreciate its value."

Ruby sat down on the couch across from me. "You have a pretty good insight about people, don't you?"

"Sometimes. Not always. I've been wrong before. I hope I'm not wrong about Jill."

"You have some doubts?"

"I'd be lying if I said I didn't. She's doing well in her work, and yes, I can tell she likes it. But she liked drugs a lot, too. I know enough about people who've been on drugs to know they have a hard time getting away from them. I just hope Jill can stay straight."

She brushed back a strand of gray hair from her eyes. "I think she'll be okay. She respects you, Mike. That counts for something. Now she's got someone she can prove something to."

I took another sip from my cup. "You don't think she has a thing for me or anything like that, do you, Ruby?"

She smiled. "No, I don't think it's anything like that. She knows about you and Tracy. I just think maybe she sees the mentor in you. You're a good man, and she can sense that. When you find a good mentor, you want to be accountable to them. You need their affirmation."

"I'm not all good. I've got my faults."

"Oh yeah? Like what?'

"I don't know. I just know there are times I don't like myself very much."

"Aren't we all like that?"

"Maybe. But I'm still a long way from who I want to be."

"It sounds like you've got a confidence problem."

"Maybe I do."

"Funny. You seem pretty self-confident to me."

I looked away. "On the outside, maybe. But there are a lot of times, on the inside anyway, I'm not so sure."

"Maybe that's a good thing."

I looked at her quizzically. "What do you mean?"

"I can only speak for musicians. It's strange, but the best ones are a little insecure. Actually, if the truth were known, some of the best of them are very insecure. Maybe that's why they drive themselves so hard. The security they want comes from creating that magic window in time when time itself is lost and the music takes on a life of its own. It's like a living being then, like a child, and the musician knows he's brought it to life. Good musicians are always trying to get on up to a higher level, to get to that place where the life within the music forms into a living being. So they're insecure. If they ever got it all together, maybe that would be the end of the quest for them."

I reached down and plucked a string on my guitar. "Music theory, Ruby?"

"No, music psychology, I guess. Or maybe just stuff and nonsense. But I think it's okay to be a little insecure. I know there are times when I'm with my piano, what you would call "playing" the piano, when I do better than at other times. In those special times, I feel a bit wistful and struggling and I'm not really confident. This is going to sound crazy, but occasionally I get a little depressed. And for some reason, those are the times when I really make my best music. I used to think it was so I would just play my blues away, but now I know it's more than that. No one likes to be depressed, but those are the moments when I sometimes, well, I can put the most feeling into the music. Does this make any sense to you at all?"

"Yeah. Some musicians seem happy and well balanced and all that. Their music is, technically, very good. But then there are others who really play their music, they really get into it. There's a drive there inside them, something the technical ones don't seem to have."

"That's true, Mike. But there's also a danger in it, too. Some musicians have gone crazy because they became lost in the music. It's like they were drawn into it, like some neurotic force pulled them into a whirlpool of swirls and feeling, and they can never reach the end of it. You've got to know when that is happening. You have to have balance. You can't let the music take over completely."

I nodded. "The same phenomenon can happen in climbing. Like playing music, it helps to be a little edgy. It keeps you in touch with your senses. You stay alert. Did you ever think making music could be like climbing?"

"No, I never saw it that way before. But I get your point. Do you get mine, though? A little insecurity in music can be good sometimes."

"But a whole lot of it, in anything, can be murder, too. I know. I've been there. At least in climbing...and in just plain old living."

"Is that where you are right now? Are you over the edge?"

"No, Ruby," I said. "I don't think so. Right now I'm riding pretty high. I actually feel pretty confident about what I'm doing in most areas of my life."

"I think maybe that's what Jill sees in you. The confidence, I mean. She needs confidence like that in herself. I think that's why she admires you."

"Then maybe that's all right. If I've got it to share, and it helps her, maybe she can get permanently straightened out. But it's really up to her."

"How well I know. I'm her mother, remember?"

"And you're a good mother, too."

"Mike, I hope you know how grateful I am to you for giving her a chance. I know what you're doing is a little risky, but I believe in my daughter. There was a time when she stood up on her own two feet rather well. No false bravery, no games. But something shook her up somewhere along the way. I don't know what it was, but that's why she turned to those dreadful drugs. If she can get just get back her balance, she'll be all right."

"Well," I said, "I'm no shrink, but I'd say she's getting there. It may take some time, but I think she'll get her life all straightened out. I just don't want her to slip and fall again."

"Nor do I."

"I guess we'll just have to see."

It was time to get back to work at the store. I got out my checkbook.

"Ruby, you are going to let me pay for my lesson today, aren't you."

She shook her head. "No, I'd rather not. I'm indebted to you."

"Come on. It doesn't seem right to me. I don't want to put a price on what I did for Jill...and you. Friendship, at least in my book, doesn't work that way. After all, I'm buying a service from you. I'd feel better about it if you'd let me go ahead and pay you."

"Honest?"

"Honest."

"Well, okay then. I tried."

"I know," I said, writing out my check for the usual amount for the lesson. "I understand how you feel. But it's just better this way for me."

"Okay," she said, taking the check from my hand. "If it makes you feel better."

"It does. Thanks."

I got up and went to the door with my guitar in its case.

"That was a good lesson today, Ruby," I said before leaving.

"Yes, it was. You're improving."

"I've got a good teacher. I'll see you next week."

When I got back to the store, I saw Jill standing by the display of backpacks. She was frowning, as if she were angry with herself for some reason. I could see it in her blue eyes as she stood beside the glass counter, holding up a red internal frame pack. She was looking at the sales tag fastened by a strand of plastic to its side.

"What's wrong?" I asked after I walked over to her.

"Oh, I just did a stupid thing," she said. "A man came in here a while ago, and he wanted one of these new Kelty internal frame packs. He was a big man, about six-foot-four. He said he wanted an 'extra-large' pack and I thought I had sold him one. I was just looking at the sales slip though, and I sold him a 'large' by accident. I feel so stupid."

I smiled. "Lighten up on yourself. The guy should have checked the tag closer before he bought it."

"He did," she said. "But I was showing him the other pack, the 'large' one, lying on the counter beside it, and I gave him the wrong one. I charged him for the bigger one, too. It was slightly more expensive."

"Did you get his name? I'll bet it's on his charge slip or on the check."

"He paid cash. And now he's got the wrong pack. I feel so dumb."

"He'll probably be back in. Maybe he'll check it when he gets back home."

"I hope so."

A few minutes later I saw a tall, sandy-haired fellow with an anxious expression on his face coming into the store, a red backpack in his hands. He nervously walked over to Jill.

"I'm sorry," he said to her. "I-I think I bought the wrong pack a while ago. This one seems to be a 'large', and I thought I'd bought the 'extra-large' one."

She smiled, with an apologetic look on her face.. "You did get the wrong one, sir," she said. "But it's my mistake. I just goofed. I'm the one who's sorry."

I walked over to the two of them. "Hi," I said to the man, "I'm Mike Rader, the manager. My clerk here told me about the little mixup with your pack. I'm sure we can get it all straightened out."

We exchanged the packs. I double-checked the tag to be sure.

"I'm glad I caught the mistake," he said. "I'm going on a climb tomorrow and I need the extra room in my pack for some food I'm taking along. I've had it with that freeze-dried stuff. The food from the supermarket may weigh a little more, but it sure tastes better."

"I know what you mean," I told him. "We sell a lot of the freeze-dried food, but personally, I go the supermarket route myself sometimes. By the way, we don't like to cause our customers extra trouble."

I picked up a pad of gift certificates from under the counter. I signed one and handed it to him. "Here," I said. "Get yourself ten dollars worth of anything in the store. It's on the house. It's the least we can do for your inconvenience."

The man smiled at me like I was a long-lost friend. "Well, thanks," he said. "You don't have to do that."

"Maybe, but let's just say we want to."

He looked down at the certificate. "You people are good to do business with. Look, though, I'm in a hurry right now, but maybe I'll get something the next time I'm in here."

"Whatever," I said. "By the way, where are you going on your climb?"

He smiled, and a faint glimmer of adventure was in his eyes. "Eolus. We're going to try a technical route up the west side. You know anything about that mountain?"

"No," I replied. "I wish I could be more helpful, but I haven't done Eolus yet. One of these days I plan to get around to it. I've read that it's tricky, though. Be careful."

"Oh, we will. I heard some girl nearly got killed on Jupiter Peak a few days back. You know anything about that?"

I glanced sidelong at Jill. "No," I said. "Can't say that I do."

"Well, anyway, thanks for helping me with the pack. We'll be careful on the climb. I appreciate your giving me this gift certificate too."

"Don't mention it."

After he left, I turned and smiled at Jill.

She sighed and nervously rubbed her hands together. "Why didn't you tell him about what happened on Jupiter?"

"Oh, you've been through that enough. Time to put that fall you took behind you. On to better things."

"Look, Mike," she said, "you don't need to protect me. I can take care of myself."

"So who's protecting you. If I told him about Jupiter, I'd have to tell him about what I did, too. I'm tired of talking about it. I almost froze my ears off that night. I just want to put the whole experience behind us."

She smiled and cuffed me on the arm. "Okay. I understand. But I hope there's one thing you're not forgetting."

"What's that?"

"I want to go back up there...to Chicago Basin...with you and Buck. You do remember, don't you?"

I let out a deep breath. "Oh yeah, that. I still need to talk with Buck some more about it."

"Why? Doesn't he want me to go with you?"

"No, it's not that," I said. "I don't think he'll mind. We just need to settle in on a workable set of dates."

Jill fidgeted. "Today's Friday. It's probably too short notice to do it this weekend though. Why not next weekend?"

I mentally reviewed my calendar. "Maybe so. I'll talk to Buck about it. We'll see."

"I'll gather my stuff together. Just tell me when you two are ready and where to be."

"My, you sure are eager."

"I know," she laughed. "I just need a fix of the mountains again. That's my new rush from now on, Mike. Sunshine and altitude beats junk, hands down."

"I agree with you on that. Let me check on things."

"Whatever you say, boss."

"And Jill," I said, "there's one other thing."

"What?"

"You need to check the stuff you sell a little closer. Watch those tags."

She nodded and smiled. "From now on I will. I promise."

"Good," I said. "We could go bankrupt handing out 'keep-'em- smiling' gift certificates like that."

"Gotcha, boss."

I went back to the office, sat down, and looked down at my desk calendar. I had circled on today's date and written in DRUG LUNCH AT QUARRY'S.

Today was the day those "Businessmen In Action" types were having that fund-raiser at Quarry's Steakhouse. I finished check-ing over my to-do list, got up, and looked in my office closet. A sport coat and a spare necktie hung from a hanger there. Good, I thought. I wouldn't have to go by the house. I finished the morning paperwork and at 11:45, put on the coat and tie, and left for the lunch. I wasn't wild about going, but I was curious about what went on at such events.

The banquet room at Quarry's was filled with men and women when I got there. They were all business types. Suits and bland conversation were everywhere. This wasn't my cup of tea, but sometimes you go with the flow.

I sat down at a table with a group of people I knew and we spent half an hour talking about the news of the town, mainly about the number of tourists that were in Durango this season.

Then one of the leading citizens, Jake Drury, went up to the podium and tapped on the microphone to see if it was on. He talked for a while about the need to do something about the kids in town getting into drugs.

It was the standard speech I'd heard before, about funding drug education programs in the schools and things like that. It was all full of good intentions, of course, and probably some of those intentions paid off for some kids. At the end of his talk, contribution cards were passed out to all of us.

We had a budget item on our books at The Aspen Leaf set aside, like most businesses do, for charity projects. I pledged a thousand dollars toward the drug prevention project. After we passed back the pledge cards, the meeting broke up.

I stood up, getting ready to leave, when I saw a tall man walking over through the milling crowd toward me. It was Dil Cullen. I hadn't noticed him previously in the room, but a lot of people were there and I guess I'd just missed him.

"Hello, Mike," he said, smiling. "Glad to see you here today."

"Just doing my civic duty, Dil," I answered quietly.

"You made a pledge?"

"Yeah, I did. Did you?"

His eyes mocked me and he laughed. "Yeah. Kicked in five thousand. It's the least I can do. I've got kids too, you know."

I stared at him, biting my lip. I knew I had to control the anger rising inside me. "Kind'a hurts business for the drug dealers though, doesn't it?" I asked.

His laughing eyes quickly turned serious. "What do you mean?"

"What do you think I mean?"

He grinned. "I don't really know, Mike. Frankly, I hope it does hurt those drug leeches. Drugs are bad news for everyone. We don't want our kids ruining their lives."

"C'mon, Dil," I said with a smile, "you're a businessman. The guys selling drugs are just trying to make a buck like all the rest of us, aren't they? I mean, drugs are everywhere, man. Somebody's got to sell them, right? And if you use them sensibly, they aren't really going to hurt anyone. I'll bet even you tried them sometime along the way."

He colored visibly. "Mike, did you have too much to drink today? What do you think this luncheon is all about? I...sure, when I was a kid, I...well, I smoked a little grass. Everybody did back in those days. We were young and stupid. But I know it's wrong now. That's all behind me. And I know we've got to stop drugs from reaching our kids here in town."

"Funny," I said. "That's not the way I hear it. Why Dil, I hear you're downright tolerant where drugs are concerned."

His smile was gone and his mouth looked sour and tight. "I don't think I like what you're implying."

"Sorry," I said casually. "I was just kidding. I know you're heart's in the right place when it comes to drugs."

Cullen's neck was straining red in his collar. I knew I had gotten to him.

"Mike," he said evenly, "Look, I've heard those rumors about me and drugs. But that's all they are, just lousy rumors. I don't know who started them. But that's all they are, just stupid, vicious rumors."

"Whatever you say, Dil," I said.

As other people walked past us, talking jovially, there was a long moment of cold silence between us.

"I heard that Jill took you up on your job offer," he said. "How's she doing?"

"She's doing just fine."

"Well, good. Glad to hear it. I know things will work out for her."

"Oh, I think they will," I said.

He moved away and I thought to myself, Mike, you idiot. Now you've really torqued the guy off. Why? Then I remembered Jimmy Rowe and his little game with his GTO when I was out running. I guess I had to let Cullen know that I could play games too. Still, it was a dumb thing to do, like tipping your hand in a card game. I should have let it pass. But what was done was done.

I went back to the store and tried to forget about Cullen, which, of course, was impossible. How can you forget it when you've just made a guy mad?

That evening I went over to see Tracy. She could tell I was a little tense but she didn't ask me what it was. She had something else on her mind.

Tracy had been after me for several weeks to go to church with her, and she started in on me again. I didn't mind it, though. I had nothing against churches. I had grown up going to one, but after all the intervening years I had drifted away from the church life.

"Come with me next Sunday, Mike. I think you'd like it," she said.

"Tracy, if I went into a church the roof would fall in. I haven't been for so long now they probably wouldn't want somebody like me there."

"Now don't give me that. You'll like it. Will you come with me?" I shrugged and nodded. "Okay. I guess so. You really like this preacher of yours?"

"Yes, I do. He's okay. I really do like him."

I laughed. "The last preacher I remember hearing was all fire and brimstone. I'm not wild about someone putting me on a guilt trip again."

"You won't feel that way with Harry...Harry Foster. His sermons aren't like that. They lift you up."

"This...this Reverend Foster...he's the guy you were telling me about who's on the drug task force?"

"He's the one."

"Okay, I guess I'll go with you if you say so."

That was how Tracy got me to go to church with her. I must admit, as I got ready to go the next Sunday morning, I felt a little strange. When I walked up to the church door with her as all the other parishioners were going in, I wondered if they could tell who I really was. I felt like a black sheep in a fold of white ones if there ever was one. At my subtle urging, we sat in a pew near the back. At least, I thought, I could hide there.

The service was, to my surprise, quite good. The people were friendly, and they acted glad to have us there. I didn't feel uncomfortable. It was a genuine sort of friendliness, not a put-on kind. The people acted normal. I didn't get the feeling anybody was trying to put pressure on me to "join our happy church." There was a freedom to it. Maybe, I thought, I could even learn to like it.

Reverend Harry Foster was a man in his mid-fifties, medium height, balding, and he wore glasses. I watched him as he preached, and there was something about him that told me he was more than just a simple small-town preacher. Maybe it was the way he moved, which suggested that he was very strong and fit. Or maybe it was the words he used, which revealed a subtle courage and wisdom, borne of a wide range of experiences. Whatever it was about him, I hadn't expected it, and it was apparent to me that there was clearly more to this Reverend Harry Foster than met the eye.

His sermon that day was about letting go of bad memories in the past, and I must admit he spoke to me. I had a lot of things in my personal history I wanted to forget. Reverend Foster seemed to be reading my mail. Maybe he was, but if he was, his approach, thankfully, wasn't judgmental. I didn't feel any twinges of guilt as I listened to him. His sermon came across like he was a reasonable guy trying to share something that had worked for him.

Okay, I admit that I wanted Tracy to think I liked it. I didn't want her feel bad about bringing me to her church. But I actually did like the guy's sermon and the whole service in general.

After the worship service was over and we were on our way out, I saw a familiar face in the crowd. There was Dil Cullen again. It was funny how I kept running into him.

Cullen had his beautiful blonde-haired wife and two small boys with him. They looked like the classic picture of the wholesome young successful family. They smiled and shook hands with their friends around them.

Cullen saw me in the crowd, smiled his best fake smile, and nodded toward me. I nodded back, returning his smile. It was all just peachy.

"Why didn't you tell me Cullen went to your church?" I asked Tracy.

"I guess I should have told you. I'm sorry. He doesn't come that often."

"It's okay. I'm just surprised to see him, that's all," I said.

We made our way to the door with the rest of the crowd, and Tracy introduced me to Reverend Foster. My eyes met his, and I could feel in his eyes, or maybe in his handshake, that he was a decent man. A man of deep strength. You sometimes get funny ideas about preachers, but Foster gave me good vibes.

"Hello, Mike," he said. "Glad to meet you. Tracy's told me about you."

"Don't believe everything she says," I said, grinning.

He laughed. "She's only told me good things. I'd like to get

to know you. Let's get together one of these days. She says you're
a climber. I'd like to hear about some of the hills you've done."

"Are you a climber, Reverend?"

"Oh, no, not me. I'd just like to hear about it."

"Okay," I said. "We'll get together."

After church, Tracy and I went to lunch at a little hamburger
shack we knew and liked down by the river. We ordered a couple
of burgers to go, and then drove up by the college on the road
that overlooks the town.

"Well," she said, "you made it through church. And the roof
didn't fall in either. What did you think of it?"

"I liked it," I said. "And yes, you're right. The roof didn't
fall in. You were right about the people; they're okay. I thought
Reverand Foster's sermon was pretty good, actually. I didn't even
mind seeing Cullen there."

"Want to come with me again?" she asked.

I laughed at her. "You're determined to make a church-going
man out of me yet, aren't you?"

"Maybe. Maybe you need it, Mike."

"Yeah," I said, scratching my knee. "Maybe I do."

We were looking through the window of the car down over
the sunlit streets and buildings of Durango. I thought about the
old town, about the miners and the cowboys and the railroad men
who had built the town. Like a lot of other western towns, it had
probably been pretty wild once. But then the church people came,
and things settled down.

Civilization set in on Durango then. Maybe that wasn't all
such a bad development either. One can get all carried away
thinking about the romance of a wild and wooly Old West town.
But in reality, conditions probably weren't all that wonderful back
in the so-called "good old days" of a frontier town like Durango.

I knew a little history about such places and times. I didn't
like the thought of the drunks in the streets back then, or the
sad- eyed prostitutes, or the men killing other men over petty
misunderstandings in the old saloons. And that, I knew from my
study of the town's past, was the way real life sometimes was
in the wild towns back in the so-called "good old days". It was
better when the churches came. The wild life settled down. A lot
of that violence and craziness went away when the churches came
in, and times became a lot more peaceful for everyone.

Today, just as in the past, it took people of real character to build a decent society. And a lot of that character came from the people who went to churches. Such people learned to treat other people with dignity. Oh, sure, I knew that churches had their share of fakes and hypocrites like Cullen. But there were good people there too, real people, who believed in a good, clean life. I identified with that kind of goodness.

I thought about the old "Wild West" days. In reality, a lot of those who lived the wild life back then were pretty empty inside. Many of them were case studies in broken dreams and broken lives. All you have to do is to read some of their letters to see that. Many of them were searching for a better kind of life, and they missed it. All along, it was just down the street, right there in that little white building with the steeple on top. But a lot of them never found it.

"So what are you going to do this afternoon?" I asked Tracy.

"I promised a friend, a girl at the paper, I'd teach her about how I do my photography. Want to come along?"

"No," I said. "You go ahead. Sunday's supposed to be a day of rest, right? I'll take my rest with a fishing pole in my hand, if you don't mind. I think I'll wander over to Buck's and see if he's up to putting a line in the water."

"Okay," she said. After lunch I took her back to her house and then I went by my place, changed clothes, and called Buck. He was free that afternoon. I got my fishing gear and drove over to his house.

Buck loved fishing as much as I did. A couple of hours later, we were out in the country, along a steam, looking for trout. I glanced down at a hole where I had pulled out a big one a few weeks before.

I knew the trout were big in this hole, and like all trout that are big, they got that way by being cautious. You got the feeling they could spot a fisherman or a line or a lure instantly. It seemed like the second they saw someone trying to catch them, they would all pass the word around to the other fish on the fish telephone line. Then they'd have a good laugh and go and hide under the moss someplace.

I looked over at Buck on the other side of the stream, and he nodded to me. We had played this game with the fish many times before, and we knew they were tough to persuade to take our bait. It took patience to do it right.

We were hidden behind a stand of juniper trees at the water's edge. We wore brown clothing to blend in with the brush. Surely, I thought, there are a few hungry ones down there.

I gently flipped my rod tip and the little fly flew quietly out over the water, landing like a feather on the surface. Small concentric ripples faded into the slowly moving current. We worked it that way for a while.

It was getting toward late afternoon, dinner time on the river for the fish looking for the flies and mosquitoes that came down to the water. A few moments later, Buck's fly landed on the water. We let the little brown flies float on the water for a while, before slowly, silently, reeling in the bait.

It took a lot of luck to do this just right. If the fish weren't hungry, or if they were wary, they would investigate the flies, circle them for a moment, and then move on. But a few moments later, there was an explosive splash up through the water near Buck's fly, and his line tightened as it went under. Without a word, Buck gave the line a skilled tug and set the hook in the fish's mouth.

He quietly reeled in the line. At the water's edge the trout splashed up through the surface, fighting the hook, trying to shake itself free. But Buck had a hand net under it in a hurry and scooped it out onto the bank. It was a fourteen-inch rainbow, just about right for eating.

As time went on we both caught a few more. After a while, Buck had his limit of eight. I was three behind him.

There was a quiet sound in the brush in back of me. I turned and saw Amaryllis standing there in the tall grass.

"Aren't you boys finished yet?" she asked me in a whisper.

"Buck is. He's way out in front, too," I said.

"How many have you both caught, all together?"

"Thirteen, counting the last one. Buck just caught a really nice one. He's got the lucky touch today."

"Aren't thirteen enough for the three of us?"

I grinned. "We've got to make it one more, Amaryllis. Thirteen's unlucky. Give me a few more minutes."

"Well, hurry up. The sun's going to be going down soon."

"Okay, give us just five more minutes."

It actually took me ten more minutes and several more casts, but I finally hooked number fourteen, a big rainbow that was in no mood to be taken. The fish fought powerfully, and almost freed itself from the fly, but I finally got him reeled in.

"Looks like I get the honors today, Buck," I said. "You got your limit first, so I'll clean."

"Yep," Buck said. "Fisherman's law, at least in these woods. Loser cleans. You must be slipping though. Usually I'm the one who cleans."

"I know. I guess I'm not concentrating too well this afternoon."

Buck didn't ask me what was on my mind. I was glad of that. I had let the thought of Dil Cullen crowd its way into my mind, though I wished I hadn't. I had gone fishing to forget about him.

We took the fish to a likely cleaning spot, and I got down on my hands and knees with my knife and set to work. I was glad I had a good sharp knife. Trout are easier to clean with a sharp knife.

"Sure you don't need any help?" Buck asked.

"I can manage," I said.

When I was finished, I put the messy stuff into a plastic bag so we wouldn't pollute the wilderness. I'd toss it into a litter barrel later.

We gathered up our gear and drove back to Buck's house. Amaryllis fried the fish in batter while Buck and I sat in his den relaxing.

"You ready to talk about going back up to Chicago Basin?" he asked me.

"Sure," I said. "Why not?"

He got up and went to the wooden cabinet where he kept all his topo maps. He brought out a map of the upper Chicago Basin area and spread it on the coffee table in front of us.

"Okay," he said, "look here. When we did Jupiter, we camped down here."

He pointed with his finger to a spot along the trail about a half- mile from the head of the valley where Needle Creek ran. I saw the blue line of the stream on the paper, and recognized the area where we had set up our tents.

"Our next climbs will be up Windom and Sunlight Peaks. See them here? We can do them both a day at a time for each, or we can try to bag them both in one day. Personally, I think we should do them together. Windom is basically a walk-up. To my way of thinking, it's easier than Jupiter, but Sunlight is a little tougher. Especially the last few feet."

"What's the matter with the last few feet?"

He grinned. "'I think I'll just save that as a little surprise for you, unless you cheat, and read about it in a guidebook."

"A surprise? Buck, I don't like surprises on the climbs. You know that."

"Sure, I know. But this one's okay. Trust me. It'll be fun. And I guarantee it'll add to your store of climbing wisdom if you let it come as a surprise. Don't read about it. Just let me take you there. You'll never forget it."

I was curious, but I decided to indulge him on this one. "Okay, we'll do it your way. Go ahead, surprise me."

"Oh," he said jokingly, "I will. Indeed, I will."

I looked back down at the map. It showed all the mountains surrounding Chicago Basin in their contour lines.

"Buck," I said. "It looks like it's just a hop, skip, and a jump over to Mount Eolus from the area where Windom and Sunlight are. Why don't we wander over and do that one, too, while we're close to it."

Buck muttered something I couldn't understand. He stroked his chin and solemnly looked down at the narrowing contour lines that formed Mount Eolus on the map.

"Maybe," he said. "But I don't think so. We'll see. Let's see how you look and feel after doing Sunlight Peak."

"You still think I should wait for that one?"

"I think. We need the weather to cooperate on all of these mountains, but especially on that one. Let's just play it by ear."

"Okay, I understand," I said. "Uh, there is one other thing I should mention about the trip."

"What's that?"

"Do you care if we take a third party along with us?"

His eyes narrowed. "Who do you have in mind?"

I swallowed. "Jill Carpenter."

Buck rolled up the map and set it aside. He didn't say anything for several long moments. Then he sighed and looked over at me.

"Are you serious about wanting to take her along?"

"I am. She'll be okay, Buck."

He looked away, then looked toward Amaryllis, in the adjoining

kitchen. "How's dinner coming?"

"Keep your pants on," she told him over the sizzle of frying fish.

He snorted.

"Well?" I asked. "What about Jill?"

He shook his head, then turned back to me. "Okay. We can take the lady along. But remember this: she's your responsibility."

"That's fine with me," I said. "She really wants to go up with us, Buck. She seems to have a good attitude. I don't think she'll be any trouble."

He laughed. "Hope springs eternal in the naive."

"Maybe," I said. "But hey, she's strong. She's been climbing before. Trust me on this one, okay?"

"Yeah, like I trust the footing on Eolus. You're a sucker for the birds with the broken wings, aren't you?"

"Probably. But this bird's got her wings healed now. She'll fly all right. And she needs to get out into the hills, same as you and me."

He leaned back against the sofa. "But why does she want to go with...us? Surely she's got other friends she can call on."

"Maybe she wants to see what it's like with somebody new. But it's really okay with you, then?"

"Like I said, as long as you take the responsibility. Just don't expect me to play nursery maid with the girl. It ain't my style."

"Look," I said. "Don't be such a hard-nose on this. We both know we're both going to wind up helping her. And she'll help us too. That's the way it is on a climbing team."

His eyes squinted at me. "Okay, but do you remember what I told you on Jupiter, when we were going back up after her?"

"You mean if you see something wrong and you blow the whistle, we abort the climb and go back down?"

"Yeah. That. That's my deal."

"Okay, I can handle that. You're the leader, Buck."

"No," he said, "I'm not just the leader. I'm the dictator. What I say goes. That's the deal. Remember that."

"I can live with it."

"You'd better."

"Yes, Massuh Buck," I said, smiling, nodding submissively.

"I ain't jokin'."

"I know. No, that's okay. I'll talk to her about it. It'll all work out. When do you want to go?"

He sighed. "Let's check our calendars. All three of us. Together. Then we'll see about it."

"Okay," I said. "Fair enough. I'll set it up with her."

Amaryllis stuck her head around the doorway. "Hey, you two knotheads. You ready to eat? The fish are ready."

Buck turned to her. "Yes, woman, we're ready, too."

"Then get over here and make the iced tea. I'm about to set the food on the table."

"Okay," he said. "We're coming."

The meal was long and satisfying. We talked about other times Buck and I had made fishing trips together, about wildflower- gathering hikes the two of them had made together, and of other days and times. I loved the way these two people joked and laughed and mock-argued with each other. It was good to see the love that had lasted through the years for them. It gave me hope for what might happen to me someday, if I was so lucky.

Life is hard on couples in these times. The minute you get something good going together with someone, it seems like somebody or some thing is always out there trying to mess things up for you. You have to work for what you've got and get tough with the outside influences. Otherwise you're in a revolving-door kind of life, single- couple-single, and you never get to go on through that revolving door and go into the main room. Buck and Amaryllis had been in their main room a lot of years, and it worked for them. It showed.

It was dark outside when I left their home. The cool night air made me wish I had a jacket on. The sky was clear and a quarter-moon hung low amid the twinkling stars, over the western sky above the mountains now.

I slowly got into the Blazer and drove toward home. At the house, I went in and locked the door behind me. There was a message waiting for me on my answering machine. It was from Tracy, asking me to call her.

"Hi," she said when she heard my voice on the phone. "Where have you been?"

"Out in the woods dueling the wily trout. We had a great meal over at Buck's place. How are you doing tonight?"

"Fine. I wanted to ask you something."

"Ask away."

"I think there's someone you should talk to."

"About what?"

"About Dil Cullen."

I felt my senses suddenly on alert. "Who do you want me to talk to?"

"Reverend Harry Foster, my minister. Remember how I told you he knew a lot about Cullen?"

"I remember."

"He can fill you in on some details I can't. He really does know a lot about the man."

"So you told me."

"Well, how about it? Do you want to talk to him?"

"Sure. I guess. I told Foster I might get together with him. When should I go see him?"

"Well, you can probably catch him tomorrow morning. I hope you don't mind, but I called him this afternoon and asked if you might see him then. Can you make time for him in your busy schedule?"

"Yeah, I can. So he's expecting me, then?"

"Yes. I think it would be good for you to get to know him better."

"Okay, I'll go. Do I have to dress up in a suit or anything?"

"Heavens, no. He's a normal person, Mike."

I sighed and yawned. "Whatever you say."

"You sound awfully tired tonight."

"No, not really. Just full of a good meal and ready to get some sleep."

"Okay, I'll let you go. Maybe I'll see you tomorrow."

"I hope so. Goodnight, sweet princess."

"Goodnight," she said.

I got undressed and took a hot shower. I pondered what the good reverend might have to tell me. Who knows, I thought, maybe Tracy's right. Maybe the guy could help. I wasn't excited about talking about Cullen, but I was smart enough to know that I had better learn all I could about him, nonetheless.

I got into bed and strummed my guitar. Out my window, the crescent moon was down low now, hanging there over the mountains, shining down on someone else's evening far to the west. Durango was peaceful tonight. Maybe I could find some peace as well. I set the guitar aside, turned off the light, and rolled over into sleep.

Chapter Six

I went to Reverend Harry Foster's church the next day. It felt funny to be going to a church on a weekday. Actually, it was strange for me to be going to a church on a Sunday, too, the way I'd been living the last few years.

The church looked nicer than I had noticed on the Sunday I had gone to worship there with Tracy. It had a clean look, with a trimmed green lawn and tastefully appointed landscaping. I saw a small white sign by one of the walkways that said: "Office." I walked up to the door and went in.

The secretary met me. She was a nervous little woman with frizzy blonde hair, about forty. She was very polite and friendly. I told her why I was there.

"Do you have an appointment with Reverend Foster?" she asked.

"No," I said, "But I think he's expecting me."

"I'll buzz him," she said with a smile.

Reverend Harry Foster came out of his office and shook my hand. He looked a little different without his clerical robe. I could see now that he was a slightly hefty man. He looked as I had remembered him, balding on top, with ridges of black hair on the sides of his head. He was dressed casually in slacks, a gray V-necked sweater, with a shirt and tie underneath.

"Good to see you again, Mike." he said, "Come on in. Tracy said I might expect you to come by this morning."

He took me into his pastor's study and closed the door. I thought he would go to the high-backed chair behind the desk, but there were two chairs in front of it, and he gestured for me to sit in one. He sat down in the other. I was glad we didn't have the desk separating us.

"I'm really glad you came," he said. "Tracy told me a number of things about you."

"I hope she didn't scare you, Reverend. I've not been what you'd call a regular church-goer in the last few years."

His smile was warm. "I know that. You don't scare me. Call me Harry, Mike. I hate being formal. And don't assume I'm going to judge you and act all holy and churchy because you've been out of touch with the church. Tracy told me you haven't been a regular churchgoer. Was it always that way?"

I sighed. "No. Not really, Harry. I grew up going to a church, but after I went away from home and went into the army, I guess I just got out of the habit. It's been that way for a lot of years now. Maybe one of these days I'll get back in church again."

He looked out the window. "I know what you mean. It happened that way for me once, believe it or not. I know how easy it is to get out of the habit."

"Oh?" I asked. "Sorry, but I wouldn't have thought things would be like that for you. How is it that a man of the cloth stops going to church?"

He laughed and looked at me thoughtfully. "I haven't always been a minister, Mike. I used to live a completely different life before this one. Believe it or not, I was once a cop."

Surprised, I scanned his features with interest. "A cop? What made you change careers?"

He shifted restlessly in his chair. "It's a long story."

I could have let it go, but I was curious. "Do you mind sharing the story with me?"

He had his elbows on the arms of the chair, his fingers together, steepled. His eyes held me for a long moment, as if sizing me up, wondering what words he should say. "No, I guess I don't mind telling you. I was on the police force in Chicago."

"What were you? A traffic cop?"

He smiled and laughed lightly, as if what I had said was somehow quite ironic. "No, I was assigned to work with juveniles in South Chicago. Ever been to Chicago, Mike?"

"Once," I said. "I was just a kid. My dad was in a service club and we went to a convention there."

"Downtown? The Loop?"

"Yeah. We stayed in a big hotel most of the time. We went on the tourist outings and that sort of thing. You know, the zoo, the harbor cruise, and the big stores and museums and all."

"Then you...probably didn't get to see South Chicago, did you?"

"No, I didn't. Why?"

"Well, it's not on the average tourist's itinerary, I'd say. It's pretty rough down there, a little different from the parts of the town you saw. That was where I spent most of my life. They have a lot of gangs in South Chicago. The kids grow up fast and play pretty rough. Drugs, drive-by shootings, crack houses. We had our hands full."

I pondered his words. "A lot of drugs in that part of town, huh?"

"Yeah, a lot. That was how my trouble started. I helped a young kid out of a jam with his gang, and he became an informer for me. There were drugs everywhere, and it's hard to fight it. Oh, you know, we arrested the junkies and the kids selling it on the street, but we were supposed to turn any big investigations over to the narcs. I, well, that kid I told you about? He led me into something pretty big. I didn't have time to bring in the narcs. I had to make a quick decision right there, on the spot. And sort of like John Wayne, I tried to take care of it on my own. I thought I had no other choice."

"So what happened?"

Harry looked down at the floor, then back up to me again. "I arrested some kids who were doing a pretty big business pushing drugs. They had the stuff with them. It was a big stash, bigger than I'd ever seen. The only trouble was, I collared a couple of mob guys along with them. One of them was the son of a Capo, a big leader in the mob. I didn't know it at the time, and I leaned on the kid pretty hard. He was a real smart-aleck, so I got mad and put the squeeze on him. Bad mistake."

"Uh-oh," I said. "Let me guess what happened then. After you arrested the guys, the mob tried to get rid of you."

"You got it. I was like a sport fisherman who hooked into 'Jaws the Shark'. They came back after me big-time. I couldn't walk my beat safely after that. One night they cornered me and nearly did me in. Backup got there in time, though, thank God, so I got off with just a few cuts and bruises. And, oh, yes, a three-inch knife cut in my stomach. I recovered. After that, my boss had me transferred to another part of town. But that didn't stop them. They tried again. Serious, persistent dudes, those mob boys. I wanted to go on living, so I guess you'd say I took early retirement. Maybe it was God's call, but I disappeared."

"You resigned?"

"Yep. Started a whole new life here in Colorado. I went into the ministry. That's more or less how I got where I am today."

"Scary business, Harry."

"Yeah," he said, suddenly turning and looking at me intently.

Very slowly, he said, "That's when I learned to keep a low profile where drugs are concerned, and to let the professional drug enforcement people handle the cases."

Now it was my turn to stare at him. I wondered what he was driving at. "Meaning?" I said.

He grinned. "You're pretty quick, aren't you?"

"Maybe. What are you getting at, Harry?"

"Tracy told me you're on to something here in town. I know you're concerned about some people involved with drugs, but I wouldn't want you to get hurt. The drug players play mean, and they play for keeps, Mike."

I sighed. "So I've been told. Look, Harry, I'm no John Wayne out looking to ride into trouble. I'm just a simple businessman trying to help a friend, or rather, a friend's kid. Tracy's obviously told you about Jill Carpenter. So let me ask you. What would you do in my place?"

His eyes narrowed. From his expression, he looked like a cop now, all business. "I would stay out of the line of fire, and watch my back. Listen to me. Druggies used to be my business. I know how these guys operate, Mike."

"It sounds like it. But it's not that simple, Harry."

He nodded. "I know. It never is. But if you're going to mess around with a man like Dil Cullen, at least use your head. I heard about what happened between you two at that Businessmen In Action luncheon."

I did a double-take. "Tracy told you?"

"Uh-huh."

I bristled. "Well, so much for confidentiality."

He shook his head. "Oh, give me a break. Confidentiality can take a hike on this one. You're messing around with guys who'd cut off your head—and other significant body parts, too—and bury you deep out in the desert, just as soon as look at you. Tracy's only trying to save your life, man."

I swallowed hard. His cop's eyes told me he knew exactly what he was talking about.

"You're pretty graphic for a man of the cloth, Reverend."

"Graphic? I'll show you graphic."

He got up and pulled open a file cabinet. Taking out a manila folder from his files, he turned and plopped it down on my lap.

"Open it. Take a long look."

I opened the folder. There were several color 8X10 glossy photographs inside. Police shots of dead people. Lots of red blood splashed all over the place in the pictures, too. Mayhem.

"Anybody you know, Harry?"

"Civilians, mainly. People who got in over their heads with the drug players, Mike. People who thought they were heroes. But they didn't know what they were up against. I'd hate to see you wind up in a picture like that."

"Yeah, me too," I said, swallowing hard. I handed back the folder.

"Then I hope you get my drift," he said. He put the pictures back into the filing cabinet.

"Loud and clear, Harry," I said, trembling a little. I reflected mentally on this minister, who had seemed so mild-mannered and cheery in the church service last Sunday. The man might know about heaven, but he also knew about hell on earth.

"So what do you think I should do about Cullen?" I asked.

"For starters, back off. Cool it big-time with the man. You've already ruffled his feathers. Don't even joke around with him, Mike. You've got another "Jaws the Shark" there. Please believe me on this."

"You know a lot about Cullen, then?"

"Enough."

"So tell me what you know. That can't hurt."

He regarded me with cautious eyes. "You sure you want to know?"

"Look," I said. I'm not exactly a newcomer to the subject of drugs, Harry. I was in 'Nam. I saw drugs over there up close. The whole scene. I was sitting in a Saigon restaurant once when two guys walked in and calmly shot the woman at the table next to me over some drug deal. I had to wash her blood off my uniform. And when I got back to the States I ran into drug people a time or two again. I never did drugs myself, but I've been close to people who did. The dealers I've seen were all pretty rough trade. Which makes Cullen such a mystery to me. He just doesn't fit the profile I'd expect for a drug lord. He's too chamber-of-commerce. He's apparently successful in his business enterprises here in Durango. The man has a nice family. Why, he even goes to your church."

Harry coughed. "Yes, I know he does. We have a $300,000 budget, and do you know what Dil contributes? The guy makes out a pledge card for $35,000, and he pays it every January in one shot. So, as you might imagine, the congregation is somewhat dependent on him. But I don't have to like him. I sort of tiptoe around him here at church. I shake his hand and smile. And yes, I know he has legitimate businesses, too. Real estate development and all. And his whole persona, his image, is carefully cultivated to look squeaky- clean. But underneath it all he's dirty as they make them."

I grinned. "Sounds like your sermons aren't exactly getting through to him."

He laughed. "Okay, that's a cheap shot, but you're right. All I can do is hope and pray on that one. I really feel for his wife and kids. They're good people. They're the one's who'll really get hit if he ever goes down."

"I still don't understand," I said. "The man's apparently got enough money and power by anyone's standards. He's respected by a lot of people here in town. On the face of it, he's got it made. How do drugs fit into his picture?"

He held out his hands in helplessness. "You've got me. I'm as puzzled as you are. I don't know all of the background on Dil, but from what I can see, money and power are the real driving forces in his life. They are, if you will, his real gods. Maybe he got into drugs in college or someplace like that. You know as well as I do there's a lot of money in that business. And it's all tax-free. Maybe he uses the cash to prop up his land and real estate investments."

"But...drugs, Harry. Doesn't he know what they do to people?"

"He probably bought the lie that drugs don't hurt anybody any more than liquor does. You probably know the old saw among drug sellers about how 'if it's good for the majority of people, it's just too bad if a few get hurt.' So, they say, why cut out the fun for the majority who get off on drugs with no ill effects? The hard-core players in that business will tell you that people get killed in traffic accidents every day, but that doesn't stop us from letting people drive. So, they say, why all the fuss about the bad side of drugs? In their minds, it's not a crime. It's just a logical extension of a recreational business, just like any other business."

"Yeah, and it's okay if so many people get hooked on drugs that to get cash for their habits they burglarize and steal, and the crime rate skyrockets. That's just a part of life in today's world, according to them, huh?"

He nodded. "You've talked with these guys, too, I see. Once you get started rationalizing, you can make it all seem like the straight people are the ones who are nuts, so it's all right."

"Oh, sure," I said. "They've got it all figured out. If they think like that, how come Dil's into supporting drug prevention work like the 'Businessmen In Action'?"

Harry chuckled. "That's just calculated hypocrisy on his part. It fits the civic-minded, public-citizen-image for him. A few bucks as a sort of write-off to make him look good while he pulls in tons of bucks from the bad side. Kind'a smart, actually. It'd sound good coming from a high-priced defense lawyer in a courtroom if he ever got caught. Might even hang a gullible jury."

"I guess so. How big is he in the trade, Harry?"

"Bigger than you'd think. He's what they call a 'regional'. Do you know how drug sales work on a large scale today?"

"I've never looked into that part of it. Never really wanted to."

"Okay. Remember 'Jaws' again? Think of America for a minute as if it was a big tank filled with sharks. Sharks respect each other unless one gets weak, then the others tear into him and take his share away. In this tank, as it were, each shark has his own territorial zone around himself. He's safe from the others as long as he stays strong and keeps in his zone."

I nodded. "Sounds like the smart way to do it."

"Yeah. The really big dudes mark out their own territories and leave each other alone. In some ways, it's like a series of buffer zones for them. The people in the zone next to you get caught and you tighten up. The drug busts you usually read about in the papers aren't the big 'shark' dealers anyway. Most of the time they're the little 'barracudas,' so to speak, the nickle-and-dimers, the ten-kilo hustlers who're trying to haul it across the country in the back of a van. Maybe they know a connection with an airplane that can fly low across the Mexican border at night and risk getting caught by the DEA."

"But 'sharks' like Cullen don't fit in with that crowd?"

"You've got it. The 'sharks', like Cullen, are real different. Around the big metro areas they belong to the mob, the organized crime families, and they've got that all sewed up with interlocking trade agreements done up by their crooked lawyers. Out in the hinterlands, like here in Durango, each 'shark' has his own independent operation. Oh, they loosely cooperate on a national level with the other 'sharks', but they're basically on their own, and their territories are mutually respected. That is, as long as they stay strong and don't talk. That's why Cullen's tabbed as a 'regional'."

"I get the picture. Where does Cullen get his stuff?"

"He gets it where all the American suppliers get it today. Though a huge amount of it comes out of Asia, most of what you might call the really bulk supply starts out, as you may know, in South America. In the old days airplanes did most of the smuggling. Fill up a DC-3 in Colombia and fly it across the Caribbean. Drop the shipment to guys waiting below. Wait a while and go back for more. But airplanes have gotten easy to take down. Today, the cartels prefer to use boats."

"Boats? Doesn't that take too long?"

"These are big boats, freighters, Mike. Boats like that are a lot slower, sure. But the cartels have got the security angles pretty well figured out. Don't forget, a big boat can carry a much bigger load than a DC-3. And freighters don't always sail straight across the Gulf of Mexico and Caribbean either, like you sometimes hear about. Container ships go all over the world. Send a trailer-sized container full of drugs, with a lot of other containers, on a ship out of some Peruvian port, well disguised with some legitimate cargo. Take that container off in one midway port and put it on another boat sailing to America. Why not route it through Europe or Asia and then to the States? Takes a little longer, but the cartels can wait.

"They've got all the time in the world, huh?"

"Why not? The drugs aren't going to spoil if they're packaged right. They've got the shipments all timed to keep the flow going. And with container ships, it arouses less suspicion that way. The DEA has to rely on informants, and they dry up quick where big money and death squads hold the juice."

"Where does it come into the country, though?"

"You name it. You can use any port of entry you like. The bigger the 'shark' group, the less obtrusive. They could route it through central Canada with a load of maple-leaf candy, and from there right on into America, if they wanted. It could come into Seattle from Japan with car or computer parts. Most of it still comes in through south Florida, though. When the drug business was really taking off a few years ago, the cartels developed an infrastructure of people down there around Miami they could trust. And trust, like in any business, is the key. Many of their loyal people, the real pros, are still in place there, so that's the most reliable shipping destination."

"What about Cullen? How does a guy like him set up his deals?"

"Cullen probably gets his junk through Florida. Like I said, that's where the main pipeline still empties out. As a regional, he has less clout, and it would take a lot of advance negotiations with the other 'sharks' to set it up any other way. So that's probably his safest bet."

"And then he has trucks bring it here to Durango?"

"No, he's probably having it flown in. Once you're in the States, planes make more sense. An aircraft crossing an international border is one thing, but the DEA has a harder time watching domestic airplane travel. Especially planes like corporate jets and the like. Trucks and cars coming up to Durango from Florida are easier to tag and bust. And once a highway route and a pattern are established, the narcs can tighten things up. No, somehow he probably has an air connection on his loads."

"But the DEA hasn't figured it out yet?"

"It's a tricky business. Real safe, from Cullen's perspective. The feds are spread thin as it is, and Cullen knows where they are. These drug guys aren't stupid. 'Sharks' may be competitors, but they do share information for mutual protection. It boils down to computers, the internet, e-mail, encryption, and all that. His surveillance people, and others, know where and when to fly in the goods. Durango has an airport. So does Farmington, New Mexico. So do a lot of other nearby places, like Aspen, Alamosa, Monticello, and Moab. And there are plenty of little airstrips a small plane can land on all around here for all the tourists who visit this part of Colorado."

"What happens then?"

"Then ground transportation does take over, but for short-term hauls. Cullen can truck it in by a lot of different roads once he's got it off a plane. He's probably got several safe places where he can stash it around here. Lots of cabins back in these woods. They'd have security systems, of course, and they'd probably be well- guarded. Build a few special weatherproof underground cellars, and you've got perfect little hiding places for the drugs and the money to be laundered."

I sighed and sat back. "Okay, Harry, so that's how it gets here. But if you know about Cullen's operation, surely the police and the feds do, too."

"Yeah, but at that point the 'regionals' handle it through an assortment of middlemen. Cullen himself never touches the product, and his money never leaves a paper trail back to him, unless you go through foreign numbered bank accounts. It's all flown out and laundered, of course. He probably uses a setup similar to the one for the incoming drugs."

"But what about his laundered money when it comes back here to prop up his legitimate business operations? Surely the IRS gets interested if he's spending more than his businesses make."

"Not if it comes to him through hired dummy 'investors', most of them overseas. It just makes him look like a good guy to back with money. It leaves him out of the loop as far as the IRS is concerned. The problem is, as we know, it was his money to begin with. And don't forget, the man is not above using some of that money to bribe certain vulnerable people, if it helps him grease the skids."

"Like the Durango cops?"

Harry shook his head. "Oh, no. That would never do. Too many local patriots, like you and me, on the force. The Durango cops are mostly honest men and women. The good guys. A local fix would soon leak out in such a small town. No, he has other ways. Other businessmen, politicians, and the like. Power is always magnetic, even if you think the guy with the power has a shady side. People weaken."

"So he's got it all covered, and his drugs get to the street through guys like Jimmy Rowe?"

"Ah, yes, the infamous Mr. Rowe. The man's got a record a mile long of attempted arrests, but no doubt Cullen's got him protected, too. He did get caught once, before he hooked up with Cullen. Spent a two-year vacation down at La Tuna Federal Prison near El Paso. But that was his only real bust. And the snitches who told on him aren't alive any more. Rowe's dangerous,

Mike. Cullen holds his leash, but Rowe's not above free-lancing a little muscle or even a hit or two if it suits him. Cullen lets him have the leeway. He knows the bully-boy's going to blow off steam every now and then.

"He'd let him do that?"

"There's method in the madness. So long as it doesn't hurt business or point any fingers back to Cullen, the boss man's going to look the other way. To a degree, anyway. Cullen's probably not above using the evidence of those capers as leverage with Rowe either, to keep him accountable. Yes, Jimmy-boy's dangerous. That's why you've got to watch out. Rowe might decide to pay you a call."

"I think he already did." I told Harry about nearly getting run over while out for my morning jog.

"I suspect that was a sort of first warning. He wanted to nudge you, see how you'd take it, to make you respect him."

"I respect him. The way you respect a rattlesnake."

"Then he did what he intended to do. He got your attention. Just a small taste of intimidation. It's just like in that war you fought in, Mike. Initial intimidation, and if that's not enough, the game will get hotter and there'll be more."

It was almost too much for me. The good reverend really had it all down.

"Okay, Harry," I said, "I know you were a cop. But you sure seem to know a lot about all this."

"Maybe," he said, narrowing his eyes at me. He was silent for a long moment. "But that's not all I know. I know about guys like you, too, Mike. Would-be heroes. Like I told you, I once did something like what you're thinking of doing, trying to be a hero. That kid I told you about in South Chicago? I worked with him for two years to get him clean and straight. I was like a father to him. Maybe that was a mistake; I got personally involved. So when the action went down I couldn't think of anything but trying to save him. I made some errors in judgment because I loved that kid. He got killed because of it, and I nearly did, too."

"I'm sorry, Harry."

"Thanks. But you see, when I think of you getting your back up protecting that girl, Jill Carpenter, I see me and that kid all over again. It doesn't have to end up that way. Think about it."

I stood up and walked around the study, my arms crossed. "So you think I should just let Cullen have his way with her?"

He got up and faced me. "That's not what I'm saying. I'm just telling you to keep from crossing him any more. You can't control what the girl does. You can talk to her, sure, but if she goes back to him, don't stand in her way. As much as it pains me to say this, you've got to be nice to Cullen. Think 'sharks' again. Stay out of his way, and he won't bite you."

"What about me opening a line of cooperation with the cops on this?"

His smile was knowing, patronizing. "As a former cop, let me give you my experienced opinion of what they'll think of you. They'll congratulate you on being a good citizen, concerned about the drug problem and all, but they'll tell you you're out of your league, and you're in their way. Essentially, they'll tell you to mind your own business and cool it if you want to go on breathing."

"Just like you're doing."

"Yeah," he said, "just like what I'm trying to do. Think about it. Look at it from the cops' point of view. They all want Cullen, sure. But they're pros. They don't want you, an amateur, getting tangled up in a professional thing. If you were a cop, I promise you you'd see it the same way, Mike. Too many would-be heroes wind up like those people I showed you in those pictures."

He was right. He made sense, too. I sat down and thought about it some more.

"Harry," I asked, "why did you ever decide to go into the ministry, anyway? You sound like you'd still be good back on somebody's police force."

He sighed, as if I'd touched something deep inside him. "No," he said. "Not me, Mike. I've done my part in that business. I know what happens when people do evil things.".

"But why did you...?"

"Why did I become a minister?" He laughed. "Maybe I've got this crazy idea that I used to deal with the effects of evil, and maybe, through this kind of job, I can work on the other end, where the causes are. You see, people go bad when they decide that bad things like drugs are really not so bad after all. Maybe I can reach a few of them before they get to that point. Maybe I can even change a few who've gotten into it, and convince them that there really are good things and bad things in life. Maybe I can convince them that just calling something bad 'good' doesn't make it that way."

I grinned. "Pardon me, reverend, but it sounds a little idealistic to me."

"I know. But Mike, it works. At least with some people it does. I've seen it."

"What about Cullen, though? He's so used to doing bad stuff, how could you ever change a guy like that?"

Harry sighed. "Men like Dil Cullen are hard cases, Mike, that's true. But they're still men. Somehow, even with a man like Cullen, so caught up in evil, there's still hope, a chance. Maybe someday, somehow, something will happen to make him look at life differently. I know it would be easy to write him off as so much human garbage, and the world would be better off without him. But from my religious standpoint, I have to believe that there's hope even for a man like him. Foolish? Maybe. But there's a divine foolishness in it. Maybe someday you'll see it that way, too."

I paused, feeling a coldness within myself. "I doubt it, Harry. Remember the bodies you showed me in those pictures? Men like Cullen are behind the murders like that. Can you forgive them for that? Can you actually think there's a shred of hope such dirtbags could change into good people again?"

He sighed. "Like I said, it must sound rather foolish, especially to a man caught up in anger like you are. But if you move beyond your anger, you'll see that the evil in evil men is not always a permanent condition. Men like that really can be subject to change. I'm not asking you to see it my way yet. I've been where you are, believe me. I know how enraged something like this can make you. But perhaps in time, you'll cool off and take a second look."

"Maybe," I said slowly. "I don't have a lock on all the truth in the universe. I just know what I've learned from being careful. I've killed people, Harry, in war. It seemed like the right thing to do at the time. I was like an animal, a killing machine once."

"And now you're a changed man?"

"Yes, I've changed. But war is different. If I was in a war situation again, I'm not sure I wouldn't do the same thing all over again."

"You'd feel justified in such killing?"

"Probably. You were a cop. You've seen how drugs can destroy people. Wouldn't you?"

He shook his head. "That's a tough one. I killed two people in the line of duty. And you're right. At the time, shooting them seemed like the right thing to do. I felt justified. But I only wish I could have gotten to those people earlier in their lives. Maybe things didn't have to turn out that way for them."

"You can't always get there ahead of time, Reverend. You don't always have that luxury."

"Maybe so, Mike. But you and I are 'there' now, ahead of time, so to speak, where Cullen is concerned. So you might try thinking about it that way. You changed. Maybe he can, too."

"I'll work on that one, Harry," I said. "But something's still bothering me. If you know so much about Cullen and his operation, and he's not so dumb, as we know, why doesn't he make it hot for you? He knows you work on the Drug Task Force. You seem like a perfect target for him. At the least, it would seem that he'd try to get you removed from the church and moved far away or something."

Harry smiled and sat back in his chair, thinking about it for a moment. "Maybe he knows I am trying, forcing myself, to see some good in him. I think every man who comes to church hopes his pastor sees some good in him, even if he's as big a phony as Cullen. Maybe that's why he leaves me alone, as you put it. He knows I really don't hate him. I just want him to become something better than what he is."

I smiled at the minister. "Harry, this may offend you, but do you know what you remind me of, in a way?"

"What?" he said, his eyes wide with expectancy and yet knowing I was going to be critical.

"I know some women, nice women, who are attracted to thugs and bad guys like Cullen like gypsy-moths to a flame. They're drawn to them with some obsessive need to reform them, to change the bad little boy inside such a man into a good little boy. Of course, do- gooder women like that always get crushed and abused in the process. But they'll tell you they can't help themselves. They've just got to try their hand at reforming the stupid creeps."

He let the words hit him, and nodded thoughtfully before he

replied. "No, the difference between me and people like that is that I know full well the bad ones may not change. I don't rush in like Florence Nightengale trying to work a miracle. I'm cautious with them, and I know them for what they are. I'm well aware that they are people who use people and then throw them away once they've drained them of anything useful. But sometimes, Mike, even with the worst of the rats, God can give you an opportunity. There's an old saying in the ministry: 'Man's extremity is God's opportunity.' Maybe some day such an extremity, such an opportunity, will happen even for Dil Cullen."

I smiled sarcastically. "I think I understand your feelings, Harry, but don't bet the farm on it. Cullen's dirty, and, as you say, a bona-fide user. Yet his drug of choice isn't really cocaine, it's power. It's squeezing the life-blood out of people and controlling them. He's drunk on that. That's the one sure thing. You can see it in his eyes, if you look close enough."

Harry sat back and gave me a long stare. "And you? Are you, the grand crusader, drunk on the idea of squeezing the life-blood out of him?"

"I don't know," I said quietly. "It all depends on him."

He shook his head in despair. "Okay, I tried. If you won't let it go, if you won't back off, at least I did my best."

I shifted in my chair. "Wait a minute, Harry. I didn't say I wouldn't take your advice. As a matter of fact, I probably will. But that doesn't mean I still don't want to see him go down. That part hasn't changed."

He was silent for a moment. At length he said, "Well, I guess that's fair enough."

"I hope so," I said. "I'm still human, Harry. I mean, that...is allowed, isn't it?"

"Sure. Just as long as you think about being open to a change in the man. Just think about it. And keep your distance from him. Don't make him mad. That's all I'm asking."

"I'll think about it. I respect you, Harry. I know you're trying to do what you see is the right thing. You've given me some facts to consider. Especially about my own safety. And Jill's."

"And what about Tracy? Have you thought of her?"

My eyes narrowed. "What about her? You think she's in a vulnerable position here, too?"

"Mike, open your eyes. In South America, even in South

Florida, these people don't just go after a man who's a threat. They'll go after his family and...friends, too. Give some thought to it."

It sobered me. I really had not considered that possibility. In a way, it kindled my anger against Cullen even hotter. Yes, he might try something along those lines. But at his absolute peril.

"It sounds a little far-fetched, but I'll remember it."

"Good. It's a complicated game, Mike."

"So it seems."

I started to get up. "Well," I said, "I'd better let you go. You've probably got a sermon or something to write this morning."

"No," he said. "I just gave you my sermon for the day. But I do have a few things I need to do. I hope you'll come back in again. If I can help you get through any of this, let me know."

"Thanks," I said. "You've been a lot of help already."

"I hope so. I hope I've been the right kind of help."

"You have."

I shook his hand and we went out of his study together. I nodded to his secretary as I passed her, and left the church.

I hadn't expected to hear what he had told me. It was good though. Now I had a bigger picture of Cullen and his operation. And I had learned a lot about Harry Foster as well. He was one interesting ex-cop in shepherd's clothing.

It was mid-morning, and I was ready for a cup of coffee. I drove back downtown to Mario's, a coffee bar I knew. Mario's was on the second floor above a clothing store. They had an open-air seating area where you could sit at little round tables with umbrellas over them while you drank your coffee, looking at the mountains. I ordered a cup of cappucino from the waiter, and waited as I looked at the clouds grazing the hilltops.

The cappucino came quickly, and I sipped it. It was sweet and mild, French vanilla, very hot. I like cappucino but I have to watch it. It's so good you can really get hooked on the stuff. But the kind I like, like the French vanilla, has a ton of calories in it and that's not so good, if, like me, you watch your weight.

"Mike Rader," I heard a voice call out as I sat there.

I looked up. The sun was in my eyes as I tried to see who it was. The dark shape was that of a tall man, and I had to shield my eyes before I could make him out. Speak of the devil. It was Dil Cullen.

"Hello, Dil," I said.

"Mind if I join you?"

"Go ahead," I said, gesturing to an empty chair.

He sat down and the waiter came over. "What are you having today?" Dil asked.

"Cappucino, French vanilla," I answered.

Dil looked up at the waiter. "Sounds good. I think I'll have one, too."

The waiter nodded and went over to the bar. "You know cappucino's not good for you," Dil said.

"So I've heard."

"It's hard on a climber's body. Besides, it's like a drug. It can get addictive. You, uh, aren't addicted to it by chance, are you?"

It was a small jibe, but I rolled with it. "I don't let it become addictive, Dil," I said. "I know when to quit."

"But it is a sort of drug, you know. The caffeine, the sugar, that sweet French vanilla flavoring; it all has an effect."

"Did you come here to talk to me about drugs, Dil?"

He laughed. "No, look. You and I seem to have gotten off on the wrong foot with each other. There's no need for that. I think we can be friends."

I thought about my conversation with Harry Foster. The minister had said to go along with the guy, and to avoid crossing him. Be friendly, he had said. Okay, I could do that.

"Fine," I said. "Maybe you're right. Look, I'm sorry if I came off a little cute at that drug-prevention luncheon. I was just popping off. Maybe I was out of line."

"I understand," he said. "This whole business with Jill had gotten us all a little edgy."

I nodded. The waiter brought him his cup.

"Besides," he continued, "I guess you've heard all those nasty rumors about me. I think they were started by some competitors of mine in the land development business. I don't know, it's my own fault I guess."

"How so?"

He sipped his cup and set it on the table. "Well, we've all done some things we aren't too proud of. When I was a young guy, just getting started in business here, I ran with a pretty fast crowd. My wife and I were only a couple of years out of college, and I wanted to get connected and make a lot of money quick. You follow me?"

"Sure," I said. "I can see how that could happen."

"The problem was, the guys I ran with then were all hustler types– you know, they were into all kinds of hot deals. Quickie schemes, and all that. We all lived on the edge in those days. Adrenaline city. Sometimes... well, hell, we even stepped over the edge. There were wild parties with some of the, uh, shall we say, less innocent ladies from around the town. And yes, there was some weed and some blow there, too. We all thought we were having a good time and it was okay as long as nobody got hurt. It was sort of expected that you went for all of it, all the way. If you didn't go along, you were branded as a weakling, a wimp, a traitor to the group. Hell, call it peer pressure. I went along with the rest of them."

"I understand," I lied.

"But, fortunately, I somehow got a wake-up call before I got in too deep. I saw that it was wrong, Mike. I cleaned up my act. I left that group. I found the Lord, thank God, and I'm a better man for it. You saw me in church, didn't you?"

"Yeah," I said, "I saw you there."

He sighed. "It's hard to shake a bad reputation in a small town once you've been doing some things you shouldn't have been doing. And even now, years later, my competitors have made hay out of my, uh, youthful indiscretions. Sure, it hurts my business when they do that, but I'll outlive it in time."

He appeared so sincere, I actually wanted to believe him. But my visit with Harry had killed that idea. Still, I knew it was best to play along. Yet it would be in character for me to query him with a few probing questions at this point.

"Can I ask you something?"

"Sure," he said. "Anything. I really want to clear the air between us, Mike."

"Okay," I said. "Look, I don't want to pry. I can understand about the wild times in your past. But tell me some more about those rumors about your being a dealer."

He nodded like he had been expecting the question. "Like I said, they're just stupid rumors. You know and I know that I'd be a complete idiot to be mixed up in that kind of stuff today. No, I've sown my wild oats and I've learned my lesson. I wish it had never happened, but I can't undo the past. That part of my life is all behind me now, though."

"What about Jimmy Rowe?"

He took a drink from his cup before he spoke. "Oh, Jimmy's all right. He's a little rough around the edges, but he comes by it naturally. He helps me out with my construction projects. If you know construction people, you know you've got to be a little tough with them at times to get things moving. Those people drag their feet sometimes. Jimmy's a motivater. He gets them moving again. That's why Jimmy's on the payroll. But he'd never do anything really out of line, at least to my knowledge. Sure, it's true, I can't watch him all the time. He's got a rough edge. He could be mixed up in something I don't know about, but I don't think he'd do anything really bad. He's got a sweet setup working for me, and he doesn't want to give that up."

"And if you did find out he was mixed up in something bad?"

Dil cocked his head to one side. "Then I'd probably have to let him go."

"Did he tell you he tried to run me down with his car when I was out running the other morning?"

Cullen's face registered shock and surprise. "He did? Oh, that Jimmy. I'm sorry about that. He does have a rather childish streak of bully in him, and he likes to play the macho dude role at times. He gets in that GTO of his and sometimes he reverts to his younger days. But I'm sure he was just playing around. No, if he really did such a stupid thing, I'm sure he didn't mean anything serious by it. Just the same, though, I'll speak to him about it."

"You say he was just playing around?"

"Oh yes. Jimmy likes to clown around. If he really wanted to hurt you, he'd have parked and tried to beat the daylights out of you with his fists. He's into all that kung-fu martial arts stuff. You know what I mean?"

"Yes," I said.

Dil regarded me with humor in his eyes. "Come to think of it though, I'm not sure I'd want to mix it up with you. You look pretty fit, and...weren't you a soldier once?"

"Uh-huh. Where'd you hear that?"

"Word gets around. When I found out you were friends with Jill, and I hope you'll pardon me, but I asked around about you. I hope you don't mind. I...I look out for my friends, Mike, and Jill is my friend. I heard you were in the Rangers in Viet Nam. Is that correct?"

I wondered how he learned that. Then I remembered what Harry Foster had said about how these guys were masters at getting protective information. Dil could have accessed my background from several sources. He probably even knew the balance in my bank account. Okay, I said to myself, this is no time to get paranoid. Play along.

"That's right," I said. "Were you in the service yourself, Dil?"

"Oh, no. I was still in high school when Nixon pulled us out of Viet Nam. Still, I'm impressed by your background. Did you see some action over there?"

Where was this going, I wondered. "A little. Spent most of the time polishing my boots, I'm afraid."

"But you were in the Rangers. Those guys are supposed to be the toughest of them all."

I grinned. "Naw," I said. "Oh, we were okay, I guess. But you know how it is. All the so-called elite service groups think their group is the toughest. The truth is, they're all about the same. We just did our part."

He nodded. "So what do you think about that war?"

Oh, boy, I thought. I'd heard that question before. "That war was pretty messed up. We all went in thinking it was the right thing to do. I guess it just got fouled up somehow. Politics and miscalculations. Maybe the intentions were right, but it turned into a mess. There's enough blame to go around for everyone."

"Were you bitter about it later, I mean when you came home, and, as I would suspect, nobody cheered you?"

I had to laugh. "I didn't go over there for the cheers I might get on my return, Dil. I did it because, like I said, it seemed like the thing to do at the time."

"Well," he said, "you seem like you've adjusted well enough from it all. I know some Vietnam War vets who really cracked up when they got back."

"Yeah," I said laconically. "A lot of them...a lot of us, did. You really can't blame them though. If you weren't over there, I doubt if you'd understand. But that was years ago. Life is a lot better now."

"You seem to be moving on rather well in your life, I'd say. I know the owners of The Aspen Leaf. They say you're a good store manager."

My paranoia rose inside again. The veteran thing was another string for him to pull, maybe. But I had to be cool. Maybe I could change the subject.

"I try to put in a day's work. Same as you, I guess, Dil. How's your business going?"

He frowned a little. "It could be better. It's a little slow right now getting buyers for the new homes we're building. But I've learned to weather the ups and downs in the local economy. You have to trust in the long-term growth curve. We're making headway. Durango's just starting to be what it's destined to become, Mike. One of these days we'll be up there with Aspen, Vail, and Breckenridge. There's still room for good people to get in on the ground floor on the real opportunity end of things. You know, I don't want to sound like I'm being pretentious, but you yourself might want to get into it."

"How so?" I asked.

"Easy. I know you probably like what you're doing now, but I might be able to make room for a guy like you in one of my businesses somewhere."

That caught my attention. "Doing what?" I asked. I had a feeling something like this was coming. The stick and the carrot. Yes, he was good. He didn't say it, but I knew he was thinking it. "I might get you fired, but if you're extra nice I might see about getting you hired for something better." It was a pretty deft approach.

He downed the last of his cappucino with a quick, hard swallow. "Well," he said, "from the looks of what you're doing at your store, you know how to manage people in a business operation. Your experience in the Army probably makes you qualified to handle some responsible management assignments, I'd guess, even those involving physical labor. You've kept yourself in good shape for your climbing. And, from the way you're trying to help Jill, I can tell you have the trait of loyalty. I do value loyalty in my organization. But I also like the way you're unafraid to stand up to people, even people who, and let's be honest here, have a bit more clout than you do. Not everyone will do that. I admire that in a worker."

I sat back and crossed my arms, smiling. "You really know how to make a man feel good," I said. "Do you always size up everyone that way?"

"No," he said, grinning sheepishly. "But I am careful about people. If I have any gift, I think I can carefully evaluate somebody who I think might make me a good employee."

Or an adversary, I thought. "Well, I'm flattered, Dil."

He coughed. "Flattery wasn't my intention."

"I know that. Mind if I return the favor?"

He bent closer in his chair. "What do you mean?"

"Oh, I've done a little research on you, too, Dil. From what I've heard on the street, and from what you've told me, I can see that you're intelligent. You'd have to be in the games you play. You're smart enough to put together an organization that's successful in a very competitive business. For what it's worth, I suspect that you're probably something of a workaholic, too. Am I right?"

He shrugged. "Maybe so. But I like what I do, so I work fairly consistently at it."

"And yes," I continued, "I've heard some, well, less than flattering rumors about you. They do say you're involved with drugs, Dil."

He stiffened again, staring at me. "I thought we covered that."

I smiled. "Now, wait just a minute," I said. "Don't go all huffy on me. I'm willing to listen and to take you at your word. I know about unfair rumors. You say you're clean and straight. I'll go along with you on that."

"Well, I hope so," he said. "Look, I'm leveling with you, Mike. That rumor stuff is a bunch of lies. I could never forgive myself if it were true. Besides, it could wreck everything I've tried to build up. My business, my marriage, my family, everything."

"Okay," I said, nodding emphatically, "let's say I believe you. But back to the rumors. Think them through with me. Why would any intelligent man running a successful business get into drug- dealing, or stay in it? Let me play devil's advocate for a minute. In business terms, it could provide a heavy influx of capital if such a businessman was extended to his limit on his business deals."

Dil shook his head. "No. It won't wash. It's too complicated. You don't know the feds like I do. The IRS has a hundred ways to spear you if you show up on somebody's paper trail with more money than you report. I know people who've tried it. It's a game you can't win. And that's just for openers. The DEA's no agency to mess around with either."

"But somebody's doing it around here. Look at the drugs in this town."

"Yes, Mike, but that's all from your small-time dealers, the midnight back-alley toughs who come into Durango with their car trunks loaded with the dope. Nickle-and-dimers out to make a cheap score. Mike, a high-profile person like me wouldn't stand a chance running a large drug operation. If the IRS didn't get you, the DEA or maybe even the FBI would catch you sooner or later. A person in my position could not take stupid risks like that. I'm far too exposed. Think about it."

"Like I said, I'm willing to believe you, Dil. But I can see how some folks might find that a juicy rumor."

He sighed and shook his head. "Look. When you're big, the people are always trying to find some way to throw rocks at you and trip you up. Your competitors love to hurt you that way. People love scandals. That's human nature."

"But you can be rough at times?"

"That's part of it. I'm not saying I've always used the kid-glove treatment when it comes to a deal. When you make money, though, it gets a little rough. I've been burned by more banks, insurance companies, and contractors than you can shake a stick at. It's a tough game, but I've learned how to survive. You get real close with the financial sheets and the fine print in the contracts when everything's on the line. Yes, I've had to get a little rough myself a few times when I thought that somebody was out to put the thumbscrews on me. I call it self defense. And I've had to gamble a lot to get the investor cash I needed for some of my projects, and that weighs on your mind. But it's all been strictly legal. I don't sell drugs, and I don't go out of my way to hurt people. If I've hurt anybody, it's just in dealing with people that tried to hurt me first. That's just business. It's the way it is on my level of the game, as you might call it. Do you get the picture?"

"Yeah," I said, "I see, Dil. Pardon me if I pushed you on that. I just wanted to know how you saw it."

He was measuring me with those quick eyes of his again. And, he was right about one thing. He wasn't going to be taken easily. Not by me or anyone else. He had to hold the upper hand in an iron fist. It was an essential talent for an entrepreneur of his caliber.

He grunted. "No," he said, "I don't really believe you do see what I mean."

"Wait a minute," I said. "Stop looking at me like I'm some high- priced insurance company lawyer trying to shake you down. Give me the chance to believe you. I'm just testing, trying to put that rumor stuff in perspective, Dil. Something would help me clear my mind on it, though. Again, if you don't mind my asking you a rather personal question, what about your relationship with Jill Carpenter? You say she's just a 'friend'. Is that really all there is to it?"

He smiled and laughed softly. "You really do get to the heart of the matter, don't you?"

"If we're going to be friends, we've got to be honest with each other. I was just wondering about her. And you."

"Well," he said, "my dealings with Jill are rather personal, but, so what, okay, I'll tell you. But first let me reassure you, though, that I have a good marriage. My wife and I have been married for seventeen years. I don't cheat on her. We have a great home life. We go to church with the kids on Sunday. You can believe me on that."

"Fair enough. I believe you. But where does Jill Carpenter fit in?"

He swallowed hard and cleared his throat. It was plain that he didn't like talking about her. "Well, when it comes to Jill...Mike, look, we're both men, and we've both been around the block a few times. Have you ever met someone you wish you'd met when you were younger, someone really special? Someone who really does it for you? Ever had that feeling?"

I nodded. "Sure. I know the feeling."

"Look, I know Jill's young enough to be my daughter. And I have to admit to you in all honesty, man-to-man, I'm, yes, deeply attracted to her. But let me be crystal-clear on this. I'm not about to have an affair with the girl. I don't do things like that.

I'm faithful. And I don't want to ruin Jill's life with some cheap affair, either. But I can't stop the caring I have for her, and wanting to protect her. She got mixed up with drugs, but she's a good girl. I just want to make it possible for her to have a good life. I don't even care if she falls in love with some other guy and gets married. I just want her to be happy. Understand?"

"I think so," I said. "So you love her like a daughter. Is that what you're saying?"

"If I were single, closer to her in age, it'd be different. But I'm not. And I really am in love with my wife, and I dearly love my kids. So all I can do is try to help Jill the best way I know how, by being a caring friend."

I let it sink in. Most of it had a ring of truth. I even felt a little sorry for him. He was only human, and people get attracted to other people at all stages in life, whether they are married or not. He really was in love with Jill, but she didn't feel the same way toward him, or so it seemed. But beyond his persuasive words, I wasn't so sure he'd let marital fidelity stand in his way if he had a chance to get his hands on her. I had known other men like him. Once they had that drug of ultimate power going, morality was often no barrier, no problem. Yet he was trying to make it sound good, so I went along with him. I wanted to sound believable to him.

"I see your point, Dil," I said. "And though I'm not attracted to her, I share your protective feelings toward her. It seems we want the same things for her."

He nodded. "I know that now. I can see it in how you've handled all this. Yet, I must confess that I was a little worried about you and Jill at first. But, and again, you'll pardon me for looking into your life, but I know you're, uh, romantically involved with someone else. Her name's Tracy Diamond, isn't it?"

It was my turn to be surprised. It was hard not to stumble when he mentioned Tracy's name. I guess I would have been a fool to think he hadn't found out about Tracy and what she meant to me. Word travels fast in a small town.

"That's right," I said. "Tracy and I are seeing each other. Jill's not in any romantic plans I have."

"I didn't think so. So I know Jill's just a girl you want to help. And you are helping her, from what I can see. I don't want to sound like some old fool sugar-daddy, Mike, but if I can offer my services to you in helping her, I really do want to."

I smiled inwardly. Before, he had tried to use a power play to keep her away from me. Now he had to come at me with the friend-to-friend approach. That was okay. It might even keep us on good terms with each other and maybe Jimmy Rowe would keep his distance. Besides, Dil could keep an eye on her and he'd know if anything irregular was going on.

"I can see that, Dil," I said. "As they used to say, I can see that your intentions are honorable toward her, too."

He laughed. "Well, that's a relief. We understand each other. You know, Mike, I'm beginning to like you. We seem to share a lot in common. You may not know me very well yet, but I hope we can talk again like this from time to time. We might even become pretty close friends."

"We might at that, Dil."

He glanced down at his watch. "Well, you hit it on the head when you said I was a workaholic. I've got to be somewhere. I'm glad we had the chance to talk all this over. Just remember, though, those dumb rumors about me having some shady business on the side is a lot of claptrap. Do you believe me now?"

"Sure," I said, trying to look as honest and sober as a judge. "Small town rumors."

"Good. I'm glad we're on the same side. I believe in the win-win deal, Mike. We'll both come out ahead that way."

"You're right," I said. "Win-win." I decided to put some positive spin on it. "And Dil, I do enjoy working at The Aspen Leaf. But listen, if that ever changes, I may want to talk with you about coming to work for you."

He seemed a little surprised. "We might work something out." He smiled a thin, canny smile. "Of course, before you came to work for me, you'd have to take a drug test first. Think you'd pass?"

"I don't know," I said. "Would they accept me if they found traces of cappucino in my blood?"

He laughed heartily. He got up from his chair and tossed some bills on the table.

"Cappucino might not pass muster, but maybe I could make an allowance in your case. Got to leave a little slack in the line sometimes. Anyway, if you ever do get the itch to get into the land development business, give me a holler. For now, take care of that Jill, will you?"

"She'll be okay," I said.

His tall silhouette was lost in the sunlight blinding my eyes as he walked away.

Okay, Harry, I did what you said, I thought. Sort of, anyway. Dil and I are bosom buddies now. Maybe things really would have a chance to work out for Jill. And maybe I could keep my health, too.

That evening I was still thinking about what Dil had said. Maybe there really was a heart down deep inside the guy after all. Maybe Harry had it all wrong about his drug business. Even cops can be wrong. Maybe it really was all just a collection of rumors, blown out of proportion. But then I caught myself. Too many other facts weighed in favor of it. No. Dil was a drug dealer deluxe.

I needed to get away from it all. Dil was good, and he had messed my mind up. I went out to the garage and turned on the light. There, gray and still, the Cobra sat like a crouching panther.

I got out my tools and opened the hood. I lost myself in checking the clearances and fluid levels. After a while, I got in and backed her out onto the street. I drove around a while, quietly, slowly, just listening to her soft, throaty rumble.

I turned a corner and saw a cop car sitting beside the curb. As I passed him, the cop turned on his red lights and came up behind me. Uh-oh, I thought, what have I done wrong now? I pulled over.

I used to get out when a cop pulled me over, but once a cop friend told me they like you to stay inside. He said they think they have better control over you that way. I waited as he walked up beside my door.

"Hi," he said, looking at me and shining his flashlight along the Cobra's flanks. What was he looking for?

"Evening, officer," I said. "Something wrong?"

"No," he said, a little sheepishly. "I just had to see this car. 289 Cobra, isn't it?"

"Uh-huh," I said, coolly covering my relief.

"And a real one, too. Not a kit car?"

"It's the real McCoy," I said.

"I've seen pictures, but I've never seen a real one up close. Is it...is it really as fast as they say?"

I chuckled. "Probably not. All that speed stuff you hear about has probably been pretty exaggerated."

He shone his light on the speedometer, which went all the way to 160. "Looks like it'd do well over a hundred if you floored it in fourth gear."

I sighed. "When it was young, yeah, I guess so. But this thing's just an antique now. The engine shows its age. It's had its day. I just like to cruise around in it and remember the good old days."

He laughed. "You're putting me on. I bet she really hauls."

I smiled. "Maybe a little. Want to take a ride?"

"No," he said. "I'm on duty. Tell you what, though. I was just about to take a break. Will you let me buy you a cup of coffee? I'd like to ask you a few things about the car."

Next you'll want my autograph, I thought. "Sure," I said.

He got back into his squad car, and I followed him to an all-night donut shop. We parked and I went in with him. We took a booth and introduced ourselves. He said his name was George Barker.

Barker was a young policeman, mid-twenties I guessed, and he had the air of a good, well-disciplined cop about him. I got the feeling he was ex-military. Maybe it was because of his ramrod-straight posture and bearing. Then I saw the Airborne tattoo on the back of his left hand and I knew for sure. He was tall, though not quite as tall as I was, razor-thin, with careful brown eyes that were friendly yet held an air of caution as he measured you.

"Where'd you get that Cobra?" he asked.

I told him the story, and he seemed duly impressed. He asked me a string of questions about the car, and I tried to give him straight answers. He was just like any auto enthusiast, and like most cops, he knew what he was talking about when it came to cars. These guys have to know the competition out on the streets. George Barker did.

"If that car's what you say it is," he said, "and if you had it in shape, it'd be one of the fastest street machines in La Plata County."

I laughed. "Well, like I told you, it's not really in tip-top shape." That was only partially the truth, of course. A few twists and turns of the tools and it could be all that it ever was, but why brag about that? Especially to a cop.

"George," I said, "you sound like you're familiar with some of the faster iron around town."

He grinned. "Oh, yeah. We can spot the locals who have the fast mills on sight. Believe me, they stick out like sore thumbs when your business is law enforcement. Got to catch them speeders, ya know. Got to make that old quota."

"You really have a quota?"

He laughed. "No, but everyone thinks we do."

"I understand," I said. "All in a day's work. If you don't mind me asking, just what kind of the speedier cars do we have here in Durango?"

He seemed pleased that I asked. "Some fairly exotic machines, actually. Oh, you know, there's a lot of kids with hot-rod junk, drag- racing types with add-on stuff. They can do their quarter-mile dance but that's about it. But there's quite a few very expensive production sports cars around, too. Rich guys' toys. Italian and German marques, and a few American. Some of those babies can top out near 200 miles per hour, and we keep an eye on them."

I nodded and bit my lip. "What about Detroit iron? Ever see a big black GTO tooling around town?"

George was raising his coffee cup to his lips. He stopped in mid-raise and stared straight at me. His friendly eyes suddenly hardened, turned cold. The cop in him switched back on.

"Jimmy Rowe," he said softly. "You know him?"

"I know...of him." I said.

"Then I hope you don't have any business dealings with him, Mike. I was starting to like you."

"No, I have no business with him, George," I said softly.

He drank a sip from his cup and put it down. "Rowe's one very bad hombre."

"So I've heard. Mind if I ask what you know about him?"

The professional suspicion was all there in him now. "Why?"

"I'm a runner. I was out for a morning run not long back and Rowe tried to run me down in that GTO."

George smiled and chuckled. "Figures. Stay away from him, Mike. Rowe's a sadistic punk, a real hard case. He likes to hurt people. He's a stone killer, too, but we can't pin anything on him yet. That is, until he slips up."

"What else do you know about him?"

He hesitated, wondering if he should tell me. I guess he decided to give me a little of what he knew. Maybe he figured I might know something that would be useful.

"Not a whole lot," he said. "Rowe came here a couple of years ago from Miami. Somehow he's mixed up in the drug trade. Does that tell you anything?"

"Yeah. It tells me to stay away from him."

"You'd better. They say he's got quite a collection of guns, a Uzi and all that macho junk. But we've never caught him with them. Keeps it all stashed away somewhere. I think he likes to use his knife better though. Yes, I'd definitely stay away from him if I were you. Why'd he try to run you down, anyway?"

"I don't know. For kicks, I guess."

"Did you file a complaint?"

"No. It was out of the city limits and I didn't get his license at the time. It would have probably made a pretty shaky case for you or the county guys. And I guess maybe I thought if it didn't stick, he might come after me."

George nodded. "Well, that's smart. If I were you I'd put as much distance between that punk and myself as I could. You know, you have your small-time hoods and your bar bullies and all that. But Jimmy Rowe is different. Like I said, he's a stone killer. He enjoys hurting people. And he's smart as a whip to boot. He's got a guy who covers him with legal talent, too, if he ever slips up, which I suspect he rarely does."

"Solid citizen, huh?"

"Oh, the best."

"What about the GTO? Funny for a guy like that to be driving an old muscle car from the sixties."

"He seems to like it. The rumor is that he took it away from some guy down in Santa Fe one night after he'd removed one of the guy's legs with his knife. Drug debt or something. Cut the leg to the bone and just snapped the bone clean off. A real pro deal."

"Ouch," I said.

"Yeah. I guess he took the car rather than the guy's life. Look, Mike, let me warn you again. Rowe is major trouble. You take your little Cobra and stay away from that dude. Don't mess with him. You'll live longer."

"I read you loud and clear, George," I said.

I got up, and George thanked me for filling him in on my Cobra. I left the donut shop and got in the car.

Well, Cullen, I thought as I drove home, your story about cleaning up your act looks shakier and shakier. If Rowe's on your payroll, you ain't no boy scout. But I'll stay out of your way as long as you stay out of mine. You've got it all thought out. Your setup's all bombproof. But if you make a slip, then to use your own words, I'll have to speak with you about it. And when I do, I won't be your friend anymore. Count on it.

Chapter Seven

Tracy had the afternoon free, and she called me at my office. Business was slow at the Leaf, and I was spending my time swinging a fly swatter, trying to chase down one of the little buzzing pests, when she called. I was losing my battle with the fly anyway, and I was glad to hear her voice.

"Hi," she said. "You busy?"

"Not really. Things are sort of dead around here this afternoon."

"Can you take the rest of the afternoon off?"

"I might. What have you got in mind?"

"I was going out to shoot a couple of rolls. I could use some company. Interested?"

"Sure," I said. "When?"

"Is now okay?"

I glanced up at the clock over my desk. It was two o'clock. "Sure," I said.

"I'll be over in a few minutes then."

"Good. Do you want me to bring anything?"

"Well, we'll be going out onto some old forest service roads. We'll probably be back kind of late. Do you want to cook out or anything?"

"I can handle that. I'll get some stuff together. Come on over."

I went into the store room and found a large portable stove we were testing. I filled it with white gas and stowed it in a stuff sack along with some cookwear, dishes, and utensils. I carried these back to the office, then went out onto the floor and found some camp food and other articles which I signed for before taking it all back to the office to put in the sack.

Tracy knocked on the door a few minutes later. She looked wonderfully happy to see me, eyes shining.. I hadn't been spending much time with her for a day or two, and I was eager to spend some time alone with her today.

"Ready?" she asked.

"Yeah," I said. "I need to get away for a while. It'll do me good to get out."

"I thought it might."

I told Barry I was taking off, and we went out to Tracy's Suburban. I stowed the carry-bag in the back and we headed north out of town.

Tracy had found that the old four-wheel-drive Suburban was just the kind of vehicle that she needed for her photographic excursions. It was big enough to carry her cameras, tripods, film, boxes of lenses and other equipment, and the four-wheel-drive came in handy on some of the rougher mountain roads. She had bought it in those first days when she came to town, trading in her Chevy sedan.

When I first saw the Suburban, I had doubts about it, though. Almost a hundred thousand miles showed on the odometer, but it had obviously been well taken care of by its former owner. I ran a compression check on the cylinders, looked for seal leaks, and checked a few other things on it, like the brakes, the transmission, and the suspension. After checking it out, it seemed to be in reasonably good shape. Old protective me, I didn't want Tracy getting stuck out in the woods.

I also suggested that she invest in a cellular telephone. The cellular people had installed a few relay antennas on some of the nearby mountaintops, and that way she could call for help if she got stranded and needed it. She balked at my suggestion at first, but then she went ahead and got one. Now she was glad she did. She had never been stranded, but it was comforting for her to know she could call for help if she ever needed it.

"So where are we going?" I asked. I had gone out with her on such outings a few times before, and it was always interesting to see what she had planned.

"Cross-Creek Canyon. It's about twenty miles north of town. I got a look at it a month ago when I was scouting locations for my pictures. There's a waterfall and some old mines. I think you'll like it."

I looked out at the sky. It was blue, with puffy white clouds. It was her kind of day.

"Well, your light looks good," I said.

"I know. It's supposed to rain tomorrow so I thought I'd better grab the opportunity."

The highway north out of Durango was always a picture of loveliness to me any time of the year. It follows the Animas River until the flood-plain narrows and the mountains get steeper, then it winds its way up along the mountainsides. The narrow-gauge railroad line more-or-less follows this route also, and as we drove along we passed one of the slow-moving tourist trains. The passenger cars were filled with happy summer people on holiday waving to us from the windows as the engine blew clouds of thick black smoke into the afternoon air.

After thirty minutes of driving, we turned off the highway onto a dirt-and-rock road with overhanging tree branches. Then we drove along a creek beneath towering mountain walls. Gaining altitude now, Tracy dropped the transmission down into four-wheel- drive. It was a good decision, for the road became rough and steep and began to switchback sharply up the side of the hill.

Higher up, the road leveled off in flatter meadows mixed with stands of green aspen trees. The green leaves trembled in the breeze as we passed by. We went a few miles farther up the trail. Then Tracy pulled over to the side of the road.

"We're here," she announced.

I looked around at the mountains. "I don't see any waterfall."

"It's a couple of miles off the road, Mike."

"Then I'm glad I came prepared for a hike."

"You always like to hike. You know that." She gestured toward the back of the Suburban. "You see that tripod back there? Would you carry it for me?"

I saw it. "Sure," I said. "Now I know why you invited me along. You just needed a beast of burden."

She laughed. "Well, you got the beast part right, anyway. I'll get my camera gear."

We set out on a wisp of a trail across a meadow through knee-high green grass that led to the first stand of trees. Tracy was in front of me, carrying her camera equipment in a blue daypack. Her perfume carried behind her through the air to me, and my eyes followed her. She walked along the trail like a woman, everything bouncing in good order, and that was very enchanting. She looked so good to me this afternoon. I became keenly aware of how much I loved being near her.

Soon, through the trees, we heard the dull thudding roar of the waterfall. Passing through the white-trunked aspens, I soon saw it up ahead. It was about a hundred feet high, and its narrow white plume of froth-water poured out of the rocks far above us. The spray of water splashed and thundered into a maze of jumbled rocks at the base before roaring off to join the silver stream in the valley.

"Well," she said, "what do you think of it?"

"Wow," I said in true amazement, "it's beautiful."

From her broad smile, I could tell she was glad I was impressed. She set her daypack full of photo gear down.

"I wish I could camp here on some night when there's a full moon. I'd love to take a fast-film time exposure of the moonlight on the falls. Wouldn't it be a wonderful shot?"

"Yes," I said. "Maybe we can do that some night."

She laughed and turned liltingly to me. "You'd like that, wouldn't you? Get me all alone up here on a romantic moonlit night."

"Are you telling me you wouldn't like it?"

"No, not at all," she said. "It might be kind of fun. But we'd have to watch ourselves though. I'd be good."

"I might not be." I said, smiling wolfishly at her.

"Oh, I don't know," she said. "I expect you might be very, very good."

I shook my head. "You and your double meanings. My, but you do tempt me, lady."

"You'd better be careful. I might push you under that waterfall just so you'd take a cold shower and cool off."

"Killjoy," I said. "Are you going to stand here and get me all excited, or are you going to take your pictures?"

"Oh, yes, the pictures," she said. "I almost forgot about them."

"I'll bet."

For the next half-hour Tracy led me up and down the hillside to various places, looking for a suitable spot to capture the waterfall on film. It wasn't easy. There were no designated Kodak Picture Spots here, and the branches of the trees were usually in the way.

She was using a couple of 35mm Canon camera bodies and trying to find the right wide-angle lenses to go with them. As a pro, she almost always used two cameras in case one malfunctioned in some way. The light was becoming a bit of a problem, too. The little puffy clouds we had seen earlier had decided to come together and form larger clouds which hid the sun from time to time.

Tracy had been through the artist's game of finding the right camera spot many times before, in many places. She finally found a spot where there was just enough of a clearing in the aspens to get the whole of the beautiful waterfall and the rocks below. She took the tripod from me and set up one of the cameras. She viewed the shot. After fiddling with the focus and the f-stop rings, she beckoned to me look through the viewfinder.

"Now that's interesting," I said as I surveyed the scene in the viewfinder. "You're using the oval-shape of the clearing of leaves on the trees to make a natural frame for the view of the waterfall."

"That's the idea," she said. "My, but you're observant. You're starting to develop a photographer's eye, Mr. Rader. Now let me put in the cable release. We'll see what the light does for us."

Somehow, by maneuvering the f-stop ring and shutter speed dial, she had the oval of framing leaves just slightly out of focus, fuzzy and flowing together. The sharply-focused waterfall in the center was enclosed, accentuated by the natural frame.

Tracy looked up at the sky, at the moving clouds. Then, just after the clouds uncovered the sun, the shimmering white plume of the waterfall, trailing hazy stands of mist, seemed to flash in the sunlight like a dazzling white veil. Tracy took a succession of shots and quickly switched camera bodies to take more. All in all, it took just three or four minutes, and then another cloud obscured the sun and the vision of the waterfall was gone.

"Well, that's it." she said.

"You mean that's all?"

"Yep. I got my waterfall. We can go now."

"It didn't take you long."

"If you know what you're after, and the light cooperates, it doesn't take much time."

"If you're a pro, huh?"

She grinned at me. "That's right. You're learning."

Just then a fat raindrop fell on my arm. I turned and looked to the sky behind me. A gray thunderhead had formed and was moving above us, up the canyon.

"Rain. Very timely, I'd say," I said.

"Yes. That's why I had to move fast."

Another raindrop fell, and then another, and Tracy was putting her cameras away into the daypack. The raindrops then started falling in earnest, and we hurriedly made our way back through the woods toward the Suburban. We got wet, of course, and as we made a mad dash across the meadow I wished we had our rainproof parkas.

We got in, set the camera gear and tripod aside, and hugged each other for warmth, giggling like a couple of kids. Outside, the rain began falling in wavy silvery sheets, and now the blasts of thunder rocked the Suburban.

"Well, that rain was a surprise," I said. "did you see that storm coming?"

"Yes," she said, "and it helped. The sunlight was coming through the rain before it got to us and it added a sort of mystic glow or something there at the last. I hope I got it on the film in those final shots."

"After what we just went through, getting drenched like that, I hope it was worth it."

"Oh, come on, Mike," she teased, her brown eyes shining merrily, "I thought you were the kind of guy who liked to go walking in the rain with a girl."

"Walking, yes. But running for my life, no. And besides, any time I go out walking in the rain with you, you can be sure I'll have a rain parka on. I almost got a chill out there. I felt like I really was standing under that waterfall."

She grinned again. "The cold shower probably did you good."

I hugged her close. "Yeah. Call it a preventive gesture. By the way, do you know what, Tracy?"

"What?" she asked, looking up at me, warm against me.

"You're very good at what you do."

"You mean the photography?"

"Yes. I'm constantly amazed at how good you really are. You seem to know and to sense so much about your work. It's a wonder you aren't as famous as Ansel Adams."

She trembled, but not from the cold this time. She was smiling up at me in pure delight. "You really think so?"

"Oh, yes. I really enjoy watching you at your work. You, lady, are such a worthy gift to this little world of ours. I wish I had half your creative talent. I become stronger inside just watching your skill and confidence out there with your cameras."

She rubbed herself against me like a purring cat. "Mmmm, you do lay it on thick, don't you? You must want something."

"Hey," I said, "this may sound like some kind of line to you, but I really mean it."

"Well, it's nice to be appreciated. Mike, I've never told you this, but my ex-husband never, ever, saw that in me. He just ignored my creative abilities in photography. I think a few times he even called my work childish, and said it was something anyone with a box camera could do. You don't know...it...well it touches me to hear you tell me you like...not just my finished work itself, but the way I go about creating my pictures."

"Well, you deserve to be appreciated for that. I'm sorry your ex never saw that in you. Maybe he was jealous or preoccupied with himself or just thick-headed or something, but you, dear lady, are supremely gifted. I never want you to forget it."

She hugged me even closer. Tears were in her eyes now. "Thanks, Mike," she said with trembling lips. "Thank you. It's so good to hear that from someone that means a lot to me...someone I love."

I kissed her brow. "So you can say it out loud now?"

"What? That I love you?"

"Yes," I said softly, tentatively.

"Well, I do love you, you know."

"Do you know what?"

"What?"

My voice was breaking. "It's...it's good to hear that from the woman I love, too. You don't know how good it sounds."

"Oh...," she murmured softly as she buried her face in my neck.

The rain outside continued for a while. Then, as quickly as it had begun, the rain let up as the storm moved on. That's the way of mountain storms in the Rockies.

The sun was going down now behind the mountains. It was obvious that we were through taking pictures for the day. I was content there with her, but I was hungry and I knew she probably was as well.

"You ready for supper?" I asked her, finally.

"Sure. What's cooking?"

"I'll surprise you. The mountain gourmet has to get the stove working first, though."

I went out into the damp and cool evening air and soon had the stove going with small blue flames flickering up from each of its two burners. In the meantime, Tracy had, at my behest, gone to a nearby stream and filled two aluminum pans with water. When she came back I emptied a freeze-dried food package into one of them and set it to boiling. I made coffee in the other. In about twenty minutes I served supper in a couple of bowls, with coffee in two bluestone mugs.

"This is delicious," she said, as she ate food. "What is it?"

"Shrimp cooked in a special wine and cheese sauce," I said. "Just a taste of old New Orleans here in these highlands, m'lady."

"They have that in freeze-dried food packets now? I thought all you had was chili mac and spaghetti and other boring stuff."

"Oh, but no," I said. "It's a whole new world now in freeze-dried foodstuffs. When I was a boy scout, years ago, the state of the art was yukko dehydrated potatoes and such. But the backpacker boom really made for a lot of improvements in the outdoor kitchen."

"This would be good back in my own kitchen at home," she said as she ate.

"Maybe, but it's still a bit pricey. You'd pay a half to a third for the same ingredients if you got them in a supermarket. It's just faster and more convenient this way. Of course, it's a light load in a backpack, and it'll keep."

She quickly finished her bowl and looked out at the blue twilight on the peaks around us. "It's heavenly out here this evening."

And romantic too, I thought. I don't know what it is, but far from the city, when things are quiet and secure, being out in the wilderness with the one you love, it gets all the feelings deep inside you going. Every time I glanced at Tracy, I felt deep love for her.

After we ate, I put the stove and the cook stuff away. We drank another cup of coffee sitting in the back of the Suburban, leaning against the walls with our legs stretched out. It would have been good to stay outside, but it was darker and much cooler now, and our clothes were still damp from the rain. We had the radio on and soft music was playing.

"This is so good being here with you" she said, as she finished her cup and put it aside. I had already finished mine and was blinking as my eyes adjusted to the fading light.

"Being together with you is always good," I said. I pulled her close beside me.

"Mmm, you feel good," she said. "Good and warm."

I kissed her, and her lips opened warmly to greet mine. Her lips were a perfect match for mine tonight, warm and sweet, like they had been waiting for years to come together with mine. It was as if some mystical circle of life was now complete.

"Now, I suppose you wish we had a full moon," I said, tracing my tongue over her red lips.

"I don't need a moon tonight," she whispered. "Just you. That's all I need."

We kissed again, and my head was swimming with delight as she relaxed against me.

"Tracy, Tracy," I said. "Are you still...afraid of me?"

"No. Not now," she said. "Not now. Not any longer."

We both felt the closeness within. It was like a new person-hood had been formed, a beautiful state of being we shared. It was no longer just me and her. It was us. I rocked her gently against me, her scented hair brushing my face. Reality blended into a dream.

"I think I'm finally ready now, Tracy."

"Ready for what?" she asked.

"Ready to be with you all the time."

She smiled. "Is that a proposal?"

I kissed her eyelids softly. "Yes. I guess it is. What do you say?"

"I say yes. Will you always carry my camera gear up and down these mountains, like today?"

"I'm good for that. And other things."

She grinned. "How well I know. I want that, Mike."

"So do I. It's late, though. Maybe we ought to head back to town. Control is slipping away."

"Well, we can't have that, can we? Okay, onward and up-ward. Time to bring the photo-safari to an end."

We got up from the floor of the Suburban and moved to the front seats. Tracy started the engine. I buckled my seat belt, and we made our way back down the mountain road.

I always feel very cautious going down a lonely mountain road in the dark, but now I was full of warmth and satisfaction, and something else, too. Confidence.

Back there where we had shared that special time together, only a few words were spoken between us. We had been content to let our feelings flow, to enjoy the closeness, the energy of the moments together. And yet somehow, within those moments, there was the joy of a promise, a promise even greater than our words had spoken. That, I knew, was the wellspring of my confidence.

We drove into town about eleven. During our return drive we had encountered more rain on the highway. Now the streets of the town were rain-slick. They reflected black and wet in the glow of the neon motel-sign lights and the street lamps.

"You were right about the weather forecast," I said. "How long is this rain supposed to last?"

"I don't know," she said, yawning. "A day or so, maybe."

"I hope it lets up by Thursday. Buck and I are planning to go back up to Chicago Basin this weekend. By the way, we have a tag- along. Jill's coming with us."

Tracy turned and looked at me with eyes full of surprise. "She is?"

"Yes," I said. "Is that a problem?"

She turned and looked ahead at the street in front of her. "No. I trust you. At least I think I do."

"I hope so. Especially after tonight."

She reached over and gripped my hand. "I do trust you. I know you're just playing good Samaritan with Jill. But what about her feelings? Do you think she might have a thing for you?"

I smiled and shrugged. "No, I don't really think so. I may be fooling myself, but I think she just wants to go climbing with some new people. She likes us, Buck and me. At least, that is, I know she likes me. She hasn't really seen Buck in action. He can be a little stern sometimes."

"But Buck agreed to having her go along?"

"Yeah, reluctantly. But he's with me on this. In his own way, I think he understands."

She pulled the Suburban up in front of my house. "Well," she said, "at least she's an experienced climber. You shouldn't have any trouble with her up high. It's what might go on in camp at night that I'm concerned about."

"Don't be," I said. "We're all taking our own tents. I'm safe. It'll be just like a daddy-daughter campout, believe me."

She laughed. "Okay, 'daddy'. Just don't tuck the little girl in to sleep at night, okay?"

I grinned. " 'Daddy' is not into that, sweet lady. I hope you know that by now. This 'daddy' has someone else he'd like to tuck in one of these days, though."

"Oh?" she said innocently. "Anyone I know?"

"I'm looking at her."

She smiled suggestively. "I could go for that."

"You could?"

"Of course. It's been years since anybody's tucked me in. I'm not a little girl any longer, you know. But maybe deep down inside I've got a little girl there somewhere who needs tucking in from time to time."

"Yes," I said, sweeping her with my eyes. "I know."

"You, you...rogue!" she said, laughing.

I kissed her. "I think you secretly like rogues, my dear."

"Only one," she said. "Only one."

I sighed and pulled away from her. "Well," I said, "I'd better be going in. I guess I'll go to the store early tomorrow. Whenever I play hooky, there's always a few matters to catch up on the next day."

"I like playing hooky with you, mister. I'll have the contact prints of the waterfall ready to show you in a day or two."

"I want to see them. Call me when they're ready."

"I will," she said.

"Tracy," I said, "we'll talk some more about what we spoke about back there in the mountains."

"About marriage?"

"Yes."

"You meant what you said, didn't you?"

"I've never meant anything more seriously in my life."

"Neither have I."

I kissed her one last time, then retrieved the stuff sack with the stove and camp groceries out of the back of the Suburban. I shut the door, and watched as she drove away.

I'd love to tuck you in tonight, Tracy, I thought as I watched her taillights disappear around the corner. But all good things can wait.

It was stormy over Durango the next day. A front had moved up from the Gulf of Mexico and had brought rain clouds up from

New Mexico to drench the San Juans. Even with the rain, I was in a good mood when I got to the store.

Occasional stormy weather in the summer usually meant that the tourists who would normally be out tramping or driving through the mountains would all come flocking back into Durango. With time on their hands and money in their wallets, they were usually in a mood to buy things. They often came to an outdoor store, like the Leaf, to browse and to buy. Today seemed to bear out that pattern.

The downtown mall was packed full of shoppers, and the Leaf had more than its share. The cash registers were ringing, and most of our employees seemed to revel in the sudden surge of business. But when Jill came in and went to work, it was plain that she was not sharing the good mood of the other workers. She looked disheveled, tired, and she just did not appear to be herself as I watched her dealing with the customers.

Around eleven o'clock, I walked up to where she was working. She had dark circles under her blue eyes. She looked away from me as I approached her.

"You look like you need to take a break," I said. "Why don't you come back to the office with me for a minute?"

"Do I have to, Mike? I'm having a rough day, and I'd...I'd rather not talk about it."

I knew when to leave it alone, but I went ahead and pushed her a little. "I was going to discuss the climb this weekend with you. I'll be pretty busy the rest of the day, and right now is the only time I've got."

She rubbed her face and said, "Oh, okay. I guess we'd better take care of it, then. Pardon me if I just act a little strange today."

"Hey," I said, "you're allowed. We all have bad days. Let's just take care of this and I'll let you go back to work."

"Okay," she said.

We walked back to my office, and I closed the door. I sat down behind my desk and she sat in the chair next to me.

"You must think I'm really weird," she said.

"No," I said. "Not really."

"I'm sorry if I seem less than friendly today. I had a bad night last night."

"You don't have to tell me about it, Jill."

She looked at me with haggard eyes. There was a trace of fear in them. I felt a pang of fear myself, for I wondered if she had slipped back into her old ways.

"I've changed my mind," she said.

"About going on the climb?"

"No...not that. About telling you about last night."

I nodded. "Okay. If it's any of my business, I'm listening."

She crossed her arms and looked out the window. She appeared to be very hesitant about discussing whatever it was that was on her mind. She turned and looked at me with uncertain eyes. "Starting a new life is...is harder than I thought it would be," she said simply.

"What do you mean?"

"Last night, I went out to a bar. I guess I thought I was testing myself. It's the one Dil goes to sometimes. It's also where, well, where you can get the stuff. There's always someone there you can connect with if you're in the market.."

"And that's why you went?"

She sighed and shook her head. "No. No, I, well, I know it was foolish of me, but I suppose I wanted to see Dil. I wanted to tell him that whatever we had, it was over."

"I see," I said, glancing out the window at the rain. "So what happened."

She bit her lip. "I was pretty nervous about it. I sat there for a while, talking to some friends, and I almost got cold feet and left. But he came in around eleven. I went over to him and told him I wanted to talk to him. He suggested we go for a ride. I didn't want to do it, but it seemed okay."

"So you left the bar with him?"

"Yeah. We got in his car. I was so afraid of him. I mean, I didn't think he'd hurt me or anything like that. I just knew he'd get angry, though, when I told him. I started to tell him about how I wanted things to stop between us, and he didn't get mad. He just started in with that smooth line of his about how I was so important to him and he needed me and everything."

"Compassionate old Dil, huh?"

"Yeah. Real compassionate. I guess I started to weaken a little, and before I knew it he had stopped the car. Then he was all over me. He wanted me to come up to one of his houses and spend the night with him. He said he needed me, and it was tearing him up, and he wanted me. I had to fight him off, but he was so strong. I actually thought he was going to, well, you know..."

"Rape you?"

Her eyes were wide. "Yes. I've never been so frightened."

"Did you get away from him?"

"Yes, finally. I had to promise I'd see him again though. It was terrible, Mike. I didn't get home until two a.m. I didn't sleep a wink all night long. I'm really shook up about it."

I sat there, doing a slow burn. Mr. Nice Guy had finally done it. I felt cold rage inside, and a vein in my neck was throbbing. I could sense it pounding away.

"I knew it," I said.

She slowly looked up at me. "Knew what?"

"I knew he'd come on strong to you sooner or later. That Mr. Charm act was just a front."

She gripped her arms with her hands and shook. "Oh, I wish I'd never gotten mixed up with him. That man just...he just tries to control me, Mike. It's like he has these steel claws, and he just reaches out and squeezes you to death. He makes you do things you don't want to do."

"Nature of the beast," I said.

"What?" she asked, blinking.

"Nature of the beast. The man's a predator. He consumes people. Right now, he's after you."

She nodded. "Mike, what can I do? I feel so trapped."

I looked at her for a long, hard moment. "You hang on," I said. "Cullen hasn't gotten you yet. And he's not going to either."

"But what can I do, Mike?. He's so powerful."

"Yes. But he's also got his good-guy image to think about, too. I had a little talk with him the other day. He promised he wouldn't try anything like this. Now he broke his promise. Maybe I can do something about it."

She sat up straight. "No, look. I don't want you to fight my battles for me. Mike, please stay out of it."

I gave her a smile. "Hey, I'm your friend, remember?"

"No, forget it. I know what I'll do. I'll just go away somewhere. I'll disappear for a while."

I shook my head. "No, Jill. That's not the way. You have the right to live here just like anyone else, without being afraid of a man like Dil. Don't you?"

A look of helplessness filled her eyes. "I...I guess so. But he's so big, Mike. I'm just..."

"One of what he calls, 'the little people'?" I interrupted.

"Well...yes. I guess I am."

I scowled. "Listen to me, Jill Carpenter. The only people who are 'little' in this world are those who let schmucks like Cullen make them accept the lie that they're that way. It's all in the mind. Dil gets up every morning the same way you and I do. He's no bigger or better than anyone else. He's really just a gilt-edged bully, down deep. And you can't let bullies run your life for you. Sure, he fell into money and power. But take them away, and he's just another Joe walking the streets same as you and me. You've got to see him that way, or you've lost."

She wrung her hands. "Mike, I know that, but listen, forget about this. I won't see him again. Please, just stay away from the man."

"Let me think about it."

She relaxed somewhat, relieved. "Okay. Just, please, don't try anything. I just want to forget about what happened."

I smiled. "Okay. I think I know one way to help you forget it. Let's talk about our climb."

"Yes," she said, letting out a heavy sigh. "Let's do."

We discussed our expedition into Chicago Basin. The weather reports said it was going to be clear by Thursday, so we planned to get started on that morning. Friday we'd camp. Saturday would be the climb day, and we would come out on Sunday. After we had sketched out the details, she got up to go back to work out on the floor. She was in a better mood by then.

After she left my office, I picked up the phone book. I had told her I would think over the matter with Dil, and now I had.

I found Cullen's number and called him. His secretary said he wasn't in his office, so I asked for his cellular number, telling her it was important. She gave it to me, and I dialed the number.

"Hello?" a man's voice in the phone said.

"Dil?"

There was a pause on the other end. "Yes, this is me. Who's this?"

"Mike Rader. Did I catch you doing something important?"

"I'm out here at my new subdivision west of town, Mike. I'm a little busy right now with one of my investors. What can I do for you?"

"I've had a talk with Jill today, Dil."

There was a long silence on his end. "And?" he finally asked.

"You put a move on her last night, buddy. That wasn't in our agreement. It was the wrong thing to do."

Silence again. "Look, Mike, I thought we were friends."

"You said you were going to leave her alone."

"Aw, nothing happened. I meant her no harm. I just wanted to talk with her."

"You did more than talk."

"So, we both got a little carried away last night. Look, this is between me and her. I'd appreciate it if you'd keep your nose out of this and leave us alone."

"Not where this sort of thing is concerned. You're the one that's going to leave her alone, Dil."

There was a long pause. "Is that a warning?"

"I'm just telling you she doesn't want to see you again. Cut your losses and give it up. And, by the way, it goes without saying, but no, I'm no friend of yours any more. Don't ever call me your 'friend' again."

Another long pause. "I'm not accustomed to being threatened, Mike."

"You don't always get what you want in life, Dil. Sorry. Live with it."

I hung up. I didn't have anything else I wanted to say to him, and I was fighting to control my anger. I got up, shoved my hands into my pockets, and looked out the window at the rain. I wasn't so naive as to think he'd let it go at that, but I wasn't prepared for what happened next.

A half hour later, the looming form of Jimmy Rowe was standing in my office doorway, dripping rainwater onto my floor. Barry was right behind him.

"You Rader?" Jimmy asked in a soft, cotton-mouthed tone as he stared at me with hard eyes.

"That's me," I said, slowly getting up from my chair.

This was the first time I had seen Rowe up close. He was a stocky brute of a man, probably in his late twenties. He was almost six feet tall, with unkempt black hair and piercing, menacing black eyes. A stone killer, George Barker had said.

Rowe had a slightly nervous manner about him. He was dressed in a black leather jacket and he had on a brown shirt and tie underneath. Your everyday gentleman drug dealer and enforcer, I thought.

"And you are Mr. Jimmy Rowe, right?"

He gave me a thin, broken smile. "At your service, old son."

Barry looked over Rowe's broad shoulders at me. "He barged right in, Mike. I'm sorry."

I watched Rowe's hands, his body stance. The old Ranger instincts came over me. This guy was on a mission. I looked for an opening, a cue. But Rowe was smooth, and he had the look of a man who had done this many times before. The Great Intimidator.

"It's okay, Barry," I said evenly, "He's obviously got something he wants to say. Spit it out, Rowe."

"In private," Rowe said, shooting Barry a glance.

"No, I think not," I said. "Say what you're here for."

Rowe spat onto my floor. "Suit yourself, buds. It don't really matter to me. It's all the same either way."

"What's all the same?"

Rowe grinned eerily, the eyes cheery and menacing at the same time. "You. I know all about you, big man. Outdoor type, ex-Ranger. A great big boy who likes to put on his little shorts and go running for fun."

I watched him closely, still waiting for that cue. "What about you, Rowe? You get off by scaring runners with that big bad muscle car of yours? The car makes you feel like a big man, huh? I remember how you played your little game in the GTO the other day. That's too nice a grown-up car for a little boy like you to be driving."

He laughed. "Gave you a good scare, huh? Maybe I should've left you just a red smear on the side of the road that morning."

"But you didn't. The guy who holds your dog chain wouldn't have liked that, now, would he?"

Rowe's smile disappeared, and he took a step forward, then stopped. "You puke. Talk like that'll get you cut, buds. I go my own way. I could have taken you out if I'd wanted."

"I doubt it. Say whatever it is you came for, and get out. You stink, and you're getting my floor wet."

He glowered at me and started to move forward, but stopped himself again, abruptly. His sick little grin returned.

"Real cute. The big hero. That's how you see yourself ain't it, Rader. The big mountain-man rescue hero. Well, let me tell you something, Mr. Hero. You're getting on my nerves. And you're getting on the nerves of my friend, Mr. Cullen, too. I got one thing to say to you, Hero. Back off on that chick Jill Carpenter. Get out of the way. The next time I have to come and straighten you out, there won't be anything left to put back together. You hear me?"

I moved closer to him. "My, my. That does sound a little threatening, Jimmy-boy,"

He looked straight at me, chewing his lip. "Maybe you didn't hear me, Rader. Do I have to show you what I mean?"

His hand shot quickly forward as he grabbed for my throat, but my own hand came up and caught his wrist in mid-air. My knee slammed into his gut a half-second later. I twisted his wrist and pulled his arm around, turning him, so that his arm was locked painfully behind him. My free hand found that soft, vulnerable place between his jaw and his ear, and my thumb pressed down on the nerve ganglia. He jerked violently to free himself, but instead he wrenched his arm in its shoulder socket. Surprised, he cried out in agony.

I held him in a tight grip. "Okay, Jimmy-boy, enough of the little game," I said. "I think it's time for you to leave. I've heard you out. Can I let you go, or do we have to call the cops?"

He relaxed, shaking. "Turn me loose. I'm cool."

I let him go as Barry stood on the other side of him, waiting. The punk was smart enough to know a scene in the store was bad, even if he had wanted to put some muscle on me. With both Barry and me there, and a store full of people outside, I didn't think he'd try anything else. Too many witnesses. And now he knew I wasn't an easy target.

Rowe rubbed his sore arm and his neck. His voice was just above a whisper. "A very bad move, Rader. Very bad."

I moved a step toward him and stared at him with cold eyes. "You're done here. Haul yourself out of my store, errand boy."

He spat on my floor again, glaring at me angrily, turned, and pushed his way past Barry, leaving.

Barry and I watched him as he walked away. Before he got to the door, he turned and looked back at me, and made a gesture I had heard of, but had never actually seen before. Two fingers, in an upside-down V, below his chin. The Cartegena salute. The kind the death-squad boys of the drug cartels flashed to a target when they intended to put a hit on him. He turned and left.

I was shaking with adrenaline now, trying to control myself. I had held it back, but now it was raging through me.

Barry looked at me with wide eyes. "Uh, boss," he said.

"Don't say it, Barry," I said. "I know what you're thinking."

"Sorry," he said, "but that dude looks like he wouldn't mind at all putting your lights out for good. Good grief, I will say one thing though. You moved pretty fast there getting that hold on him. Did they teach you that in the service?"

I tried to smile. "I'm still breathing, Barry. The Rangers taught me a few tricks, I guess. They just came back when I needed them."

"Well, they worked for you this time. But what about the next time?"

"I don't know. I guess we'll let next time take care of itself."

Barry gripped my shoulder. "Look, Mike," he said, "none of that would have happened if..."

"I know, Barry," I said angrily, pushing his hand away. "It never would have happened if I hadn't started looking out for Jill. But it's done now and that's that. I don't want Rowe or his boss, Cullen, to hurt that girl."

He paused. "You may not have any choice."

"I know."

Jill came into my office then, and she was alarmed. "Mike, I saw Jimmy come in here. What did you do?"

I said nothing.

"You called Dil, didn't you?"

I looked at her and turned away. "I'm sorry. I said I'd think it over. I did. I called Dil and told him to stay away from you. He didn't like it, so he sent Jimmy-boy a-callin'."

Anxiously, she asked, "Did he...did Jimmy hurt you?"

"No," I said. "I'm okay."

Barry laughed lightly. "But Mr. Rowe got a very sore arm and neck out of the deal, though."

"Oh, wow," she said. "Look, I think I'd better just leave town and go somewhere. I didn't mean to drag you into this."

"No Jill," I said, giving her a hard glance. "Don't run away from this. Rowe failed in his little intimidation attempt. Cullen will hear about it. He just may cool it for a while."

She shook her head. "Dil doesn't like failures. He may let it go for a while, but he won't stay that way. I know him, Mike."

"Well, let's just see."

Barry grabbed my arm again. "Mike, I think we should call the cops. We ought to report this."

"I thought of that. Cullen'll just claim I threatened him and he sent Jimmy to politely ask me to stay out of his private life. With his legal eagles, they'd work it to keep Jimmy clear of any assault charges. Hey, man, they might even try to hang a charge like that on me."

"They might yet," Barry said, releasing my arm.

"I don't think so. Cullen wants to keep this whole matter private."

"So what do you do?" Barry asked.

"We forget it and go with the flow. That's what we do."

Barry sighed. "Okay, it's your crusade, Mike. But I hope you'll stay away from those dudes from now on."

"I intend to. As much as possible, anyway."

We went back to work. That night, after I had gone home, I did something I hadn't done in a long time. In my bedroom, I got my "nine" out of a wooden box and cleaned it. My "nine" was a Glock 17 9mm pistol. I wasn't wild about the idea of keeping a loaded pistol near me, but after crossing swords with Jimmy Rowe that afternoon, it seemed like the prudent thing to do.

Paranoia can go to your head, though. It was just like back in wartime. If you let the fear get to you, you go nervous and wind up doing something stupid. Most of the time your fears never resulted in things the way you had imagined. You had to keep your head on straight.

Still, it was comforting to have the Glock by my bedside. The neighbors on both sides of me had dogs, and more than once they had scared off would-be prowlers in the night. Of course, a pro like Rowe knew how to take care of a dog if he decided to pay me a nighttime call to make a hit.

Then it came to me. Me, Mike Rader; I could be a hit man's target. Over Jill? Probably not. I knew enough about criminals to know that a real hit from Rowe would be pretty risky for Cullen. After all, Barry had heard him threaten me using Dil's name and Jill knew about it, too. Too many witnesses for that. Besides, Cullen wanted Jill for his romantic intentions, such as they were. He'd score no points with her by having me hurt or bumped off by a midnight caller at my house.

He might try some other way, but sending Jimmy over with a knife or a gun would most probably not be his style. A story in the paper linking him as a suspect might ruin him in Durango, in spite of his lawyers and his connections.

Still, the Glock looked comforting lying on my bedside table. For a while it did, anyway. I thought some more about it. It was a symbol that I was surrendering to fear, and that I didn't like. Disgusted, I finally got up and put the gun away in the wooden box.

If I'd heard a noise in the night, I might have gotten up and shot myself in the foot or done something equally stupid. So the nine was best left put away.

It was time to try to forget the fun events of that day. I crawled back into bed and pulled the covers around me.

If the weather broke, we could go climbing in a couple of days. I was more than ready for that. I hoped the mountains would be ready for me, too. And for Jill and Buck.

Chapter Eight

It was a cool Durango morning, alive with bright sunlight. I walked toward the old tourist train depot with my mountain gear slung over my shoulder. I was ready to get away, far away, to go out where I could think clearly and be free again.

It had been too many days since I had been in the mountains, and I was itching to slip into my climber's persona. There, in that beautiful world, hard exercise would awaken that more primitive being down inside me. It also meant I could forget about the sordid circus with Cullen and Rowe for a while.

I was wondering now what it would be like having Jill along. She would be a new element to fit into the personal chemistry Buck and I had known with each other. I would discover how it would work before long.

I had left the Blazer parked in a motel parking lot on Second Avenue a couple of blocks from the tourist train depot. I knew the motel manager there. He had waived the parking fee that he usually charged to people leaving their vehicles there for a few days while they went off into the woods. It was a case of locals trading help with locals. I'd return the favor with a discount for him at the Leaf one of these days.

I could have parked downtown at the Leaf and carried the pack several blocks to the station. Maybe it was lazy of me to drive those extra blocks and park at the motel, but it made things easier on the return. When the train got back, I would only have to carry my stuff a short distance to the Blazer. I liked it that way.

I had on my heavy leather climbing boots, a blue denim work shirt, cotton pants, and a floppy white sun hat. Some outdoor purists eschewed cotton as a clothing for hikers, but it worked for me. The purists said if it rained on your cotton clothes, you got cold and you stayed cold. Cotton soaked up water and took a while to dry. The way I figured it, though, if it started to rain, you quickly put your rain gear over your clothes. No matter what you wore, you stayed dry that way. Cotton kept you cool when you were walking in the hot sun, sweating your way uphill under a heavy pack load.

The night before, I had carefully packed all the needed items into the heavy backpack. The interior of the pack held most, but not all, of my belongings. My extra clothes were in one stuff sack there, my food in another. Above that was my daypack with a few items of climbing gear. At the top was my hard plastic climber's helmet.

The side pockets of the backpack contained the water bottle, the one-burner stove, a half-filled fuel bottle, and my camera. There was still room for little extras like my bandana, leather rock-work gloves, a small FM radio, and a flashlight. The upper back pocket contained a map and compass, and a little notebook and pencil for recording walking/climbing times and other information. The middle back pocket held a red rainproof nylon pack cover in case it rained, my Goretex rain-wind pants, and my Goretex mountain parka. These were located in the middle back pocket so you could get to them in a hurry if a storm came on.

In the bottom back pocket I carried emergency items. My first-aid kit was there, and a flare, a little bottle of sunscreen, and a plastic bottle I used for a night-owl. Strapped to the frame at the bottom, in a waterproof stuff sack, was my goosedown sleeping bag. Below that was my lightweight tent in a green stuff sack. Across the top I had a sleeping pad rolled up, cinched down, and my nylon climbing rope. My ice axe hung down the middle of the pack in back, strapped on with nylon webbing.

All in all, my backpack was actually what you might call a portable house. It was, functionally, a bedroom, a clothes closet, and a kitchen. It contained the other necessities of camp life as well.

The tourists at the station who were ready to embark on their day-long excursion on the train regarded me with curiosity. There I was, looking like an alien in their midst, a tall, slender man with this enormous thing on his back. As I ambled toward the front door of the depot building in my heavy lug-soled boots, I felt like Paul Bunyan entering the crowd of vacationers.

One fat little man in a Guadalajara shirt and plaid shorts and sandals walked up to me. He looked like some salesman who had spent too many years behind a desk in an office building. Maybe he was the type who went in for too many martini lunches. Now he was taking his big vacation out West with the wife and the kiddies.

The guy fingered the camera strap that hung in the middle

of his chest and looked me up and down quizzically, like I was some zoo oddity. Usually, I was as friendly as I could be with the tourists that came into the Leaf. But this little weasel sent a buzz up me the wrong way.

He grinned a sour, crease-eyed grin. "Er...where you going with all that camping junk, big fellow?"

"For a little hike," I said, not really interested in giving out a long explanation about our plans.

"Yeah, I can see that, but where are you going exactly? You look like you're going to be out overnight or something."

I sighed. "Well, about halfway up the train line from here to Silverton, there's a water stop. That's where I'll get off. I'll be spending a couple of days out in the woods with some friends."

He smiled. "Sounds like more work than I'd want to do. I did all the camping I ever want to see in the army. You can have it, woodchuck."

"I know," I said. I ambled past him, on into the station. I sat down on a long wooden bench to await Buck and Jill.

The tourists were thick as bees around a hive in the station house now, excited, jabbering away. They gripped their little papers and purses and cameras and were impatient to board the morning train.

Jill arrived a few minutes later. She carried her pack with her, much like mine, and she was dressed in a tee-shirt and shorts. She smiled her pretty smile and took off her baseball cap. Her hair was pulled back in a pony tail.

"Good morning, boss," she said.

I looked at her in mock seriousness. "Jill, please don't call me 'boss'. Let's leave that kind of talk in town, if you don't mind."

"Okay, I see," she said with a grin. "No rank on this trip, Mike. Anyway, good morning." She looked around at the people. "Is Buck here yet?"

"No, but he'll be here. His wife's dropping him off."

"Have you got your train ticket yet?"

"Nope. I always wait till Buck gets here before I buy it. Just a habit, I guess."

"You afraid he might not show up?"

"He'll be here."

She sat down next to me, placing her pack at her feet. "Are you sure he doesn't mind me going along with you guys?"

"I'm sure. If he didn't want you to go, he'd have told me."

"But he's not real excited about it either."

"Don't jump to that conclusion. Buck's all right. He just takes a little getting used to, Jill. Go easy with him. It'll all work out."

"If you say so."

Buck joined us a few moments later, wearing his old pea-green Boy Scout shorts that showed his stocky legs, thick as tree trunks. He slung his backpack to the wooden floor with a heavy thud, sighed, and nodded to us.

"Good morning," he said with a snort and a wide grin. "Are we all happy campers this morning?"

I smiled up at his moon-round face, staring at the silvery-lensed sunshades that hid his eyes. "We were doing okay till you got here, all cheery and bright-eyed."

He chuckled, and reached for his wallet. "It's your turn to go get the tickets. I went last time."

Jill turned to me. "Something I need to know about?"

"Oh, Buck doesn't like to stand in line with the hoi-polloi of tourists. It's the hardest part of the trip for him. He thinks they're like a bunch of giddy kids and he hates rubbing shoulders with them. He's afraid it'll weaken him and somehow drain away his macho strength. They ask him all sorts of questions and it makes him edgy."

"You can have them," Buck said.

Jill laughed. "Well, I don't mind being the one to go after the tickets. Just pony up the money and I'll go get in the line."

We gave her the cash. The steam-powered Durango tourist train is one of the few remaining narrow-gauge lines still operating in America. It travels some forty-plus miles up the winding track from Durango to Silverton through some of the most beautiful mountain scenery in America.

Although it is well worth the trip, the excursion ride isn't cheap. Because of the demand for tickets, you have to get reservations ahead of time. I had taken care of our reservations earlier in the week. Though our tickets were priced somewhat less than the full fare, since we were only going halfway up the line to Needleton, still, I was always a little reluctant to shell out the necessary cash.

Nonetheless, riding the rails was the best way to get to the

Needleton hiker's trailhead. Oh, you could drive up Highway 550, the road Tracy and I had been on earlier that week. The highway more- or-less follows the train's route. A scenic and precipitous road, it was called "The San Juan Skyway" in the tourist brochures.

You parked at a highway waystop called Needleton. From there, you could take an eleven-mile trail hike down through the woods to the same Needleton trailhead the train met along the Animas River. However, most of us preferred to take the train and avoid the extra twenty-two miles of in-and-out walking. So we paid.

The first time you take this train, your mouth is usually open in wonder as you stare at the natural splendor you see in the Colorado wilderness. It really is exciting on that first ride. The raging Animas River, the high cliffs, the summits, and the mountain forests all combine to mesmerize you and stir your blood. But after the fourth or fifth train ride, the thrill isn't quite the same. You just sit in your train seat, resting for your hike. The tourists around you excitedly stare out the windows and tell each other how wonderful it all is. Today the three of us simply wanted to get to the trailhead and start hiking.

Our tickets were for the early train. Three or four trains make the run each day, but the early train gets you to Needleton by mid- morning. Once there, you have a six-mile hike ahead of you. The trail climbs some three thousand feet, from about 8300 feet of elevation, to around 11,200 feet in the upper Chicago Basin area. With a heavy pack on your back, you needed all the hiking time you could get. This was especially true if a thunderstorm caught you somewhere along the trail.

Jill brought the tickets over to us as we sat on the bench. Not long afterward, the loudspeaker called out for us to get aboard. We got up, went out to the train, and loaded our packs into a baggage car. Then the three of us boarded one of the passenger cars.

Jill and Buck sat together in one seat, and I sat across the aisle from them. We settled in. The old train began to move, leaving the station in slow chugs that became faster.

A young man who looked like he might have been a lawyer on vacation sat next to me. He was in his forties, thin, with glasses, and had a shock of brown hair that kept falling in his eyes. Two little girls were with him, and they sat a couple of seats away from us. He was quiet and friendly.

"You folks look like you're going up to Chicago Basin," he said.

"Yes," I said. "Have you ever been there?"

"I helped sponsor a group of teenagers on a youth trip up there once a few years ago. We went in too early in the summer though. Late June. We were going to try to hike over Columbine Pass and go down Johnson Creek to Vallecito Lake. But the snow on the north side of the basin was way too deep. No way we could make it up to the pass. We camped for a day or two, and then came back out to Needleton and rode the train down."

"I know what you mean about the snow pack up there. It takes time for it to melt out so the trail to the pass is clear. Better to wait until late July or August."

"You live and you learn," he said. "We had a good time anyway. I think that basin's the prettiest place I've ever seen. You think you're in the Swiss Alps or something."

"Yeah, it'll do in a pinch," I said.

"So what are you going to do up there? Just camp?"

"No. We're into climbing. There's a couple of the Fourteeners we're going to try."

He hesitated. "You going to do Eolus?"

I glanced over at Buck. My old friend pulled the brim of his hat down over his eyes and turned his face toward the window. No, Buck, I thought, I'm not going to drag you into this conversation.

"No," I said. "This time we're just going after Windom and Sunlight Peaks."

The fellow smiled. "I hear Windom isn't too hard, but I've also heard that Sunlight Peak is a little tricky. I guess you know what you're getting into, though."

"I hope so. We've done a few of these mountains before." I smiled. "Excuse me."

I got up and walked down the aisle toward the refreshments car. I wanted a cup of coffee. Though the fellow had been friendly enough, I didn't feel like a long conversation about our climbing plans right now. I got my styrofoam cup of coffee and stepped out onto the platform where the cars were coupled together. You could go out there and get some fresh air along with the other folks.

Though I really didn't want to think about them, my mind kept going back to Dil Cullen and Jimmy Rowe. I wanted to put those two out of my mind. Yet even here, where I should have had my mind on the climb, it was hard. I sipped my coffee and thought about Rowe, and his gesture, the 'Cartegena Salute'. Would the punk really try something on me? It seemed likely. After all, we had made him look bad. I wished he hadn't forced me to put that little move on him, but he left me little choice. Now his pride was injured, and, no doubt, he had to have his revenge. No, Rader, I thought to myself, that was a dumb thing for you to do. But maybe it was the only thing I could have done at the time.

I finished my coffee and went back to where Buck and Jill were. The young man who had sat down by me was gone now. Buck was snoring in the seat beside Jill.

"Looks like Buck's got the right idea," I said to Jill, who was reading a paperback book. She put down her paperback as I sat down across from her.

"He probably needs to rest," she said.

"Maybe. So how are you doing?"

"I'm okay. A little nervous, though."

"Nervous? Why?"

"Oh, this is a little different from the way I usually make this trip. The last couple of times I rode up here with Ron Hamby, we were just laughing and joking the whole way."

I sighed. "Well, I guess it is a little boring going out with a couple of older guys."

"I don't mind. I don't know what I'm so nervous about."

"Whatever it is, you'll soon get over it. Once we start the hike, you'll be okay."

"Probably," she said.

The weather stayed clear and sunny as the train puffed and chugged its way on up the canyon. That was good. I liked it sunny and I liked it warm. I knew how to hike in the heat.

At mid-morning the train stopped for water at Needleton, beside the noisy rapids of the Animas. The three of us stepped down off the train and got our backpacks from the baggage car. There were perhaps thirty or forty other backpackers, and we all helped each other get our packs down from the car and we separated the stuff into piles. The other backpackers picked up their gear and divided themselves into their groups. Then they marched off toward the suspension bridge that took you to the other side of the river.

Buck, Jill, and I got our own stuff and we followed them, now strapped into our packs and getting accustomed to the extra weight on our backs. My pack felt right at home, heavy but comfortable.

We ate some trail food as we hiked along. High altitude hiking with 50 pounds on your back burns a lot of calories, so you eat a little food every now and then as you go along. I carried my own trail mix in a plastic baggie. It consisted of nuts and raisins and M and Ms, giving me a little hit of salt and sugar and chocolate. Buck always stuck to hard candy, though; I think trail mixes gave him indigestion. Jill preferred strips of beef jerky as her trail food. Everybody has his own preference, but the purpose is the same. You want to keep a steady stream of calories flowing into your bloodstream as your body goes into unaccustomed exertion and burns energy.

The trail up toward Chicago Basin is steadily uphill, at places rather steep. Yet it was always enchanting to me as it climbs and makes its turns through the forest of aspen and pine. The path we took was actually an old miner's road. It ascends above Needle Creek, a noisy sidekick splashing silver-white down below. I could smell the wet aspen bark and the pines as we walked along. The fragrant aroma brought back good memories to me, memories of friends, of mountain trails long past.

Buck, as usual, was slow but steady in his stride. His knees and lungs had seen many trails, and he was like the proverbial tortoise, ambling along. As you watched him, you wondered if he was really going to make it all the way. Yet if you knew him, you were aware that he was just conserving strength. Buck knew his body. He could go on and on when those with a jackrabbit pace would be winded halfway to the destination. Sometimes on the uphill stretches he would tell me to go on ahead of him, he'd catch up. On the downhill parts of a trail he was sometimes faster than I was. Those sturdy, oak-like legs of his really moved when he was on the descent. And, just as it had been coming down off Jupiter Peak, he would push me along.

I was in the middle of our threesome, with Buck behind me and Jill up in front. Sometimes the three of us were close together, but more often, we were spaced apart. That was okay. When I first started hiking in the hills I stayed close to my hiking partners, sometimes crowding them, right on their heels. But as I grew more experienced I realized you didn't have to do that. There were times you liked being close together. But other times it was fine to be somewhat separated from the others, off a ways by yourself, just ambling along in silence. We tried to stay in sight of each other, though, as we followed the uphill path toward the basin. Jill was really moving out. But why not? I thought. She was young and lean and energetic, and she needed to let her spirit free today. As she walked in the lead, she would stop and wait on us every so often.

"Am I going too fast?" she asked as I drew near her at one of her stops.

"No. You're doing fine," I said, catching my breath. "We old men just take a while on these uphill stretches."

"Watch out who you're calling old," Buck said, catching up with us and drawing deep lung-fulls of air into his mouth.

The hiking was joyful, but still, quite strenuous with the heavy packs. Every mile required an average upward climb of 500 feet, and you really felt that elevation gain, too. Some hikers in poor condition often stopped along the way in the area where we had come to now. You could see where they had made their camps. There were several fire-rings in the narrow flat places where they had pitched their tents.

After three more hours of hiking, the trail became easier as we entered the first meadow of lower Chicago Basin. We saw tents back under the trees here, and people were lounging against logs, resting and talking. They waved at us as we passed, and we waved back.

We moved on. We could now see the peaks ahead of us forming a semi-circle at the head of Chicago Basin. On the left was the oblong shape of Mount Eolus, of course, with its bare gray crags. Jupiter Peak was on the right, and I remembered our most recent excursion to its domain. Straight ahead of us, up the valley, was the triangular form of Mount Windom. Hidden behind an adjoining sub- peak next to Windom, named Peak 18, I knew, would be Sunlight Peak. I still wondered what surprise Buck was waiting to show me on Sunlight Peak.

Along the hillsides we passed, through the green grass on their slopes, you could see where a lot of the mining activity from back in the 1880's and 1890's had been. Prospect holes, with their piles of rust-colored rocks, sprang up along the sides of the mountains. They evidenced the hard work and hard men who had once put their sweat into the digging that had taken place in Chicago Basin. Most of the mining activity had ceased along about 1905, but the scars of that industrious era were still easily visible now, almost a hundred years later.

Finally, we made it to the head of the basin. You can tell when you've arrived there because the trail circles around to the south and climbs through the forest toward timberline. It proceeds on up the side of the mountains to Columbine Pass, thousands of feet above us. The pass is an obvious dent in the ridgeline there. We caught up with each other here, at the basin's head.

Buck slung his pack off his shoulders and laid it on the grass. He looked up at the sky, his eyes peering through his sunglasses for signs of clouds. It was clear overhead now.

I had been watching the mountains all along the trail, but the view of them from here was gorgeous. There was still some snow on the brownish-gold treeless summits above us. With all the greenery below, and the clear blue sky overhead, you felt you had arrived in a place out of a dream. It was a place where mountains were truly the kings of the world.

Buck watched me in silence, then he looked over at Jill. I dropped my pack, as did Jill.

"Well, here we have a choice to make," he said.

"I know," I said. "Make camp or climb some more."

"Climb some more?" Jill asked.

"Yeah," I said. I pointed to the northeast, to a steep trail on a grass-and-rock slope that went up to a ridge high above us.

I nodded to the trail. "There's a flat place, a sort of plateau, way up there over the high ridge, called Twin Lakes Basin, Jill. Some climbers like to go on up that trail and make camp there on top. You can get to the three Fourteeners, Eolus, Windom, and Sunlight fairly easily from up there. The only trouble is, it's another thousand feet of climbing to get to that ridge. It'd be pretty steep hiking with these full, heavy packs."

"And," Buck said, "to be honest with you, I just don't feel like going up there this afternoon. So I say we camp here and do that little thousand-foot jaunt up to Twin Lakes Basin in the early morning, with just the daypacks. Is that okay with you two?"

Jill shrugged. "It's fine with me," she said.

"Yeah, it's okay with me, too," I replied.

Actually, I was glad we decided to camp where we were for several reasons. Like Buck, I didn't relish the thought of lugging my 50-pound backpack on up that steep trail after the hike we had just made. Besides, I liked it down here at the head of the basin. We would be better protected from the weather if a storm came. There was also plenty of water to cook with from nearby Needle Creek here. Topping it off, the view of the mountains was unbeatable.

So we left the trail and walked back over into the trees and found a good campsite. We made camp, setting up the tents.

I carry along a little two-man, flyless, waterproof tent that I've had for years. Light-green, it blends in with the scenery. It only weighs about four pounds, and yet it's got all the room I need for my rather large body. It's strong in the wind and weather, too. Best of all, I can set it up quickly if rain starts to fall. Not having a tent with a rainfly is lighter and more convenient, but you have to put up with a tradeoff.

Waterproof tents, like mine, tend to build up condensed water on the inner walls at night. Your sleeping body sweats, the sweat evaporates, and then condenses on the night-chilled fabric of the nylon tent walls. The moisture can run down and soak your sleeping bag and other gear. So unless you wanted to sleep in cold, sauna-like conditions, with water dampening your sleeping bag, you have to keep such a tent well-ventilated. The vents let the evaporated moisture out. Flyless waterproof tents aren't very popular for this reason. The tradeoff, though, was that you saved the weight from carrying along a rainfly. I was willing to make the concession, but I always made sure the air vents on the sides and ends of the tent were open when I staked it out.

I finished setting up my tent, then I went inside it and unrolled my insulated ground pad and laid out my sleeping bag on top of the pad.

The tent had a separate area, outside the door flap, covered by a sheet of nylon, called a vestibule. The vestibule covered a little space of ground. This was a sort of anteroom, where, if you had to, you could do your cooking protected from the rain. It also sheltered your backpack from the weather, too. I got everything arranged and crawled back out of my tent into the warm sunlight again.

Jill was still setting up her tent, a dome model. Dome tents are interesting, but I saw one blow off a mountain ledge like a parachute one time. I've never been much of a fan of them since that day. Still, if that's what she liked, it was fine with me.

Buck's tent was a conventional green triangle-sided shelter, a sort of oversized pup-tent. It had a rain fly and was a by-the-book affair. His tent weighed a bit more than mine, but Buck had grown accustomed to it over the years. I tried to get him to buy a lightweight, high-tech little number like mine, but he hung on to his old one, probably for sentimental reasons. It was reliable, too, of course, but I still always thought it weighed too much.

After Buck's tent was up, he got out his one-burner stove and made a pot of coffee. Out here, you drank liquids frequently to keep your body well hydrated. You could sweat away a lot of critical body-water and not even be aware of it.

"The weather looks good so far," I said as I walked up to him. "I'll check the report on my radio tonight."

"Won't do much good. You know that."

"I know. The mountains make their own weather. Still, it might be good to know if the local clouds are going to get any help from a front moving in."

He poured a mug of coffee and drank it, scanning the mountain walls of Mount Eolus above us.

I smiled at him. "Still don't want to try that one, huh?"

"No," he replied. "Not on this trip. Let's see how you handle the other two peaks first."

"You're the doctor."

The sun was starting to go behind one of Eolus's ridges as we began the evening cooking ritual. There was a fire ring not far from our tents. We made that our cooking and dining area. We prepared our suppers and sat on logs as we ate.

"I loved that hike up into the basin," Jill said.

"Yeah, it's nice," I said.

"I wish I had your youth and vigor, Jill" Buck said to her. "You went up that trail today like a gazelle."

"Thanks, Buck," she said. "You looked pretty strong yourself."

"For an old man?"

"I didn't say that."

"Yeah, but you were thinking it."

"No, not really. Buck, I really don't think of you as an old man."

He had taken off his sunglasses now, and he smiled at her. "You know, I almost believe you."

She gently poked his arm with her fist. "Give me a break, Buck. I know you didn't want me coming along."

"Who told you that?"

"Oh, no one had to tell me. You've been quiet today. You've got your defenses up. I can tell."

He shrugged. "I'm sorry if I seem that way. I'm just not used to having, well, a girl along."

"I'll do my fair share," she said. "Just give me a chance, huh?"

"Okay," he said. "I just keep thinking about that night we came down off old Jupiter Peak over there," he said, gesturing at the mountain across the valley.

Jill looked over at Jupiter. "I was pretty weak that night. I've got my strength back now."

Buck sighed. "I believe you do."

I cooked and ate my dinner, a bowl of vegetable stew, in silence, listening, smiling inwardly. I knew he'd come around once he got to know her a little better.

Later, after we finished eating, we knew night was coming and the air was soon going to get cooler. We put our coats on and built a small campfire. Then we listened to the hiss of the steam in the damp wood and the crackle of the embers. The leaves of the aspen trees near us rustled as a breeze came up.

The stars appeared in the twilight sky and they seemed to dance in the sky above the rising, flickering sparks of the campfire. The three of us were silent for a long time.

"I was wondering," Buck mused, at length, "what it was like for those miners who lived up here a hundred years ago."

"It probably got a little lonely for them," I said, "far from the comforts of home."

"Maybe," he said. "I get a little lonely, too, sometimes out here in places like this. Funny, the loneliness always seems strongest on the first night out."

"Do you miss your wife?" Jill asked him.

He turned and looked at her. "Yeah, Jill, I guess I do. I brought Amaryllis up here with me once, one summer. She really liked it."

"Why don't you bring her along again some time?"

He looked at the fire. "Oh, I might. It was just the two of us that time, and I was doing some solo climbing. She doesn't like waiting around all day for me when I'm up climbing, though. She said she'd rather be doing something with me than sitting alone in camp."

"She must love you a lot," Jill said.

"Yeah, I guess she does. We've been married for over forty years now. I'd be lost without her."

There was a long silence as the fire crackled. "I...I wish I could be married to someone like that someday," Jill said.

Buck turned and saw her face illuminated by the fire light. He seemed to be looking at her with a new understanding. "No reason why you can't, Jill. It can happen for you."

"I hope so." She said. She turned and looked at me. "What about you, Mike? Have you ever been in love like that?"

I smiled and laughed lightly, prodding at a stick with the toe of my boot. "I think I'm in love that way now, Jill."

"With Tracy?"

"Yeah. We're a pretty good pair, I guess."

She waited a moment, then asked, "What is it about her you like?"

I kicked at the stick. "You're getting a little personal, aren't you?"

"Sorry," she said. "I don't mean to be."

"Oh, it's okay. To answer your question though, I guess Tracy just, well, she sort of gives me the freedom to be myself. She knows what I'm really like, and she loves me anyway. I get a little crazy sometimes, and yet she accepts that part of me. She has a way of making me feel a sense of freedom about myself."

"And, do you give her that freedom in return?"

"I hope I do."

She looked off into the night. "It would be great to find a man someday I can be with, like that."

I pulled my coat tighter about me, feeling the night air's chill. "Well, they're out there, Jill. I'm sure some guy out there has your name on him. It's just a question of time till you find him. Keep looking."

"I wish I had your confidence about that."

I reached down and poked at the fire with the stick. "Oh, you'll meet him some day. Just don't settle for second best."

"I don't intend to."

Buck slowly got up from his log, stretching. "Well you two campfire kids can stay out here and talk if you want to, but I'm going to sack out. My old bones are calling me."

"Okay," I said. "I doubt if we're far behind you."

He walked away in the darkness, toward his tent. Jill and I stayed by the fire, watching the embers glow.

"You see, Jill," I said softly. "He's warming up to you."

"You really think so?"

"Yeah. He wouldn't have talked about Amaryllis that way if he was feeling tight and withdrawn. He's letting you in on the man inside of him."

She pulled her coat around her body. "I hope you're right. I really do want him to accept me and like me. I'm not a bad person."

"I know. After we climb together tomorrow, he'll probably be like an old friend to you. You'll see."

"I want that," she said. "I really do. I like him. I just want him to accept me."

We watched the fire a little longer, then we put it out and went back to our respective tents. I crawled into my sleeping bag and got out my little FM radio. Putting on the headphones, I dialed in a station down in Durango. Soft classical music played piano sonatas. I thought about Tracy, back there in her warm bed in town. I missed her, even after just a few hours away from her. I wished she were here with me to share this quiet night in our camp at 11,000 feet. I realized, the same way Buck felt about Amaryllis, how much the lady meant to me.

I wondered if Jill was lonesome, too, over there in her tent. Dream, Jill, I thought. Dream of the man you'll find some day.

As I lay there, near sleep, listening to the radio, I finally heard a weather report at the station break. The announcer said a front was coming in slowly, and so it was probably going to be a clear day in the mountains tomorrow. Sure, I thought. I've heard that one before. Still, it was reassuring. I switched off the radio to save the battery and stashed it, along with the headphones, in a side pocket of the tent.

The night air was becoming much colder now, so I pulled my wool balaclava over my head. The balaclava is like a big woolen ski mask, and it keeps the head good and warm. If your head stays warm, that's more than half the battle against the cold. I was comfortable now, and my last thoughts were of Tracy as I drifted off to sleep.

My inner alarm, that clock in my head, woke me early the next morning. The others had awakened, too, by now. It was clear but cold as I dressed. I had a quick breakfast, a couple of fruit bars, and loaded my day pack for the climbing that lay ahead. I looked out of my tent. It was still dark but dawn was giving a little light. I saw Buck's dark silhouette as he stood by his tent.

"Morning," I said. "Do you think we'll need the rope today?"

He saw me. "Not on Windom," he said, "but there's a place or two on Sunlight where it might come in handy. Better bring it along."

"Okay," I said. I crawled out of my tent with my daypack, found my braided nylon rope, and lashed it over the top of the daypack. It added another four pounds of carry-weight, but it was probably wise to take it along if Buck said so.

We left camp as dawn grew brighter, and walked in the cool half-light up a steep dirt trail through the trees. Again, as on the day before, Jill took the lead. I walked in the middle, and Buck brought up the rear.

We came out of the aspens at a grassy, boulder-strewn meadow, and not long after it we came to the steeper part of the trail. Up ahead, above me, I could see the thousand-foot climb to Twin Lakes Basin.

A couple of other climbers, young men, came huffing and puffing up the trail behind us. They overtook us, said hello, passed us, and went on ahead.

"Looks like they'll get there first today," Jill said.

I said nothing. Buck just smiled.

When we arrived at the foot of the steepest section of the trail, Buck said, "Hold up just a minute."

We waited on him as he slowly surveyed the way the rocky trail angled near-vertically up the mountainside. Then he said,

"Here, we start using the mountain-step."

The mountain-step, or rest-step as some call it, is a way of walking that lets you make efficient use of your oxygen as you climb. You place a bootstep on the path, stop a second or two, take a deep breath, and then you step higher again and do the same thing over again. Discipline, timing, and listening to your breathing and heartbeat are the keys. It's a slow way to go, but it feeds a lot of air to your lungs and heart at high altitude, and you can move better that way. Once you get the hang of it, you can climb much more easily than just stubbornly charging forward, uphill, nonstop.

A couple of hundred feet up the trail we met the two young men who had earlier passed us, coming back down. They looked sweaty and red-faced in the early morning light.

"We couldn't make it," one of them said, huffing and puffing. "That trail's so steep, it's a killer. Our hearts were pounding too much. We felt like we were going to have heart attacks. We're completely winded."

"Take it easy," I said. "Rest a bit. You can do it. Watch how we do it."

Jill, Buck, and I passed them and ambled upward on the steep incline. We went at a snail's pace, mountain-stepping. The two watched us go, and a few minutes later they turned back up the trail and began to follow us, imitating our mountain-step.

After gaining several hundred more feet of elevation, we topped out on the first flat place on the trail. The flat stretch didn't last long. More steep climbing followed, more flat ridges, and then we slowly negotiated our way horizontally across the loose rocks of a roaring stream that ran below a small waterfall. I noticed ice on the green ferns alongside the stream.

We scrambled up a grass-and-rock slope, and then began the climb to the highest ridge. It led directly into Twin Lakes Basin. We reached it, and saw that the landform around us curved into a rocky plateau that looked like the arctic tundra.

Huge, rounded boulders and piles of rock were everywhere amid the sparse patches of green grass. The lakes which gave the basin its name lay ahead of us.

The lakes were two connected glacial tarns cut into the upper valley by masses of glacial ice and snow from ancient times. The place made me feel that we had moved backward in time to an era thousands of years before. I took out my altimeter and saw that we were now about 12,500 feet up.

There were a couple of small, silent tents along the shoreline of the farther of the two lakes. Whoever had made camp here was nowhere to be seen, probably already up and climbing on the surrounding peaks. I admired the stamina of whoever had lugged their packs up to this altitude. At the same time, though, I was glad we had decided to make our own camp back down at the head of the basin.

Beyond the lakes, I saw, to my amazement, the surprisingly well-preserved remains of a wooden miner's cabin. Some hardy souls from many years before had actually packed lumber up that steep trail and had worked their claims here. I made a mental note of the location of the building. It might make a good storm shelter if the weather should turn bad.

We decided to take a short rest. The sky was brightening now as the dawn gave way to pale blue overhead. Dropping our packs, we sat back against the cold granite slabs of the boulders. Buck looked as strong as ever, but Jill was starting to show some signs of strain.

"How are you doing, Jill?" I asked.

"Oh, I'm all right," she said. "Those guys we saw at the bottom of the trail were right. That really was a killer climb."

"You did okay though. Grab a bite of something to eat."

"All right," she said, and she reached in her pack for a granola bar.

"I guess I'm just a little nervous," she said as she ate. "It isn't like me, you know. I mean, I used to go up rock faces with a lot more exposure than anything we're doing. There's just something about coming up here today that's getting to me."

"I think I know what it is," Buck said.

She turned to him. "What?"

"It hasn't been that long since your fall over there on Jupiter Peak, Jill. A lot of climbers, after they have a bad fall, well, they get the shakes the next time out. We're not far from where all that happened. It's only natural for you to feel a little apprehensive. You'll get over it."

"I hope you're right," she said.

"You'll do fine," he replied. "Just take it easy."

Good old Buck, I thought. It sounded like he was starting to warm up to her. I thought he would in time; he just had to gain a little trust in her. I had been a little worried that when we got to the tougher climbing Jill might slow down and Buck might get irritated with her. But no, he was showing his approval of her, and that was a good sign. The old macho man could open up after all. This was the real Buck I knew. Soon, before the lactic acid settled in our muscles and made us stiff-legged and sore, we got up and resumed our trek.

Peak 18, the one that obscured Sunlight Peak from down below in the basin, was now somewhat ahead and to our right, with Mount Windom's lofty crest beyond it to the east. The climber's trail led around beneath the base of Peak 18. There, the trail climbed steadily up along the ridge between the two mountains toward the summit of Windom. We made our way up to the saddle between the two mountains.

Windom Peak looked incredibly high from here, probably because we were getting a little tired by now. Yet I was feeling alert and able as we moved upward, and I sensed we would make the summit without any problems. It would be my first Fourteener, and I was happy.

From the saddle between the mountains, we looked across the narrow valley to the north toward Sunlight Peak. We watched two climbers negotiating their way down through the rocky slopes on their way back from the mountain. I wondered if they were the ones from the tents beside the Twin Lakes. Their route of descent looked a bit tricky, but they were moving well as they approached the valley floor.

"Sunlight," Buck nodded. "That's where we'll be heading next, after we do Windom."

"Looks like fun," Jill said, watching the far-off climbers coming down.

"I hope so," I said.

We turned our attention back to Windom again, and resumed climbing. The footing was good through the scattered rocks along the ridge. We were following cairns now. It was reassuring to know that we had not strayed from the correct route.

We gained the windy summit of Windom by nine o'clock. The rocks around us here at the top were rugged and orange-red, weathered into rounded shapes by the winds and weather that swept these summits.

The view was indeed breathtaking. From our perch we could see Chicago Basin stretched out below us like a green, folded carpet below the steep walls of the Needles. I thought I could see all the way down the valley to far-off Durango. I wished Tracy had been with me to share the moment.

"Well, congratulations. You got your first Fourteener," Buck said to me, shaking my hand. I shook it, then he shook Jill's, as did I.

"Mine, too," Jill said nervously. "I'm glad I came along."

We set down our packs and signed the summit register. Buck got out his camera and took some pictures of us. I had trouble moving around. I was transfixed by the joy of our accomplishment and the beauty of the view. A few moments later, though, I got over my elation and found my Canon rangefinder camera in my pack. I took a few pictures. Then Buck reached into his pack and withdrew a can of lemonade.

"A toast for the victorious climbers," he said.

"Wait," I said. Reaching into my pack, I withdrew two cans, and handed one to Jill.

"You brought one for me?" she asked.

"We can't very well have a toast if you don't have a can along with us," I said.

"But," she said, glancing down at my pack, "the extra weight— you should have let me carry it."

"Next time you will, but this one's on me," I said.

We clinked our cans together and gladly sipped the cool lemonade. Then, almost as one, we turned around and looked back across the northern valley toward Sunlight Peak.

Buck silently regarded us, perhaps trying to measure our levels of fatigue. "Are you game for a go at old Sunlight over there?" he asked us.

I nodded. "Whenever you're ready, fearless guide."

"That okay with you, Jill?" he asked.

"Sure, I'm ready," she said.

"Okay. You'd better let me take the lead though," he said. "Getting over there will take a little bit of routefinding, and I've been there before."

So we went back down, at first following the way we had come up. We arrived at the upper part of the valley floor. Then we went off-trail, contouring our way through the boulders over to a high ledge. We looked up at the rugged walls of Sunlight. A reddish- colored couloir full of sand and loose rocks led upward. Buck told us it was the most accessible way to get to the top.

We scrambled our way up the red couloir as best we could. The footing was tricky on the sandy dirt, mud, and small loose rocks. From time to time we kept sliding back down, and I thought for a while we would never reach the top of it.

We finally made it though, right to the saddle between Sunlight Peak and a pinnacle named Sunlight Spire. We moved on up to our left through a window between the rocks. Following cairns again, we pulled ourselves up over some rather large boulders. Then we came to even higher boulders, and I knew they would require the use of both hands to get us up and over them. Buck must have had the same thoughts.

"Let's leave the ice axes here, Mike," he said. "We'll be coming back down this same way and we can get them then."

"Fine with me," I said, laying my axe where I would see it when I returned.

We made it up and over the huge rocks, and found ourselves on a somewhat level place again. Here, there was some exposure to falling however, and Buck thought we should use the rope for protection. I unstrapped it from my pack and uncoiled it. We tied in and belayed each other over the exposed section.

Jill was climbing well, but I could see that she was becoming very nervous. It concerned me, but I said nothing.

We stopped and rested, and I saw Jill turn away from us for a moment. Then she took a long drink from her canteen. I didn't think anything more of it, and we started our ascent once again.

We passed beside another large opening in the rocks, and finally we found what Buck called "The Keyhole." We scrambled through this narrow window, and on the other side I saw that the next stretch was going to be quite steep and exposed.

Again, we tied ourselves to the rope, belaying each other, and made our way to an inclined ramp in the rocks that led upward another hundred feet or so. We then crisscrossed back above the lower route on a new ledge until we came to a narrow crack which afforded some handholds. The crack in the rocks took us, finally, on up to the flat, boulder-strewn summit area. At first, I thought we had at last reached the top of Sunlight Peak. I was glad.

It was now about 10:30 in the morning, and the clear skies

were still in our favor. Then I saw that we still had not quite reached the top. Ahead of us, a high pinnacle of rock jutted up into the sky. This was the true summit, and I saw that it was going to be a challenge to climb it.

"What's that?" I asked.

"That's the surprise I was telling you about," Buck said, laughing. "You haven't finished climbing this mountain until you've done that thing."

The pinnacle was composed of a huge, narrow, angled slab of rock leaning against another, taller rock. I could tell it would require a higher level of skill and courage than I had ever used to make the last ascent to the true summit of Sunlight.

"Are you going up there?" I asked Buck.

"No," he laughed, "Not me. I've done it before. But if you two are going to say you've been to the top of this hill, you've got to scramble on up that thing."

I took a deep breath, laughed, and turned to Jill. "Okay. I'll take a shot at it. Are you game, Jill?"

She acted a bit uncertain, glassy-eyed now, as she stared at the summit block. I hoped her apprehension was merely from the exertion of the climb and not something else, like mountain sickness. I had to admit, though, looking at the boulders made me a little queasy as well.

"S...sure," she said, in a strange, relaxed voice. "You go first, Mike. I'll watch."

I tied the rope in a bowline around my waist and had Buck belay me. At first I tried to crab my way up an inclined slab of rock, but I just couldn't muster what it took to do it. I slipped back down; I just couldn't find the purchase. There had to be another way. Buck suggested another way up, a sort of block-to-block jumping route along another side of it.

There was about a four-foot space between the block at the edge of the flat area over to another block that led to the top. I'd have to jump the distance. A fifteen-foot fall was the penalty if you missed the jump. I saw that if you did land on the far block as planned, you had to grab on for dear life. On the other side of that block was a drop of at least a thousand feet, straight down.

Okay, I said, steeling myself, other people have done this. I walked over to the ledge, mindful of the rope, sucked up my courage, and jumped. I made it across the gap and hung on to the block, hoping the rope would catch me if I somehow slipped off.

I leaned out over the rock I gripped and looked down. The precipitous view down the north side made my body shake with fear and adrenaline. I slowly turned and pulled my body five feet on up over the top of the very last boulder. Then I lay prone on the true summit, clutching the three-foot-wide rock for dear life.

An image flashed into my mind. I remembered a picture I had seen in a book several weeks before. It had shown some brave climber from long ago actually doing a handstand on a narrow summit block like this one. At the time, I hadn't taken much notice of the caption. Now, I remembered where the picture had been taken. It was right here atop Sunlight Peak. I was lying where the guy had actually done his handstand. But I wasn't about to do anything like that today. Shaking like a leaf, I eased my body back down onto the lower block, then hastily jumped back to the safety of the flat area. I rolled on the rock surface, relieved that I had completed the climb.

"Did you like that?" Buck grinned, looking down at me as he coiled the rope.

"Yeah," I said, getting up and dusting myself off. "It was pretty stimulating. So that was your little surprise, huh?"

"You got it."

"Well, I can't say it's the easiest thing I've ever done, but at least now I know it can be done.."

I turned to Jill. "You want to try?"

"Uh...sure," she said unsteadily. "It's what we came here for, isn't it?"

She roped in, and went over to where I had jumped to the far boulder. Then she acted oddly relaxed about the whole thing, almost too relaxed. For some reason I felt a pang of worry for her. But she made the jump, and clung to the far rock.

Buck and I shouted, "Hooray, Jill!" We watched as she followed what I had done, pulling herself on up over that final rock to the top. I was about to shout more congratulations, but then, to our surprise, she began shaking like a leaf. Then the unexpected happened. Jill said nothing, she just grew limp, and she let go her hold on the rock. She slipped off the summit to the far side, with nothing for a thousand feet below her but thin air, and nothing holding her but the rope.

Buck immediately tightened the rope. It snapped taut and caught her before she went down very far. Thankfully, Buck had been sitting in a protected belay position. His legs were wrapped around a rock, the rope in front of him. Jill's body weight pulled him tight against the rock. She hadn't fallen very far, maybe five feet or so, but we heard her screaming as she hung there above the abyss.

"Blast it!" Buck yelled, holding her, "what happened?"

"She just slipped off!" I said, rushing to the ledge.

His eyes bored into me. "But why? She wasn't in any real danger. She was holding on to that rock just like you did. And then it looked like she just let go!"

"I don't know what happened," I said, looking across the ledge, wondering if I should jump unprotected.

It was tempting for me to try to jump that gap again and somehow help her get back up, but I kept my head. Jumping the gap without a rope could have meant a second problem for us, possibly a fatal one. Instead, I went over to Buck and helped him pull on the rope. A few moments later we had Jill up to the top of the summit block again.

She was trembling with wild fear as she wrenched her body up onto the ledge again. She was weak, shaking. Then, as she lay there, clutching the granite, she seemed paralyzed and afraid to move any further.

"Jill!" I yelled. "Are you okay?"

"No, but I'm...I'll be all right," she said, gasping for breath.

"Then climb back down to us!"

Weakly, she slowly began to move her arms and legs, and gradually made her way back down to the top of the first rock. She stood at the gap between the rock and the ledge on our side. I stood at the edge of the ledge, ready to catch her when she jumped over.

"Jump!" I said, and as she leapt forward through the air I reached to grip her arms. It was a good thing I did, too. She didn't quite make it over the gap all the way, and her boots slipped on the lip of the ledge. Holding her arms now, I pulled her on across and we rolled to the ground. I hugged her trembling body.

She was shaking so badly she almost fainted. I couldn't help thinking back, remembering how I had held her like this on Jupiter Peak. Deja vu. I hugged her until her shudders subsided somewhat. She seemed so small, so vulnerable in my arms, like a scared kitten.

"Boy," I said, looking into her frightened blue eyes. "You gave us quite a scare there."

Buck was standing over us. There was a serious glare in his eyes. "What happened, Jill?" he asked stonily.

She looked up at him. "I...I just fell off," she said simply.

He was silent for a long moment. "I know that, but why?"

My eyes squinted at him. "What are you driving at, Buck?" I snapped angrily, "She told you, man. She just fell off!"

He ignored me, continuing to stare straight at her. "No, it all happened too easily. People don't just fall off like that. What really happened, Jill?"

She began to cry as I held on to her. Then she seemed to recover again, breathing deeply, quietly. I was furious with Buck. Didn't the man have an ounce of sympathy after what she'd just been through?

"Buck...," I said.

Jill wiped her eyes. "I'm sorry, so sorry..."

Buck continued to stare at her. "You haven't answered my question, Jill," he said evenly. "What caused that fall? You were holding on like you were supposed to. You were fine. But why did you suddenly go limp like that and let go?"

I was just about ready to jump up and move in on my old buddy, but Jill slowly reached into the pocket of her parka. She held out a small plastic medication bottle. Not believing what I was seeing, I took it, opened it, and found some white pills inside.

"I...I took some of them," she said.

"Drugs," Buck said, spitting on the ground. "I thought so."

"What...?" I asked, looking bewildered at her, shaking my head.

"I'm sorry," she said. "I...I just thought...if I just took a couple of them...back there...it would relax me...help me make the climb better. I was getting so scared...the heights, I guess it just all got to me...."

Buck quickly took the bottle from my hand, looked at it, capped it, and with a furious cry he threw the bottle far out over the cliff.

"That was the stupidest thing I've ever seen anyone do on a mountain!" he shouted at Jill. "I knew we shouldn't have taken you along on this climb. I guess it's true: once a druggie, always a druggie!"

Jill began to cry again, and I hugged her, though by now I was angry at her too. Still, I knew our anger wasn't what she needed at the moment. She'd nearly been killed again, and was almost catatonic with fright.

"He's right, Jill. Very stupid," I said.

"I know, I know, I know...," she moaned. "I know that more than either of you do."

Buck walked away, across the rocks, muttering disgustedly to himself. I continued to hold her until her sobbing gave way to gasping breaths.

"Okay," I said, lifting her chin, looking into her eyes. "Look. What's done is done. It's over. You're okay now."

"No," she said, letting out a deep sigh of abject defeat. "I'm finished. Over and done with. Buck's right. I'm just no good."

I shook my head and sighed. "Okay, Jill. You blew it. You went back to the old ways. It nearly got you killed. But you're safe now. The danger's over."

"But I'm such a failure," she said, looking down.

"No," I said. "You made a big, a colossal mistake, sure. But you know you're not a failure. What were those blasted pills, anyway?"

She sighed again. "They were tranks. Tranquilizers. Dil gave them to me. He said if I was going climbing, I might need them to help me mellow out. But they only made me dizzy. I just couldn't hold on up there."

I stared down into her blue eyes. My anger returned, but it was not directed at her now.

"Good old Dil," I said softly. "Good old Dil, once again. Every time he comes around and gives you one of his little 'gifts' it leads to trouble. Don't you see that by now?"

"Yes, yes, yes!" she said. "I see! Look, why don't I just get up and jump off this stupid mountain and get it all over with. I'm a rotten person. Let me finish it all, right here!"

"No," I said slowly. "That's not the way, Jill. You're not rotten. You're good. It's just the drugs that are bad."

Buck was walking back to us now. "Well," he said, "we can't undo what's done. But we'd better get down off the mountain anyway." He gestured toward the western sky. "The clouds are starting to build."

He turned and looked down at Jill for a long moment. Then he let out a loud sigh of exasperation. "Jill," he said, "look, I'm sorry I lost my temper. But good Lord, girl, can't you see what you did was the wrong thing to do on a climb?"

"I know, Buck," she said wearily. "I know. I'm...I guess I'm just...weak, that's all."

He knelt down beside us. He seemed to be struggling for patience as he rubbed his brow. "Jill, you don't have to be weak like that! You were doing fine! You don't need drugs to help you make it in the things you do, girl. You've got plenty of power to make it without them!"

She stared up at him and blinked away her tears. "You don't know me very well, Buck."

He leaned down, taking her from me, lifting her in his arms. He helped her to her feet. Then, gently holding her by her shoulders, he said, "Jill, I know you better than you think I do. Do you think you're the only person who's ever had problems? You can make it, girl, if you try. We might even be able to help you. Just stay away from those blasted drugs!"

"Okay, okay," she said.

I was surprised at Buck. Really surprised. What was going on inside him? Maybe he was beginning to see Jill for who she really was. Maybe he saw who she might, with a little help, become.

I glanced upward. Buck had been right about the clouds. To the west were the summits of Eolus and its sub-peaks, and the dark clouds above them were drifting our way. It was as if the mountain were sending us a nasty present, special delivery.

"The clouds, Buck," I said. "Time to kiss the summit bye-bye and get down lower."

He turned from Jill, looked at the approaching storm, and nodded. "Yeah, I guess so."

We didn't bother with pictures or the summit register now. We grabbed our gear and quickly began making our way back down, belaying each other again over the steep sections.

I had wondered if we'd have to assist Jill in her downclimbing. I had expected her to be weak and fearful. But now, for some odd reason, she was stronger and surer about her descent moves than either Buck or me. Maybe the drugs had worn off. Maybe it was anger at Cullen, or maybe it was something else, but she went down the trail with rock-hard confidence, as sure-footed as a mountain goat.

We picked up our ice axes where we had left them. The three of us breezed down the red couloir, sliding, almost jogging through the loose dirt and pebbles. At the bottom of the couloir, we scrambled our way over the rocks of the valley between Sunlight and Windom. Then the wind and rain, and then the snow began to beat on us in earnest. It was a slashing, nasty, snowy rain in our faces now, challenging us, punishing us. I could barely see through pale shrouds of wind and weather. Then, on ahead of us, I recognized the dim shape of the old miner's cabin.

"Let's make for that cabin," I shouted to them. "We can ride out the storm there and go on down to camp after it lets up."

Their parka hoods nodded agreement, and we moved as quickly as we could. We arrived at the old miner's cabin as the storm blasted us with furious, torrential sheets of cold rain and snow. We hurried into the building.

The cabin was rather delapidated, drafty and decaying with a few boards missing along its walls, but we didn't care. All we wanted was basic shelter, some place to hide from the ferocity of the storm. The cabin was as welcome to us as a king's mansion.

We were cold and soaked to the bone, even in our protective clothing. Fancy protective clothing is good up to a point, but it isn't perfect. When you went through the kind of weather we'd just been through, you still got wet. Buck turned and stood in the doorway, looking out at the rain, as Jill and I went back into the interior.

"I'm freezing," Jill said, and I hugged her. She had worn shorts that day, and beneath her storm parka her legs were white as chalk from the cold and the wind.

"Did you bring any other clothes? You ought to change into something warm."

"Okay, I will. That is, if I can stop shivering."

I helped her off with her pack, and she opened it. I looked inside. She had a wool sweater in there and some jeans. "Here," I said, lifting them out, "put these on."

She reached deeper into her pack and pulled out a change of dry underwear. She gave me an embarrassed little smile. "I'd...I'd better put these on too. I'm turning to ice."

I nodded. "Well, we can't have that," I said. I turned toward Buck. "Buck, keep your eyes turned away. The lady's changing."

"Okay," he said.

I walked over to him while Jill changed her clothes behind us. We peered out at the driving rain in silence.

"Mike," he said, quietly, "we shouldn't have brought her along."

"It was a gamble, Buck. If I had thought she was going to use drugs, I never would have considered it."

He shook his head in consternation. "So what do we do now?"

"Well, today we got the two Fourteeners we wanted. That's what we came for. I guess we go back to camp and leave the basin tomorrow, just like we'd planned."

He gestured his thumb over his shoulder. "I meant, what do we do about her?"

I stared out at the lonely silver rain, falling on the gray stone walls and ramparts of Sunlight Peak high above us. It was still raining hard, but less so than a while before. I knew it would probably quit soon as the dark clouds moved on.

"Well," I said, "you'll probably think I'm crazy, but I say we forget about what happened back up there."

He turned to me. "Forget it? You mean we should just let it go?"

"Yes."

"Just like that?" "Just like that. I think she's learned something from all this,

Buck. I really do. I say we let it go and move on from here."

He regarded me with narrowed eyes for a long moment in silence. "Okay," he said. "Maybe she did learn her lesson. We'll do it your way this time. I don't know. Maybe you're right."

"I don't know either. It's just a hunch."

He kicked at the ground with his boot, looking down at it. "You think I was too hard on her?"

I laughed lightly and shook my head. "No, probably not. Maybe Jill needed to hear what you said. Sure, you were pretty rough. But I'm glad you eased up on her before we came back down. Did you see how she made the downclimb? She was making better time than we were."

"I saw that," he said, smiling faintly. "To tell you the truth, it surprised me. Maybe you're right about her. Maybe she'll wise up now. I can see that she's a good girl at heart. Maybe she really can put all that garbage behind her."

A few moments later I felt an arm around my back. Jill was standing between both of us and she had her arms around both of us. I hugged her for warmth, and her young body pressed against me.

"The lady is decent now," she said.

"Aw, too bad," I said with a grin, hugging her closer.

"Hey, careful now," she said to me, "you're already spoken for."

"So am I," Buck said, joining in our hug, "but that doesn't mean we're made of stone, lady."

"You're both too old for me," she said, laughing, wiggling against us." You two probably need to put on some warm clothes yourselves."

"She may be right," I said, smiling at Buck. "Care to change your outdoor recreational attire, my good man?"

Buck snorted. "Oh, I'm all right," he said. "You do what you want to."

By the time I had changed into warmer clothes, the rain and snow had quit. The wind was still strong, but we decided to chance it. We left the cabin, walking off across the rocks.

Reaching the twin lakes, we saw the tents we had seen earlier. A young man and a young woman were now standing near their tents. They waved to us from across the lake as we passed by on the other side. Waving back, we walked on.

We came to the windy crest of the ridge above the basin as the sun came out from behind the clouds. That sun was a welcome sight. I looked to the west. Through the rocks, I saw a faint snow- whitened climber's trail leading horizontally across the tundra-like slopes. It turned upward in a narrow ravine toward the summit of Mount Eolus.

Buck was standing alongside me. I gestured toward the trail with the point of my ice axe. "So that's the trail, the way you go, to get to the top of Eolus, huh?"

"Yeah, that's the way you normally go. But not on this trip."

"Not even tomorrow?"

"No, not even. We wouldn't have enough time to get back up here to Twin Lakes, make the Eolus climb, and go back down. If we did those things, we'd still have to pack up and get on down the lower trail to the train in time to be picked up. We'll save Eolus for another day."

"Buck," I said, "do you think I'm ready for it now, after what we did today?"

He rubbed the stubble on his chin. "Probably. Yeah, probably. You looked okay back there, especially scrambling up that summit block. I guess if you can handle Sunlight you're ready to take on Eolus."

Jill didn't say anything. I wondered if she wanted to come with us when we came back to make the Eolus climb. I knew after what she had been through today, she might not want to come along. After all she had been through, she probably had her fill of mountain climbing.

We headed on down toward camp. It was a slippery hike down the steep incline that led to our tents. We arrived at about five o'clock, muddy and exhausted. We didn't have much time to rest before night set in, so we cooked our suppers and ate while it was still light and the air was still comfortably warm. We were exhausted, tired of conversation, and we went to bed soon after that. My sleeping bag felt good after the long day.

The next morning, under cloudy skies, we packed out and made our way down to the train. We loaded our packs into the baggage car and got aboard. All three of us slumped against the windows. We slept all the way back to Durango, oblivious to the noisy tourists all around us.

They were enjoying the ride and the scenery. After all, they were on an adventure, and they were enjoying it.

Chapter Nine

Sunday morning when I awoke, I was still bushed from climbing the two Fourteeners. It would have been good to just catch a few more hours of sleep, but I remembered that Tracy wanted me to go to church with her. I looked at my watch and rolled out of bed. After dressing in my best suit, I had a quick breakfast. I drove over to Tracy's, hoping I wasn't late. She was ready when I got there and we drove to the church.

I felt good to be going to church with her, and I was starting to like Reverend Harry Foster and his sermons. But I had another reason for going today. I wanted to see if Cullen and his family were there.

No, I wasn't going to talk with Dil about the pills he had given Jill, at least not there at the church. I just wanted to see the guy and his upstanding-family-man image and how he worked it.

Dil and his wife and kids were all there, sitting down near the front pews, proper as could be. As I looked at him I couldn't stop thinking about Jill and that little bottle of white pills.

Tracy and I sat a few pews back from the front row. I listened carefully as Harry gave his sermon. He was preaching an interesting message this morning. Harry looked confident, gesturing with his glasses in his hand as he spoke.

" 'What does it profit a man if he gains the whole world, and loses his soul?', the scripture says. What does that mean for us, the modern people who live here in Durango? Are we trying to gain wealth, and power, and influence over other people, even to sacrifice our immortal souls? Can we ignore the command to care for the people around us, especially the young, while we do things that destroy their dignity, their very lives?"

Yeah, Dil, I thought, as I sat there listening. This one's for you, baby.

Harry went on with his message. It was a good sermon, aimed straight at Dil and others like him. But the definition of a "good church sermon," Tracy had once said, cynically, was a message that went straight over your head and hit the guy in the pew behind you. I suspected that this one went straight over Cullen's head. It hit me, though.

After the service we filed out the door. I was close enough to Cullen to hear his words as he warmly shook Reverend Harry's hand.

"Great sermon today, Preach," Dil said. "You really hit the nail on the head."

"Why, thank you, Dil," Harry said diffidently, nodding to him, before shaking the hand of the next person in line.

When I took his hand, I said to him quietly, "I heard you talking to Dil. Do you ever get tired of the hypocrisy?"

He winked at me with a wry grin. "Patience," he said. "It takes a long time for the water to wear away the stones, Mike."

"Some stones don't wear away too well, Harry."

"You've got to hang on to hope."

"Well, you've got a lot more hope than I do, Reverend."

"Maybe so. But I'm glad you came today."

"Thanks. See you, uh, 'Preach'."

Reverend Harry smiled at the way I had imitated Dil's word. We went past him out into the morning sunlight.

We left the church and got in my Blazer. I was ready for some quiet conversation with Tracy. I was still thinking about Jill though, and Dil's pills that had almost cost the young woman her life on Sunlight Peak.

We had lunch at a local restaurant, The Lazy Onion. As we sat eating, Tracy could tell I was on edge about something. I was quieter than usual as I ate.

"What's wrong?" she asked. "Is it me? Did I say something that got on your nerves?"

"No," I said. "Not you, lady."

I wasn't in the mood to talk about what had happened back there on the climb. "I'm just a little worn out from the trip I guess. Maybe I need my hot-tub therapy, and my therapist, of course. That's all."

"Oh," she said. "Well, perhaps that can be arranged. So how was Jill? Did your climbing with her go okay?"

Maybe it wasn't lying if I merely sidestepped the truth. I didn't like telling half-truths to Tracy, but I did anyway.

"It went okay. We got two Fourteeners, Windom and Sunlight. It was worth going."

She was still puzzled. "You don't sound too excited about it."

"It's okay. I'm just tired, that's all," I said.

She gave me a long look. She was beginning to know me too well. "Okay, you can tell me about it later if you like. I can see that your brain's been on overdrive too long."

"Thanks," I said, relieved.

After lunch I took her back to her home, telling her truthfully that what I probably needed the most was sleep. I took a rain check on the soak in the hot tub. Back home, I sacked out for the rest of the afternoon in my waterbed.

At seven that evening I woke up, got dressed again, and I called George Barker. He was the cop that I had met the night he had admired my Cobra. George wasn't on duty that night, so I arranged to meet him at the donut shop where we had met before. I told him it was important; that it was about Dil Cullen.

I arrived a little before he did. I stepped out of the Blazer and watched George park his old blue Dodge in front of the donut shop beside me. I thought we would go on in, but he motioned me over to his car window.

His lean, stern face looked up at me. He regarded me with serious eyes. He had that air about him, all cop.

"Get in," he said "Let's take a drive."

I got in beside him. "We can talk better as I drive," he said, "that is, if you don't mind."

"Fine," I said. I told him about the climb and about Jill and her fall and the pills. Then I told him about Dil giving them to her.

"You didn't save the bottle of pills, by chance?" He asked.

"No, George. Buck threw them over the edge of the mountain. I guess it was an impulsive move on his part, but he was mad. That bottle of pills is probably a thousand feet down the north side, buried in a crack in the rocks somewhere. Maybe we should have brought them back. Would they help?"

"They might. We might have lifted one of Cullen's prints off the bottle or something. That could be a direct evidence tie-in."

"We didn't think of that at the time."

"Citizens usually don't," he said mirthlessly.

I shrugged. "So what can I do about it? He illegally gave her pills, and they almost got her killed. Look, I want to get this guy, George. Isn't there anything we can do?"

George smiled at me. "Yeah. Look the other way."

"What?"

"You heard me right. I said look the other way. Forget it."

"You're kidding."

He grinned. "Gotcha. No, I know where you're coming from. I know what you want to do, too. You want us to collar the guy. I've been there, I know the feeling. But like I told you before, this is a police matter. I'll pass the info along to the narcs. But I've got to be honest with you, Mike, it's really just hearsay without any evidence. And the only evidence you've got would be that pill bottle. It would be pretty thin. As they say, anorexia."

"Oh," I said.

"Besides, Cullen can always claim they were legit prescription drugs. He'd say he just gave them to his friend Jill out of the kindness of his heart. People give pills to other people like that all the time. It's not strictly legal, but everybody does it and it's hard to prosecute. The D.A. would laugh in my face if we tried to take something like that to him. So would the grand jury."

"But Jill was nearly killed. Cullen was responsible. If we hadn't been there..."

"Yeah, but you said she made it back down okay. The hard fact is, no victim, no crime."

"You're saying it would have been better if she had gotten hurt or killed?"

"That's the cold, hard fact of the matter. We might put something together with an injury, or worse, but she wasn't hurt, just scared. If you want to make a crime out of it, you've got to show me a victim. Look, I'd like to be more help, Mike, but there's no luck in it. And another thing. All Cullen did was give her the drugs, right?"

"Yeah."

"Then she was the one who made the decision to take them from him and to actually use them. If the D.A. wanted to prosecute anyone, it'd probably be her for knowingly ingesting someone else's medication."

I crossed my arms and clenched my fingers around my biceps. It was maddening. "So Cullen covered himself on that one, too."

"Looks that way," George said. "An innocent man, trying to do a good deed. He couldn't help it if she took those pills at a time that endangered her. Nice try, but no luck."

We drove back to the donut shop and he let me off. I was

wide awake now, still steamed, but frustrated. I drove home and called Tracy.

"What are you doing, right about now?" I asked.

"Watching TV. There's nothing much on though. Why?"

"Care for some company?"

"Sure. But don't you have to go to work tomorrow?"

"I slept all afternoon. I'm awake and hungry now. If you'll let me, I'll make us some hotcakes. Are you game?"

She paused. "Game and hungry. Come on over."

The bacon sizzled in the pan as I cooked our late supper. I served it up on her plates, and we were both ready for it.

Tracy and I don't always eat at the table. Tonight we sat on the living room floor on a big Indian rug, watching the fish in her aquarium as we ate. Finally, our conversation got around to what we had been talking about earlier that day, Jill and the climb.

"Want to tell me about your trip to the basin now?" she asked.

I set my plate aside, and looked at her in the dim lampglow. "I didn't lie to you today. We did climb those two mountains. But what I didn't tell you this afternoon was that Jill had another fall. She nearly got killed again."

"Oh, great," Tracy said, setting down her plate. "This sounds like it's getting to be a habit."

I told her what had happened on the summit of Sunlight. I told her about my going to George Barker, too, and what he had said. Then I told her about Jimmy Rowe's little visit in my store office.

She shook her head. "This is all getting way over the line, Mike. You've got to get out of it before you get hurt."

"You think I should stop helping her?"

She shook her head in frustration. "I don't know. It just seems like you're getting into this thing deeper and deeper."

"Yeah," I said. "But I'm in too deep to quit now. I'm still betting that Cullen will keep his distance from me, though. I haven't really done anything to hurt him."

"Or so you think."

"Or so I think, yes."

"Well, I don't like it at all," she said.

"Somehow, I didn't think you would." "You were right. It's too crazy."

I stretched. "I really am beat, Tracy. But would it be okay if I took a soak in the old hot tub now?"

She smiled and relaxed. "Only if I can come, too."

"I was counting on that."

We cleaned up the dishes and she got the tub ready while I changed into my swimsuit. I was glad she was so agreeable. I really didn't want to quarrel with her.

The water was warm over our bodies in the tub. I don't know what it is about a hot tub, but there's something primitive and relaxing about a soak. A psychiatrist would probably say it's the return to the womb memory, buried deep down in your mind. You felt safe there in the warm water, comfortable. And if you were with someone you loved, you felt nourished and protected. The return to the birth-cave. That was fine with me.

I felt really numb after the soak, my muscles all jellied and all my energy gone. Tracy sent me home and I stumbled into bed again.

The next day, Monday, I worked through the morning out on the floor with the clerks. The day wasn't overly busy, and I like to spend time out on the floor at least one morning each week. You stay in touch with the customers that way, and you learn which clerks are doing their job right.

About noon, a guy I knew came in. Occasionally I play a little tennis, and the guy who usually called me up to play was a chiropractor named Dan Nomhaden.

"Hey, Big Mike, how's it going?" he asked as he saw me.

"Okay, Doctor. How's the back repair business?"

"Pretty good. Too many of your backpackers carry a pack too heavy for them, and they keep me busy trying to fix the damage. Feel like playing a little tennis tonight?"

"Tonight?"

"Yeah. I'm busy all afternoon with appointments. I've got to do a real job on a guy today and it'll take a couple of hours. I need a little tennis to get the kinks out. I'll reserve us a court at the racquet club if you can go."

"I think I can arrange for that," I said. We set the time for seven o'clock.

I knew I'd be rusty at tennis. I hadn't played for weeks and I was still fairly fatigued from the trip, but I thought it might do me some good to get my muscles moving again.

That evening I put on some old denim shorts and a tee shirt. I got my racket and went to the club.

Dan met me in the lobby. As always, he wore a clean, white traditional tennis outfit. He was a straight-arrow kind of fellow, a young professional, always well-scrubbed with a hint of cologne on him.

Dan was a little younger and a little better than me at tennis, but then again he got in a lot more games than I did. It helps to stay in practice. But sometimes, when the moon was right or something, I managed to take a few games from him.

I was really fatigued as we started playing. I knew my body wasn't fully recovered yet, but it was fun, anyway. Dan was quicker though, and very accurate with his placements and ground strokes. He won the first set 6-2. Between sets we sat on a bench, had a coke, and talked about how the summer was going for us.

"Are you still dating that photographer?" he asked.

"Yeah. We're still seeing each other."

"Anything serious, uh, developing there?"

"Just having a good time," I said.

"Good," he said. "Maybe something will come of it."

"We'll see," I said.

I don't know exactly why, but I was a little annoyed when he asked about Tracy. Maybe that's what got my competitive instinct going for the next set.

I came alive, and with a flurry of finely-carved placement shots I had him running all over the court. I don't know where those placement shots came from, but while they lasted I felt right in the zone.

He didn't give me an easy fight of it, though. He came back on me as my accuracy faded a bit. But I finally pulled out the win, 8-6. I was tired and breathing hard when we finished and sat on the bench, wiping off the sweat.

He wiped the moisture off his racket with a towel and said, "Still game for a third set?"

"I guess so," I said. "Give me a minute to get my heart rate back down to normal."

We got up and began the third set slow, with easy volleys at first. I noticed that he had little trouble putting his passing shots out of my range. He won the first three games. As we went on, for some reason he acted a little tentative with those passing shots, like something was on his mind, distracting him.

I won back the three games and we were even. He got tough again in the seventh game and took it after a long battle of hard baseline volleys, but then I went into the zone again.

I knew it probably wouldn't last long, so I decided to take advantage of it and speed up the game. Somebody, the old tennis star Rod Laver, I believe, once said if you're playing tennis badly, play faster.

I increased my pace and cracked off three more winning games, and before I knew it, I had him: game, set, match. When it was over, I was gasping for breath and I felt like I had overextended myself. I thought I was going to collapse right there on the court.

"Well, you got me," Dan said, coming up to the net to shake my hand.

"Lucky night," I replied, sucking in air, shaking his hand.

"Not bad, not bad," he said. "Got time for a little refreshment before you go?"

"Sure," I said. "I could use something right about now."

As we went up to the lounge, the clock over the bar said it was nine-thirty. We took a table and palmed the sweat off our arms and faces with our towels.

"You slowed down there a little toward the end, Dan. Everything okay?"

"Oh sure. I guess I'm a little tired tonight."

It didn't seem like him. Usually, he got better by the third set and took the match running.

"You thinking about that back un-twisting job you did this afternoon?"

"No," he said. "My tennis was okay. Just winded a little. Maybe I thought you'd fold and I'd have it easy."

"Not tonight," I said. "I just had a lucky streak. You'll probably get me next time."

The waiter came over and we ordered a couple of lemonades. They make great lemonade at the club, and tasting it reminded me of climbing, of the cans of lemonade Buck and I used to toast each other on the summits.

"So you've been doing pretty well these days?" Dan asked, leaning back in his chair..

"Yeah, pretty well. The store's been moving a lot of merchandise in the last two weeks. It's been busy, but I like it that way."

Dan nodded. He acted hesitant for some reason. "That's, uh, great, Mike. Uh, do you mind if I ask you something kind of personal?"

I thought he was going to bring up Tracy again, and I didn't want to talk about her. But I decided maybe I was being too guarded about that. She was, after all, a very important part of my life now.

"No," I said, setting my drink down. "I guess not."

Dan downed half of his glass of lemonade, and set the glass aside, the ice cubes tinkling. "Uh, maybe this is none of my business, Mike, but what's this I hear about you and Dil Cullen?"

I stiffened. "What exactly have you heard, Dan?"

"I hear you two have some kind of feud going, that you got mad and threatened him or something. Is it true?"

I wasn't quite prepared for this. "He's been bothering a lady friend of mine. I told him to back off."

"Is it Tracy?"

"No. A girl named Jill Carpenter."

Dan looked at me with curiosity. "Jill Carpenter? Who is she?"

"Just a young lady who works in the store for me."

"Well, what did Dil do?"

I studied Dan's face. I couldn't figure his line of interest. "Well, for openers, I think he's been giving her drugs."

"Drugs? Dil?" he asked, as if unbelieving.

"Uh-huh. Cullen's supposed to be some kind of drug dealer here in town."

Dan frowned at me and shook his head. "Oh no, Mike, that simply can't be true. Not Dil. Look, Mike, I've known Dil Cullen for years. All those stories about him being some kind of drug dealer are just a lot of hogwash. I know the man. I know him well."

"How do you know him so well?"

He sighed. "Look, our families are real close. His daughter used to babysit my kids. Heck, Mike, my family, well, we've taken vacations with the Cullens. He's a good man. Don't swallow those nasty rumors."

I frowned. "Then how do you explain the stuff I've heard about him being mixed up with drugs?"

"Like I said, that's just a lot of bunk stirred up by the gossip- mongers. Honestly, sometimes I think Dil himself may have started them. He likes to make people think he has a shady side, a sort of adventurous streak. But it's all a big sham. Now look, think about it. If Dil really was some kind of big drug dealer, the cops would have been all over him a long time ago. He may push the edge a little, but he's not really a bad guy once you get to know him."

"Really Dan? What about that tough guy that works for him, Jimmy Rowe?"

Dan laughed. "Oh, I know about Jimmy, too. But he's not all that bad. Yeah, sure, he comes on like a tough guy and tries to scare people. But that's all for show. Dil just likes him to keep some of the rougher people he has to deal with in line. Don't let him scare you though, it's all just a big act."

I frowned. "Are you sure you know these people, Dan?"

"Yeah, I do. And I really know Dil. He's helped me personally, and he's done a lot of good for this town. He headed up the United Way campaign two years ago and got more contributions than anyone ever did before or since. He's helped build buildings for his church. His kids are on the town sports teams. Mike, I'm telling you, forget that drug stuff and leave him alone."

"What about the girl, Dan? He put the make on her."

Dan shook his head, smiling. "I don't know that girl, Jill Carpenter, but I suspect that she's just a little young. Maybe she's one of those girls you hear about, just a little bit wild. It sounds to me like she's the real problem here."

"I don't think so."

"Look, all you've heard is the story she told you, her side of it, anyway. A lot of young good-looking bimbos in Durango would like to steal Dil Cullen away from his wife, Amanda. The girl probably tried to seduce him so she could use it to her advantage. Happens all the time. Dil has a soft spot for helping people, and sometimes he goes too far. But he and Amanda have a good marriage. Look, Mike, I like you. But you're making waves, man. We all need to keep Dil Cullen happy. He's good for the town and we need his leadership. Don't go making a lot of trouble for him."

I couldn't believe that Dan was defending Dil this way. Was he completely blind? Maybe so. Sometimes, in the name of peace and harmony, people denied the truth about others. They wanted things to stay peaceful so much they would look the other way and go to great lengths to keep everyone happy. In their attempts to please everyone, people like Dan got to the point where they didn't care about what's right or wrong anymore. They would even tell you so. And that is a very dangerous state of mind to be in.

The real tragedy of it was that Dan himself was a good man. But a good man who denies the truth, lets it erode away, and defends a living lie can have an effect just as bad as a man who truly is bad. Yet I could see that arguing with Dan was going to get me nowhere. You poor, blind idiot, I thought. You fool yourself more than anyone.

"Dan," I said, "I can see where you're coming from. And yet everything I see points to conclusions different from yours. But I've got an open mind. I won't bother Dil as long as he stays away from Jill Carpenter."

He laughed. "He won't bother her. I know him too well. But it would be good if you'd give him a call and apologize to him for upsetting him. That'll make him happy."

I wanted to laugh. The guy was really in the bonko zone. "That would be like a rape victim apologizing to her rapist for not being more accommodating."

Dan's congenial mood faded. He grew red in his face under his balding, wiry gray hair. His little watery-blue eyes glinted in erratic hostility, like tiny ball bearings. "Rape? Now that's pretty strong language, Mike."

"I know, doctor." I said. "And I meant every word of it. I'm dead serious."

He glared at me, biting his lower lip. "I just can't get it across to you, can I? I thought you were reasonable, and could see how much we need to keep people like Dil happy in our town. Come on, Mike, think of the contributions he makes."

"We all make our little contributions to the town's well-being, Dan," I said softly.

He laughed sarcastically. "Contributions? Look at you. What have you done for the good of the town? You were lit- tle more than a vet bum on the run when you came to Durango a few months ago. You got lucky and got that job at The Aspen Leaf. Since then you've been a sort of hanger-on, a newcomer who's made a few bucks and had some fun. What would a...a person like you know about civic contributions, about the hard work of building up a place like Durango?"

I calmed myself before I spoke. "Dan, Durango got along just fine before you, me, or Dil Cullen ever set foot here. It's a wonderful town with many good folks. All of us have a right to be here; we're all citizens of Durango. With the time and energy we've each respectively had, we've all done our parts, big or small. So don't give me some vested-interest, chamber-of-commerce lecture about who is supposedly a more valuable person than another to the town. We're all parts of it, buddy, we're all equals here. It's just that I happen to think your friend Cullen is one of the dirty parts."

Dan got up angrily from the table. "Then I guess I'm dirty, too. Is that how you see it?"

"No, Dan," I said, looking up at him. "Just blind to the truth. And maybe a little under the influence of your friend's wealth and power, and whatever other hold he has on you. But wealth and power ain't what cut it in the end, friend."

"And I suppose you know what does 'cut it in the end' as you call it?"

"Yeah. I think I do. Try the word 'honor', Dan. I'd rather be honorable than rich and influential any day of the week."

He snorted. "Honor? A hell of a lot a small-timer like you know about the word. Your self-righteous ideas about who's who in this town will get you into a lot of trouble around here. You got your store job easy, but you may lose it and find yourself on a rail out of town. I may help see to that. I know who gave you that job. They won't take kindly to their store manager giving their business a black eye."

I stared straight at him, squinting. "You probably would do something like that, too, wouldn't you?"

"Yes." he said. "I can get a lot of other tennis partners."

I got up. "Well before you do, Dan, I hope you'll think about your friend Dil just a little bit more. Check out where he spends his time in town at night. Check out the talk on the street. Then go home and look at your kids. Ask yourself if you really want people like Cullen and Rowe leading the way in the town your kids are going to grow up in."

He was unmoved. "You leave my kids out of this. You'd better start thinking about where you're going to live after you leave Durango. You keep it up and you're finished here, buddy."

"We'll see, Dan," I said. "We'll just have to see about that one. It's just sad to see a good guy like you give in to what Dil and his kind are offering you. Kind of like watching a back go bad."

His face turned red and he stammered and snuffled like he was going to try to do something to me physically. Then he caught himself. At least he had the good sense not try anything. Still clutching a few shreds of dignity to himself, he angrily turned and walked away, carrying his tennis racket. I just stood there, perplexed. I was glad we were the only ones at the tables in the club that night. I got up, shaking my head, went out, and drove home.

I hate to see friendships end. Two people meet, they get to know each other, they have a little fun. Then something comes at you out of the dark, and blooey, it's over.

In this case, young Dr. Nomhaden had just sold out to the town power brokers, and had deposited whatever honor he had in the great ash can of life. Maybe I should have been a little easier on him, a little more understanding, and then I might have sidestepped the terminal disagreement. But I was tired of tiptoeing around the main event. Dan typified in my mind the proverbial 'good man' who stands by and does nothing but look the other way while evil wins the day and takes over. That kind pave the road of triumph for the bad guys.

So mark one friendship up in the loss column, I thought. It hurt a little, sure. But, I mused, that's the price you sometimes pay for being true to what you believe in. It's uncomfortable, but it allows you to smell clean, untainted by the odor of rotting human dignity.

I was all jangley and agitated when I got home. I went out to the garage. Opening the garage door, I flipped on the light and closed the garage door behind me.

"Hey, little Cobra," I said as I walked over to the car. I took a soft cloth and wiped the dust off the sides.

I looked down at the gray primer paint. Many times I had mulled over what color I would want if and when I ever got around to having it painted. Red? No, a little too flashy. You got attention, but I wasn't driving it to get attention. Black? No, the Blazer was already black. I didn't want to be known as 'the guy who has those two black cars.' White? Maybe, but that made me think of white sedans you see all over the tourist highways. No, maybe I would paint it metallic blue. That was the color of so many of the old racing Cobras, so it would fit in with the heritage of the car. It was a good balance between the traditional and what I really liked. So yes, maybe metallic blue. Maybe someday. I closed the garage door and went in to bed.

The next afternoon after work I went over to Buck's real estate office to see him. I told him about my tennis match with Dan Nomhaden, and the conversation that had taken place after we had played.

Buck smiled and shook his head. "Don't let that little hypocrite Dan Nomhaden get to you," he said. "I know him. He's one of those guys so well educated in his field and so good at his profession that he thinks he's an expert at everything else, from the schools to the church to the business community."

"I know, Buck," I said. "But I hate to lose him as a tennis partner. Players on my level of the game are hard to find."

"The next time you choose a partner for tennis, get someone who doesn't like to talk much. Find a real soft-spoken, mild-mannered guy. You'll save yourself a lot of grief."

"Somebody like you, maybe?"

"Yeah," he grinned. "Somebody real nice and quiet, like me."

That night when I went to bed, I reminded myself that tomorrow was Pioneer Day, a town holiday. That meant the store would be closed and I wouldn't have to work. I was ready for the break.

Chapter Ten

Pioneer Day dawned hot and clear, and I was ready for it. I needed a break from the routine of work. The town holiday celebrated the founding frontier days of Durango. And, since I didn't have to work, I relaxed as I got ready for my daily run.

A cloudless blue sky was overhead as I went out onto the streets in my shorts, tee-shirt, and running shoes. Since I had plenty of time, I decided to take a longer run than usual, heading south of town this time. Seven easy miles passed before I was through. I didn't push it, taking it really slow in the last two miles. I felt good when I got back to the house, with my leg muscles all firm and puffy from the exertion.

After I showered and dressed, I went down to a coffee shop where I sometimes met with Buck and some of his buddies. They were a group of old-timers and businessmen who met there every morning except Sunday.

In every small town like ours, groups of locals gather each morning at coffee shops like this one to visit. They talk about the town and solve the problems of the world. During their spirited conversation, they often came up with simple and idealistic solutions to various matters, like what the government should or should not be doing. I sometimes wondered if the ideas they occasionally concocted might not be precisely right on target. It was populist democracy in action.

Today, as usual, they were gathered around two tables pushed together, as they normally did, jabbering away. Buck was already there, getting in his viewpoints as he always did. I sat down with them and the waitress brought me a cup of java.

The world-problem-solving discussion time was over though, and now the old-timers were getting ready to get up and leave. However, before they left the shop, the coffee had to be paid for. To handle that bit of unfinished business they played what they called "the game."

"The game" had three rounds: one to pay for the coffee, one for the tip, and one for the pot. It involved a simple game of chance.

An old man, a sort of dealer, took a paper napkin and secretly wrote a number between one and a hundred on it. Then he hid his chosen number, turning the napkin over on the table. Each other man at the table tried to guess what the number was. The trick was to avoid stating the correct number, so when his turn came, each spoke another number. The object was to try to get some other unlucky player to speak the real number or the number closest to the one on the napkin, and thus lose.

On the first round, if you lost, you had to pay the tab for coffee for everyone. On round two if you lost, you had to pay the tip. But on round three, everybody set a dollar bill on the table. This time if you guessed the secret number or a number closest to the secret number, instead of losing, you won all the money in the pot. If you were very lucky, you could lose on round one and win on round three and just about break even.

Normally, I don't get in on stuff like this. I had learned the hard way not to gamble for money when I was in 'Nam. One night some Marines cleaned me out of a month's pay in a five-card draw game in Da Nang. After that, I swore off gambling for serious money. I guess I'd rather gamble on people, like Jill. But just for fun, today I decided to share the game, as I had on a few other occasions.

"You want in on this?" Buck asked.

"Sure," I laughed. "Why not?"

Round one started. Buck guessed 39. That was the closest number to 40, the correct number, so he had to pay for everyone's coffee. Naturally, he howled and there was a pained expression on his face as the dealer smiled at him and told him of his bad fortune. The other guys just laughed.

"Lady luck not smiling today, Buck?" I asked him. "Yeah," he muttered. It really didn't matter though. He had paid for the coffee many times before.

We moved into round two. The guy on my left lost on his number and winced as he knew he had to pay the tip. He wasn't much happier than Buck had been.

Then we moved on to round three. We all put our bills into a neat pile in the middle of the table. I guessed 52, and, strangely, that combination turned out to be right on the money. The dealer showed me the number, written on the back of his shredded napkin. Then he pushed the stack of dollar bills over to me.

"You win, Mike," he said.

"My lucky day," I said, taking the cash as most of the men

got up to leave.

"Your lucky day," a disgruntled Buck said to me. "Yeah, I guess so. What are you going to do with all the money?"

"I don't know. I'll probably feel better if I give it to some worthy cause, huh?"

He snorted. "How about donating it to the 'Buck Corwin Coffee Fund'? That's a worthy cause, amigo."

"I'm sure it is." I laughed.

He smiled. "Yeah. By the way, where were you around eleven last night? I tried to call you."

I thought back. "I was probably out in the garage with the Cobra."

"You really like that toy car of yours, don't you?"

"Everybody needs a hobby. I heard that from a shrink somewhere."

"Very original. You ever take the Cobra out on the highway anymore?"

"Sometimes. Not much though. It has this nasty habit of drinking gas like it's in cahoots with a fuel refinery somewhere."

He smiled. "Then I know what you can do with that money you won. It's a perfect day for a nice long drive. Why don't you take your winnings, gas up the little sporty car, and head for the hills? A ride like that'd be a freebie, and you need to get out and get some clean mountain air."

I turned the idea over in my mind. It really had been a while since I had taken the Cobra out for a spin up the highway. Today, as beautiful as it was, it looked like the perfect day for it.

"I may do just that. Want to come along?"

"No, but thanks anyway. I'm helping out with the carnival over at the fairgrounds for Amaryllis's club. Ever been to the 'Bear Pitch'?"

"No," I said. "What's that, anyway? Do you throw bears at people or something?"

He chuckled. "Sounds like it, doesn't it? No, we've got this little trailer rig with stuffed toy teddy-bears in the middle, along with a bunch of drinking glasses and junk. They put these little glass saucers on top of all the bears and the drinking glasses. Then the rubes, uh, I mean the customers, toss dimes from behind a railing around the trailer. If your dime lands on a saucer and stays there, you might win a teddy-bear or a glass. Since you're so lucky today, I think you ought to try it."

I grinned. "Just how hard is it to land your dime on one of those glass saucers?"

"It looks easy, but only about one out of twenty-five tosses makes it. It's tougher than it looks. Those dimes add up. We usually net about $500 a day or so for the club."

"My kind of game," I said. "What would I do with one of your teddy-bears if I won it?"

He grinned like he had a sudden wild idea. "You could give it to Tracy. Or you might give it to your young friend Jill. I'm sure she'd appreciate it."

I smiled and shook my head. "Jill might, at that. No, Tracy would want it. She might be just a tad annoyed if I gave it to Jill."

He nodded. "I can understand why she might. She ever say anything to you about Jill?"

I shrugged. "Oh, she knows what I'm doing. But I'm fairly certain she knows who I'm really interested in when it comes to women."

He cocked his head to one side. "What about you, Mike? You sure about who you're interested in?"

It was a good thing we were friends. I had to pause before I replied. "Yes, Buck," I said, "I'm sure."

"Good. Say, I was wondering, after the little mishap we had with Jill on Sunlight Peak, are you still thinking of taking her with us next time, when we go after Eolus?"

"Eolus?" I asked, surprised. "Does that mean you really think I'm finally worthy of such a grand climb, O hallowed mountain guide?"

"It's the next one on the list for you. You looked okay dancing around on that summit block back on Sunlight. I guess I'm ready to chance it with you, if you feel up to it."

I coughed. "As I recall, I wasn't exactly dancing up there on Sunlight, Buck. I was hanging on for dear life."

"I know. But I'll never tell."

I sighed and became more serious. "What about Jill? Do you feel okay about her coming along this time?"

He stiffened and considered it, wrinkling his brow. "That's a whole 'nother matter, old buddy. You remember what happened the last time. Would you trust your life with her on the mountain, if it came down to it?"

Without hesitating I said, "Yes. Buck, you saw the girl too. She's a good climber when she behaves herself."

His eyes narrowed. "But that's the real question, isn't it...will she...behave, and stay away from the funny little pills. In my mind, I'm not so sure."

I rolled my eyes. "I don't know, Buck. I guess we could always search her pack and clothes before we headed out, just to be certain."

"Oh yeah, sure. No, I'm going to ask her one time before we head out if she's going to do it clean or not. One time. If I think she's lying, either she stays at home or I don't go, and that's it. I've had enough shenanigans with your young charity case."

"Then you don't mind her going, if she's in the clear as far as the drugs go?"

He shrugged in resignation. "No, I guess not. You're right about one thing, though. She really is a natural-born climber. I just hope she can do it without chemical assistance from now on."

"She will, Buck," I said, hoping I was right.

At least I had faith that she would. Ever since that debacle on Sunlight Peak, Jill had seemed like a changed woman. I wasn't sure exactly why, but I think it was because Buck and I had talked it over with her. Now she looked up to us with a new light in her eyes. She had been a very good worker at the store ever since that day, too, dependable and knowledgeable in every way. Even Barry admitted that she had turned into a good hand.

"Okay," Buck said. "You set up a climb date with her, let me check it, and we'll see what happens. But you remember..."

I interrupted, "I'll remember, Mr. Hardnose. You just do what you do best, pushing our carcasses up that hill. I bet we'll have a good climb, and a good time, too."

"I hope so," he said.

Then he did something I'd never seen him do before. He reached across the table and took me by my arm. "Mike, you do know why I'm serious about this, don't you?"

I looked down at his hand on my arm. "I think so."

"Heck," he said, "I don't like to come on like General Patton about her, but I want her to stay alive as much as you do. I want us all to come back in one piece, too. I'm getting too old to die on some fool hill just because a young kid does something stupid. I don't want to see you get into something bad either. I'm just tired of the nonsense."

"I know that, Buck."

"Look," he said. "I'm getting older every day. My biology isn't what it used to be. I don't have too many climbing days left for the big hills. I want to knock off a few more of them before I retire from the mountains and start using my old ice axe as a trowel for my garden. I don't mind showing you the way up some of these hills, because you're pretty careful. But I've got to be honest with you, Mike. Sometimes you let your soft-hearted ways cloud your judgment."

I nodded. "Okay, I understand, Buck. Actually, I'm glad you're playing devil's advocate about it. I need to look at it from your angle just to be sure my head's on straight about it."

"Well what I'm telling you is just good common sense, when you boil it all down."

"I agree. But trust me. I think Jill's come around. I'll get with her on the climb dates and let you know."

"Fine. I'll be waiting. Be sure to read up on Eolus good in the guidebooks before we set out. I let that summit block on Sunlight come as a surprise for you just for fun, but we don't want any surprises on this one."

"I've done some reading on Eolus already."

"You've heard of the 'Sidewalk in the Sky', then?"

"Yeah. It's a long ledge connecting Eolus to its companion peak North Eolus. About a hundred yards long and averaging two feet wide on top. It has a drop of some two-hundred feet down one side and about a thousand feet or so down the other. A real near-knife- edge with a kicker if you slip off. The books say to be real cautious on it."

"Those books are right. The 'Sidewalk' will test what you're made of the first time you cross it, for sure."

"Sounds interesting," I said.

"That's one way to describe it. It'll get your blood pumping." He sat back in his chair. "Well, I'd better be going. Got to get that Bear Pitch game going. Are you going to take that little drive I recommended?"

"I think so. You're right. I need to get out of town for a few hours and get some fresh country air. Besides, the Cobra's probably ready for a little highway running."

"What about Tracy. You thinking of taking her along?"

I shook my head. I had already thought that one over. "No," I said. "I'll go solo this time. Just me and the car. I guess maybe I just need to be alone."

"Whatever. See you later." We left the coffee shop together. I went back to my house, had a bite to eat, and went out to the garage.

There she sat, my gray-primered little Cobra. It had indeed been several weeks since I had last taken her out onto the highway, but I knew she was as ready to go as I was. Mechanically, she was tuned as well as I could tune her and all the settings were where they were supposed to be, even on the sometimes finicky eight-barrel carburetor.

I had already made up my mind to take the road they call the "San Juan Skyway" up to Silverton, some 45 miles to the north. A run up the road to Silverton and back would be well worth it today. The green trees of summer and the mountains against the blue sky would make it one of those scenic days you never forget. I could already picture seeing Engineer Mountain's lofty crest on the road beyond.

I got in, turned the ignition key, and heard the familiar satisfying rumble of the pipes. It was almost as if the Cobra was waiting to go, as if she had been cooped up in the garage and in the city for far too long. I buckled the seat harness and checked the gauges. Yes, she would need some gas, I saw.

I backed out of the garage and drove over to a Chevron gas station and filled the big fuel tank. I cleaned the dust off the windscreen and checked the tires.

"Got your Cobra out today I see," Jim, the station attendant said.

"Yeah," I said. "Just thought I'd go out and blow out some of the carbon. Just a little run up to Silverton."

"Watch it, Mike," Jim said. "This being a holiday, the smokies are probably out on 550 thick as fleas on a hound dog. You got a radar detector?"

"No."

"Want to borrow one? I got a good Escort you can take along. Beeps on all the bands."

"No thanks, Jim. I'll watch it."

"Hey, they see that Cobra coming and they'll be laying for you."

"I know. It's happened before. I'm just going to cruise a little."

"Suit yourself."

"Thanks, Jim."

I paid for the gas, got back in, and drove off. There was a lot of traffic on the streets for the Pioneer Day festivities. I wondered how Buck and the "Bear Pitch" were doing. He'd probably tell me later.

I left the north end of town, and the road was stretched out in front of me like a winding ribbon of black. The sky was clear and the mountains were as beautiful as ever. I slipped on a pair of sunglasses and gripped the wheel as I rounded the long curves leading northward.

Surprisingly, the traffic was lighter as I followed the road north along the river. The flat, grassy fields of the flood plain were green as I passed by the little airport, the sailplanes in the field waiting for a tow to the skies. I glanced over at a little waterfall on the hillside off to my left, and headed on up the road toward the Hermosa Cliffs area.

Further on, the steam locomotive of the tourist train came into view, belching out its cloud of black smoke. As it passed, the passengers waved and shouted and I waved back. Everyone was in a good mood today.

I listened to the Cobra's engine as we moved on up the valley. It sounded great, like it was having the best day of its life. In some ways, this seemed to be the best day of my life, too. In spite of my troubles back in Durango, it all seemed to fade away now as the wind raced through my hair with the Cobra growling, the world passing beneath me.

I left the Animas River Valley as the road climbed higher. The river, I knew, cut over to the east now, over into its deep canyon there. The highway ascended up into the mountains, up through the pine and aspen forests. Several undulating miles passed by on the odometer, and I came to the buildings of the little village called Needleton. You could see the tall spires of the Needle mountains several miles away to the east from here. The golden crests of Pigeon and Turret Peaks, steep spires more then 13,000 feet high, scraped the clouds. Mount Eolus was over there too, if you knew where to look, standing tall and forbidding, though somewhat hidden behind the slightly lower summits.

Along the highway here, near Needleton, was where the hikers' trailhead began. From there, you could walk those eleven miles down to the Needleton trailhead by the Animas River. Once again I was glad I had always taken the train to the trailhead. Still, it might be fun to do the hike some day to see what it was like.

Up the highway, on beyond Needleton, was the entrance to the Purgatory Ski Area. Passing by, I glanced up at the ski area, and saw the snowless grassy ski trails cutting through the trees. Memories came back to me, memories of winter days when I had been with friends, carving my way down those beloved crystal-white runs like Nirvana and Styx. Next winter, I would show Tracy those trails. She would come to love them, too.

Ahead of me on the skyline was Engineer Mountain, as beautiful as I had pictured it in my mind. I was feeling more adventurous now, and I urged the Cobra up to a higher speed. She had no trouble, even though we were in thinner air and the slope was getting steeper.

I was in a kind of driver's euphoria. I had passed a few cars along the road, and as I saw Engineer Mountain coming nearer, I began braking for the turn leading to the long, slow, climb full of curves that led to the high pass. I glanced into the rearview mirror and saw a car looming there, far behind me, but closing fast.

At first I thought it might be a highway patrol car. Looking down at the speedometer, I checked to see if I was doing anything illegal. Braking for the winding road ahead, I saw that I was just within the speed limit. Thankfully, I glanced back again at the approaching car, and suddenly I recognized the car.

It was no highway patrol cruiser back there. No, the car was an ebony-black sedan, a GTO. I knew it probably belonged to one man. Jimmy Rowe. And judging from the way it was closing on me, Jimmy had the pedal to the metal.

My pulse quickened. Then I relaxed a bit. Okay, I said to myself, so it's Rowe. He's just out for a drive in the mountains, just like me. He's just enjoying the nice day, just like I was. Maybe even goons like Rowe liked a country drive every now and then. It was a perfect day for cruising the hills, and it's a free country. No reason why we shouldn't be sharing the road together. I'll just let him pass me and then he'll be gone and I can forget about him.

Rowe's GTO came closer and its dark shape filled my rearview mirror. As we came to a long uphill stretch where he could pass me, I slowed down a bit, moving over, thinking he'd pull on around and go by me. But Rowe slowed down too, apparently content to remain a few feet off my bumper, tailgating me. I could see his toothy smile, his taunting eyes; the whole of his menacing face.

Okay, Jimmy boy, I thought, what's the game? You want to hang back there on my tail and try to scare me, go ahead.

That is exactly what he was trying to do. I accelerated, becoming a little concerned, but good old Jimmy stayed close behind me. He was anticipating and following my every move. Then as we headed down a long straight portion of the road, he moved up very close, and I felt his bumper tap mine.

The tap was light, but it was enough to make the hair rise up on the back of my neck. I glared back at him through my mirror. What was the guy trying to do? Then it dawned on me. He had said he would pay me back for the way I had humiliated him. This would be a perfect place for friend Jimmy to try to run me off the road, but I wasn't in the mood to play his game.

The road was clear and there was a slower car, a sedan full of people, ahead of me. I swung over into the left lane and roared up just ahead of the slower car. Rowe followed me. I got just past the sedan, and, carefully avoiding a collision, deftly swung back into the right lane just in front of it. This startled its driver and caused him to honk at me in angry frustration. I couldn't really blame the poor guy, but I had left Jimmy with no room to follow me into the gap.

Rowe eased up beside me. As he pulled even with me I saw his passenger-side electric window rolling down. I expected to see his ugly face, but along with his face with its thin smile, I now saw something else. It was a small-caliber pistol, its one-eyed barrel pointing straight at me.

I floored the gas pedal just as I heard the crack of a shot ring out, and felt a bullet whistling past my head. Now it was all too clear. Jimmy Rowe meant business, and he didn't care whether someone else witnessed what he did or not.

This guy's really crazy, I said to myself in surprised anger.

He's determined to kill me, either with his gun or with his car. And he doesn't care if he takes out another car full of people along with me as he's doing it.

I knew he probably wasn't going to miss with the pistol if he got another chance at a clear shot. I'd just have to figure out a way to get away from him.

The Cobra was very fast, but so was the GTO. I roared off down the mountain road, the GTO close behind. Fortunately, the road was clear as I downshifted for a hard, slow bend at the bottom of a canyon. I stood on the brakes, the tires screaming.

The Cobra's rear tires were now breaking away from the pavement as I rounded the turn. I went into a four-wheel drift, gunning the motor, steering into the slide. I was no practiced race driver, and the drift was clumsy and amateurish, but I kept the steering under control. I straightened the Cobra's nose out and headed up another long stretch of road. After leaving the turn, I expected Jimmy to be far behind me now, but it was clear that he and the GTO had driven at speed before. The big 389 engine underneath his car's black hood was screaming. He soon closed the gap between us again, and he was surging the GTO menacingly, as if to smack it into the back-end of the Cobra again.

A steep cliff with no guard rail was on the side of the road. As I gripped the wheel I was afraid I might go shooting off the edge if he bashed into me just right. That was what Jimmy was hoping for too, I knew. If he didn't succeed in forcing me off the road, he wanted me to panic and drive myself over the cliff. But I stayed glued to the blacktop, swinging this way and that as he skillfully mimiced my evasive maneuvers.

The road was clear on up ahead, and he gunned his accelerator and surged into the left lane. He was a bit quicker than I was in the moment. As his car drew up alongside my rear wheels, without warning he swung the nose of the GTO into my left rear wheel panel, trying to push me off.

There was a grating sound as metal scraped against metal. The Cobra's back-end was pushed toward oblivion. My heart was pounding. My right rear wheel was kicking up gravel inches from the edge, and I fought to maintain traction. Somehow I managed to surge forward again and swing back toward the center of the road.

I couldn't avoid smashing into the GTO's nose, sending his

car weaving this-way-and-that-way. I hoped he'd crash into the hillside or else back off, but he recovered. A moment later, he was right on my tail again, mean as ever. The guy was very good.

Now everything I had ever learned about high-speed driving came into play. I knew it was either this or my life. The curves ahead found me quickly, and I had to pass several slower cars in succession. Their frenzied drivers must have wondered who these two crazy idiots were, racing each other on such a dangerous mountain road.

I dropped the shifter into high gear and gained some distance on him, but Rowe was using every skill at his disposal, too. I was praying now that a highway patrol car would come along and see what was going on. Only they could stop the madness and save me now. I knew that Rowe would not be satisfied until I was dead, either run off the mountainside or else left crashed with a bullet in my head. If he shot me and I went over the edge and crashed at the bottom of some valley, that would do it. It might be a while before they discovered my body. And Jimmy would be long gone.

We topped out over Molas pass, our exhausts blasting noisily as we roared over the high-altitude road. We began the final descent down the winding highway toward Silverton. My fears had condensed into cold anger.

Who was this guy, this hardened piece of low-life, to try to take my life, I thought. All right, Jimmy, I said to myself as I clutched the wheel and downshifted. All right, now I'll play your game. But there are going to be a few new rules.

The road on that stretch down to Silverton follows a rim of rock cut right into the side of the mountain. There is a cliff on the right, several hundred feet above the Animas River below. Of course, there are also numerous curves in the road.

Our two cars passed a startled racing bicyclist, barely avoiding knocking him into the canyon. We headed for the next bend in the road. It was a blind curve with the bend in the oncoming traffic lane hidden by the mountain wall.

Another car, a van, was ahead of me now in my lane, approaching the bend. I quickly weighed the odds as to passing the van.

Only a true idiot would have passed on such a curve, not knowing what might be coming up the road from Silverton. But, praying that another car was not coming up the grade, I cast safety to the winds and quickly swerved over into the left lane as if to pass the van. Jimmy saw the obvious danger of passing, and hesitated to follow me. He was probably wishing I would collide with a semi truck. Instead of going around the van, though, I surprised him by standing hard on the brake pedal.

As the Cobra's huge disc brakes protested, screaming and smoking, I slowed down. I pulled back, even with Rowe's GTO beside me. Glancing over at his window, for a split second I saw the uncomprehending look on his face.

What I had done had been suicidal, and in the brief flash of time it took for him to consider all this, he took his eyes off the road ahead of him to stare at me in unbelief. The van turned around the blind curve, as did I, in the left lane. I knew if a vehicle was coming, I was dead. Jimmy was unnerved, frozen in disbelief and in the sudden array of choices.

In that half-second, his momentary lack of concentration was enough. The speeding black GTO missed the turn entirely, going straight ahead. It was far too late when he finally stabbed his foot at his brakes.

The GTO roared straight off the cliff edge. Like some big, black, metal bird in slow-motion flight, it sailed out into space over the deep canyon.

I whipped the Cobra back over into the right lane, seconds before an oncoming eighteen-wheel semi, air-horn blaring, would have smashed into me. Quickly glancing out to my right, I saw the blur of the GTO arcing slowly downward. It was turning end-over- end now, like a tiny toy car. I stood on the brakes hard. Taking another quick glance, I saw the GTO explode against the rocks far below in a thundering plume of fire and flying splintered metal.

I felt shock coursing through me.

"Gone," I whispered in a shudder, slowing the Cobra, breathing hard.

I pulled the Cobra over, off the road, onto a very narrow parking space. My head was spinning and a wave of nausea seized me.

Shaking like a leaf, with trembling fingers I got the harness unbuckled. I jumped out of the car and looked down toward the river, far below. Yes, he was gone. What had once been the

Jimmy Rowe's muscle car was now a mangled, burning, smoking smudge of black down there on the rust-colored rocks lining the river. I knew Jimmy Rowe would never trouble anyone again.

Other motorists stopped to see what had happened. The excited drivers got out and asked me what had happened. I was too numb to say anything. Through blinking eyes, I saw the white-faced bicyclist we had passed wheel on by, a stunned look on his face. He seemed frozen in bewilderment, frightened, not even bothering to stop.

I was shaking like an aspen leaf. I went back to the Cobra and sat there, drained. My ability to speak slowly returned. When questioned by the other drivers who had stopped, I mumbled to them that it was all a terrible accident, just terrible.

Somebody must have called it in. In a while the highway patrol cops arrived, sirens blaring, red and blue lights flashing everywhere. I got out to meet them. They led me over to the side of the road and I told them who I was, showing them my driver's license, and who I thought the driver of the GTO was. Then I told the cops how Rowe had tried to run me off the road, and more-or-less how he had reached his sad end.

The highway patrolmen detained me a long time, asking all the expected cop-questions, and I answered their questions cooperatively. I told them how I had been verbally threatened by Rowe back in town, but I omitted the details about Cullen over Jill. I didn't want Jill dragged into it. Not yet, anyway. And I wasn't sure I wanted Cullen's name added to the discussion just yet, either.

The cops had me look over the cliff again. I watched in silence as some of the highway patrol cops drove along the river below us on a dirt trail in a blue four-wheel-drive jeep. They made their way to the crash site.

Other patrolmen called in on their car radios. I knew their computers were checking my license ID, and anything else they could dig up on me. They wanted to find out what they could about my story on Rowe.

Then they led me back to one of their black-and-white cruisers, and ushered me into the front seat. I sat in the seat beside another highway patrolman, a sergeant. He seemed to be the one in charge.

The sergeant was a big, burly man with a mustache and horn-rimmed glasses. He was in a bad mood, and was more than a little nervous and suspicious as he regarded me silently for a moment with an air of distaste. Chewing on a toothpick, he looked me squarely in the eyes, measuring me like a good cop will do.

Finally, he said to me, "Okay, we found the guy's body. He was really barbecued down there, as you might imagine. We ID'd the tags on that GTO. They were pretty badly burned, but we got the numbers anyway. We called it in and got the vehicle registration. You were right about his name. James Rowe. Just like you said."

I nodded.

"Do you know who that character was, Mr. Rader?"

I let out a long, strained sigh. "I don't know much about him, officer. I heard he was mixed up with drugs or something, back in Durango."

The sergeant continued to stare at me, biting his toothpick in half. He waited, watching my reactions.

" 'Mixed up' is hardly the phrase I'd use, Mr. Rader. Jimmy Rowe was a serious player in the contraband drug trade around here. I normally have respect for the dead, but I'll make an exception in his case. The world is a better place without him in it. Believe me."

"Oh?"

"Yeah," he said, crushing the remains of his toothpick between his teeth, chewing at the splinters. "But to tell you the truth, I'm...well, I'm still a little puzzled about you, Mr. Rader. How do you fit into all this? We checked you out on the computer records. We know you work at a store in Durango called The Aspen Leaf. Your record's clean. Durango PD has nothing on you that would tie you into the drug trade. That is, unless there's something here you're not telling us."

"I'm clean, sergeant," I said.

"Maybe. The narcs at Durango PD verify that you reported that Rowe was leaning on you, though. But why?"

I decided I'd better give the sergeant more to go on. He was probably going to find out anyway if he kept on looking, which he probably would. I didn't want to be seen as withholding evidence.

"Sergeant," I said, "I have a new employee in my store. Her name's Jill Carpenter. She's an ex-druggie. I, well, I look out for Miss Carpenter. Rowe came to my store trying to get her back on drugs. I more-or-less politely told Rowe to leave her alone. I guess he didn't want to cause a fuss at the store. He backed down, but he threatened me. That's probably why he came after me today."

The sergeant wiped his glasses. "That's all? He tried to kill you over that?"

"That's the truth as far as I know it. He was a pretty brutal and determined fellow. I guess he thought I was interfering in his business. I got in his way, and maybe he thought taking me out would send a warning to others who might interfere in his dealings."

The sergeant looked at me with a hardened, professional gaze. "So he...he tried to kill you over...that? Just because you made him look bad? Seems pretty strange, Mr. Rader. Funny that he should try it with a car, of all things. Usually that kind...well, from what I know, they like to do it less, uh, publicly."

"Yeah, I know," I said. "But look at the two cars involved, sergeant. He had a muscle car, a GTO straight out of the sixties. You see the kind of car I'm driving? Do you know what it is?"

He looked through the windshield at the Cobra. "Of course I know what it is. I've never seen a real Cobra up close till today, but I've heard of them. I've seen pictures. A real hot rod, I'm told."

"It's a pretty fast car, sergeant. Jimmy had a fast GTO. Maybe he not only had a grudge and wanted to kill me, but maybe he wanted to beat my Cobra while he was at it. Guys like that have a lot of pride. Maybe he wanted to take me out in a radical way, a way he'd really remember."

"The man and his car both, huh?"

"Yeah. Something like that. Who really knows what goes on in the mind of a man like that? He seemed pretty twisted. Maybe he saw it as a grudge match between the cars as much as anything else. It'd be sure to make a big spash in the papers. When word got around, it would warn other people to let him alone and not cross him."

He eyed me curiously and shrugged. "You're a regular Sherlock Holmes, aren't you, Rader?"

"It's just a theory."

He tossed the splinters of his toothpick out the window. Then he wrote something on a sheet on the clipboard and set it aside.

"Yeah, interesting theory at that," he said. "Anyway, he lost out."

"That's for certain, sergeant."

He stared coldly at me again, probably still wondering if there was more to my story. I tried to look as if I'd told him everything.

"I may as well tell you, you aren't completely in the clear on this incident, Mr. Rader. From what I've heard from the other witnesses, you yourself were breaking a number of motor vehicle laws in that Cobra of yours during that little race you had with Rowe. You could have killed some other people on the road."

"I was running for my life, sergeant," I said.

"Maybe. Anyway, since none of us cops saw you doing it, and since you were, as you say, running for your life, we aren't going to arrest you. Right now, that is. And, I suppose, since this has resulted in the elimination of one of the nastiest bad guys around, in a way I could call this justifiable homicide, or motorcide, or something. Hell, you've probably done us all a favor. Maybe some judge'll sort it all out; I don't know right now. But all the same, Mr. Rader, I think you'd better stick around Durango. We might have a few more questions to ask you. Don't leave the area. Understand?"

"I don't intend to leave," I said. "I've got a business to run."

"I suggest you do that, and stay away from people like the late Jimmy Rowe."

"That's my plan, sir."

"Good. By the way," he said, suddenly giving me a cold grin, "you know you are one lucky dude. If I'd have been betting, from what I've seen here, I'd have bet that except for a thin piece of luck, you and your cute little Cobra would be down there along with Rowe and that burned-out GTO right now, laid out for the morgue."

"I know," I said. "Just my lucky day, I guess."

"Yeah, real lucky. And another thing, Mr. Rader. Maybe I don't have to tell you this, but the drug trade around here is a lot like the Old West. Revenge is the operative word. You'd better hope Mr. Rowe didn't have any friends who'll want to come after you and even out this score. You get my drift?"

"Perfectly," I said. "I'll watch it."

He relaxed a notch or two. "You okay now?"

"I think so."

He picked up his clipboard again, glanced over it, and laid it aside. "Okay, Mr. Rader. Thanks for you cooperation in the investigation. We're done with you for now. Stay in touch."

So they let me go. I walked over and looked over the edge one last time. The GTO was still down there, but the fire had been put out. The wrecked car was merely a mass of black, smoking metal on the otherwise beautiful river bank.

I drove slowly on down into the village of Silverton, where I got out and I checked the body damage the Cobra had sustained. The back left fender was crumpled in, and the tire in the wheel well had taken a beating where the metal had been scraping against it. The steel tire threads were exposed. They revealed how the rubber had been sliced off by the friction of the knife-like paring action of the metal fender. If the tire had taken worse damage, it might have blown out back there on the cliff road and I might have gone off the edge. Again, the day was just plain lucky.

I always carry a crowbar in the Cobra's trunk. With a few well-placed pulls and bends on the bodywork, I gave the wheel the clearance it needed. Then I changed the tire, putting on the spare.

I knew I could have the bodywork straightened out with a minimum of trouble in a body shop, but the ruined tire would have to be replaced. The rear quarter of the car looked like a mess, but the Cobra was drivable. Considering what it had gone through, it was still good enough to get me back home.

As I prepared to get in and try driving it again, I heard a noise behind me and I looked up. The bicyclist we had startled on the highway was wheeling up next to me.

He was a lanky young fellow, good-looking, with blonde hair and a smile. His arms and legs looked lean but strong from long hours pedaling his racing bike, no doubt. The young man trembled with nervousness as he approached me.

"You...you were one of those guys racing back up there, weren't you?" he asked.

"Yeah," I said. "Sorry you got caught up in that. Who are you, anyway?"

"My name's Darren," he replied. "I was training for a bicycle race on that road. You two almost killed me."

"I know. Like I said, I'm sorry about that. The guy in the GTO didn't leave me much choice back up there. I was trying to get away from him. Did you see what happened to him?"

"Yes, I saw," he said. "I didn't stop, though. I guess I just wanted to get away from it all."

He looked back toward the highway coming down the hill, and shook his head.

"I understand. You all right now?" I asked.

He relaxed. "Yeah, I'm fine," he said with a smile. "I could tell that he was after you and you were just trying to escape from him. I could see he was trying to push you off the road. Do you want me to tell that to the cops or anything?"

I smiled. "No, Darren. Thanks, I appreciate it. Are you sure you're okay?"

He laughed nervously and showed white teeth. "It shook me up, but I'll be all right. What about you, though? You sure you're okay, mister?"

I nodded. "Yeah. I'll make it. My car got dented up but she'll drive."

"Why was that guy trying to do that to you? Why was he after you?"

"It's a long story. I'm sorry it ended the way it did, but it's over now. I'm going home."

"Well," he said, "see you around. But not like that back there again, I hope."

"I hope not either, Darren. Have a safe ride."

I watched him silently pedal his bicycle away. It's strange how the innocent sometimes get caught up in the stupidity of others, and it's always interesting how they react to it. Maybe I'd meet with this young man, Darren, again some day. I hoped so. He seemed like a good kid.

It was getting late in the afternoon in Silverton, and the chilly winds were dusty and promised a cold night. It had been a long time since I had anything to eat, but I had no appetite, even now. The aftershocks of what had happened were starting to sink in on me. I still felt the nausea, but I repressed it.

I slid back into the driver's seat, fired the beast up, and headed back toward Durango. As I passed the spot where Rowe had gone off the road, it was empty and quiet there now, a little eerie. All the cars of the cops and the onlookers were gone. Only a pair of black tire marks heading straight toward the cliff showed where Rowe had made his futile attempt to brake before making his final flight into eternity. Shameful waste of a beautiful GTO, I thought.

I had little remorse for what had become of Rowe. Still, I couldn't help feeling somewhat guilty and sorry for the man. Once he had been someone's little boy, a toddler on someone's knee. Maybe they had good thoughts about his future. Who knew what forces had shaped his young life? Something had instilled that bitterness in him, had turned him into a bully-boy, and then a drug man and a killer. Once, somewhere along the way, someone might have turned him around. But that road was never taken in his life, and now all that was left of him was in a black body bag in some morgue.

Yes, I had feelings of guilt, but not many. Jimmy made his choices, and when it came down to him or me, he was the one who lost. It could just as easily have been me. I drove back home through the hills and the trees in silence, my mind throbbing like a drum, replaying the chase.

The story about the accident was on the car radio when I neared Durango and home. The cops must have given the news people the story that it had just been another fatal traffic accident.

When I got to my house, I went in and slumped into a chair and flipped on the local TV channel. The news was on.

"A fast-driving Durango man was killed this afternoon going off the edge of the road near Silverton," the commentator said. "Going well over the speed limit, the man failed to round a curve and was killed when his car fell into a canyon."

He said nothing about another man, driving a Cobra. That was fine with me. I went to bed.

The next day Barry met me in my office. He had a big grin on his face. "Boss, you know that Rowe guy that came in here the other day making all that noise?"

"Yeah. What about him?"

"He got killed in a car wreck. Went off the road up near Silverton."

"I heard the story. I guess he won't be coming around anymore to bother us."

"I guess not. Are you relieved?"

"Sure."

"Thought you'd be."

"Thanks, Barry."

"Sure, boss," he said, and he went out.

The cops didn't call me with any more questions. I decided I'd phone one of them with a few questions of my own. After work that night I called George Barker. I told him about Rowe, the chase, and the crash.

"I heard the inside scoop on that down at the station," George said. "I thought I told you to stay out of it."

"I was 'out of it', George, at least I thought I was. But Rowe pulled me back into it. Unavoidably. He just made a move on me. I wanted out, but he wouldn't let me stay out."

"And so he died."

"Yeah."

"I'd watch my back, Mike. Dil Cullen won't forget about this, you know. Rowe was a valuable player for him."

"Do you think Dil knows about my part in the accident?"

"You can make book that he knows by now."

"You sure?"

"Of course. He's a pro, Mike. You'd better sleep with one eye open."

"I will," I said. "I've sort of gotten used to doing that. Thanks, George."

I hung up and thought it over. As I sat there, morbid thoughts came to me. I now saw, in my mind's eye, Rowe's body when they got him out of the wreckage of the GTO. His body would have been crumpled and blackened, more a charred cinder than a human body. But in my dark vision I swore I could see his face, smiling from death, staring at me. The blackened lips seemed to whisper, "You, too, will die soon."

I went to bed. Sleep came only after I was too exhausted to think another thought. I tossed and turned all night, haunted even in dreams by the staring face of the man who had been killed that day near Silverton. Even in death, Rowe had the power to frighten me, as did his former employer, who was still very much alive.

Chapter Eleven

Reverend Harry Foster came to visit me the next day at the store. I was a little surprised to see him. As he came into my office, he smiled as I offered him a chair. Harry looked very tired. The creases around his eyes today were more pronounced than usual. I wondered what was on his mind.

"Good to see you, pastor," I said. "How's it going with the church?"

He sighed. "Oh, pretty well, Mike. It could be better though. The summer slump has caught up with us, I suppose."

"What's the 'summer slump'?"

The beginning of a smile tipped the corners of his mouth. "You don't know much about churches do you?"

"I guess not."

"In the summertime, a lot of my parishioners seem to take long vacations from coming to our worship services. These fine summer Sundays we have around here are just right for fishing or camping or otherwise playing hooky from going to church. There are Sundays when I wish I was a Catholic. Unlike Protestants, our Catholic brothers and sisters consider absence from attending worship a sin, so maybe they're a little better about their faithfulness to church."

I laughed. "I've not been a very good example of that either, I'm afraid."

"I know. But you've been away from the church, Mike. You were out in the cold a long time."

"That's true. But if this is confessional time, I'd have to tell you that I'm feeling more and more like becoming one of your Sunday morning regulars."

He smiled and drew closer in his chair. "And why is that?"

"Well, for one thing, I just sense there's something good there in your church I can't find anywhere else. I don't know. Call it cleansing of the soul or something. I just feel like I need it."

"Even on the Sundays when my sermons aren't the greatest?"

"If you'll pardon me for saying so, Harry, your sermons have very little to do with it. To be honest with you, I like your sermons, they're good. But I don't come to church just to hear the orator."

He frowned. "Well that's a backhanded compliment if I ever heard one."

I smiled. "Did I hurt your feelings?"

He grinned. "Heavens, no. Not really. I wish all my people had that attitude. I hate being the determining factor on whether someone attends church; every pastor does. We're only human, you know. Some Sundays we preach a clinker of a sermon. But if it's not 'the orator', as you put it, what does really draw you to church? Being with Tracy?"

I shook my head. "No. Tracy got me coming to your church in the first place, sure. I like sitting next to her. But it's more than that. Something down inside me, I guess."

"What is it, then, if you don't mind my asking?"

I scratched my head. "Harry, even though I haven't been to church in a while, I'm not exactly Biblically illiterate. A long time ago, when I was a kid, they made me read the old Book in Sunday School. I remember reading something there in the Old Testament. Back in the really early days of the Bible times, when those old Hebrews were out there wandering in the wilderness, I recall that they worshipped in a thing called a tabernacle. If memory serves me, it was a big portable tent or something."

"They did, at that."

"Now, the Bible doesn't say much about sermons, or choirs, or hymns back in those days. The big draw was that tabernacle. They came to be close to God there, in a special way, like friend-to-friend. I guess you could say that's what it means to me to go to church. I feel, well, a presence there, a mystery. A good kind of mystery, though. God maybe, I don't really know. All I know is I feel cleansed and better after I've been there. Free."

The minister shook his head. "Wow," he said. "That's amazing. How'd you like to preach a sermon on that at my church some time?"

I laughed out loud, long and hard. "No, I don't think so, Harry. I'll leave the preaching up to you if you don't mind. Besides, if I saw Dil Cullen out there in the congregation, sitting in the front pew where he can be on display as an upstanding citizen, I'm afraid I might preach a sermon we'd all later regret."

Harry smiled and nodded. "Perhaps so. Dil is the reason I came to see you today."

I shuffled uneasily in my chair. "I thought it might be about him. Why come to me about him, now?"

Harry drummed his fingertips on my desk. "You know I'm a retired cop. I still see the boys in blue occasionally. I had breakfast this morning with a local policeman I believe you've met, an officer named George Barker."

"I know him."

"Officer Barker told me about what happened to you yesterday on the way to Silverton."

"He told you about Jimmy Rowe?"

"Yes, God have mercy on the man's soul."

I winced. "You have more faith than I do on that one," I said, with a rasp of bitterness in my voice,

"I know I do. But that's okay. Maybe God can sort it out for him, somewhere out there in eternity."

"God would have to be the one to do it, Harry. He tried to kill me."

"Yes, I know. I'm certainly glad his attempt failed."

"But...you came to see me about Cullen, right?"

"Yes."

"Why?"

"Because I'm afraid that now Dil will be more interested in you than ever. With Jimmy gone, you've no doubt forced him to make some big changes in his plans."

The telephone buzzed and I picked it up, a frown on my brow. Jeannie, my secretary was on the line.

"Yes, Jeannie?"

"Boss, I know you have someone there in your office with you, but a Mr. Dil Cullen is on the phone and he wants to speak with you. Shall I tell him you're busy?"

I looked over at Harry. "No," I said. "Put Mr. Cullen through."

"He's on line two."

I switched on the speakerphone so Harry could hear the conversation. I punched line two's button and cleared my throat. "This is Mike Rader," I said, trying to sound casual and relaxed.

"Mike, Dil Cullen."

"Good morning, Dil. How are you today?"

"I've had better days. I need to talk to you."

"What about, Dil?" I asked calmly. I heard his long sigh through the speaker. "It's about Jimmy Rowe. I heard about what happened with you two on the road to Silverton, and how he got himself killed. I want you to know something. I had nothing to do with that stupid stunt. I just can't understand why he tried to do it. Did you say something that made him come after you that way?"

I hesitated. "I think you know what happened, Dil. He came into my store a few days ago and threatened me. He said if I didn't get out of your way with Jill, I was going to have some massive trouble ahead. You know anything about that?"

I looked at Harry as we waited through a moment of silence. Dil sighed again and spoke. "Oh, I did tell him I was a little frustrated about the situation with Jill. But I certainly didn't tell him to do anything to you about it. I'm just sick that this whole thing has happened."

I cringed. "Yeah, me too, Dil. It didn't have to be this way."

"I just wish he hadn't done it. This has all gotten way out of hand. Listen, I'm rather busy this morning. Could I get together with you today at that coffee bar where we met the last time we talked? We've got to get this sorted out. We don't need bad blood between us. We're adults, for heaven's sake. It should never have come to this. Let's put a stop to it before anything else happens."

I looked at Harry as I turned the proposal over in my mind. "You're right, Dil. Maybe we can work it out. I'm a little busy right now. How about us getting together around four o'clock?"

"That sounds good. I'll see you then."

We hung up and I looked over at Harry. "What do you make of that?"

He shrugged. "Same old Dil, trying to cover himself."

"What do you think he really wants?"

Harry steepled his fingers and mused on it for a moment. "He's probably telling the truth about one thing. He probably does want a truce between the two of you."

"I'm not the one at war, Harry."

"Oh, yes you are. At least, that's the way he sees it. The very fact that you're protecting Jill and giving her your protection and counsel is a threat to him. That's what he sees as your act of 'war', as you put it."

"Harry, Jill's working here at the store by her own choice."

"Yes, but it's a choice you made possible."

"So I'm the one at fault?"

He shook his head. "No, no, of course not. I'm just trying to look at this through Dil's eyes."

I turned and stared out the window. The tourists were milling in the streets. It seemed like there were more of them than ever, more and more coming to Durango. Many of them were escaping into a fantasy of the Old West, far from their urban areas, far from things like the disease of drugs. Well, we've got it here, too, friends, I thought. I remembered Jill, and all the other drug-trapped people like she had once been, using Cullen's merchandise.

"Harry," I said, turning back to him, "yesterday, when I was watching Rowe's car down there at the bottom of the canyon, do you know what I was thinking?

"What?"

"I was wishing it was Cullen down there, along with Jimmy. I wished Cullen was totally erased from the world. Dead meat."

His tired eyes fixed me. "You really do hate him, don't you."

I shook my head. "I don't know about that one. I hate what he's doing, that's for sure, and I hate how he's complicating my life right now. But as for the man himself, no, I don't know if the word 'hate' applies."

"Yet you think killing him would be the answer to your problems?"

I felt his eyes looking into my soul. "Harry, remember back when you were in Chicago, back when you were a cop? Weren't there some days when you wished some of the people you were after would somehow wind up dead?"

"Of course I did. That's human. But don't you see, Mike, the problem here isn't really Dil Cullen, the man. It's what he's thinking, what he's doing."

I felt my anger rise. "What he's thinking and doing are pure evil, Harry. That makes the man himself evil in my book."

Harry sighed. "That may be true. But even a man doing evil things can change. I learned that, too, as a cop. I saw men change. It can happen with some guys. The right word, the right event at the right moment can make the crucial difference. That's what really led me into the ministry, friend. Even the worst of sinners can be changed."

I cocked my head to one side. "Changed? How, Harry? Dil comes to your church most every Sunday. He sits there, looking pious and respectable. He listens to your sermons and you preach it straight. You tell people to clean up their acts. He hears that along with the rest of us. And he lives in this town, too, along with the rest of us. He knows what happens to the people who get on drugs, and he ought to know what he's doing is wrong. So you see, Harry, the way I look at it, he's had every chance in the world to change. But it just hasn't happened. I'm sorry, but I don't share your optimism on him changing into a different kind of man."

Harry leaned forward. "He can change, though, Mike. Weird as it sounds, I still believe it. Maybe the right opportunity just hasn't happened for him yet."

"And what if he doesn't...change? What if he just goes right on poisoning people? How many more lives does he have to ruin?"

Harry sighed and sat back again. "I don't know. But I do know this, and I'm speaking now as your friend. You've got to stop letting this eat away at you. If you stay angry at him, you're letting him control you, don't you see that? You may become just as bad as he is."

I thought of something I had once heard, that little proverb that says, "Be careful who you choose for your enemy, for you will become like him." No, I didn't wish to become a mirror image of Dil Cullen.

"I don't think I'm anything like him, Harry."

"Oh no? We know he can kill, and you killed a man yesterday."

"That was different. It was totally self defense. Yesterday it was either Rowe or me."

"But you did manage to create the conditions leading to his death, Mike. And you seem to show little remorse for doing so. You act glad that he's dead. That certainly seems characteristic of how Dil would feel about the death of an enemy."

I shook my head. "Look, if I have little 'remorse', as you put it, it's because I consider Rowe's demise a good thing for the world. Even you've got to admit, Harry, he was one bad hombre."

He nodded in agreement. "I suppose so. But the one I'm getting worried about now is you, Mike. You've turned cold. This thing between you and Dil is changing you, making you bitter, deadly. Listen, bitterness is an acid that destroys its own bottle. I know that from personal experience. Whether you admit it or not, you're turning into something very nasty. You're not the man I knew before."

"Well," I said, sighing, "you're probably right about that. But for now that's just the way it is. And in spite of what Cullen says about wanting peace between us, I don't believe it for a New York minute."

Harry nodded. "Nor should you. He may just be looking for an opening, a weakness, some opportunity to get at you."

"Okay, Mr. ex-cop. Let's say he just called to cover himself. What do you really think he'll do if I talk with him?"

"It depends on what you two have to say to each other. I would expect him to let this whole matter go for a while. He doesn't know if you mentioned his name to the cops or not when you told them what had happened. He's got to have the appearance of innocence, at least for a while."

"And then what? Does he send out another goon like Rowe to try to kill me?"

"Maybe. But for now I'd say things were safe for you. He can't afford for conditions to get too hot. He has that upstanding citizen image to protect, you know. That image holds his little house of cards together. But in time, things will cool off again, and then you may be vulnerable to danger. It's what lies in the future, down the road, that you've got to worry about."

"So it seems. What do you think I should I tell him when we meet today?"

"Just tell him the truth. Tell him Jimmy tried to kill you and you couldn't help that he went off the road. Dil may buy it. But be careful."

"Oh, I will," I said. "I will."

"Good. I'll keep you in my prayers this afternoon at four o'clock. You may need those prayers."

I smiled. "How well I know."

Harry said goodbye and got up and left me there. What a strange way of looking at the world this ex-cop turned Man of God had, I thought. He knows there is evil out there, but he clings to the hope that people caught up in evil can somehow turn into good people again. I never thought cops let such thoughts cross their minds. But then, Harry was no longer a cop.

On my lunch hour I went over to Ruby's for my guitar lesson. She was very nervous when I came in.

"Can we talk, Mike?"

"Sure," I said. "About my lesson?"

"No, not that. Oh, we'll get to it. But I've heard a rumor about you and I want to check it out."

I had to laugh. "A rumor? Me? Ruby, whatever could you mean? You know I've been living a pretty dull life lately."

She frowned. "Don't clown around with me, Mike. This is serious business. I heard you forced Jimmy Rowe's car off the road and killed him."

I stopped smiling. "Where'd you hear that?"

"From me," another voice said. I turned and looked in the doorway to the hall. It was Jill. "Is it true?" she asked as she joined us.

"Not exactly. Jimmy tried to run me off the road. As a matter of fact, he tried half a dozen times on the highway between here and Silverton. He was driving pretty recklessly, and at one point I just pulled over out of his way and he didn't brake in time. He went over the edge. All I was doing was trying to stay alive, I swear it."

Jill and Ruby stared at me for a long moment. I couldn't tell if they were happy or angry over what had happened. As it turned out, they were more afraid than anything else.

"Well, that may have been the case," Ruby said, "but most of the folks who knew Jimmy think you killed him."

"And they're angry about it?"

Ruby gave me a little smile. "Oh, no, quite the contrary. To them you're like Dorothy in the Wizard of Oz. It's as if you'd killed the Wicked Witch of the East, or whoever she was. Rowe was a bully of the worst kind, and they all despised him. They admire you for what you did."

"Yeah," Jill said, "they talk about you like you're some 1880s gunfighter out of old Durango, shooting the bad guy in a showdown at high noon. I even heard one man say they ought to give you a medal."

I put up my hand. "No," I said. "What they ought to give me is a nice protective custody cell in some prison or safe house far, far away. I have a feeling Dil Cullen may want my head on a platter for what happened."

Jill and Ruby looked at each other. "That's what we're afraid of, too," Ruby said.

"Well," I replied, "I'm not much on being cooped up in a safe house or a prison. And I doubt if Dil is going to try anything foolish in the near future."

"How can you be so sure?" Jill asked.

"Just a hunch."

Ruby frowned. "Mike," she said. "you know he won't let this rest. If the word's out on the street that you nailed his main boy, he'll probably try to get back at you pretty quick. He has to show who's got the power in this town. He'll want to let people know that no one can do that to him and get away with it."

I again shook my head. "No, he's too smart for a quick reactionary hit like that, Ruby. He knows that's just what the cops are looking for, a quick response. In that sense, he's vulnerable. It might be different if he were just some full-time professional criminal out to settle a score."

"But he is a professional criminal, Mike," Jill said.

"Maybe, but Cullen's got those other legitimate businesses and his precious civic image to think of. No, he may try something, but it'll be down the road.

"You think so?" Jill asked.

"I'm banking on it. He may actually get smart and look at it through the eyes of a businessman instead of like a criminal. Maybe he'll see that Jimmy was just a loose cannon, and that revenge against me would not be in his best interests at all. In other words, he may decide to cut his losses and forget the whole matter. He called me this morning and he was all sweet talk and apologies over what had happened. I'm supposed to meet him this afternoon and smoke the peace pipe with him."

"He's called you already?" Jill asked.

"Yeah."

Jill's eyes narrowed as she thought about it. "You said he might think of it like a businessman would instead of a criminal. But there's one other possibility you may have overlooked, Mike."

"What's that?"

"He may be looking at it like...a lover."

Ruby shot Jill a glance. "What?" she asked her daughter.

"Look, Mom, I know Dil better than either of you do. This isn't really about drugs or business or even about revenge. It's about me. It's me he wants."

I considered it. "You may be right, Jill. In which case, I don't think he's ever going to let it alone."

"Why?" Ruby asked.

Jill turned to her. "What he means is that Mike stopped Dil once again from getting to me. Mike's like a wall between Dil and me. Take away that wall, and he thinks he can just come and get at me. And if that's the case, maybe I'm the one who should leave town. That would solve everything."

"No!" I said emphatically.

"Why not?" she demanded. "With me out of the picture, the problem's over."

"No," I repeated slowly. "Like I told you before, there's more at stake in this than just you and me. It's all got to stop, here and now. Cullen doesn't have the right to control your life or anybody else's, just because he wants to. It's just not right and I'm getting tired of it. No, running away isn't the answer. Jill, I've said it before and I'll say it again. You have no reason to give up your life here just because Mr. Big has the hots for you. He's got to learn to back off and leave other people alone."

She crossed her arms and turned away, then looked back to me. "But that doesn't make sense. Can't you see, Mike? You've been a hero long enough. As long as I'm around, you're in danger."

I glanced at Ruby, then back to Jill. "I don't think so. Like I said, he wants, at the very least, a cooling-off period on this whole thing. Right now the last thing he wants is more trouble. No, I say we all just stay put and stay on course."

Jill laughed. "Now who's trying to manipulate my life?"

She had me there. "Okay, okay. But the big difference between me and Dil is that I'm on your side."

She sighed and walked over and hugged me. "Yeah, I guess you are. But what do we do then? I'm so confused about all of this."

And frightened, I thought. "What do we do? We just go on about our business and do what we've planned to do, one day at a time. And for openers, I've got some good news for you. Buck has agreed for you to come along when we climb Mount Eolus."

Her face brightened into a smile. "Eolus? Really?"

"If you still want to go."

"If I...of course I want to go. But only if you really think it's okay if I stay on here in Durango."

"I thought we'd covered that."

"Then when are we going up?"

"That's up to you and your schedule. You've been working Saturdays, subbing in for some of the clerks at the store while they've been out climbing and whatnot. In my book that means you've earned some vacation time. How about you taking off a few days in the middle of next week?"

She laughed. "Do you think the boss'd let me?"

"He might. He knows you've earned the break."

"That's good enough for me. And you said Buck was agreeable to me coming along?"

"Yeah. He came around. But no funny pills on the trip this time."

Jill glanced at her mother. "You can bet on that. Wow, this is crazy, but it's fine with me. Besides, this is probably a good time to get away from all this stupid mess."

"I sort of saw it that way, too," I said. I looked down at my watch.

"Yes, I know," Ruby said, watching me. "You have to be getting back to the store soon and we haven't even started your lesson. Tell you what, all this has made me pretty flustered. I don't think I'd be a very good teacher today anyway. How about if we just take a rain check on it? No charge for today."

"Okay by me," I said. I left them and drove back to the store.

Time passed slowly at the Leaf as I waited for my four o'clock meeting with Cullen. I busied myself at my desk with a new trail guide that had just come out covering the Weminuche Wilderness, the vast area of the San Juan Mountain country in which the Needle Mountains were located.

The trail guide had a section discussing the weather in the wilderness area. The writer said that before heading out on a trip, one should consult the weather maps published in the newspapers and to observe the weather reports on the TV newscasts for some time before heading out. That made a certain degree of good sense.

If you really wanted to be sophisticated about the weather, you could do what Buck did. He had a good computer, and with his online service he could call up a satellite weather map of the

San Juans any time he wanted. He could even zoom in on a small area of the wilderness and see what was happening to a particular mountain range.

The trouble was, between the time you checked any of that and the time you hiked in to your base camp, the capricious mountain weather could turn on you. Still, you tried to play your best odds, so you checked out the weather before you left home.

The major storms that headed for the San Juans usually came down from the Northwestern United States, the Oregon and Washington area. Storm fronts could also boil up out of New Mexico from the Gulf of Mexico. You took all that into account when you made your plans.

I had been watching the TV weather map for several days, and it looked like there would be clear weather ahead next week, unless something broke open. There was a small band of clouds coming down from the northwest, but with any luck, we'd be okay when we set out for Eolus.

Weather can be the bane of the climber, especially one who had only a few precious days in which to get his climbing in. And August weather can be very unpredictable. A few hours of clear weather can suddenly shift and the next thing you knew you'd be battling rain and lightning. You had to understand lightning to stay out of its way.

Back on Jupiter Peak, we had gambled with it, but you didn't ordinarily want to do that. Lightning often strikes the highest exposed object on a mountain, like the summit, a high tree on the timberline, or even a hiker standing alone on an open flat area. But sometimes it broke the rules. It sought you out even if you thought you were safely down out of harm's way. You just had to play your odds as best you could and use your head if the worst came.

I always liked to read what a new guidebook had to say about lightning. You could never learn enough about the subject. The thing nearly all the mountain guidebooks said was that if you were caught in a lightning storm, you should get rid of all metal objects, which attracted the bolts of electricity.

I never carried much in the way of metal except for my ice axe. I could toss that away at almost any time, so I wasn't too worried about that. But I was a tall person, and I had a nagging suspicion that some day, on some peak, I might be the highest point on the hill. And Mr. Lightning Bolt might come visiting. It was one of the few times in life I wished I could make myself shorter.

I flipped through the pages of the guidebook and finally set the book aside. I looked up at the clock on the wall. It said three-thirty. I went out onto the floor of the store and found Barry tending one of the cash registers.

"Barry," I said as he looked up, "I'm taking off for a while. Got to go see a guy."

His eyes were curious. He knew I rarely took off this time of the day. "Anything I ought to know about?"

I was mildly surprised at his undisguised curiosity. "I don't think so. Why?"

"Just a suspicion," he said. "Jeannie said you got a call from Dil Cullen today."

I grinned wryly at him. "My, my. Whatever happened to the rights of telephone privacy?"

"Sorry, Mike, but they don't apply when Dil Cullen calls on you. There's too much at stake. Namely, you. You going to see him now?"

"That's the plan."

"You want me to tag along? Say, keep a little distance, but keep an eye on you?"

"No thanks, Barry," I said. "I don't need a chaperone. What's the matter? You afraid you might have to become the new manager if I turn up missing?"

He smiled thinly. "The thought had crossed my mind. But you know what I mean. I don't want anything to happen to you, guy. I've sort of gotten used to you, and we both know Cullen can play rough. Especially now after what you did to Jimmy Rowe."

So Barry had heard the "rumor" too. "Look, Barry, I didn't kill Rowe. He drove himself off that cliff. It was an accident, plain and simple."

"That's not the way I heard it."

"Are you going to believe me, or whoever told you that crazy story?"

"Oh, I believe you. You know that. But isn't the point that everyone else in Durango thinks you nailed the creep? Even Cullen must think so."

"Cullen knows Jimmy brought it on himself."

"But you were there. He won't let that go, Mike. You know that."

I sighed. "I don't think he wants it causing a problem right now. Bad for his business."

"You really believe that?"

"It fits, Barry. Anything happens to me and everybody points the finger at Cullen. No, he's not going to hurt me. Not now, anyway."

"Then what does he want with you?"

"He just wants to talk things over. Man-to-man, with me. Alone."

"So, you don't want me coming along?"

"No, Barry. But thanks anyway."

"All right, then. It's your funeral."

I was mildly annoyed with Barry, but I knew he was only trying to protect me. I probably would have felt the same way if I were in his shoes. Still, it was good to have him ready to take a stand for me. You didn't see too many folks willing to do that kind of thing these days. Oh sure, I had stood up for Jill, but that was because of Ruby. Maybe that was what real friendship was all about though, I mused. When it gets dark, as they say, that's when the stars come out.

I got to the coffee bar before Cullen arrived and I sat at a table. I ordered a cappucino from the waiter, as I had the time before. I had made sure that I had selected a table far apart from the others who were there. We needed to be alone when we talked.

There was a mild breeze blowing over the deck. I could hear the wind in the pines down on the back streets, softly whispering.

Cullen walked up silently behind me. I sensed his presence there, and his movements were casual. I was glad of that.

"Still staying with the cappucino, I see," he said.

I lazily turned my head and looked up at him. He was dressed in an expensive western-style tan sport coat, with sharp creases in his jeans. He had on a monogrammed white silk shirt, open at the throat, a gold chain necklace there. His shiny lizard-skin cowboy boots looked brand new. The man's eyes were hidden by dark brown lenses, and his white teeth were on display, like piano keys, as he smiled.

"Yeah, cappucino," I said. "I was going to order herbal tea, but I decided to break training again. Sit down, Dil."

The metal chair scraped the tiles as he settled into it. A waiter joined us and Dil ordered a Perrier.

"Well, I guess you've heard the rumors on the street. A lot of people seem to think you took Jimmy out on your little excursion up to Silverton."

"Yeah, I have heard that," I said. "People believe what they want to believe, I guess."

He laughed and sat back in his chair. "I guess they do. How does it feel being made out to be the man who killed Jimmy Rowe?"

"Not that great," I said. "Especially since it's not the truth."

He chuckled softly. "Well, I wouldn't worry too much about it. As long as you and I know the real truth, that's what really counts, wouldn't you say?"

"I guess so, Dil," I said. "But I'd rather all of them believed the facts about what happened."

He laughed again. "Don't people say, 'When the legend is bigger than the truth, go with the legend'? You sure don't like being called a legend, do you?"

I shook my head. "No, I'm no legend, that's for sure. And I don't find the whole idea very funny. Sort of pathetic, actually."

He stopped laughing. "No, I suppose it's not all that funny. Jimmy was a wild one, but he was still a man, and in some ways a pretty good man. I guess we shouldn't laugh at the expense of the dead."

"No. And there's more to the rumor, of course."

"What do you mean?"

"A couple of folks have speculated that Jimmy's boss might be thinking of making up for his loss by taking me out."

Dil stared at me. "Well, I hope you're not thinking that. Sure, I liked Jimmy. He was a useful resource to me. But I'd never do anything like that. Oh, when I first heard about it, I was shocked, as anyone in my position would be. But Mike, I know that you were the...the victim...in that little fracas. At least I think you were, weren't you?"

"From my standpoint, it sure felt like it at the time. I didn't want it to end the way it did. But Jimmy was the aggressor. I just pulled out of his way. He was the one who did himself in."

Dil nodded. "Then the way I see it, you're blameless."

At least he sounded convincing. I wondered what his angle was.

The waiter brought him his glass and bottle of Perrier. Dil took it, poured his glass full, and set it on the table. He was one cool fellow. The thing I couldn't get over was how well he was playing it.

"Dil," I said, "You mentioned blame. In all honesty, I don't know if I was absolutely blameless. Jimmy was mad at me at the time, let's be real about that. But he had to prove he could force his point. That's what really did him in."

Dil sipped at his glass, removing the lemon resting on the edge and putting it into an ash tray.

"I hate these lemons," he said. He looked up at me again. "I guess you're right. And I guess that's what we need to talk about."

"Maybe we do."

He pushed the glass away and took out his schedule book. He flipped it open.

"You see this? It's full of appointments. Things to do, people to see, meetings to attend."

"I see it. What's the point?."

He put the little book back into his coat pocket. "The point is this - - I've got a million things to do, Mike. I'm always busy. I don't need any intrigue going on in my life. I run a big string of businesses, you know that. And right now I'm on the ropes with some of the guys who are backing me on my real estate developments."

"Bad, huh?"

"It could be better. Property sales aren't moving quite fast enough. And I'm, well, a little over-extended at the moment. In my business, everything hinges on investor confidence. This matter about Jimmy and you and me isn't good for making my investors feel very confident about things. It needs to fade away quickly."

If he was telling me the truth, I knew he was right. I had been counting on that investor pressure to countervail and take the heat off me.

"Why tell me this, Dil?"

His lips broke into a smile. "You don't get it, do you?"

"No, I guess I've missed something."

"Mike, this may sound crazy, but I need your help."

"You want...my help?"

"That's right, guy. Look, I know we've had our differences over Jill. But I also know you're a smart man. There comes a time in any business when you've got to eat a little crow and work it out with somebody with whom you haven't been on the best of terms. What I mean is that I want to bury the hatchet and just let everything that's happened up till now be forgotten. This may sound a little crazy, coming from me, but I really want us to be, well, hell, to be friends. It would be good for both of us. We've got to have some peace. Oh, I know it's good business to do it that way, but I suspect you want that, too. Or don't you?"

"Sure I want it. But what about the matter of Jill?"

He took a long drink from his glass. "You still don't want me around her, do you?"

"That's the general idea."

He scratched his head. "Mike, I just don't understand that. I mean her no harm."

"That's not the way I see it, Dil."

He bit his lip as he stared at me from behind those shady brown lenses. "All right. I know when to ease up. You've got the leverage on this one. Jill's in your camp, so to speak. Let's just not talk about it. I concede the point."

I had to laugh inwardly. 'Concede the point'? I thought. Is that how you see her, just a 'point'? Not a person, just another point in the game?

"If you say so," I said dryly.

"Hey, look at the big picture," he continued. "Let's think about the larger issues here. As I said, I've got a lot of businesses to look after. It's my whole life, man. I can't let a bunch of rumors threaten that. My family, all my people, everything I've worked to build up here in Durango, it all hinges on how people look up to me. I can't afford to mess all that up, Mike."

I waited a moment. "You're saying there's a chance you could lose all your businesses?"

He frowned and took off his glasses, cleaning them with the cloth napkin. "Well, my bankers aren't very friendly these days. It was getting pretty tight for me before, with sales drying up, before Jimmy took his run at you. I can see now that Jimmy wasn't all I'd hoped he would be."

"That's an understatement," I said.

"All right. So he was the bad apple in my apple barrel, so-to-speak. When people found out about him in the papers, naturally his name got connected to mine. That doesn't help my image. Or that of my operations, either. And with people thinking you did the town a favor by getting rid of him, all I need now is everybody saying I'm having some kind of ongoing quarrel with you. You see what I mean? I have no choice. I've got to come to terms with you, Mike. Terms of real peace. Like I said, it's in my best interests, and probably yours, too, in the long run."

If Cullen was being straight with me, this was the best news I had received all day. It all made sense.

"Okay," I said. "What can I do to...help?"

He downed the rest of his Perrier. "Good question. I've thought about it. Look. This may sound absolutely crazy, but once before I talked to you about coming to work for me. I'm making you the same offer now. I'll even give you Jimmy's old job, going around and making sure the contractors are coming through with their jobs on time. I'll pay you three times what you're making now at your store. What do you say?"

I was mildly stunned. "That's quite an offer. I'd have to think about it," I said.

"So think. I'm dead serious. It's important to me."

"But Dil, what about the...the other things...Jimmy did for you?"

He frowned. "You mean all that stuff about drugs? Mike, I guess I was misinformed about Jimmy. Jimmy apparently did have some kind of illegal drug business going on the side. But it was strictly something he was doing on his own. He hid it all from me, and I didn't have anything to do with it. Hell, I swear, I didn't know about it. I guess that's how those rumors got started connecting me and the drug business...through Jimmy. And you can rest assured that part of his work ain't in the job description for the position I'm offering you."

I tried my best to act as if I were taking it seriously. "Well, it's a lot of money. Let me think it over," I said.

"That's okay," he said. "Listen, though. Normally I keep my job recruiting confidential, but would you have a problem if I told some people I know that I've made you this offer? I'd like them to know that you're considering it."

I laughed. "That'd really make it look like we'd kissed and made up, huh?"

He smiled. "You're downright perceptive. Look, I'm past pride at this point though, Bucko. I'm sweating, and an arrangement like this might help me a lot, and make you a little richer in the process. Yeah, that's the story I want folks to hear. It would at least show that we're not exactly at each other's throats anymore. Is that too much to ask? Mike, a lot of good people who work for me are depending on me. If I go down, they and their families will suffer."

I nodded. "I guess it's not too much to ask, Dil. Maybe it really would put a stop to some of the hogwash people are bantering about these days. That would be good for both of us."

"That's the plan. Good. You think it over. Just call me when you've made a decision on it."

"Give me a little time. I'll tell you my decision."

He got up. "And Mike, look." He sighed deeply. "Again, about Jill. Don't sweat that one, either. Like I promised, I'll ease up. I may not want to, because she's such a fine kid. But even though I know how you feel about me and her, your feelings may change in time. You just need to get to know me better. I'm not such a bad guy. If we were working together, I'm confident that you'd come to see it that way."

"Maybe so," I said. "Maybe so."

He seemed satisfied with the way I took it. "By the way," he said. "Do you like going to our church?"

I was surprised he'd mentioned that. "It's a good church, Dil. Yes, I like it."

"We love that church. And I like Harry Foster, too. I'm glad you've been coming there. Maybe I'll see you there Sunday."

"You probably will, Dil," I said. Then I added, "Harry's sermons have a lot to say to guys like you and me."

He gave me a quick second look, then chuckled as he turned and left. I watched him go over to the cashier. He paid for our tabs and left the coffee bar quickly. I was alone in the afternoon breeze.

Dil's words had caught me completely off guard. Of course, that was his style, and it probably worked in his negotiations most of the time.

A job offer, of all things, I mused. A real temptation to sweeten things between us. I couldn't help fantasizing just a bit about what a salary three times my current one could mean.

Oh, man, he had found my greed button. In a different place in time, with different circumstances, I would have jumped at the chance for such a high-paying job. But that little yellow caution light in the back of my brain was winking on and off.

The guy is using you, testing you, I thought. And he really knows how to get to you, too. The bait was good. New clothes, money in the bank, and all the rest. It all was very tempting. Too tempting.

I left the coffee bar and went back to the store. The Aspen Leaf was nearing closing time when I got back to my office. Barry couldn't restrain his impatience to talk to me.

"Well, I see you're still in one piece. No broken kneecaps or anything. How'd it go with the bogeyman?"

"Real peaceable," I said. "Almost too good. Guess what? He even offered me a job in his outfit."

Barry's mouth fell open. "He what?"

"He wants me to have Rowe's old job. Imagine that."

I told him about the conversation, and Barry swallowed hard as he listened, his eyes wide.

"That's a lot of money, Mike. So...are you going to take him up on it?"

I laughed. "You'd like that, wouldn't you. After all, you'd probably get to move up and be the manager here. Oh, I could try to muddy the water with the owners about you and they might go looking for somebody else. But for the right kickback I'd put in a good word for you, Barry."

"You idiot," he said, shaking his head. "Come on, what are you going to do about his job offer?"

"I told the man I'd think it over. No harm in that."

He glowered at me. "But you're not serious, are you?"

"The bucks do look good, Barry. Three times what I'm making here would pay off a lot of back bills. I might even get the Cobra painted."

"But, Mike!"

I grinned broadly. "Oh, hang on to your hat, Barry. I know what you're thinking. But I told the man I'd consider his offer, and I intend to do it. Let's just leave it at that."

He got up, and without another word, walked out. I knew he was angry with me, but maybe that was okay. Barry would tell other people what had happened. Now the rumor of peace between me and Cullen would spread. Maybe folks would ease off about the trouble between me and Dil. They'd think I was a rat, of course, but that wasn't my major concern. I simply wanted the whole mess to cool down.

We closed the store at six and I called Tracy. She said we could eat at her house that evening. It was my turn to cook again.

Chapter Twelve

Cooking dinner that evening at Tracy's, I decided to be a bit creative. I made a stir-fry dish with marinated strips of beef and vegetables. It turned out a lot better than I had expected.

A lot of good cooking depends on the meat you get, of course. I had discovered a good little meat market over on the road from Durango to Bayfield, and I kept the meat in a rented frozen food locker in town.

We sat at the table and enjoyed the quiet of the evening as we ate. Tonight Tracy had dressed up a bit, wearing a beautiful blue silk blouse over her white skirt. Her hair looked lovely, framing her face, and there was scent of soft perfume and woman in the air. Her eyes seemed deeper, wider than ever before tonight, holding a special glow.

The room was quiet as we ate together. She had placed candles on the table and turned the lamps low. Outside now, a soft rain began to fall.

I looked around at the wood-paneled walls and cabinets of her dining room, noting her touches of elegance. The mind and imagination of the creative photographer showed there, in the little details. They revealed that the person who lived here valued beauty, the kind of beauty a lot of people do not normally see.

Tracy put down her fork and dabbed her napkin to her lips. "If you ever decide to give up working in an outdoor store, you could probably get a job as a chef somewhere," she said. "This stir-fry is fantastic."

"Thanks," I said, "I'm glad it turned out good. It's a recipe I picked up down in Texas from an oriental friend, a refugee from Viet Nam. Anyway, I'm glad you approve. If I ever bomb out in selling outdoor stuff, maybe I could get a job in a Chinese restaurant."

An easy smile played at the corners of her lips. "Have you ever been to China?"

"No. When I was in Nam, China was the last place I wanted to go. Why, have you?"

"Yes. It's a beautiful country. I went on a photo expedition there a few years ago. The people are lovely, especially the children. Maybe we could go there sometime."

I looked at her face, her eyes. "Would you be my tour guide, Tracy?"

Merrily, she said, "I'd guide you anywhere."

"Anywhere? I may take you up on that."

She smiled and said nothing. Her mood was drawing me in, more and more.

After dinner we washed the dishes, put them away, and then we returned to the living room. She showed me some of the photographs she had been taking lately, pulling them from a large brown portfolio.

Tracy had a little makeshift darkroom in her house, but she only used it for her black-and-white test prints. If a scene looked good, she'd consider it for her color work with her Hasselblad or her Canon 35mms. Once she had narrowed her choices, she did her serious work with these, sometimes using an original or sometimes going back and re-shooting a scene.

When she had selected the best of her good color negatives for the "finalprints," as she called them, she sent the film strips to a professional color lab back in New York City run by one of her friends. Tracy knew how to do color enlargements and how to develop and work with color film, but it was rather complex and tedious getting everything to work right with her enlarger and all the chemicals and light settings, so she didn't often deal with it in her home lab. She wrote down explicit and detailed instructions on how she wanted each of the prints to look when they came out, and then sent her edict along with her film to the lab guy. He was a good collaborator, she said, and he knew her nuances, wants and dislikes. Her prints normally came back to her looking just the way she expected.

The current prints she laid out on the coffee table before me were of the wilderness waterfall on the shoot we had made together. I was captivated by the pictures. Once again, I noted that she saw things I had missed when we were out at the shooting site. These subtle details showed up in her creations. The pictures had a haunted spell to them, somewhat mythological, like a scene out of a barely remembered dream. Shafts of light bent through the cascading water, catching crystalline gleams against the gray rocks and the green leaves of the trees.

"The scenes look even better than when we were up there, Tracy," I said. "It's like magic."

"It's the light, of course, as always. But the right filters and the right development work can help create the magic, too," she said. "When I'm out in the wilderness, I'm in two worlds. I'm thinking of how a scene looks in nature, and at the same time I'm thinking of what my friend in New York can do to enhance it. Darkroom work is sometimes even more important than the actual shoot. The result is usually a combination of both visions."

"Sort of like a being movie director. You edit the movie film after all the shooting into the movie you want."

"Something like that."

There really was a certain fluid poetry to the photographs, that haunted quality. I could almost hear music in the pictures, soft strains of mysterious harmony from some faraway musician, playing out his almost-hidden tunes. The waterfall seemed to be alive and flowing in the pictures. Tracy was pleased that I liked them. Her smile broadened in approval as I studied them at length.

I set them aside and pulled her closer. Her body was warm, gentle, but full of strength. "So the final key is in...the developing, huh?"

"You might say that."

"It makes me think...do you think we're developing right, lady? Is what we're creating between us coming out right? I feel some magic of our own happening tonight."

She gave me a conspiratorial wink and moved closer, brushing her hair against my cheek. The warmth of the curves of her body through her silk blouse seemed to flow toward me.

"Maybe so", she said. "You know, in the development stage, you have to get the chemistry just right if you want something beautiful to happen when the picture comes true."

I kissed her, my mouth covering hers hungrily. She pressed her warm, open lips to mine, and she moved sensuously against me.

"The right development takes a little time, though," she whispered, "you've got to go slow, and move with care and patience."

"Time, for once, we've got, my beautiful lady."

And we took that time, as the dance of desire and warmth swirled around us and clouded our senses.

"I love you so much," she whispered, her fingertips brushing my cheek.

"And I love you, sweet one."

I ran my fingers through her hair. Love carried us on its slow, confident sojourn, down a river of souls who were not lost, but had found another, and had found new life in the journey. The waves and swells of the river pulled us under, over the flowing steam, down some mountain valley into bright grassy meadows of the heart. The warm waters of love seemed to bathe our togetherness, to drown us, and yet to raise us up high, to give us back our breath of life. Our spirits were aglow with the fire, yet we restrained and tamed the fire, savoring the joy. It was good.

Much later, holding each other near, we sat back against the couch, our arms entwined, our breathing now easier. The soft rain continued to fall outside, the droplets pattering against the window pane. I glanced down at her face. The lamplight was golden on her velvet-soft skin. Her fingertips were slowly stroking my hand.

"I feel so close to you tonight," she said. "It's like I've finally shut the last page of the chapter on my past, Mike. All that pain is gone now."

"I know," I said. "I can tell."

"How about you? Are you still fighting your demons of the past?"

"I think I must have closed my own chapter on them some time back. All I want to do now is spend my life with you."

She smiled up at me lazily through half-closed lids. "I guess that means we're serious about this, huh?"

"Yeah, I guess so," I whispered, kissing her brow.

"I love being together with you. Sometimes I need your nearness so much. I want to ask you something. I feel so alive when you're with me, like I can see and feel so much more than I do on my own. It has an effect on my picture-taking. Would you go out on another shoot with me tomorrow? I want to take some shots up near Ouray, and I'd like you to be with me."

I hugged her and laughed. "You don't really need any help with your pictures, Tracy. They're beautiful any way you take them."

"Maybe, but I'd love having you along with me. Do you think you can go?"

"I think I can swing it. Let me call Barry."

The phone was on the end table, and when I called him Barry

said he'd watch the store, to go ahead and get away. I hung up and looked at the time. It was late.

"You want to go to the Ouray area, huh?" I said. "If that's the case we'd better get an early start."

"I was thinking the same thing."

"I guess I'd better go then."

The smile in her eyes contained a sensuous flame. "Can you wait a while longer?"

"Yes. Yes, I can."

So I stayed another hour. And I was glad I did.

I drove home later, and I felt more relaxed than I had in weeks. Maybe it was the way the evening had gone for us. Or, I thought more circumspectly now, maybe it was the fact that Cullen didn't seem like a threat anymore. More than likely, though, it was the knowledge that this wonderful, natural closeness with Tracy had grown so much between us.

Home, as I lay in bed, I wished she was with me. Her laughter and her smile were pulling at me, bringing me home again to myself. I did want her near me all the time now, and the time was coming when I would have to make that a reality. We'd have to have a visit with Harry Foster down at the church. I whispered her name as I fell into sleep.

At six the next morning, I returned to her house, and we left together in her Suburban. She was cheery and anxious to go to work and play with the mountains and the dancing sunlight she loved.

She wanted me to drive this time, so she could load her cameras and get the gear ready. Along with her cameras and gear, she had packed a picnic lunch for us and brought along a thermos of coffee. Stopping at the donut shop, I bought a half-dozen donuts and we ate them as we drove out of town, up along the Animas River Valley toward Silverton.

The morning light made the mountains come alive, and several times Tracy resisted the urge to have me stop for a picture. It was tempting to her, but she knew she wanted to get to the Ouray area in time for the mid-morning light to be just right. So we drove on.

When we passed along the highway near Silverton, we came near the place where Jimmy Rowe's GTO had made its death flight off into space. The expression on my face changed from happy to somber. I told her again about Rowe and the chase. I slowed down.

"There's where it happened," I told her, pointing to the edge of the road.

She looked out the car window down at the tire marks, then at the cliff edge, and she shuddered. "That must have been a nightmare," she said.

"That's an understatement," I replied, trying vainly to see if I could spot the wreck from where we were, here so far from the valley below. It was impossible, of course. We would have had to stop the Suburban and get out, and we wanted no delays now.

I told her about my conversation with Cullen, and how he had wanted a truce. I told her about how he had even offered me a job, and had said he would stay away from Jill. She was glad that Dil and I had buried the hatchet. Now we could get on with our lives.

I drove on down the mountain and passed Silverton. Then we turned north and went on up through stands of trees into the higher highway elevations toward Ouray.

The mountain scenery became even more wondrous as we went along, evoking visions of the Swiss Alps. We passed by waterfalls and old mine buildings. High, gray granite summits were all around us.

We topped out on Red Mountain Pass and started our way down the winding staircase of a road that leads to Ouray. The highway there is quite spectacular as it clings precipitously to the mountainside above an incredibly deep and dangerous-looking canyon. The road passes by avalanche chutes, some covered, some not, and you look for falling rocks from above and on the road surface. A driver has to be attentive.

I thought we were going on down into the town of Ouray, but Tracy had other plans. A mile or two before we got to the town, Tracy had me slow down and take a forest service road off to the west.

"Where are we headed?" I asked.

"Yankee Boy Basin," she replied. "Ever heard of it?"

Indeed I had. Yankee Boy Basin was well known to climbers. That was where the trailhead to another rather famous Fourteener named Mount Sneffles was located.

Sneffles was often photographed from a few miles to the

north, beyond Ouray, out in the flatter country in an area called the Dallas Divide. The beautiful image of the Sneffles mountain massif, taken from the northern vantage point, often graced calendars and coffee- table photo books about Colorado. In many ways, it symbolized the grandeur that was high Colorado. I had yet to climb Mount Sneffles, but it was on my list for a summit attempt some day in the future.

The gravel road entered the forest of pine and aspen. Then it narrowed. It began a long ascent up a valley, along a rim-rock mountainside trail, where the bed for the road had been blasted out of the rock. There was a deep canyon hundreds of feet below us on our left, and without a guard rail, you had to drive very carefully. Your heightened adrenaline now reminded you how close the cliff- edge was. Fainthearted drivers must have found the drive here overwhelming.

In one place, the rock wall overhung the road like a half-tunnel. I prayed as the Suburban made it on through the narrow overhang section. I had a strange fear that though the rocks above us looked unmovable, they might yet fall on us. It was the sort of feeling you might have if you had to walk beside a sleeping dragon, trying not to awaken it. Some day that overhang would fall. I hoped it wouldn't be today. The uneven rocky floor was wet there as water from underground springs seeped down from the overhang. We passed through slowly.

"Nervous, Mike?" Tracy asked.

"Uh-huh," I said.

"Relax," she said.

"I'm trying."

On beyond the overhang, the road became steeper and I dropped the transmission down into four-wheel. We climbed the gravel road further, the engine groaning in protest, and finally we topped out into the alpine meadows of Yankee Boy Basin. I parked on a level spot where the bare rock gleamed.

"That was some road," I said.

"I'll say. It does tend to give you white knuckles on the steering wheel, doesn't it? I didn't think it would be that hard getting up here."

"I'd hate to drive it in a storm."

"Yeah. It's exciting enough in good weather."

We got out of the Suburban. Yankee Boy Basin was a wide,

grassy, horseshoe-shaped valley surrounded on all sides by the high peaks. The wildflowers bloomed in the rolling green-grass meadows, between mounded, rocky formations and little lakes. There were a few mine cabins here, and a hiker's trail led to the northwest. Mount Sneffles crowned the chain of the mountain walls to the north.

Tracy hardly knew where to begin with her picture-taking. The sky was clear and blue and her light was right. She set up her tripod and began taking her shots while I carried the camera bags for her.

"Oh, this place is lovelier than I had imagined," she said gleefully.

"That it is," I said, stirred by the beauty all around us.

After shooting a couple of rolls with the Hasselblad, Tracy put the lens cover on it and picked it up with the tripod still attached. We took the hiker's trail on up toward the direction of Sneffles.

We were at high altitude here, and I could tell. Breathing required a greater effort than back in Durango.

We walked for a mile across the rocky, tundra-like landscape as I looked up at the summits, concentrating my attention on the big mountain.

Sneffles was named after the fictional "Mount Snaefel" in Jules Verne's famous turn-of-the-century novel Journey to the Center of the Earth. The early explorers to Yankee Boy Basin thought the landscape and the mountain looked like they had come straight out of the novelist's description.

I remembered from the guidebooks where the climbing route up Sneffles was located. I saw the steep rocky gully that led to a saddle from where you made the final ascent up a narrow, sometimes snow-filled couloir. I could see snow in the couloir today. Tracy saw my longing gaze.

"You aren't going to climb it today, are you?" she asked.

"Not today," I said, smiling. "It's a temptation, but I haven't got the time or the equipment. From the looks of the snow up there in the high couloir, I might need a partner and a rope. One of these days I'll come back here for it, though."

"You and your climbing," she said.

I laughed. "Do you disapprove?"

"No. As a matter of fact, I'd like to tag along on one of your trips some time. I wouldn't want to climb, though, just see what it's like to be in your base camp."

"We might work that out. Buck and I are going back up to try to do Mount Eolus with Jill in a few days. What about coming along on the hike in?"

"Yes, I'd like that," she said. "Do you think I'm in shape for it?"

I couldn't resist. "Don't ask me to comment on your shape, Tracy."

She made a face. "You know what I mean."

"Yes, I do. And yes, you're fit enough to hike into Chicago Basin. I can tell that from the way you're moving here today."

"Good. We'll see, then."

She took more pictures. As I sat on a rock nearby, waiting and watching, two tired-looking climbers came down the stone-filled gully from Sneffles. I called out to them and they came nearer. They were noisily breathing deeply of the thicker air down at our lower elevation.

One of them was a stocky-looking, friendly man with glasses. His companion looked a bit older, and he wore glasses as well. The second man had an air of quiet steadiness to him that let you know he was mentally very tough indeed.

From their bearing and from the looks of their equipment, you could tell that the men were veterans of the Colorado highlands. They looked like they had climbed many mountains together.

"You guys go all the way to the top?" I asked when they were close to us.

"Yeah," the stocky man said, unstrapping his red daypack and setting it on the ground as he took a drink of water from his canteen.

"We've done old Sneffles before," he said. "We've done all the Fourteeners, but Sneffles is special. The view from up on top is the one of best I've ever seen." "You feel so blessed to be up there," he continued. "You can see most of the San Juans from the summit. We spent a half an hour just naming mountains we've done and remembering those climbs we made together."

"Where are you fellows from?" I asked.

The stocky man smiled. "We're actually scientists. We work down in New Mexico, at Los Alamos."

"At the National Laboratory?"

"Yeah. We love to come up here though. It's good to get away from the lab and do a peak or two. It clears your head. The lab gets to you some times."

"How was your climb up Sneffles today?"

"It wasn't bad. The fun part is that snow-filled couloir up there on the southeast side. It has a little character. I was glad we had a rope along today. We heard that some kid slipped on the snow up there in that couloir last year and got himself killed. Poor kid, if he'd been on a rope it probably wouldn't have happened."

"Then I'm glad you two had a rope," I said.

The stocky man smiled. "Standard equipment. We always take a rope along on something like Sneffles. It's the only way, fellow, unless you're looking to cash it in."

The climbers looked over at Tracy, who was busy with her tripod and camera.

"Your friend looks like she's serious about her photography," the stocky man said. "This is a great place for picture taking, isn't it?"

"I'm not sure you could find a better place," I said, looking around at the scenery.

"You're so right. Well, we'd better move on down. We're ready for a hot soak in the springs back in Ouray after that little hill. We've done things with a lot more challenge, but Sneffles was still a nice outing."

I nodded. "I do a little climbing, too. Maybe we'll meet on a mountain one of these days."

The man smiled. "Maybe we will. You usually meet some pretty good folks climbing. We've spent some of the best days of our lives in these hills. And we've got a few more to do before we're through."

He slowly turned to his partner. "Right, Bob?"

The older climber smiled. His eyes looked wise, as if he were thinking of something distant, something far away. "Oh, probably so, Chuck," he said softly. "If my legs keep on holding together."

The stocky one grinned at me and winked as he lifted his red daypack to his arms. "Don't let him fool you. Bob can outwalk and outclimb anyone half his age. He's the best climbing partner a man could ever have. He's as tough a climber as you'll ever meet."

"I believe you," I said. "Enjoy your soak down there in that hot tub. Like I said, maybe I'll see you again one of these days."

The stocky one nodded to me and smiled again. Then, as if an afterthought, he waved goodbye to me, and they started on their way.

There was something about them that made me think of that word: legend. The two climbers trudged on down the pathway together. They were like ancient warriors going home from a victory. Then they disappeared, lost in the turns and folds of the mountain trail, and the soft wind blew on my face.

I wished I had been with them on their climb. Even in the chance moment we had shared together, I could tell that these were my kind of men: tough, adventurous, and genuinely friendly. What tales of the mountains they could probably tell. What a blessing of freedom they had enjoyed. They would carry those memories with them long after their last campfires had died away.

I walked over to Tracy. She was putting the cap back on her camera lens. She had watched them go.

"I'd forgotten that," she said.

"Forgotten what?"

"I heard what the man said about that boy getting killed on Sneffles. It was in the papers. I'd almost forgotten that people sometimes do actually die in these mountains. I just push the thought of such danger from my mind when I think about you and your climbing. Sometimes I forget how dangerous it can be."

I shrugged. "Oh, it can be dangerous, Tracy. But if you're smart you minimize the dangers any way you can, just like in anything else in life. You're probably more at risk in your car on the highway approaching a climb than you are on the mountain itself."

"If you say so," she said. "Are you getting hungry yet?"

Time was moving toward lunchtime now. "Yeah. Have you got all the pictures you want here?"

"I've taken enough for today. This may sound a little crazy, but I'd love to be back here with the camera when a storm is blowing through. I can just imagine the fog swirling around these summits and the clouds that would pass low over the basin. It would be a wonderfully dramatic scene in a color print."

I chuckled. "It is beautiful, in a way, but you can have it in a storm. When it's blowing a gale up here it can be like hell on earth, believe me. I'd just as soon be down in some place like Ouray snug in a cabin or something."

Her teasing laughter was in her eyes. "Well, I'm surprised. Where's your spirit of adventure?"

"Call me a sunshine climber. You can have all the mountain storms you want. Just don't include me."

"It'd still make for some great pictures, Mike."

"For you, maybe. But not for me. I've been in storms like that. They can take the fun factor away in a hurry. Anyway, let's get back to the car. I'm starting to get hungry."

We made our way across the rocky hiker's trail over the up-and-down land folds, and about an hour later we were back at the Suburban. Tracy laid out the food and drinks on a big rock and we ate sandwiches and enjoyed the view. My mind was here with her, but occasionally it would drift elsewhere.

She looked again at the mountains, the sky, the wildflowers. "I wish I could just bottle this day and carry it with me all the time," she said. "On a cloudy day I'd just uncork the bottle and here I'd be, with you in the sunshine with these gorgeous mountains all around us."

"That's a nice thought," I said, kicking at a pebble near my foot. "We need to save the nice days."

She put her sandwich down and kissed me. "You're a little preoccupied today. What are you thinking about?"

"Oh," I said, "even in a paradise like this I can't really free my mind all the time. Things get to you. I was thinking about Durango, about Cullen again."

"Cullen? I thought you said things were okay now between you and him."

"I still can't quite see it that way, Tracy. I told you all about his little peace-making overture, about offering me the job and all that. But still, something doesn't feel right. I don't know what it is. Bad vibes, I guess."

"You're just paranoid. It'll be all right with you and Dil. He really is friendly these days. Did I tell you what happened to me the other day at the supermarket?"

I turned toward her with a surprise in my eyes. "No," I said, frowning at her. "What happened?"

"I'd been grocery-shopping in the supermarket. I was push-ing my cart full of groceries out to my car, and who should come walking behind me but your dear friend, Mr. Cullen. He was all full of smiles and he even offered to help me load my groceries into the car. I let him; I couldn't see any reason not to. He really is a charmer."

I bristled hotly at the thought of Cullen with Tracy, and I was surprised at myself, at the depth of my anger.

"Did he say anything to you?"

"About you?"

"Yes."

"No. He just acted real warm and friendly, like he was wanting me to like him."

I chuckled sarcastically. "And how did you feel about him?"

She sighed. "Oh, I don't know, Mike. I know what he's done, but he seemed, well, changed, relaxed. He didn't act like what I thought he'd be. Maybe he really is going to leave you alone."

I turned and looked back at the mountains. "I wish I could believe it, Tracy."

"Oh, lighten up, Mike. People really can change. Who knows, maybe this whole thing about Jimmy's death finally convinced him to drop the drug stuff and play it straight from now on. You know what Harry Foster says. People really can change if the truth hits them at the right moment."

"Yeah, Harry told me that. Maybe you're right. But I still say it would take something pretty big to turn a man like Cullen around."

"Maybe it already has. Jill's managed to change, hasn't she?"

"That she has. But Cullen's a different breed."

"How?"

"The guy's been into the bad stuff too long. When you do that, you pile up layer after layer of lies until you start to believe it's all the truth. Maybe that's the ultimate evil, Tracy. Maybe the devil is not just some guy with horns and a pitchfork after all. Maybe he's just a big layer of lies laminated over and masquerading as the truth. All I can say is it'd take a lot of real truth to make Cullen turn away from all those lies in his mind. And to change."

"Like I said before, maybe it's happened. Maybe Rowe's death shocked him into it."

"Maybe," I said. "But I doubt it."

We finished eating and drove back to Durango. On the way into town we stopped a few miles before we got there. The light of the fading sun seemed to cast golden rays over the valley leading to Durango.

"Look Tracy," I said. "There's your 'Durango Light'."

"I see it. It's beautiful this evening."

"I know now what you really mean about the light here. It's very special."

"Yes," she said, looking down the valley. "Like heaven itself." Durango lay ahead. I wanted to believe that heaven could be there. I really wanted to believe it.

Chapter Thirteen

The night before we set out on our trip to climb Mount Eolus, I checked the TV for the weather forecast on the San Juans, paying particular attention to the Needles Mountains area. The weather map didn't look as encouraging as I had hoped a few days before. A late-summer cold front was moving down from the Northwestern states, bringing a band of nasty-looking clouds our way. I called Buck, who had also checked the weather with his satellite hookup through his online service.

"Well, do you see the same thing on your computer I saw on the TV?"

"You mean that storm front?"

"Yeah," I said. "Well, what do you think?"

"I don't know. It's a tossup. I've seen bad weather like this approaching before a climb, but anything can happen in the Needles. Sometimes the storm clouds will go around them. Sometimes it looks bad at first, and then you get a window of clear weather and you can do the summit. The whole thing's a gypsy's guess."

"And sometimes it looks like it's going to be bad, and it is bad, real bad, up there too, right?"

"Oh, sure. That can happen. But I'm leaving the decision to you on this one. It doesn't really matter to me one way or another. I did Eolus a long time ago, so it's your show, buddy. You call it."

"Thanks," I said sarcastically. I considered our options. Several days before, Buck had agreed to allow Tracy to go along with Jill and me. The four of us had all met over at Buck's for dinner one night to plan the final details of the trip.

That night we were all in good spirits for the climb, including me. I was itching to go. But now, as I thought about that cold front coming, my enthusiasm was waning.

"Buck," I said, "Tell me the truth. What's the worst that could happen to us up there?"

He thought it over for a moment. "Well, I guess we could get up to Chicago Basin and be pinned down in a monsoon rain or possibly a hail or snow storm. It would be unpleasant, to say the least. But hey, we've got the equipment to ride out a storm if it comes to that and wait for it to clear. If it doesn't clear off, we can just stay dry in the tents until we can walk out of the basin. Or if we got caught up on the mountain in bad weather, we just go back down like we always do. I don't think there's all that much to worry about. We're prepared for the messy stuff."

"You sure sound optimistic."

Buck paused. His tone changed. "Look, Mike, I hate to tell you this, but you don't always get picture-perfect weather like we've had this summer when you go out climbing. Sometimes you start with a little bad weather, and you just have to gamble that it will turn good enough for the ascent. We've just been lucky where the weather's concerned. So what's your decision?"

I felt caught between a rock and a hard place. "Okay," I said reluctantly, "I guess it's a go."

He laughed. "That's the spirit. But do be sure you take along your rain and cold weather gear. And make sure Tracy's got some, too. I expect Jill already has that covered."

"I'll call the women and tell them we're still going."

"Fine. I'll see you in the morning."

I called Jill first, and then Tracy, and told them about the weather and that we were still planning on going. Both of them were game and glad. They thought it would be a fun trip either way the weather went. I didn't want to be a wet blanket, but I still wasn't so sure about the whole thing.

The next day the sky dawned red over Durango, dampening my spirits even more. Yet we went ahead with the trip. We all met at the station as prearranged, got our tickets, and boarded the early train.

Tracy sat beside me in one seat, with Jill and Buck in the one in front of us. Buck, as I might have predicted, rolled his head against the window while we were still at the station and fell asleep. This was a neat trick, because the train was more crowded than usual, and it was noisy as a hive of bees in the passenger car. But Buck had miraculous powers of tuning out the sounds of the world around him when he wanted to get some rest before the long hikes. He was dead to the world, snoring away even as the tourists babbled and moved around in their excitement.

"Lots of tourists on the train this trip," Tracy said, turning to me.

"Yeah," I said. "It's almost time for the schools to start,

and I expect a lot of these folks are getting in their last summer weekend in the mountains."

"It's good that we got our reservations a few days early," she said. "I think every seat is filled and they had to turn a few people away."

"I know. Glad you thought of it."

"Your mind was on so many other things we needed for this trip. Getting the train reservations was the least I could do."

It had been fun outfitting Tracy for the hiking. She had little gear for real backpacking, so I had found a few of the better items the store had and took them out on consignment for her. Most of the outdoor stuff she already had for her photography jaunts was mainly day-hiking apparel. Since she wouldn't be joining us in the climbing, a lot of her standard hiking stuff would suffice for this kind of trip. Still, she needed a few other items, like a warm woolen guide sweater, a wool balaclava and some wool gloves.

I had developed an appreciation for wool with experimenting and hard experience, and it was still the best thing to wear in cold weather conditions, at least in my book. The ads touted the virtues of the synthetics, but I stuck with wool whenever I could.

I got these clothing items for her, and I also found her a good internal frame backpack and a sleeping bag and pad. The last pieces of hiking equipment I found for her were very important: a Goretex parka and some matching wind-rain pants. They would keep her dry on the hike "in the wet," as they called it. She already had a set of good leather trail boots, and I'd waterproofed them with Snow- Seal. After that I knew that's about all she would really need for hiking into Chicago Basin, camping there, and getting back.

I planned on carrying the other gear she would need in my own backpack so her pack's weight wouldn't kill her. I had a couple of her cameras, extra lenses, and her film. She could sleep in her bag inside the two-man tent I carried with me. She could eat her meals from the extra cook kit stuff I had, too. It didn't really add all that much weight to my own gear to carry her camping articles.

Since this was her first time to go to a high elevation camp, I really wanted her to carry a relatively light pack so she would enjoy the experience. It was light, too, about twenty pounds, all in all, when we weighed it. I knew it should be just about right for her.

As the tourist train moved northward, I glanced out the window. High clouds were moving in above us. I didn't like it, but now it didn't matter. We had paid our money and we were on our way.

Unlike Buck, I didn't feel like sleeping on the train this morning. This was not Tracy's first journey on the Durango-to- Silverton run, but it was the first one we had taken together. I wanted to stay awake and talk with her, to savor the experience together. It was good to point out the sights along the way, to tell her about things she might not know about, and to see her reactions.

After a while, Jill looked over the seat in front of us. She had her hair in a kerchief, and merriment was in her eyes.

"You two seem to be having a good time," she said.

"We are," Tracy said, laughing.

"I can tell. I bet it's nice to be going on a trip like this with someone you...well, someone you really like."

"It helps," I said. "Someday you'll do the same, Jill."

"I hope so," she replied, smiling.

The train chugged its way on up the canyon, and outside the skies were turning dark and gray. It was windy in the canyon, windier than I had ever seen on the train trip. Now and then rain would spatter against the window. In spite of having Tracy near, I could not share her jovial mood.

Needleton arrived quicker than I thought it would, and Jill shook Buck awake. We got down off the train and walked back to the baggage car. Today we were the only backpackers there, and it felt strange to be the only ones.

The baggage attendant slid open the door on the side of the car and climbed in. He turned and looked up at the cloudy skies. There was a cold mist in the air. Then, with doubtful eyes, he looked down at us as we stood there beside the rails.

"You folks sure picked a great day to do your hiking. That weather doesn't look so good to me."

Buck spat on the ground. "We like it this way. It's less crowded on the trail."

"If you say so," the attendant said, handing down our packs. "Still, I think you're a little crazy to go hiking with a storm front moving in."

Jill tried to look nonchalant. "We like it crazy," she said.

We got the packs down on the ground and took out our parkas and put them on. Then we hoisted the packs to our backs and walked toward the suspension bridge that crossed the Animas River, Buck leading the way. Jill followed him, and Tracy was in front of me.

"How are you doing, Mike?" Tracy asked, turning back to me.

"Oh, I'm okay. That baggage guy was right though, you know. I don't like heading out in nasty weather like this."

"Oh, don't be such a pessimist. Maybe it'll turn all sunny once we get to Chicago Basin. Cheer up."

"Okay, I'll try," I said, unconvinced.

Yet try I did. Buck was right about not always having good weather when you started on a trip like this. And, as he had said, the weather might get better. But some distance up the trail my dark mood returned as we came to the little wooden box where you sign in on the register for your hike. The register told the forest service people where you are going and how many are in your party in case they had to come looking for you.

There was a sign over the registration box that had a warning in bright red letters. It reminded us that the mountains we were approaching were dangerous, and that several climbers had bought it trying to climb Eolus.

I had seen that sign before, and had read its words before, but never had its meaning come home to me so explicitly. I had wanted to do Eolus for so long now, but at that singular moment I felt a gnawing, pained reluctance come over me. The mountain liked to kill people. I just hoped it wasn't going to be one of us.

The steep trail up to Chicago Basin had never been so wearing on me as it did on that cool, windy, rainy morning. The rain would hit us in wind-driven showers every so often, and we had to stop and huddle for shelter under the swaying trees, waiting it out.

"You sure about all this, Buck," I said once.

"Look," he said, a little impatience in his voice now, "like I said before, Mike, it's your call. We can go back any time you want."

Yet I didn't really want to go back now. It was an honor thing, a commitment thing, and we were headed to the destination. "No," I said, "let's see how it goes."

Maybe, I thought, things actually would change once we had arrived in the basin and had made the base camp. We trudged on higher, the brown mud slippery beneath our boots.

Finally, about three hours after we started on the trail, the terrain grew flatter and I knew we were in the lower basin area. The fog and clouds were low over us, hiding the mountains.

"Well, Tracy," I said. "I apologize. I told you this was as beautiful as Yankee Boy Basin, but I guess it doesn't look that way today."

"But it's beautiful, in its own way," she said. "You just have to look at it that way."

"Oh, I forgot. You like it stormy. I hope your cameras are working. Well, you may get a lot of pictures of this stormy weather you seem to like. At least you won't go home empty-handed."

She stared at me. "Mike, would you please just lighten up? The weather may change, dear."

"No, I don't think so," I said.

But I was wrong. When we finally came to the lower basin, the fog and the low clouds blew away and it was hazy blue overhead. From out of the clouds now, like ghosts, the gray, barren mountain summits appeared against the turquoise sky. There, to the east, was Jupiter Peak, and to the north, were Windom and Peak 18 hiding Sunlight Peak, as always. Above us on the west was our goal, ominous-looking Mount Eolus, still capped in a sheath of flat clouds.

It was still quite cool and windy along the trail, but now I felt some degree of hope returning. Maybe we would get in our climb after all.

We made camp in the same place Buck, Jill, and I had set up when we climbed Windom and Sunlight Peaks a few weeks before. In the cold, wet wind we didn't talk much as we erected the tents. After we had them up, another column of dark clouds came scudding over the mountain walls from the northwest, sending more rain down on us. We got into the tents for shelter, and I lay in my bag next to Tracy in hers.

"What a messy introduction to backpacking, Tracy," I said to her as we huddled together. "I wish you could have come up here on a better day."

"I just wish you'd stop being so concerned about me," she said. "I'm enjoying myself. Look, it may be raining out there, but I'm warm and dry in this little tent of yours, here out in the middle of nowhere. And I'm with you. That's all that matters to me. Why are you so down today?"

"I don't know. I guess maybe I'm thinking about tomorrow. Camping's one thing. Climbing's another."

"Oh, so that's what's on your mind. Well if it's bad you don't have to climb the mountain, you know. If the weather's rotten in the morning, you just won't go. It's as simple as that."

"I don't know. Buck seems awfully determined on this trip. I can't figure it. Usually he's the cautious one."

"Look. He just wants you to get the peak, Mike. But even he knows if it's too dangerous to make the climb you won't go. Relax; don't be so gloomy."

"Maybe you're right. We'll just have to wait and see."

After about a half hour, the rain subsided, and we all came out of the tents to fix dinner. My little stove was balky about firing up in the cold wind, and the grass and rocks were wet everywhere. But with a little wheedling and coaxing, the fussy little stove finally came to life, hissing and fuming. Buck's stove was like mine, but Jill had hers going well before we did. She was a modernist when it came to backpacking stoves. Her stove was one of the more contemporary propane-gas units you light instantly and you've got your fire going. The old-fashioned white gas stoves like Buck and I had have to be primed and cajoled and fiddled with before they will start their ragged, reluctant burning. Even so, they've never failed us yet. They may be cantankerous, but they get the job done. And we were too stubborn to switch to the newer kind.

After I got mine aflame, I cooked a heavy meal of beef stew for Tracy and me, and it tasted good after the long hike in the cold afternoon. We ate until we were full. Then we had several cups of hot chocolate as we sat on the wet logs around the blackened fire- ring along with Buck and Jill.

None of the four of us talked much as we sat there. There was a quiet, humorless mood over our little party. We were all trying simply to eat, stay warm, and conserve our energy.

I resisted the urge to say what I thought about our situation regarding the possibility of climbing in the morning. I was tired of sounding like a Jeremiah. Buck and Jill, the other two who would be making the climb, knew how I felt anyway. Yet I thought we'd still better at least talk about the ascent tonight.

I turned to Buck. "Looks like it'll be a cold-weather climb in the morning," I said.

He gave me a look that said my words were obvious, but he didn't give me the sarcastic reply I thought he would. "We'll get warm soon enough once we get going. Just take along your coldweather stuff in case we get into something really dicey up high."

"Will we need crampons?" I asked. I had packed mine along just for luck.

"No," he said. "I don't think we'll need the foot-claws. We shouldn't be crossing any snowfields this time of the summer. We'll just take the rope and the ice axes; they should be sufficient. But do wear your helmet, Mike. The footing's probably going to be a little greasy."

"Greasy" was Buck's favorite term for slick footing on mud or ice or frost-covered grass. I fully expected it to be greasy where we would be heading.

"How soon should we get up in the morning?" Jill asked.

"Oh, about like before, Jill," Buck said. "Maybe around five. We'll have a look at the weather. If we're not completely socked in, we'll talk about it." He looked over at me. "That suit you, Mike?"

"Sounds okay," I said woodenly. I was still about as pessimistic as I had ever been before a climb.

Buck's eyes were whimsical as he stared at me from under the hood of his parka. "Did you study up on the guidebook about Eolus like I told you to?"

"I did," I said.

"If we should get so lucky as to make it to that catwalk up there, you know the one they call 'The Sidewalk In The Sky,' just remember something. That's the place where we'll probably want to use a rope. It's steep and messy on the final part of the climb up to the summit, but that catwalk's where a lot of crazy stuff can happen. Especially if the rock is wet or icy. You did bring a rope along, I presume?"

"Yeah, I've got a rope. It's in a bag in my pack. Any other words of wisdom?"

"Uh-huh. Get a good night's sleep. You're going to need it tomorrow if we decide to go up."

I pulled my parka around me against the cold and the approaching dark. "Buck," I said, "you really think we'll get to climb this thing?"

Buck turned from me and looked up at Eolus' heights, hidden in the clouds above him. "Mike, you've been after me all summer to guide you up this hill. You did Jupiter, Windom, and Sunlight. You're ready for Eolus, and it just might be ready for you. I say if there's any way at all possible, we go for it, friend. Does that answer your question?"

"Yeah, it does. I just..."

"You just what? Are you going to tell me you're getting cold feet again?"

"No. I just wondered why you're so intent on this climb. It seems like an obsession with you this time."

He gave me a guarded smile. "It's the moment of truth, Bucko. We're here. You either put up or shut up. If there's a break in the weather, we try it. If not, we don't. It's that simple. This is a new level of climbing for you now. You wanted this mountain, and now you're going to get it. What's more, if it's any comfort, I think you can do it. You're just a little edgy tonight. Everybody has that feeling sometimes. Get over it. You'll be all right."

"Okay," I said. "I think I understand now."

After dinner, we all retreated to the tents again. Tracy and I crawled into our sleeping bags and put on the wool balaclavas. Soon we were warm again.

I carry a little candle lantern on the backpack trips some times, and I had it with me now. With cold, stiff fingers, I tied it with a string to the top of the tent and lit the wick in the glass case. It gave us some light and a little cozy warmth as we lay there.

"Did you drink enough water?" I asked Tracy. "You're probably pretty dehydrated from all that hiking, and water in your system will help you stay warm tonight when it really gets cold."

"I think I drank enough."

"If you get too cold in the night, I've got some chemical warming packets in my pack."

"I think I'll be okay," she said. "Buck really laid it on the line for you out there, didn't he?"

"Yeah, but I'm glad he did. Now I know where his head's at. It helps."

"I just hope his head's really thinking clearly about the weather and climb," she said. "He does seem a little on the macho side about all this."

I shook my head. "No, Buck's got it figured out about right. I'm the one who's on the conservative side. Probably too conservative, really."

She shifted her position in her sleeping bag and looked up at me. "Is it because I'm along on this trip? Are you thinking about me? Is that why you're so restless?"

I shook my head. "No. it's not that, Tracy. I just never figured on a winter-conditions climb of Eolus. Even though it's August, with this cold rain down here in the basin, it's probably snowing up high on the mountain. I've got a feeling it's like wintertime up there above the twelve-thousand-foot level. There's probably snow and ice glazed all over the mountaintop tonight. It even feels a little like winter here in the tent tonight. Look at my breath."

Sure enough, as I spoke, little puffs of white vapor came out of my mouth.

"You'll stay warm," she said. "You've got the right clothing for it. And when you start huffing and puffing up the trail to the top, you'll probably work up a sweat and you'll have to peel some of your clothes off. And you can handle the snow and ice if it comes to that."

"Maybe," I said.

She reached from her sleeping bag and put her hand on my head. "Mike, I hate to be a pest, but I think you ought to get some sleep now."

"Yes, Mom," I said, grinning at her. "Anyway, as cold as it is, there's not much chance for romance in this tent tonight."

"Later. When we're back home. I promise you a long hot soak in the hot tub. Then we'll see what...develops. How does that sound?"

"I wish we were there right now."

"I know. But go on to sleep. I'll blow out the candle after I'm sure you're down for the count."

"Okay. I'll see you in the morning."

"You can bet on it."

I closed my eyes and tried to relax, but Eolus haunted me again. Always before it had been the unreachable mountain, the challenge, the one I was so eager to tackle. But tonight it only brought deep, black fear to my soul. It was an irrational fear, I knew. But still I felt a foreboding about the mountain. A deathly warning bell was bonging away deep in my brain. Eolus had become the mountain of my fear. But it was too late to back out now. Like Buck had said, we were here, at the doorway to the climb.

That fear was like a chain around my neck in black water, dragging me down, down, down as I tried to sleep. When sleep finally came, I still felt the fear; and even in my dreams it pulled at me, taunted me. I slept restlessly, tossing and turning in my bag.

It was well past midnight, when, in my dreams, I felt a hand on my brow. It was a hand so distinct, so dreadful, that I almost cried out in the darkness. But then I felt the hand becoming warm, and I knew it was not a hand to fear. Its fingers were warm and caring, stroking my brow. I knew it was Tracy's hand, coming to me from out of the darkness, reassuring me that everything was all right. I turned upward and kissed her fingers.

Only then did I fall back into sleep again, for the first time in the night feeling some semblance of peace. I held her hand close as I drifted on the calmer waters of the night, straight on till morning.

The alarm of my wristwatch woke me at five o'clock. I moved up from my warm sleeping bag and looked out the tent flap. It was a cold, windy morning out there. Dark clouds were smeared across the sky, and spit-snow was in the air. My little thermometer said it was 15 degrees. Great weather for climbing, I thought dejectedly.

Normally, in such conditions, I would have told Buck I wasn't going out on such a miserable morning, but I didn't get the chance. He was already dressed in his climbing clothes, eating a breakfast bar as he ambled over to my tent door.

"I heard your alarm go off. It's not so bad out here. I think we have a chance if the weather breaks."

"I was afraid you'd say that," I said.

He grunted. "Jill's already dressed. Get some clothes on and grab something to eat. It's time."

I tried not to awaken Tracy, but my rummaging around in the small tent for clothing and food had disturbed her sleep. When I was at last ready, she got up and kissed me goodbye.

"I'll be with you up there, in spirit anyway," she said. "You come back to me."

"That's the plan," I said as I scrambled out of the tent into the cold, damp, windy morning darkness.

We slowly left the base camp at six. Jill was in good spirits. Buck was stoic though, ever the wary mountain guide. We were dressed warmly, of course. I had on my wool-blend underwear, woolen guide sweater, and balaclava under my mountain parka. The day-pack on my back felt surprisingly light. I clutched the ice axe in my gloved hand as we walked forward.

At Buck's insistence, we stopped for a moment and put on our hard plastic climbing helmets. I snugged the strap on mine into place. Jill was looking down at her hard-hat.

"I don't see why we have to wear these darned helmets," she complained. "The guidebook said that we won't be climbing any cliffs, where rockfall might come down and hit us on the head."

"Don't argue," Buck said simply. "That may be true, but your helmet has another purpose today, Jill. If you slip on the ice and hit your head on a rock, you'll be glad you're wearing that helmet."

"Okay," she said, reluctantly putting hers on and snugging her chin strap into place. "You're the guide, Buck. And I promised I'd do everything the guide said. Remember?"

"I remember," he said gruffly.

As we began walking, there was a little dawn light now, enough to see the trail. It was the steep one we had taken weeks before, up toward Twin Lakes Basin. The climb up the trail was slippery with mud and ice, and it took a lot of effort. Getting warmer now, I stopped and took off my sweater and stowed it in my pack. There was a brittle coating of ice on my parka now, but underneath I felt like I was in the tropics.

The guidebook said that the standard route up to Eolus was to go to Twin Lakes Basin. Then you were to head southwest on the climber's trail toward the mountain. But Buck had a different route in mind. About halfway to the Twin Lakes, we turned and veered straight up the steep grassy slopes and made a "diretissma," a direct climb toward the wide peak gully above.

The grass and rocks on the slope were icy and slippery and the effort made my leg muscles burn, but we took it slow enough, using the mountain step. After what seemed like hours, we reached the upper approach trail. It felt somehow more secure to be back on a trail. We were below the snow-whitened east face of Eolus now, and it looked rugged up on toward the top.

Then we got a break. The sun came out at about eight o'clock and the clouds were clearing a bit.

"Just look at that sky," Jill said, seeing the blue through the mists. "We may make it after all."

"Maybe," I said, glancing upward, and breathing deeply of the frigid, thin air.

Then, strangely, we heard the clattering noise of what sounded like a helicopter's engine, somewhere in the sky between the mountains around us. I looked for the helicopter, but I couldn't see one.

"What's that?" Jill asked.

"Probably a chopper," Buck said. "The miners use them these days to prospect and to work their claims. There's still a few working mines here in the Needles, and a helicopter ride beats hiking up here any day of the week."

"I guess it's a little different from the old days when the miners and prospectors used pack-in mules," I said.

"Yeah," Buck said. "But I'm a little surprised that they're flying up here in weather like this on such a crummy morning. But maybe they've got something they just have to do, though. Miners can be a peculiar bunch."

The sound faded, and we never did see the helicopter. We stopped to rest by a rock, and as I sat there I suddenly spotted the body of a dead deer not far off the trail. The carcass looked like it had been lying there for several months. Idly, I wondered if it was some kind of bad omen, but I turned my mind away from it.

As we rested, we all took drinks of water and ate some of our trail food. We needed those calories on such a killer climb. After a few minutes, Buck got up and we started upward again.

There was a small glacial cirque above us, and that was our next goalpoint. We arrived there, and looked to the northeast. Ramps of rock led upward to the right, and we took the second one, following cairns now. The ramp was relatively safe, slick with ice, but wide enough to traverse safely if you were careful. At the top of the ramp the wind blowing over the ridge was much colder. It came at us like the blast of a hurricane. I stopped and put my sweater back on again and buttoned my parka over it.

Moving higher, beyond the lip of the ridge, we were on a high plateau now, and there was a small frozen lake here. It was beautiful, and shining faintly red in the glow of the rising sun. An actic landscape was all around us.

"Let's take a break," Buck said. "We need to talk about what we want to do next."

We were above the 13,000' level now. Buck led the way over toward the ice-covered lake. Suddenly, quite unexpectedly, Buck pitched forward, his stocky body thudding onto the snow-covered rocky ground.

"Blast it!" he shrieked, pulling himself to a sitting position. He didn't look right as he clutched his foot.

"You okay, Buck?" I asked, hurrying over to him.

"Oh, I slipped. I think I twisted my stupid ankle pretty bad. My boot got caught in those rocks and it didn't let go when I fell. I probably hyperextended the blasted thing."

"Did you break it?"

"No, I don't think so. But it feels like I sprained it pretty good. Let me see if I can get up and walk on it."

He pushed himself higher and tried to stand up, but it was too painful for him. He sat back down on the rocks, breathing hard, disgusted with himself.

We knelt beside him and looked at the pained expression on his face. This was the last thing I expected to happen. I had never seen Buck get hurt.

"It's pretty bad, huh?" Jill asked.

He looked up toward the summit of Eolus, to the west. "Bad enough to keep me from going any higher. I don't know, I really might have broken the stupid thing." He untied his boot and gingerly felt around the ankle. "I can't feel anything like a bone sticking out or any blood, but you never know."

I sighed. "Well that's it, then," I said. "I guess we go back down, huh?"

Buck sighed deeply. "Probably so. It's a blooming shame though. We're so near the catwalk, and from there it's only a few hundred feet on up to the summit. But I'm not too keen on you two doing it without me. As slick as it is on these rocks, and as messy as the route is on up to the top, you two probably need me along. And it doesn't look like I'm going to make the summit today."

The weather was turning more ominous now. The clouds were starting to roll in again, erasing the scattered patches of blue. From far away, we heard the distant rumble of thunder.

"How are you feeling, aside from the ankle?" I asked.

"Oh, not too bad. I'm warm enough, and I've got all my survival goodies in my pack. But I just don't see how I can do any more climbing. I'll be lucky to get back down. You might have to carry me."

I looked to the west now, toward the upper slopes of Eolus. The snow-covered top of the mountain was out of the clouds, agonizingly near. So near and yet now so distant, I thought. As we had climbed to this plateau, I had realized that we had most of the elevation gain behind us. I had begun to feel a bit more optimistic about our summit attempt. Now that hope seemed to be dashed along with Buck's ankle.

As Buck had noted though, it wasn't very far from where we were now on up to the catwalk, the famous "Sidewalk In The Sky." Since I had read and heard so much about it, I wanted to at least take a look at it while it was so near.

"Buck," I said, "if you'll be okay for a while, maybe Jill can stay here with you. I'd like to go on up and see what the Sidewalk looks like. I just want to see it so I'll have an idea of what I'll be trying to go across the next time we come up here." I turned to Jill. "Is that okay with you?"

"Yeah, it's okay with me," she said. "I'd like to go up there with you to see it, but one of us probably should stay here with Buck."

I turned to my partner. "Well, what do you say? Okay if I go up and take a look?"

He stared at me for a long moment through wearied eyes, and then he nodded. "Yeah, go ahead. I'll be okay. But just look at it, okay? Don't get any funny ideas about going across that greasy thing. Two guys have fallen off that catwalk in the last couple of years, both of them when it was icy like it is today. Just take a look, Mike. But don't do anything stupid."

"I don't plan to. This is just a reconnoiter, Buck. That's all

I've got in mind."

"Okay. But be careful," he said. "We don't want any more slip-ups today."

"I'll watch it," I said.

So I left them. I climbed the nearby rocky slope, carefully scrambling and bouldering my way alone. At length I came to the beginning of the catwalk that led over to the tantalizing summit ridges of Mount Eolus.

I carefully perused the famous catwalk I had read about in the guidebooks. The sun came out from behind a cloud again, and I saw the gleam of the film of ice on the jagged rocks along the narrow traverse.

The Sidewalk looked long and tricky. I could now see that it consisted mainly of boulders, but it also had a few flat places along the way across. It looked about four-to-six-feet-wide in most places, but in a couple of spots it narrowed to only about two feet wide or so. Still, it looked like it could be done under the right conditions. It looked like it might even be easier than I had imagined.

One side of the traverse fell almost straight down, possibly 1000 feet or more. On the other side there was also a steep drop, not as far as the first, but again, almost straight down. The Sidewalk might have been more manageable than I had previously imagined, but still, it was no piece of cake.

The snow and ice on the thin walkway would make any attempt to go across extremely dangerous. Even in dry weather, a climber might want to be tied in to a rope before attempting it. Today, crossing it looked like a clear invitation to death.

Yet even so, even as I considered the formidable dangers, a strange new feeling now began to course through me. I couldn't explain it, but dangerous or not, I suddenly felt pulled toward it. It was crazy. I actually wanted to cross the catwalk, here and now. I felt a strange, irrational, growing sense of confidence within myself. For some mad reason, I felt that I could actually do it. I knew that just as I had felt that irrational fear of the mountain the night before, now I was experiencing another irrational feeling: euphoria. And such euphoria can be as misleading as fear.

No, I said to myself, you said you wouldn't. But I felt like my moment of truth had arrived. Going across seemed like it would be easy. And I simply had to do it, and do it on my own, without a rope. As if drawn by a magnet, I started on my way.

I hugged the icy boulders carefully, testing them for any sign of movement, and I made headway going several feet ahead over the slick rocks. It was as if something was tugging at me, carrying me forward through the danger, and yet I felt protected and safe, as if something was watching over me.

I didn't look down at all as I progressed. It was like a dream, this crossing, like something I had to do out of a sense of some pure mythic destiny. Or madness. I spent probably half an hour slowly negotiating, crawling, crabbing my way across the knife-edge, balancing my body on the slippery boulders at every turn. When I finally reached the far side, I was breathing hard. A sunburst of elation came over me like nothing I had ever known before. I had done it! I had traversed the "Sidewalk in the Sky!"

I looked back on where I had been and I couldn't believe I had made it. Foolish? Of course. But it was behind me now.

Buck, no doubt, had he seen what I had done, would have had some interesting words to say to me. But then again, I thought, maybe not. He sometimes spoke to me of a climber's confidence, of how you reach new levels of bravery with experience. I felt that I had come up to a new level now.

Yet my climb of Eolus was not finished. Now that I was across the Sidewalk, I was in a position to go for that elusive summit. I knew it wouldn't be easy, though. The summit was perhaps another 300 feet above me, but ahead of me there would be the ordeal of trying to climb on slippery, crumbly, unstable rocks.

I gripped my ice ax and thought it over. I had two choices for a route from where I was. Either I could go up the somewhat exposed ridge, or take what the guidebook said was "the more complicated, but easier" ledges of the east face. Conservatively, I chose the east face.

There was quite a bit of bouldering and scrambling here on the icy rocks. In a couple of places I had to pull my entire body weight up over four- and-five-foot ledges, and many of the rocks were indeed quite loose. Yet I climbed with great care, confident now in my routefinding skills. Gradually, I made my way higher. The confidence held within me now.

About a hundred feet from the top I was feeling even more assured. I decided to forego the loose rocks of the east face ledges and go on up to the ridge. The ridge was a rocky, backbonelike seam of boulders that curved upward to the summit of the mountain. I pulled myself up through the ice-coated rocks and saw the ridgeline a few feet higher.

When I got to the ridge, I had second thoughts about my choice. The dizzying thousand-foot fall was right off the edge, but the ridge was fairly level with few exposed places and many handholds to test and hang on to. For some crazy reason though, I kept feeling more and more confident. I hardly noticed the low rumble of thunder coming from the approaching storm clouds to the west.

I wondered about the ecstasy I was experiencing. Was I succumbing to the opposite of fear, the irrational elation that could make you take stupid risks? It was like a fever in my blood now, an obesssion, to bag the summit. I controlled the euphoria, reminding myself to be cautious, but it was difficult, more difficult than the climbing itself.

The storm clouds to the west did have me a bit worried though. But now, I was almost there, almost to the top, and I wasn't going to let a storm or lightning take this mountain away from me as had happened on Lost Arrow Peak. I was determined to outrace the storm, at all odds.

The rock was still slick and crumbly as I moved along the ridge, and I was glad I had my ice axe along. The axe aided my balance and helped me scrape away snow from the stones so that I could find secure footholds and handholds.

I climbed up to a place where my path appeared to be blocked. A huge boulder seven or eight feet tall was standing in the way; one last problem. I examined the boulder carefully. I moved around on the right side of it and saw a little ledge about six inches wide. The ledge slanted slightly downward and was dangerously covered with rime. One slip off that tiny iced-over ledge and you were gone into the abyss that dropped more than a thousand feet down. No, I told myself, this isn't the way.

I carefully moved back around the big rock and explored its other side. I had not noticed when I first approached the boulder, but down from it, on the left side, there was an easy ramp about two feet wide that led further downward, and then upward again. Breathing a sigh of relief, I made my way down the ramp. Then, rounding the big rock, I stopped and caught my breath. Ten feet away from me, where the mountain stopped and the sky began, was the last cairn, marking the summit of Mount Eolus. I was home free.

I left the ramp and easily walked up to the summit cairn at exactly 10:02 that morning, and I smiled. If Buck would have been angry with me for going on up the mountain, at least he might have been proud of me for observing the "ten-o'clock" rule. I could see the black storm clouds coming, flashing out lightning. I merely intended to touch the marker, stay a moment or two, and head back down.

What a feeling coursed through me as I stood on the summit of Eolus, even in the furious winds and weather! I had finally climbed the mountain of my fear, the one mountain I had fixed within my dreams of both fear and elation. I knew I could not stay on the spot long, though. I had beaten the storm, but it was only minutes away now, and the most probable target for all its lightning was right where I was standing.

I put aside any thoughts of signing in on the register, but now weariness seized me. I knew I had to rest just a minute or two to gather my strength. I sat down, setting my ice axe aside, resting against a nearby rock. Taking off my helmet, I wiped the sweat from my eyes to clear them.

I felt somewhat dizzy. It must be the altitude, I thought, as I looked up. Before my eyes was a strange vision. There in front of me, against the swirling clouds and fog, I thought I could see the slightly unreal face of a human being. It was no ordinary human being either. The face was that of Dil Cullen.

I knew it was only a bad dream, some dark trick my addled, exhausted mind was playing on me. But the dream-face then smiled at me. Then, with a stab of real fear, I knew that the face before me was no dream. It was real. My heart began to race.

Dil Cullen stood up from behind the rock where he had been sitting, and apparently waiting for me. He was clad in a hooded brown parka. Under the hood, the skin of his face looked gray and frost-chilled, but his dark eyes were intense and cunning. He walked closer to me, throwing his pack and rope to the rocks in front of me.

"Where did you come from?" I asked, as if talking to a ghost.

He ignored my question. "I was hoping you'd come," he said, "although I'd hoped you'd have the others with you."

"But how....?"

"How did I get up here? Think about it, Mike. Eolus has more than one way to get to the top. Oh, I know you amateurs read those climbing guides and they tell you all about the easy 'tourist' route to the summit over on the east side. But if you were a real climber, you'd know there are several other technical routes to get up a hill like this. I had a helicopter drop me off about five hundred feet from the top, over on the west side."

So that was the helicopter we had heard.

Dil continued. "I would have had him put me right here on the summit, but the wind was blowing too hard. So he let me off down below and I just free-climbed the last part, the way a real climber would. Of course, you wouldn't know about that. Then I waited for you here. I just thought I'd surprise you."

I felt weak. "Surprise me? Why?"

Cullen gave me a thin, ironic smile. "Be patient. I'll tell you in a moment, Mikey-boy. I knew you were coming up to the basin to climb this mountain."

I frowned. "But why did you come up here today?"

"Patience, patience," he said. "First I need a drink of water. That little free-climb got me all thirsty."

He reached down into his pack. But instead of taking out his canteen, he pulled out a small black snub-nosed pistol. He aimed it straight at me.

"Oops. No canteen. But this will do for what I'm going to do next."

"What do you mean?" I asked, breathing much harder now.

"Eolus is a dangerous mountain, Mike. People fall off all the time. You're about to join them."

I was on the ground directly in front of him, with nowhere to go. The summit was just too narrow. The muzzle hole of the pistol stared straight into my eyes. I knew there was no way out.

"But why, Dil?"

He laughed. "Oh, don't act so stupid. You know why. You messed things up with me and Jill. I had a good thing in the works going with her. A little coke, a little romance, and off to bed with the pretty little lady. She would have been so fine, just like some of the other young ladies I've entertained. But you had to put your big nose right in the middle of it, didn't you. You blew the deal. And then there's Jimmy. I trained that boy, Mike. Trained him good, too. He'd been cutting and moving coke for me on the street for three years, and he had the muscle to keep everyone in line. It was perfect. But then you had to come along and pull that little trick in your Cobra that sent him to the big coca plantation in the sky. I'd say you've earned a flying leap off this mountain, a couple of times over. Getting rid of you should balance the scales and clear the decks for me now all the way around. I'm going to take a deep pleasure in seeing you splatter your guts on the base of this mountain."

I knew moving would probably buy me a bullet, so I stayed alert but very still. "You'll have to shoot me, Dil. A bullet in my body will tie me in to you with what the cops already know."

He laughed. "Have you looked down over the north side, Mikey-boy? If you force me to shoot you, I'll just drop your body down into a pile of rocks so far and so deep they'll never find you. And if they do, it'll take them months to do it, and there won't be much left of you. The bullet wound will be long gone by then. And I sincerely doubt that they'd connect your carcass to me. Just another dead climber. So a jump or a bullet, it's up to you. It doesn't really matter much to me. Either way, you're going down, old stick."

He was counting on me to be stunned, immobilized, at the death sentence. But an explosion of thunder in the air nearby jarred the mountain, momentarily distracting him. I had been carefully moving into a crouch, and it gave me the opening I needed. I lept forward and tackled him to the ground.

He swung the pistol down and clipped my brow. I felt the sting and the warm liquid seeping into my eye as I desperately reached for his throat, pushing his chin upward. My other hand caught the wrist that held the gun, and we rolled and struggled back and forth, every nerve and muscle straining at the limits. The gun fired, and I thought I was hit, but in the half-second after it discharged, I managed to smash his gun-hand against a rock. The pistol flew out of his hand and over the cliff.

I got a knee up into his belly, then another, and I choked his neck hard. He coughed and sputtered and grew limp as I gripped him. I rolled over on top of him, pinning him down, shaking violently.

Anger, blood-red anger, surged through me. For a moment, I felt like throwing him over the edge, along with his pistol. But something stopped me. I knew I couldn't do that. I wanted to take the man down, but not that way. The death of Jimmy Rowe had been unavoidable, but cold-bloodedly killing Cullen wasn't my way.

I thanked my Ranger training for coming to my rescue. It's strange how the training comes back. Cullen wasn't prepared for those little moves I made on him during the struggle. He may have been the pro when it came to climbing, but when you're wrestling with a Ranger, even a decrepit old ex-Ranger like me, a different kind of professionalism enters the game.

I got off his limp body, checked him for any knife he might have been carrying, and, gasping for breath, sat back against a rock, looking at his prostrate body. I picked up my ice axe, ready to use it on him if he came at me again. The axe wasn't normally meant to be used as a weapon, but it would do for now.

Cullen slowly sat up, and now, surprising me, he put his head in his hands and silently began to cry. I hate to see a grown man cry. But I remembered how, so many times back in the war, both the victors and the defeated sometimes cried like this when a fight was over. They don't tell you about that in the news stories, because it detracts from the so-called glory of war, but it happens. The emotions take over. And Dil Cullen, the big man of Durango, was crying his eyes out now.

"I...I...I don't know where it all went wrong!" he sobbed.

"Where what went wrong, Dil?"

"I don't know...I don't know. I never meant to hurt anyone. I had a good life. Everything was going so good. We moved up to Durango and it was all so good."

I was still trembling with anger. "But what happened, Dil?"

"I just don't know," he wailed. "I got in with these guys...and they had these parties...young girls from in town...drugs...and I just fell into it. I couldn't help it!"

"What about your drug business. How did that all start?"

He wiped the tears from his eyes. "I started out small, just selling to some friends, you know, no big deal. I just wanted to turn people on, make them happy. And then one thing led to another. I met a Colombian, and I borrowed some cash and made a big score. Then it all just took off and...the money was good. I couldn't stop. It...it was too easy. God, I wish I'd never gotten into that stuff."

I gripped the axe, wary of him. "But you did, Dil."

He looked over at me with pleading eyes. "Mike, I was a good person...a good man once. I have a family...we go to church...I know what it means to live a good life...and now this. Please don't kill me, please don't!"

I was silent for a moment. "I'm not going to kill you, Dil."

His mouth fell open, and his eyes were red and wide. He seemed to relax. "Please don't. Look, Mike, I know I've done wrong. But I never thought things would go this far. Everything just got out of hand. And here I am now, the loser. Look, I'll change. I swear I will."

I tightened my grip on my ice axe, then relaxed it a bit, though still vigilant. "I believe you can change, Dil," I said. "You'll have a long time to think about it where you're going. One thing you've got going for you is your intelligence. Can't you see how stupid this all is?"

"Yes. I can see. You're right. It is stupid. I may go to prison, but I just don't care anymore. I'll put it behind me after that and become what I started out to be."

I remembered what Tracy and Harry Foster had said about a man like Dil changing. "You just have to have the right situation," their words came back to me. Well, maybe this was the situation Dil Cullen needed to break through his cycle of evil. Even the worst of people could reform, my friends had said. I wondered.

I looked at his pitiful form. Dil was probably right. Once he had indeed been a good man. But he had gone the wrong way. Yet maybe, even for a man like him, there was hope.

"Dil," I said, glancing at the ever-moving storm clouds coming our way, "we've got to get down off this hill. That storm's moving in on us. We'll both be in trouble if we don't move."

"All...all right," he said. "Can I get up now?"

Strange to have a man like that ask my permission. "Yes," I said, "but take it slow so I can watch you."

"No problem with that," he said, sounding drained. "I'm about done in. I just don't know if I can get down the mountain or not. I'm hurting pretty bad."

"You'll get down," I said. "One way or another."

"You won't hurt me any more?"

"No, I won't hurt you. Get your gear together and let's go."

I got up, shaking my head, thinking about the downclimb ahead. I reached down and grabbed my daypack, momentarily setting down my ice axe to put it on. I didn't think he would try anything now in his weakened state.

I was wrong. In a flash, Cullen lunged forward like a striking snake and grabbed the ice axe away from me before I could get to it.

"Finders keepers," he said, jumping up, holding it. His eyes were alive with a wild glee. He held the ice axe as if he were going to swing the sharp blade right into my stomach. I felt like a complete idiot.

"Things do have a way of changing, don't they? Sit back down," he said.

"Dil," I said, the word tasting like an ash in my mouth, "this isn't the way, man. You were right before. It can be different. You can change. You can put all of this behind you. You've got a chance, man. Don't blow it now."

"No. Sorry about this, but I'm not doing any changing today. There's simply too much at stake in my life. You're the one that's going to change, though, Mikey-boy. You're about to change from being alive to being very dead.

"Dil, think, man!"

He ignored me. "You know, I really am sorry I have to do it, too. In a way, I really do like you. But you do understand why I can't possibly let you keep on living. You're about to become the latest victim to fall off Mount Eolus. It's even better than with a bullet. It'll look like you fell on your axe on the way down. Just go ahead and take it like a man, and it'll all be over before you know it."

"Dil!" I shouted desperately, "Don't do it! You really can become a new man!"

"No," he said, softer, almost hopelessly. "It's a done deal. Not even God can change me now. Goodbye, Mike."

Cullen lifted my ice axe back, ready to swing the death blow. I knew I had one chance to fend off the axe. But my arms felt leaden, tired from all the climbing and the fighting. I might get an arm up and deflect it or grab it, but he knew that, too, and he was strong and quick. He was going to slice that sharp blade of the axe right into my skull. The hair rose on the back of my neck.

I saw him lift the axe back over his head, and instinctively, I braced myself. I saw the axe start to fall in a swift arc, and then there was a blinding white light. I heard an awesome roaring in my ears. I knew he had hit my head. And I knew I was a dead man.

Then, somehow, my fluttering eyelids opened, and I shuddered at the sight before me. Cullen's body, standing there, was on fire. His surprised eyes were full of fear and his mouth was wide open, white smoke pouring out. He had been hit straight-on by the most terrible mountain weapon of all: a bolt of lightning.

Metal, the metal of the axe-blade he held above his head, was the all too enticing target for the storm cloud hovering over us. The lightning had found him.

Still clutching the axe, his smoking body crumpled backward like a fallen tree, and he went over the edge of the summit. I could not do a thing. He was gone, lost in the winds of Eolus.

How that bolt of lightning managed to avoid killing or maiming me as well as him I'll never know, but lightning is funny that way. It has its own logic, its own rhythms, its own pathways. And, I knew, contrary to the myths, it does indeed strike twice in the same place, at least on mountain summits.

With a quick leap, I pushed myself down the east face and fell, rolling, a few feet to the ledges below. Any amount of distance from the top would be a little more protection now from the next bolt that would strike.

It came. The lightning hammered at the summit with a deafening roar, scattering stones, as if old Aeolus himself was sculpting, smashing, and reshaping the summit named in his honor. But as I scrambled on down to safer elevations, I knew that it wasn't a mythic god who had finally exacted justice on Cullen. It might have been the true God himself. Divine justice? I didn't know. The answer to that would have to wait for eternity.

My ordeal wasn't over. With no ice axe, getting down off Eolus was going to be very tricky. Dangerously tricky. Gingerly, I picked my way down the crumbly ledges of the east face. Once I misjudged a jump and I rolled right to the edge of a cliff, nearly falling off, but somehow I caught myself. This was no fun at all.

The mountain artillery, the lightning, was still striking areas all around me, and I had no place to hide. So I tried to crouch as low as I could while I moved, hoping I wouldn't share Cullen's fate. Then the lightning blasts subsided somewhat. But the wind-driven snow from the new storm clouds was back, blotting out my vision. I could only see the rocks a few feet below me. Still, I doggedly made my way back down the east face, hoping I was making my way toward where the catwalk began.

I sighed when I reached the catwalk. It was almost totally clouded in fog. I noted that new snow and ice had covered its broken rocks, and the deep abysses on both sides looked dark and deadly. I shook with new fear. Crossing the Sidewalk In The Sky now looked utterly like an impossibility. The confidence I had relished before was gone, as weariness, depression, and the memory of Cullen's death dulled my mind. I was trapped on the mountain.

Then, wonder of all wonders, from out of the cold mists I saw the form of a white-haired mountain goat. It appeared ahead of me, on the narrow ledge, about twenty feet away. The goat's gentle eyes stared at me like I was some crazy creature, lost in a dream.

I slowly crawled toward the goat, on across the ledge, hanging on carefully. I centered my gravity as the goat watched my every movement. He moved slowly back, still watching me, going further back into the mists, and stopped again, curious. I followed his tracks through the snow, for I knew he knew how to keep from falling off; he seemed, strangely, to be guiding me over to the side of safety.

"Come on, little friend, keep on leading me," I pleaded.

The last time I slipped and caught myself, the goat disappeared into the mists. My heart sank. But a moment later, the fog blew away. The goat was gone, like a ghost. And, I saw I was only a few feet from the end of the Sidewalk. My whole body trembled with relief.

I looked around for that blessed goat, but he had simply disappeared. I wondered, as I reached solid ground, could an angel take the form of a mountain goat? I don't know. But so it seemed at that moment.

I shuffled on down toward the plateau and the frozen lake below where the Sidewalk began. Jill and Buck had found a shelter in the rocks near the frozen lake, and had erected a roof made of their clothing over it.

Jill shouted when she saw me coming. "Mike! You're back!"

"Yeah, it's me!" I shouted in return.

"We waited for you, and when you didn't come back, we

thought you'd fallen off the mountain! The storm blew in, and we decided to cover up until it passed. We were going to go on down without you. We thought you were dead!"

"No," I said. "I didn't die. But I almost did, several times."

Jill saw my head wound and put a temporary bandage on my forehead. The cut Cullen had given me had almost stopped bleeding now, but it was still a bit of a mess.

Then I quickly told them what had happened up on Eolus. Buck just looked at me in stony silence as I told my tale. There were a thousand things he might have said to me, but he said nothing, during or after my brief explanation.

In a few minutes the clouds and the snow passed on, and to my surprise, a clear blue sky then came over us. The mountains around were now gloriously, crystalline white.

"Well, what do you make of that?" Jill asked.

I started to say something, but she stopped me. "I know," she said, "you don't have to tell me. 'These mountains make their own weather'."

"That's right," Buck finally said, "and now that the weather's cleared a bit, we should get down off this hill. We've had enough excitement for one day."

"Sounds like the thing to do," I agreed.

With Jill and me supporting Buck's arms, we slowly made our way on down. As we aided him, I couldn't help thinking back to when Buck and I had helped Jill come down off Jupiter Peak. We could see Jupiter now, right across the valley. And the Jovian face in the north wall, was, as always, smiling at us, smiling at all human folly.

We finally walked down into camp. Tracy greeted us, and hugged us all. We got Buck into his tent and made him as comfortable as we could, helping him with his badly sprained ankle. Bundling most of his body in his sleeping bag, he was warm and dry, safe from any more storms.

We had put ice wrapped in a cloth on his ankle, which he said helped. Jill immediately went over to the fire-ring and started cooking food for him. Tracy went with her.

I was alone now with Buck. He looked up at me with half-lidded eyes from his sleeping bag. He still had said nothing about my summit climb, nor about Cullen and what had happened to him.

I sighed and slumped to the ground outside his tent door, tired beyond words. "I guess you think I'm a fool," I said.

He ignored my remark and turned and reached in his day-pack. "I was saving these for us," he said, slowly handing me a can of lemonade. "You know we always have a toast when we get to the top. I didn't bag the peak, but you did, so I guess we can drink these anyway."

"You didn't answer my question," I said, taking my can and popping it open.

"I know," he said. "No, I don't think you're any more foolish than I've been a time or two in these mountains. I don't talk about it much, but I've done some dumb stuff in my day, just like you did up there today. You saw a chance and you took it. Sure, now it all sounds like you did the wrong thing, crossing that catwalk and going on up to the top all alone. But any time you can come back down alive I guess it's okay, Mike. I'm sure glad Cullen didn't kill you though."

I nodded. "You and me both."

He took a big swig of his lemonade and sighed. "I wasn't thinking so much about you. It'd be on my conscience forever if I guided you on a climb and I let you do something that got you killed."

I laughed. "You're all heart, Buck."

He joined me in the laughter. "Seriously, I'm glad you made it. Maybe we can forget all about Eolus now and get back to some real climbing one of these days, soon as my ankle heals up. But you look wasted right now, partner. You'd better go crash in your tent."

"You sure you're okay?" I asked.

"I'll make it. Get out of here."

With Buck now safe from harm's way, I got up and walked back over to my tent. Kneeling, going in, I lay down on my sleeping bag face down, now shaking. Adrenaline rushed to the farthest nerve endings of my body. It was over. Cullen, the mountain, and my fear. Over.

Did I feel proud? Good? Triumphant? No, all I felt was numb. There was a twisted-up feeling inside me, and yet a deep feeling of gratitude that God had somehow brought me through the whole thing alive. Even that mountain goat back at the Side-walk seemed like Divine Providence watching over me.

Tracy came to me and put a new bandage on my brow where the cut was. Then she left the tent. When she came back, she offered me a cup of tea. "No sugar, though, Mike," she said. "Sugar kills the taste, remember."

Somehow I couldn't smile. The recent memories trapped me, locked me in. That old dead climber's skeletal face now had a new companion: Cullen's blackened, fiery visage, the moment after he had been hit. I closed my eyes and sighed, then looked up at Tracy.

"Thanks," I said, taking the cup from her hands. I poured out my story about the climb, the fight with Cullen, how he died, and how I made my way back. She listened in silence.

I looked up at her with tears in my eyes now. "I tried to give the man a chance, Tracy, I really did. For a while there, I thought it really might happen. He might have somehow turned into a good man if...if I'd just gotten him down.."

She nodded and stroked my brow tenderly. "You did all you possibly could, Mike. All we can do with men who are overcome with evil is to try to help change them. But they have to see their mistakes and they have to want it. Sometimes we can help, sometimes we can't. When we can't, we just have to leave them to God."

We stayed in our camp at the head of Chicago Basin that night. The next day, helping Buck hobble along, we made our way down to the Needleton trailhead. It was good to get on the train, very good to be heading home.

Chapter Fourteen

Reverend Harry Foster twirled a pencil between his fingers as he looked at me. I had told him the whole story of what had happened back there on Mount Eolus. Now he was reflecting on my words.

It had been two days since Harry had held Dil Cullen's funeral. All they had told him was that Dil had died in a climbing accident, struck by lightning.

The funeral had been a big one, and several hundred people had crowded into the church. Harry had struggled, I knew, to give an honest eulogy. It must have been hard for him to restrain his true feelings about Dil Cullen. Somehow, though, he found the appropriate words, and he had done a good job. Or at least as good a job as could have been done, considering the circumstances.

Now Harry sat at his desk in his study as I half-reclined in a chair across from him. His eyes regarded me with wonder.

"That's quite a story," he said. "Did you tell it to the police?"

"Yeah," I said. "No way around it, Harry. Oh, at first I thought we might keep it all quiet. You know. Swear Buck, Tracy, and Jill to secrecy, and give out the story that Cullen had fallen of his own accord. Just make it sound like a simple mountaineering accident, like they told you before the funeral. But you can't really keep something like that a secret for long. Sooner or later one of us would slip up and the real story would come out. Then we'd have suspicions, an investigation, and more trouble. So I went ahead and told the police the truth."

He nodded. "That was the smart thing to do. And what did they say?"

"They made me tell it several times, over and over, to see if it hung together and to see if I would change anything. You know the drill. Then they questioned the others, too, of course. But then the cops did a funny thing. They let us go, and they told us to keep our mouths shut about the whole thing. I guess they had somebody send a team up to the north side of Eolus and they found Dil's body. He was still holding my axe because, well, because his hands...they were melted to the grip."

Harry cringed and shook his head in horror. "That's disgusting. The funeral director didn't tell me that. It almost makes me sick."

"I know. I felt the same way when they told me. Later on, the cops called me back down to the station again and the chief talked to me. He said they were going to call it an accident. I told the chief that wasn't the way it really happened, but he said I was wrong, that I was probably hallucinating up there."

Harry smiled.

I went on. "He said that I didn't know what I was talking about. Since there were no witnesses on the summit besides me, there was no one else to verify my story. Maybe he thought the whole thing would be simpler that way. I didn't argue with him. So that's the story they told you and the papers and everyone else. A climbing accident. Cullen dies in a tragic fall. No one's fault. End of story."

Harry coughed. "So no one in town is supposed to know he died up there with you with him?"

I shifted in my seat. "Like the police chief said, technically, it was an accident. You saw the headline in the newspaper. 'Climber struck by lightning.' I can't deny that part. The story in the paper didn't mention me being on the mountain with him. It only said that he'd been solo climbing and had been struck near the top. I guess, in a way, that's true enough. The pilot of the helicopter that took him up there verified that Dil had been alone when he let him off, too."

Harry gave me a little smile, nodding. "So you're off the hook now?"

I looked out the window. "Yeah," I said dryly, "I guess I'm off the hook with everybody. Everybody, that is, except me."

Harry frowned. "What's that supposed to mean? You feeling guilty now?"

I shrugged and shifted in the chair. "I guess so. Yeah. Maybe 'guilty' is the word."

Harry let out a long sigh. "So you didn't come here today just to tell me the story, did you? You came here seeking, well, seeking some kind of absolution."

I looked straight at him, thinking it over. "I guess that's what you might call it, Harry."

He smiled broadly. "But why? You were only defending yourself. What's your big sin?"

I moved uncomfortably in the chair again. "I don't know, exactly. I'd been so angry with Cullen for so long that I really, well, hell, Harry, I really wanted to take him out. You remember when I told you about how when Jimmy got killed I wished Cullen had been killed along with him? When I had him cornered up there on that mountain, just for a moment I really did want to kill him. The old feeling came back. It would have been so easy when he was lying there to just...just push him right over the edge. Man, was I tempted."

Harry nodded. "But you didn't do that, Mike." "No," I said, shaking my head. "I couldn't."

He leaned back in his chair, regarding me thoughtfully. "Do you know why?"

I looked out the window again. "No. There he was, just lying there on the rocks. It would have been so easy. But I just couldn't bring myself to do it."

I blinked slowly, turned, and looked at my minister friend again. "You know what you said to me about there being hope of redemption for a man, even a man like him? I don't know, Harry; I guess that thought must have stopped me. I think, in that moment, I believed it could be possible. And what I really wanted to do was to give him the chance to turn it all around."

Harry studied me closely, pausing before he spoke. "So what you're telling me is that...you're the one who really changed, Mike."

I looked up at him in sudden awareness. "Maybe I have changed. When it got down to brass tacks, I didn't have the nerve to go through with killing him."

He waited a moment, then shook his head. "I disagree."

"What do you mean?"

"You have plenty of nerve. But you couldn't kill the man in cold blood."

The thought sunk in. "Yes," I said. "I guess you're right."

"And you didn't kill him, anyway. The lightning got him. You know that. So the question is, why are you feeling so guilty about it?"

I looked down at my hands. They were shaking. "I don't know, Harry. I guess maybe I feel like, well, if I hadn't dropped my guard and let him grab the ice axe, he might be alive today. And he might really have changed his ways."

He leaned across his desk now, hands outstretched. "Mike, do you know what I think? And I'm speaking here both as an ex-cop and...as a Man of God. Do you know what I really think?"

"No."

"I think you gave Dil Cullen every chance in the book. In the words of old Saint Paul, you literally 'fought the good fight and you kept the faith'. But the responsibility, or what you would call the 'blame', wasn't yours, for what happened. It was Dil's alone. He had an opportunity to start setting things right. But instead, he chose the old way, the way he had chosen so many times before. He simply ran out of last chances. And he paid the ultimate penalty."

I sat back in my chair, a bit calmer now. Harry's words were important to me. They had the ring of truth in them, a feeling of moral weight, of authority.

"Look," he said, waving his hand back and forth in front of me in some vague ecclesiatical gesture, "if it helps, I absolve you of your sin."

I grinned. "You don't have to say that, Harry. I think if anyone's doing the absolving here, it's not you. It's the Man Upstairs."

"Oh, I know that," he said, smiling. "I just thought I'd say it and do that gesture anyway. I don't often have sinners coming to me for absolution, and I just wanted to say it and make that little sign for my own satisfaction."

I laughed. I was glad he saw some humor in the situation. It gave me hope. "You're okay, Harry."

"I'm glad you think so. I sometimes wonder if I'm all that okay."

I stood up. "You are, Reverend. Thanks. Well, I'd better be going now."

He got up along with me. "One more question, Mike. Are you going to be climbing any mountains any time soon?"

"I don't know. I'll have to sleep on it," I said, stretching. I turned to leave, and looked back at him. "See you in church, Harry."

He winked. "I'll be there."

"That's right. You don't have much choice, do you?"

"Not really," he said, "Not that I'd really want a choice."

He came around the desk and shook my hand. "Glad you made it back alive, Mike."

"Thanks," I said. "And Harry, thanks again for what you said. I appreciate it."

"You're welcome."

I left the church. Much later that day, I drove over to Tracy's. We had dinner, which she cooked, and afterward we sat down in her living room. It was a quiet evening and the mood was warm between us.

She had a new batch of photographs to show me. She took one of the big brown envelopes out of her files. She laid out her prints, displaying them on the coffee table. We sat together and looked at them.

"Back up in Chicago Basin, I took these while you were up on the mountain," she said.

I pulled her close. "So. You got your stormy weather pictures after all, huh?"

"Yes," she said, "and I think they turned out rather well."

I had to admit, the photographs were some of the best she had ever shown me. On the first print she had caught Jupiter Peak all wrapped in clouds, with the face looking down as ever, in a permanent expression of mirth. Another picture showed the icy patches along the banks of Needle Creek, the green reeds covered with frosty white icicles. Other pictures were of the trees, the dark clouds above, and the pits where back in time the old miners had spent their days digging for ore.

"I have something to tell you," she said. "New York called today. They like the pictures I sent them. They want to do the book with them."

I smiled at her. "That's great, Tracy. Let me guess the title. 'Durango Light'?"

"You got it. I even have a cover photograph picked out. Here, let me show it to you."

She pulled one last picture from the stack. It was a telephoto shot taken early in the morning. The left side of the picture was filled with the unmistakable heights and crags of Eolus. On the right side was the steep climbing approach route to the high mountain.

There in the picture, you could clearly see three human figures, climbers, moving upward toward the top. A shaft of golden morning sunlight gleamed from the ice and snow, diamondlike sparkles caught here and there.

"I took this the morning you three were going up," she said. "Think it'll make a good one for the cover?"

"Whatever you want," I said. I kissed her. "Durango Light," I mused. "Nice name. The light here really is special, isn't it?"

"Yes," she said. "I even wrote a poem about it."

She handed me a sheet of paper.

DURANGO LIGHT

Afternoon light
Always, afternoon light
Warm-cold, yellow light
Old, vintage light
Falling across old weathered boards
Of a hundred snow-cold winters

Light
Crossing sparkling rapids
Of the Rio Animas

Haunted light
Filtering yellow through aspen leaves
Reflecting
From the glass of broken window shards
Of the mine cabins of long ago
Filtering quietly
Into dusty rooms.
Light of lives long past
Lives of the survivors
Lives of the dead
Light that leaves its mark
On the mountain side, the cold mountain
Long after the sun
Has set.

I set the poem down on the coffee table beside her photographs. "It fits, Tracy. You really love the light, don't you?"

"Always," she said. "Always. And especially, Mike, especially...if it's in your eyes."

We put the pictures away, and looked out the window together. It was dark now, dark and stormy out there, out in those mountains.

But the light would return.

Ed Williamson is a Christian minister who has lived in
Northern New Mexico and West Texas. He began his work in
churches in 1971, and currently serves as pastor of a large church
in West Texas. He is an experienced climber and backpacker. He
received his mountaineering training from two special friends in
Northern New Mexico and from instructors of the Exum Guide
Service in the Grand Teton National Park. He has summited
many of Colorado's highest mountains, including Mount Eolus,
and has led group expeditions of young people on several mountain climbs, hikes, and retreats. His work has been published
in *Trail and Timberline*, the magazine of the Colorado Mountain
Club. He is married and has a wife and three children, a daughter
and two sons. Currently he makes his home in Big Spring, Texas.